SLEEPWALKERS

Tom Grieves has worked in television as a script editor, producer and executive producer, as well as a writer. *Sleepwalkers* is his first novel. He lives in Sussex.

SLEEPWALKERS

Tom Grieves

To Ann

with best wishes

Tom G—

30/vii/2012

Quercus

First published in Great Britain in 2012 by

Quercus
55 Baker Street
7th Floor, South Block
London W1U 8EW

A CIP catalogue record for this book is available
from the British Library

HB ISBN 978 0 85738 980 0
TPB ISBN 978 0 85738 981 7

10 9 8 7 6 5 4 3 2 1

Printed and bound in Great Britain by Clays Ltd, St Ives plc

Typeset by Ellipsis Digital Limited, Glasgow

For Ceetah. Always Ceetah

ONE

Blink. Keep your eyes open. Blink. That's it, don't go back to sleep, not yet.

I'm staring up at the ceiling in the middle of the night cos I've just had a nightmare. I get them all the time, to be honest, but they can really get to me and I know that if I try to go to sleep now then I'll just let the bloody thing back in. So I need to stay awake, just remind myself where I am, distract my brain, get the nightmare out of the system and then I'll be okay.

A car passes outside and the noise is rough and reassuring. I roll over and look at Carrie who's fast asleep. Her mouth's open and she's snoring. It makes me smile. But then the boy in my head cries out again.

In my dream there was this boy, you see. They'd tied him down to a bed and he was struggling, trying to get up, screaming louder and louder.

I sit up. Stop thinking about it, you idiot, it's always like this. I've learned to shove the memories away and I know this one will go too, in a bit, but right now it's so fresh. The way he looked at me, the way his eyes pleaded, like I was the only one who could help him.

I pull the covers off, making sure I don't wake Carrie, and slip out of the bed. She rolls over with a groan but she's gone, I can tell. I pad out of the bedroom. My clothes are just where I left them, grubby jeans on the battered armchair (ripped to shreds by the old cat) and pants and the rest on the floor by the door. I walk past them into the passage, past the stain where Carrie dropped the bottle of red wine when she was off her face. Fuck me, that was funny. Keep on walking. I feel better now I'm up.

Next to us is Joe's room. Our first. He's asleep inside and I can hear his short, quick breaths. A nightlight glows gentle greens and blues and a leg dangles out from under the sheets. There are toys scattered all over the floor. Next door to him is Emma. Her tiny face is buried in a pillow and the dummy she needs to get her to sleep has fallen under her chin. I go and sit on the edge of the bed. I could watch her forever, sit here all night, the way some people will stare into a fire. At the end of her bed is a shed-load of stuffed animals. Right now it's a camel that's her favourite. She's named him Dooley and he's clutched tight under her arm.

That boy. Screaming and panicking.

'It's alright, son, it's alright,' I said, trying to calm him down. But I was scared too. I was scared because I thought the way he was acting would cause trouble. 'Just close your eyes and it'll all go away.' Why would I say that? And then I remember that I was tied down too. I was in the bed next to him, tied down, and I was as scared as he was. 'Please, kid, shut up,' I begged him. And then I could hear people walking towards us and I looked up and the lighting was so bright and—

Stop thinking about it, you moron. Look at your gorgeous four-soon-to-be-five-year-old daughter. Look at where you are.

For some reason I check my wrists where the restraints were – well, would have been. Of course there's nothing, but I needed to check. I told you, these nightmares get to me. I budge along the bed and get close up to Emma and slip my index finger into her closed hand and she instinctively grips it tightly. I stroke her blonde locks with my other hand and then gently pull myself away. I go into Joe's room, slip his leg back under the covers and then head back for our bed. But as I come into the passage I see that I've woken Carrie, and now she's standing by our bedroom door, crumpled, hair all over the place, looking at me with her wonderful 'what the fuck?' face on.

'Nightmare,' I say.

She nods, used to it. She holds out a hand – come back to bed – and I take it. We snuggle back into each other, the covers pulled right over our heads, and soon Carrie's breathing deeply again. She falls asleep so easily, always. Once, I was trying to explain something – can't remember what – about being stressed or something. Anyway, I was saying to her about that feeling when you get into bed and you know you won't be able to get to sleep no matter what, and she looked at me as though I'd been down the pub with the boys again. And I pushed her about this and she said she just gets into bed, puts her head on the pillow and goes to sleep. Always.

Isn't that incredible? I can toss and turn for half the bloody night. Lucky cow.

Soon it's too hot and airless and I have to pull the covers

3

back down from over our faces. She's snoring again – really light, nothing gross – and I laugh quietly, half hoping I'm going to wake her, but she's so deep in it now it'd take an army. For a moment my brain lets the boy back in so I have to stare at the ceiling and push him away. I think back to the time when Carrie first led me in here, pulling me by the hand, so excited. There was a crack in the ceiling and the window sills were rotting but she couldn't be talked down. *It's perfect.* She squeezed my hand tight with her tiny fingers, trying not to let the estate agent see just how keen she was and whispered in my ear, 'We'll make babies in here. I know it. We will, we will.'

How could I deny her? Suddenly I was a part of something grown-up, something real and permanent. A family. It's something you imagine, but when it becomes real it's ... it's ... I don't know. I'm no good with words. Too simple. But we bought it and now there is no crack in the bedroom ceiling. And the colour swabs that she painted in neat, organised squares are gone too. And now the kids are growing and the house is fraying in places and life is good.

Carrie rolls over and throws an arm over me, holding me down. Just like she did when we were in Greece that time, ages ago, long before all of this. We went to sleep in the sun, drunk on the wine in the middle of the day, and woke up shivering and burnt. We spent the next three days holed up in our tiny villa, scared of the sun. I remember finally opening the shuttered windows – a lizard sped away – and we looked out together at that fantastic view. Below was a small harbour, white fishing boats moored in the bay and a sea so blue and calm. She had laid her head against my chest.

'Let's come back here every year,' she said. 'Make it a tradition. I want us to have loads and loads of traditions.'

We never did go back, but that's not so bad. We're happy and the memory feels special for it. I remember the way the leaves moved in the breeze and when I moaned about my sunburn she laughed at me and slapped me so hard on my arm I thought the bloody skin would peel off right then and there.

'Wanna see my marks?' she said, and suddenly she was doing this crazy striptease on the bed, her legs all wobbly on the uneven mattress. She was singing that pop tune that was on the radio all summer and she was singing it *so* badly and we were both laughing. Red skin, pink knickers.

She fell asleep afterwards, her hot arm pinning me down, just the same as now, and she dribbled on my shoulder. I realise that the boy in my dream has gone and I can close my eyes. Pink knickers and dribble. What a girl.

Joe's always had his mother's balls and attitude, which makes me laugh and drives her up the wall. He's just got ants in his pants, that's the thing. It never bothers me really, but keeping him still or getting him to concentrate on anything for more than five seconds can do your head in. Right now, I'm having to push him back against the wall, hold him by the shoulders so he's in place. *Stand still.* I pull the pencil from behind my ear and draw a line against the wall. He turns, excited, sees how much he's grown.

'Mate, if you'd eaten your broccoli, you'd be a giant by now,' I tell him.

'Yeah, like if you eat carrots, you can see in the dark. Nice one, Dad.' Eight years old and he's already a teenager.

Now it's Emma's turn. She's only grown the tiniest bit, so I fake it on the board and she rewards me with a sneaky grin. I look at the wall, see the uneven chart of my children's growth. Different colours, different times. I see one, Joe – three years before – remember him trying to stand on tiptoe to cheat the height. We had four different pencil lines in one day. Chose the smallest one as a jokey punishment. Laughing, I remind him of this.

'I don't remember that.'

'Sure you do. It was hilarious. Your mum had tears down her face. You were stood just there, all grumpy, arms crossed.'

He stares at me with a James Dean sneer. 'How old was I?'

'Five'

'Nah.'

'Yeah, you were five; it's this one here.' I point to the mark. 'And then you went upstairs in a hissy fit and came down in your footy boots cos you thought the studs would make you taller.'

He just shrugs. Does he really not remember at all? I try to remember other details to spark it for him. But nothing comes. The memory feels isolated from everything else. The kids stare at me as I stumble for something more. I'm trying to pull something from the back of my mind, but now everything's gone and got confused. The kids are staring at me like I'm mental but there's something, there's something I can't ... just ... can't ...

'Hi, honey.' Carrie hurries into the kitchen just as the phone rings. I answer it and someone's talking in my ear, someone I don't know but someone I like. I'm thinking this is odd, why

6

do I like them when I don't know who it is? I'm wondering about this but I answer the questions anyway and now I'm a bit hazy. Everything feels so warm and happy and it's like this cloud's coming down and . . .

I wake up with the feeling I'm late for something. A bit of a start, a jolt. I sit up and wince because my back's so stiff. I'm sure I've got scratches down it, I can't really see them properly but it hurts like hell. It's like that all day. Work at the garage was a nightmare. I seemed to be bumping into things all the time and now I'm home I just want a hot bath and a long sleep. Carrie says I'm being a drama queen. It was rugby training last night, season starts in two weeks and I'm always like this, she says. I guess she's right. The ground's still hard from the summer and you always get a bit scuffed up before the autumn sets in properly. I'm part of a veterans' team and we're all trying to pretend we're still twenty by training too hard. Half the blokes are really posh but they're alright, as it goes.

The papers didn't turn up and I was going to pop around to the late-night supermarket to get one, but she talked me out of it. I'm so pooped, I could hardly be bothered anyway. And it's not just my body. Sometimes, like today, my head feels like a fog. There are figures moving about, just beyond reach, and whenever I go towards them, they're gone.

I slump onto the sofa and look down at my arm. Bruises are starting to colour under the swelling. I switch on the TV. The news is on, but the volume's down to zero for some reason. As I turn it up, Carrie comes behind me, kisses me and whips the remote from my hand, turning it off.

'I'm going to give up the rugby,' I tell her. 'I'm bloody aching all over.'

'But you love it. You're always moaning at the start of the season, but in a couple of weeks you'll be doing all those stupid strong-man poses and talking about – what was it last year? – pop passes, and showing them the inside and all that shit.'

'Right.' I try to remember. There's that fog again. Something tells me she's probably right.

'And you've got your mates there. You won't feel like you've deserved ten pints and a fat burger unless you've sweated and grunted with Mac and Jonno.'

Mac and Jonno. Two laughing faces spring into my mind. I seem to have played rugby with those two forever. But oddly I can't remember them as younger men. Only as they are now.

Carrie must have seen my frown; she flicks my ear playfully.

'Oi! That hurts!'

'Maybe you *should* give up the rugby. I mean, if you can get your arse whipped by a girl, then you're no use to your mates.'

'You? Whip my arse?'

'Come on, big man, show me what you're made of.'

And suddenly we're racing to the bedroom, laughing. She's pulling off her clothes as she runs. I'm up on my feet – God, my bloody back – hurrying after her with a low, happy growl. As we run, we pass the kitchen and I see the lines I drew to show the kids' height, and there's something about this that slows me for a second. I stop. Something I'm meant to remember.

'Oi, fatty! Are you out of breath already or did you stop for some chocolate?'

Cheeky cow. I run upstairs and the sound of my heavy feet on the stairs has her screaming and laughing.

'Watch out, honey. Here I come, ten tonnes of fun!'

When I was five years old, my mother decided to teach me the piano. Not seriously, not like some Chinese prodigy, and my hands were too small anyhow, but she wanted me to be good at music. Said it was important, a 'life skill'. Those were the words. So she would sit me down on the piano stool next to her and she'd play a scale with my hand on top of hers so I could feel her fingers pressing down on each key. And also it'd look like it was me that was playing. I remember being scared that I'd fall backwards, so she'd snuggle up tight and wrap an arm around me, nuzzling her soft cheek against mine. We'd do it again and again and then she'd tell me to try it myself, showing me how to slip my thumb under my third finger to complete the scale. We'd do it over and over, and in the end I could do it properly. She kissed me and clapped, and I felt like a prince.

We've got a piano. It sits, lid down, near the back door. We thought it would go in the lounge but the passage was too narrow and we couldn't get it in. I got home a little earlier than planned today – work at the garage sometimes pans out that way. Anyhow, I get home, and normally I'd go straight upstairs and have a shower to get the grease and dirt off me, but coming in I see the piano and I remember my mum. She's dead now, long gone. And I'm looking at the piano and the house is well quiet. It's weird actually because normally our place is like Beirut. I lift the lid and look down at the keys, then place my heavy fingers on the notes, trying to play a

9

scale. But the notes won't obey my fingers and I'm too clumsy. I try to play a simple tune that we learned together, but can't get anywhere near it. It all sounds awful. What a dick I am. I've thrown away a talent. Mum'd be furious.

I'm about to sit down and have a real proper go when the family pours in through the back door, a bundle of shiny coats, wellies and shopping bags. Joe's screaming because Emma's scratching at him, red-faced with fury about something. I run to them, pull them apart, listen to their contradictory accusations as Carrie staggers in with the last of the shopping.

Once I've calmed down the kids by putting on the telly, I look back at the piano. The house is too noisy now and I feel bashful. I shut the piano lid. I should just stick to the things I'm good at, I guess. Maybe I could practise when no one's around, make a surprise of it for Carrie. Learn a tune then sing and play it for her birthday.

I like this, and the idea makes me turn to look at Carrie. I'm surprised to see that she's watching me. I smile. She smiles back. But I find myself turning away from her, as though there is a secret in me that I need to protect. And somewhere deep inside me a man shouts something that I can't hear, but I know that it's important. The shout echoes inside me like it's bouncing off white stone cavernous walls, and I imagine sand and sun and a glaring blue sky. I look back and Carrie's now elbow-deep in shopping bags, emptying their contents onto the counter-top. Jesus, no wonder she calls me 'Dream Boy' sometimes. I walk over, grab the bleach and put it in the cupboard where it should be, put everything in the right place.

*

'If you hold his head under for long enough, he'll soon start blabbing. Just make sure you don't kill him cos that's a real shitter.' We both laugh. 'Go on,' he encourages me. I look at his arm – see the tattoo of an eagle wrapped in flames. 'Go on.' His voice is harder now. 'Don't be a pussy.'

There's a young lad lying on the floor. He's no more than fifteen and he's been beaten badly. Some of his dark hair is stuck to the congealed blood on his face. He stares up at me, starts to beg in a language I don't understand. And I start laughing. Stamp my boots onto his delicate fingers. I hear the crunch as a bone breaks—

And I wake up.

Carrie's asleep next to me and Joe's sneaked in on the other side. Neither wakes. I don't move. I just lie there. But this time I don't try to think the dream away. Because I have dreamed this before. Not the same dream, but earlier, when I led this poor boy into the room, told him he'd be okay. Before I smashed his face in. I raise my hand up in the darkened room. Clench it into a fist. Try to imagine hitting him. The dream tells me I can. My head disagrees.

I slip my hand back under the covers. Joe sighs. A dream of his own.

Maybe I should see someone.

I'm sitting in the tiny upstairs boxroom where I sort the bills and stuff. We've got an old computer on a three-legged table while the rest of the room is stuffed full with junk. A red bill sits in front of me. I ignore it, and instead type 'dreams' into google. But there are too many sites, and nothing seems to relate to me.

Carrie pops her head around the door, comes in and starts to massage my shoulders, distracts me. Normally I love it.

'I think I should see a doctor.'

'What's wrong?'

'My nightmares.'

'Oh, hon.'

Her fingers continue to push and probe.

'Or maybe a psychiatrist. You know, all that stuff about—'

'Wanting to fuck your mother?'

'No I don't, I . . . be serious.'

'I am.'

A thumb digs around my collar bone.

'If my brain is, you know, so busy with all this shit then maybe it needs sorting out.'

'Okay.'

'And I'm fed up with them. I keep waking and it's spooking me out and . . . can you get off a sec?!'

She withdraws, stung. 'You want to be alone?'

'No. Yeah. I don't know, I just . . . I don't know.'

She looks at me, confused. Her eyes stare into mine, trying to understand what she's done wrong.

'I just want you to take this seriously.'

'I am.'

'No, you're sympathetic, but this is really . . . it's a mess, my head and I . . . I . . . it feels like it's getting worse.'

'Okay. Well, we'll go to the doctor. I'll go with you.'

'No, no, you don't need—'

'I'm taking you seriously.'

'I'm not . . . Jesus, I just meant . . .'

I don't know what I meant, but I know I should be doing

this alone. Somehow. Carrie shrugs – suit yourself – and leaves. I feel guilty now, but I don't rush to stop her. I turn back to the computer, click on the internet again. But it won't connect. The computer's gone slow. I wait for a moment but it's like the fucker's on strike.

Irritated, I go out onto the landing. We have this wall where we hang our favourite pictures in gaudy frames. There must be nearly a hundred now. Carrie calls it our Wonder Wall. I stare at them – stare at a collage of my life. In every photograph, we are smiling.

Carrie is there again. She looks at me – waiting for it.

'Sorry.'

Not enough.

'I'm a tit. But I'm not sleeping so I'm a tired tit and that's . . . that's my excuse.'

She can't help but let a little laugh slip out. I put my arm around her.

'I'll book an appointment with the doctor and you come if you'd like. I don't mean, like you shouldn't or couldn't or anything, I just . . .'

'You're just a tired tit.'

'That's me.'

'It's almost poetic.'

'Yeah, I've got hidden depths.'

We walk back to the bedroom. She has an arm around me, almost guiding me to sleep.

Work's been a pisser so I've had to cancel my doctor's appointment twice now and the woman on the phone was a bit shirty. But I've been sleeping better recently and now I think maybe

I made too much of it. I'm a bit embarrassed I made such a fuss, to tell you the truth.

Right now, I'm watching Joe play a footy game at his school. It's the middle of the afternoon so there's only one other dad. The rest are all mums who know each other well. They stand in a group further down, chatting and cheering happily. The other dad and I share a smile, but that's as far as our contact gets. I prefer it like this. I've always been a bit of a loner. I like people, for sure, but – I don't know – I guess I'm a bit shy and I don't mind being alone.

Joe's a spindly lad, a streak of piss, and he stands awkwardly away from the action, cold and unhappy. The ref is also the games teacher and he shouts over at him: get stuck in!

Joe runs towards the ball, but it's gone before he gets near it and he stops, looks around, rubs his hands on his shorts. He glances at me. I give him a cheery smile and a thumbs-up. Even I feel a bit pathetic. He shuffles on towards the action.

'That your boy?' It's the other dad. A gruff, shortish man. His jeans are paint-splattered from work. I nod, a little ruefully. A smile.

'He's shit, eh?'

I look at him. He's got a way about him that tells me he likes rubbing people up. I look back at the game. Gruff Man starts screaming encouragement to his son. I watch the boy for a moment – he's annoyingly good.

'Come on, Joe, you're doing great, mate,' I shout out across the grass.

'If you say so,' comes the wry reply next to me. I can feel the snide smile but keep my eyes fixed on my son. Joe slips

14

and doesn't bother to get up. A wind sweeps across the pitch. Man, is it cold.

Gruff Man shouts more encouragement for his boy and a couple of the other kids. There are three or four boys who like the game and are good at it. Another bunch who are less talented but try hard. And then a few, Joe included, who are there because they're told to be. I hate this. It reminds me of my childhood. My hands too cold to unlace my boots and the noise of studs on concrete.

I watch my boy pick himself up, hug himself against the cold and trudge into position as one of his team-mates implores him to make more of an effort. Joe nods, trying to please, but really trying not to be noticed.

I feel guilty.

Gruff Man barks away next to me. His son scores a goal. Everyone's delighted. I join in the applause, but do everything I can not to look at the crowing idiot.

A whistle blows and I can see the relief on Joe's face. He wanders around, shaking hands with the opposition with the same bored look that he had during the game.

The teams head back to the changing rooms. The mothers have knit themselves into a tighter huddle and are laughing like drains. I'm stuck with Gruff Man. I pat my pockets, swear quietly to myself and walk off to the car under the pretence I've left my phone there.

Joe comes out a bit later, showered but still with muddy knees. I laugh and he gives me a grin. I put my arm around him as we walk to the car.

'Football's a shit game,' I say as lightly as I can.

'You're not allowed to swear.'

'Fifty pence in the swearbox. Remind me when we get home. But it is.'

'Yeah. It's alright, maybe.'

He's groaning under the weight of his school bags and I offer to take one but he shakes his head. I notice all the other kids are carrying theirs as well. Fair enough. I walk a little more slowly to the car.

Inside, I whack the heating up and hand him a chocolate bar. He munches on it gratefully. I want to chat to him, but he's happy just to be taken home, doesn't want an inquisition, so I drive off. We pass Gruff with his son. Gruff's talking animatedly, angry about something. The boy has his head down, not listening. This cheers me up.

We drive on in silence for a while. Traffic slows us.

'I hated football when I was your age. Then I grew, and it got easier. I was quite good when I was a bit older.'

If the encouragement seeps through, Joe doesn't show it.

'You're just like me, you know.'

'Yeah, you've said.'

I glance at him, see he's smiling.

'I thought I might buy us a goal, put it in the garden. We could play after school.'

'You'll break a window.'

'Yeah. Probably trash all the flowers as well.'

'Mum said you're totally mental about keeping the grass all tidy.'

'I am. Screw it, we'll ruin the lawn. Who cares?'

Joe looks at me as though I've just crashed the car.

'Yeah, and we'll wreck the flowers, break windows and probably get mad old Mrs Moore next door foaming at the mouth. And your Mum will kill us. What do you say?'

A pause. Then a huge grin spreads across his face.

'Yeah. Let's do it.'

He laughs, thrilled with his cheek. It's a laugh that comes from deep in his belly. As we drive home we punch each other when we think the other won't notice it. He's laughing so hard at one point I'm worried he's going to puke the chocolate back up. My boy.

We're all singing Happy Birthday. Emma's dressed in a pink fairy outfit with gigantic wings that make it almost impossible for her to sit at the table. She's grinning like a good 'un, with chocolate smeared around her mouth. Carrie places the birthday cake down in front of her and our little girl blows all the candles out after four attempts. Then we have to re-light them because Joe blew a couple out and Emma started to get teary.

I hold Joe back so he can't blow them back again and even though he knows he mustn't, he leans forward, unable to stop himself. We play a gentle, happy wrestling game to keep him back while Emma huffs and puffs.

Finally the candles are out. I release Joe who immediately snatches a candle and tries to light it with the box of matches. It's relentless but it's funny too. His face is alive with mischief, his eyes wide and excited.

'Come on, get ready,' says Carrie as she holds the knife above the cake. As the blade cuts through the chocolate we all scream as loud as we can until the knife touches the plate below. To let the Devil out. It's an old ritual from Carrie's side of the family. Emma carries on screaming because it's funny and it's her birthday. Joe shouts at her to shut up, but they're both laughing.

I hide the matches while Joe's distracted, running my hand along the edge of the countertop. The floor is covered in wrapping paper. While they were at school, I hung up a cheap and rather tacky Happy Birthday sign with sellotape which won't hold for much longer (and Carrie thinks the sign's rubbish so I bet she'll give it a sharp tug when I'm not looking). My hand touches a piece of masking tape which hides the moment when Joe and Emma got 'creative' with the cutlery. On one wall is a set of plates with painted baby feet to mark their arrivals. The room's cramped and the table wobbles unless you stick some cardboard under one of the legs. There are stains on the ceiling from splashy playtimes in the bath.

Carrie hands me a paper plate with a slice of birthday cake on it.

'Happy Birthday to you, you smell like a poo.'

'Joe,' we say at the same time, with the same voice.

And then the phone rings. It's right next to Carrie, but she seems busy tidying up.

'You want to get that?' she says, her hands full of wrapping paper.

'It'll only be your mum, wanting to talk to Emma.'

'So pick it up.'

I don't like Carrie's mum, but since I barely ever see her I can't really tell you why. So I answer the phone. There's a pause. Maybe she's dropped the phone.

'Hello?' I say. And there's a voice on the other end that I don't recognise but for some reason I like. That's odd. He's

asking me questions and I can't stop myself from smiling
and . . .

It's easy to break into a hotel. There are cameras all over the
place, of course, but a hood and a screwdriver are all you need.
I slip inside with barely a pause. The room I need is on the
fourth floor, but I take the stairs rather than risk the lift.

The corridor is deserted. It's an expensive hotel. There are
large bouquets of flowers on tables and a scent of lilies in the
air. I walk along to the right number: 406. Check my watch,
Then pat my back pockets. They're there. I know they're there
but I pat my pockets to be sure.

I knock on the door and take a step back.

I wait, then hear bare feet pad upon carpet towards the door.
Then silence. She's checking through the spyhole right now.
Another silence. Then the door opens. Dumb fuck. They always
do it, but dumb fuck all the same.

I move fast. One hand hits her straight in the neck. Shuts
her up and knocks her back into the room. The white hotel
dressing gown rises up as she falls; she's naked underneath.
We're inside in a blink and I push the door shut – not too
hard, don't want the door to slam, but firm enough to hear
the lock click.

The woman sits up as I reach behind and pull a small hammer
from my back pocket. I slam it hard. Not even a yelp. I'd use
the hammer again but I don't want any blood on the carpet.
Those are the orders.

Her eyes pop open, bulging, staring at me with confusion
and panic, as my hands grab her neck. Won't be much longer.

She scratches at my hands. Her nails sink deep and draw

blood, but it makes no difference. Her legs kick and her thin body writhes. I like her for trying.

Soon it is over. I wait, check her pulse. Wait another five minutes and check her pulse again to be sure. Done. Then I stand. I must have done it too quickly because it gives me a slight head-rush. I shake it off, go to the door, open it. My man is waiting for me outside.

We head back in. Time to get her out of here.

But then my body starts to shake, as though someone has grabbed me by my shoulders. I turn to look at him but he's just staring down at her on the floor. My whole body shakes and convulses. I feel a moment's panic. I'm shaking and shaking and . . .

I wake up with a jolt. Emma and Joe are shaking me, laughing and screaming. Daylight's coming in through the window. Although Emma's in her pyjamas, she's still got her fairy wings on. She starts bouncing up and down on the bed and, still half-asleep, I imagine she's flying. I see her blonde hair lit by the sun as it floats and bounces. It's beautiful.

And then the pain hits me. Jesus Christ, I feel fucking awful. My head's crushed, my shoulders ache and my back . . . oh Lordy, I'm a wreck.

'Oh man . . .' I croak.

And that only excites the kids more. Joe and Emma are jumping and jumping and the cheap, thin mattress isn't holding out.

'Guys, come on, give an old man a break will you?'

But they're just laughing even more. Joe bounces high and hard, then crashes, bottom-first, onto me. Emma screams with laughter. Joe's wiggling his bum and I know he's trying to do a fart on my head. Emma's screaming at him to do it. *Do it!* I manage to push him off and sit up.

Christ, my hands . . .

I look down at them. They're scratched. Badly scratched and sore. And I've absolutely no idea how this happened.

And then Joe and Emma come flying on top of me again. I feel my daughter's soft skin as she wraps her arms around my neck. It's more of a cuddle than a wrestle, but she wants to be part of the game. Joe's jumping on me, using his knees to get some sort of reaction. Little bugger.

A shout from their mother stops them in their tracks. I look up – she's dressed, a smile on her face despite an attempt at disapproval.

'Come on, you two – breakfast. And you, lazybones, shift your chubby arse.'

Emma frowns. 'Is arse a swearword?'

'Not when your mother uses it. Go on downstairs, give your Dad a chance to wake up.'

They scuttle off, obedient as ever. Bloody miracle when I think of some of our friends' kids. Carrie comes and sits on the bed. She puts a hand on my cheek.

'Morning.'

'Hi.'

'So, guess where I found you last night?'

This doesn't sound good.

'Downstairs, asleep on the sofa, dribble all down your shirt, sat bold upright with Ian Botham's greatest moments on the DVD.'

'No . . . oh no . . .'

'Tragic, fat man. Bloody completely embarrassingly tragic.'

'Ouch.'

I look back at my hands.

'Hey, you want to play rugby and risk those baby-boy looks, it's your lookout. I've told you enough times.'

Rugby. Yes, of course! Slugging it out in the mud last night with the guys. Beers afterwards. Gav banging on about his new satnav. Trevor insisting that lager's full of chemicals and he never gets a hangover with real ale. So he drinks ten pints to prove it and makes us all do the same. And now my head feels as though it's in a vice. Cheers, Trev.

'Seriously, hon, you need to get up, you'll be late.'

'I know, I just ... I'm knackered. Totally grounded.'

'Pull a sicky.'

'Can't.'

'You're a bit green, babe.'

'Yeah.'

I look at my hands again. The scratches are so fine. They don't look like stud marks. More like fingernails. I look up. Carrie's watching me.

'Shift your arse, mister.'

I sink back into the sheets. They've never felt warmer or softer. I peek out at Carrie. The raised eyebrow says it all.

'Okay, I'll get up in a sec. I will! I'm like a—

'Coiled spring,' she says, just as I do. We know each other too well. She shakes her head and turns for the door. Then suddenly turns back, grabs the sheets and rips them off the bed. Cold air sweeps over me. I hear her cackle as she canters down the stairs.

'That's not funny!'

I sit up, try to shake my head clear. Then look back down at my hands again. I feel stressed about something. My chest's tight. But I can't work out why.

I'm slow to get downstairs and when I do, I feel like I've walked onto Oxford Street during the sales. Carrie's stuffing Emma's ballet kit into her bag while having a running row with Joe about the nutritional value of doughnuts. I just crash down onto a chair and help myself to some kiddy cereal for a boost. Joe's talking much much too loudly.

'It's one of my five a day!' he shouts.

'Are you kidding me?'

'Apples are fruit, aren't they?'

'Hello?'

Emma joins in. 'Apples is fruit, yes they are. Mrs Pearce said so.'

'See?' says Joe.

Carrie has her arms crossed. 'You're using your baby sister—'

'I'm not a baby!' Emma wails.

'Apple doughnut's got apples in it, right?' Joe says, as though he's talking to a thick kid. 'Simple.'

'Joe, I don't even know where to begin.'

I stare at the milk and cereal in my bowl. The milk is now brown from the cereal. It makes me feel nauseous.

'And jam's made of fruits, right? So a jam doughnut—'

'Do you have any idea how much sugar they use in jam?'

'Still, fruit, innit?'

'Innit? You said "innit"? Right, after school you and I are going to get on the computer and have a look at what too much sugar does to your teeth and belly. In fact, get your dad to smile and lift up his shirt and you'll get an idea.'

I hear the words, know that they're aimed at me. But they feel distant, somewhere else. A completely different world. Eventually I pull my eyes up. They're all staring at me.

'Right, that's it, mister. No more rugby. You. Are. *Busted.*'

Carrie offers to drive me to the garage. It's probably the only safe way to get me there, but she virtually has to kick me out of the passenger seat when we arrive. She's laughing at me for being such a dope. And normally I'd laugh too but I feel more than sick, there's something nagging at me.

Inside, I sneak into my boss's office, hoping to snatch the sports pages and maybe a kip if it isn't busy. His jacket's on the chair which means he's pissed off to the cafe round the corner. Nice one. The office is stuffy and hot, just as he likes it. I go to his desk, but there's no newspaper there; he must have taken it with him.

Jeff pops his head around the door. Jeff's a big guy, ex-army. He's got tattoos all over his arms, but the one I always notice is the eagle on his right forearm. He grins a craggy smile at me. I notice the grey flecks in his hair. They make him even tougher, if that's possible. He's a piece of granite.

'Oi, dosser, what you playing at?'

'We busy?'

'Enough. Some dozy tart's put enough oil in her car to sink a tanker. Smoke everywhere. We got to clean it out, see if it can be salvaged.'

'You got a paper? Wanted to read about the City game.'

'What do you need a paper for? I was there, I'll talk you through it. You won't be happy, though. Come on, honest day's work and all that.'

There's a paper dumped in the wastepaper bin. I see it.

'Mackey missed an absolute sitter,' says Jeff. 'Easier to have scored than missed. What a waste of money.'

I want to snatch the paper. But I can feel Jeff's eyes on me. 'Yeah, alright. I need a dump first—'

'You're not sneaking off to the bogs to read the sodding paper. It's a day's work, not a holiday, you git.'

'What, coming from you?'

'Yeah.'

He's standing still now. Suddenly this feels like the start of a fight. Now, normally I'd back down because of the size of him. But then, thinking about it, he's a lazy arse himself – he's always slinking off to do this or that. So what's the issue? So I don't move. Just look at him. And although he's bloody big and could beat me to a pulp (and the rest) he doesn't move. Instead he gives me this wolfish grin.

'Look, Ben, be fair. I want to get away early tonight. Got my stunner to see. You know, Jenny from the White Horse? Come on, buddy, give us a fair crack at the whip, eh? Not being funny, but the engine's black and all kinds of shit.'

I've never hit a man in my life. Enjoyed my sports but I'm a softy. But right now, I know if I took a step forward, he'd back off. I am alpha male. I'm Jeff and Jeff is me. And that's just too fucking weird. I look back at the paper, then back at him.

'Jesus, take it,' he says, his hands in the air. 'I don't care, but let's do this job first, and then, tell you what – you can bugger off to the pub for lunch, take your precious rag and I'll cover for you, but please let's just, for crying out loud, let's just get this one going, start the day without risking a bucket of shit on our heads.'

I wait. I like feeling like this. Jeff's smile is frozen to his face. I go to the bin, dead slow, pick up the paper, fold it under my arm and walk past him towards the cars. Jeff pats me on the arse, all chummy again.

'Well done, stroppy. Thought you were about to have your period or something,' he says with a big laugh.

We fix the car. It's a disaster, but we get it done. The radio's on, pop music. Whenever the news comes on, Jeff changes it to another channel for more shitty music. The guy's a muppet.

When we're finished, I look for the newspaper. I'd placed it under my coat on the chair in the corner. But it's gone. I look to Jeff, but he just raises his eyes and gestures towards the boss's door. He's inside, feet up, reading it. I can make out the scoreline on the back page. Just as Jeff said.

He appears at my side, pats me on the shoulder.

'Same as it ever was, Benny boy. Boss in the warm, workers out in the cold. How about a couple of jars?'

Sitting in the pub, listening to Jeff natter on about nothing and everything, I sink three pints. Partly, I guess, because I feel so rough and I want to dull all of my aches, but also because it gives me an excuse to get up and go to the bar every now and then – so I can get away from him. After three, my head's all messed up. I'm a lousy lunchtime drinker, but I slide off the bench to order another anyway. My back aches despite the booze, and while I wait for the barmaid I stare down at my scratched hands.

Rugby. I am too old.

I look back at Jeff. He's watching me. He smiles a leery grin.

26

'Come on, girly, hurry up with those beers!' he laughs his big, stupid laugh.

How did I end up with a friend like this? I'm not like him, I don't like him. But here I am. Did I choose him or did he choose me? I try to remember. Try to pull the data from my head. Try to imagine my brain as some sort of computer. But the beer's in the way.

Jeff's started singing along to the tune from some advert on the TV. He's doing it really loud, on purpose, and some people are staring at him. I'm embarrassed, but I'm also starting to laugh.

The woman at the bar is struggling with the remote control. The batteries must be flat, so she bangs it against the counter. She pushes the buttons heavily and starts to flick through the channels. The TV gets stuck on the news and everyone in the pub groans.

Jeff starts singing the same stupid song again, louder this time.

I glance up at the telly. The image changes and now there's a photo on the screen of a pretty young woman with dark hair. And something goes all jittery inside me. Next is a photo of a hotel somewhere. Looks posh. I don't know the girl, don't know the hotel, but I suddenly feel like I'm going to puke.

Jeff's at my side all of a sudden. 'Alright, matey?'

My breathing's shallow, fast. The woman clumsily stamps on the buttons with her chubby fingers and finally finds the sports channel and everyone cheers. Jeff pats me on the back. I look up at the screen, as though that girl, that hotel might linger there. My heart is pounding. Who was that woman and why, why did she matter to me? I see, somewhere in my head, a white dressing gown, but I don't know what this means. There's a stack of newspapers at the far end of the bar and I need to see them.

'Come on, buddy boy, we need to get back to the garage.'

I ignore him, grab the papers, flick through them, looking for her. My scratched hands are clumsy and I can't find what I'm looking for.

'Ben, he'll sack us both. Come on . . .'

I can't find anything, I look again, but then I see that there are pages missing. I chuck the paper down, look to the next one. And again, there are pages missing. Who did this? I look around the pub at the boozers, at the woman, but they seem so dull, there's no way they'd . . .

I look up at Jeff. He's watching me. He comes over and puts a hand on my shoulder. I want to pin him to the bar.

'Ben, what's up?'

I smile. I don't know where I find it from.

'It's nothing, I just . . . déjà vu, I guess.'

'Is that French?'

'You are such an ignoramus.'

'German?'

I sigh, playing it all normal and such. 'What time are you seeing your bird?'

'Her shift starts at seven, so we're hoping to have a ten-minute hump in my car.'

'You old romantic, you.'

Jeff laughs. I see his face relax, but his eyes are trained on me. He's been watching me all day. He's always been doing this. I feel a little sick but I'm still holding it back. I need to be careful now. It's like I've been asleep for ages. Why haven't I noticed this before?

I pat him on the shoulder and we head out of the pub.

'After you, matey,' he says as we get to the door, jolly as ever. The liar.

'No, mate. After you.'

TWO

Anna Price's car suffered from an annoying squeal thanks to an anonymous driver who had pranged it in the night while it was harmlessly parked outside her house. People would often glance at her as it passed, and Anna would wince and swear under her breath, desperately hoping no one could lip-read. As she screeched towards Saint Thomas' comprehensive school on an ordinary Tuesday morning, a prickly red rash crept up her throat and she tried to conquer her nerves. She'd worked there for two years, but it wasn't getting any easier. She could cope with the younger children, but the boys and girls at the top of the school saw her as easy meat.

Anna liked to get to school early. Normally it would just be her and the caretaker. This way she could prepare, avoid the arriving children and their big-mouthed parents, and keep things under control. But on this day she was late and the books on the back seat slid and fell as she made a sharp turn. Serious voices on the radio debated the news, but Anna's mind was busy plotting suitably sneering comebacks to Ralph Lorrison and his cohorts. Such phrases didn't come easily.

By the time she reached the school her spot in the car park had – inevitably – been taken. She found another, squeezed her car into a small space next to the scary Mr Downside (PE) and then fretted that it was too close to the kids. Indeed, just as she pulled the key from the ignition, the car was bumped by three sixth-form girls who sashayed carelessly past. Anna watched them, invisible inside the car: three long-haired sixteen-year-olds, more women than girls, wearing short skirts. They joked and laughed theatrically for the boys to see, cocooned within their ignorant, blissful adolescence. Anna envied them their confidence as they waltzed on, vacuous and happy.

She entered the school a few minutes later, with books piled high and a take-away styrofoam coffee perched on top. Burly boys with acne and aggressive haircuts marched past her. As she got to the bottom of the stairs (the staffroom was on the first floor) she was knocked by two shouty kids and some of the coffee spilled onto her cream blouse. She turned to reprimand them, but they were already gone, their voices echoing down the corridor. *Wanker, twat, mofo, gay boy* . . .

She retreated to the staff toilets. The door scraped as it opened and closed. Anna unbuttoned her blouse and tried to soak the stain in the sink. It didn't seem to help. In fact she was just making a larger, lighter-brown stain, but she knew that her cardigan would at least hide the worst. She caught herself briefly in the mirror, saw her utilitarian bra, her slender frame, her freckled shoulders. She wore little make-up and simple, plain jewellery. Anna would often try more fancy things in the shops, but they never felt like her. She'd return them, self-conscious, to the shop assistant and wonder why she'd been drawn to them in the first place. She was in her early thirties now and felt she should know better. As she looked down and dabbed away at the blouse, she heard the scuffle of feet in one of the cubicles.

She turned, mortified, grabbing the blouse to protect her modesty. But then saw the scuffed black shoes beneath the door and realised that it wasn't a teacher hidden inside but a pupil. Emboldened, she called out.

'Who's that in there?'

The feet shuffled but no one replied.

'Come on, these toilets are for teachers only. Come out, please.'

She both liked and hated the teacher's voice she used. She liked it because it didn't sound like her with its confident tone that she wished was permanent; hated it because she hated any kind of performance.

The lock clicked, the door opened and a schoolboy stepped out. He was holding a pair of wet trousers even though he was fully clothed. Fifteen years old, he was a gaunt, wiry boy with an eager, open face that made adults like him and children bully him. His name was Toby Mayhew.

'Toby . . . ?'

'I'm sorry, Miss. I just . . . I had an accident.'

Their eyes went straight to the trousers.

'Oh!' he squeaked. 'No, no, not like that! I just . . . it was a game. You know, they get you and push you against the sinks and then turn on the taps and splash you so it makes it look like you've, you know, wee'd yourself.'

He described it like a game until the denouement. And then his voice was quieter, betraying the hurt. Both of them knew that this happened a lot.

'Who did it, Toby?'

'Come on, Miss. It was just messing about! Kids, eh?'

He gave her a big smile. Please – the smile said – please don't make a big thing of this.

'Your shirt's wet as well.'

'Yeah, I've got a spare. Always bring a spare. I was just about to . . . when you came in, so I . . .'

His eyes glanced down at her exposed shoulders and she clutched the blouse to her. Two stained tops. The connection was obvious to them both.

'The bell's going to go in a minute, Toby. If you change now you'll just about make it.'

'Yes, Miss, thanks, Miss. And I won't use these loos again, it's just that, sometimes, they come looking for me to make sure I don't . . . you know. This way, I've fooled them. Ace, eh?'

'Ace. Toby, do you need help here? Want me to talk to someone?'

'No, no, I . . . thanks, but I don't think that'd help.'

'Really? I'm a black belt in origami.'

It took him a moment before the weak joke registered. 'Oh. Ha. Funny.'

They held their wet clothes to themselves, no longer sure what to do. Toby was the first to burst the silence.

'Right, well, I'd better get changed. That trigonometry won't solve itself!'

Maybe he also has a voice for school and a voice for himself, Anna thought. She nodded and he turned his back on her and pulled off his shirt. She hastily threw her blouse back on and was about to pull the cardigan tight to cover the stain when she saw his back in the mirror. And she had to turn to make sure she was seeing him right.

Toby was in too much of a rush to notice that he was being watched. But when he pulled off his wet shirt he revealed a torso that was covered in scratches, bruises and scars. Anna couldn't help but gawp. She saw dark, jagged lines scrape down from his shoulder blades to the base of his spine. A series of now-healed puncture wounds blistered at a diagonal angle and might have continued across his front, for all she could tell. She saw bruises now fading to green and yellow. They were the remnants of intense pain. It was shocking to see such brutality inflicted on such a frail boy's body. He looked like some kind of Frankenstein's monster. Then he whipped on a fresh white shirt and the spectacle was ended.

He turned round and grinned at her as he looped a tie around his neck.

'Alright, Miss, thanks, I'll see you in English. Third period, isn't it?'

'Toby . . . '

'And don't worry, I didn't see anything really. Much.'

His eyes slipped mechanically to her breasts and she didn't know what to say.

'Right. Ciao Miss, and thanks again.'

'Toby! Hang on—'

But he was gone. Anna leaned back against the basin, shocked by the violence and cruelty she'd just witnessed, so disconnected from the cheery face that bore it.

Anna did indeed teach Toby during third period, but there was no mention of their encounter. He sat at the back and when she glanced at him, he would often be staring out of the window. She didn't pull him up on this, but when she was able to set the class a written exercise, she noticed that he was the last one to find a partner. The girl he joined tried to complain, but Anna ignored her moans and watched as he let her copy from her neighbours and totally disregard him. He was happier when no one at all was looking at him.

Later, she watched him in the lunch break. She was on duty, shouting at the boys to stop jostling. Everyone was playing, everyone was happy. But Toby stood outside the play area, kicking a crumpled can on his own. He didn't even look lonely. Anna watched him and wondered why she had never noticed this awful exclusion before. Someone kicked a ball over the wire fence and it landed near Toby. Happily he went and got it then jogged over to give it back, hoping for a game. The ball was snatched off him and the kids carried on. Anna watched his face fall, then, geed up by an imaginary comment, she saw how he smiled to himself and carried on kicking his can.

At the end of the day, Anna made sure that she was standing outside as the kids headed home. It was getting dark. Most wandered cheerfully out of the gates, either to the bus stop further down the road or into town. Only a few parents waited outside. Toby's father, Michael, was one of them. In his fifties, he was a tall, imposing man. There was a natural scowl about him. He looked the type who would shout in public places when things didn't go his way. He waited for his son, standing aside from the others, unblinking. Anna spotted him, then saw Toby trudge out amongst the others, who chatted happily to anyone but him.

Toby nodded at his father, pleased to see him. Michael waited for him and neither spoke as they walked together to the car. Michael put his hand on the back of his son's neck. From Anna's perspective, what should have been a caring gesture appeared somehow more controlling. A vice, not a caress.

Michael herded Toby into his car and moved over to the driver's side. Before he turned a key in the ignition, he hit the central locking. The locks snapped down. No one could get in – or out.

As they drove off, a small cold breeze caught Anna and she pulled her coat tighter around herself for comfort. Toby's pale face gazed out of the window as they passed. He seemed happy enough. But Anna couldn't help wondering.

And then Kath was there. Kath was Anna's only real pal at the school and Anna could tell that people thought they made an odd couple. Kath was loud-mouthed, pushy and desperately single. She'd somehow decided that Anna should be her running mate in the bars and clubs – probably because it would mean that she'd get the fitter males, Anna suspected. Kath did laugh at her jokes though, although Anna didn't really think she was *that* funny. Maybe it was just that her humour was unexpected.

'So where are we meeting then?' asked Kath. Anna looked at her blankly. 'Don't you dare, don't you dare tell me you've forgotten.'

'You mean tomorrow night?'

'You know damn well I do, I've been going on about it all week.'

'Yes, sorry, Kath. You see, the thing is—'

'RICHARD JACKSON PUT IT BACK IN YOUR FLIES OR I'LL CUT IT OFF!'

Kath had a shout that could be used for military purposes.

'Kath, how about we take a rain—'

'No bloody way. This is what you do, what you always do. You say yes, knowing you're going to blow me out later. Well, you and I are hitting the town and I'm going to find out what really hides behind that trim little Miss English Teacher bollocks.'

'I'm really not—'

'I'm not listening, I'm not listening, I'm not listening, I'm not—'

'Alright! I'm coming!' Anna laughed, flushed.

'Fab. So shall we meet there? No. On second thoughts, I'll be sat waiting for half an hour before you ring and say you're stuck on Year Five homework. I'll come to yours. And if you even think you're going out dressed anything like you are now then there will be blood on the carpet. You digging me?'

'I'm digging you.'

'Good. Now, bugger off home and dust down your Wonderbra.'

Anna smiled weakly.

'You don't have a Wonderbra, do you?'

'Not in the literal term of the meaning of . . . no.'

'Lucky knickers?'

'Lucky for what?'

'Fucking hell.'

'Oh don't look at me like that, you big slapper,' Anna said, a wry grin on her face. 'I know how to party. In fact, I think you'll find I'm pretty groovy.'

Kath sighed. Terry Anderson, a wheezing asthmatic with an industrial collection of doctor's notes staggered past. Kath pointed at him, and he seemed to wither under her gaze.

'See him? That's you unless you buck your ideas up. And if you ever say groovy again, I'll burn every last one of your Jane Austen books.'

Toby's bedroom was, at first glance, every inch the classic boy's room. Football heroes adorned the walls (Mum wouldn't let him put up the poster of the pouting girl in a bikini which Martin Foster stole from his elder brother) and the shelves were stacked with books and Manga comics. But it was also incredibly tidy. You could still see the clean lines where the hoover had methodically done its work.

Toby sat at his desk. School work and books were scattered all around, but Toby wasn't doing his homework. Instead, he was writing feverishly in a battered diary. He stopped, paused, then started to flick back to previous entries. One page caught his eye – an old drawing of him (a bit stick-man but he'd got his hair right) trying to climb over barbed wire. A black dog was biting his leg. Blood spurted out theatrically from the bite and from his hands on the wire.

He flicked over the page to another drawing – this time a small boy (Toby if you squinted) held his hands up, standing on the top of the roof. Pointing a gun up at him was a soldier.

Below it, Toby had scrawled, 'And that's the last thing I remember!'

He flicked through more pages.

'What Happened Next?'

His writing was scratchy, untidy – written in a hurry.

Another picture showed a line of men and women lying in beds, with straps holding them down. One of them is reaching out towards Toby's stick figure.

'Who is the man in the bed?!'

A smudged drawing showed Toby lying on the floor, his leg bent in different directions.

'Why can't I remember??!'

There was a knock on the door and the diary was snapped shut and hidden under a school book. It was Michael.

'Dinner's going to be ready in five minutes. And Mum's gone and done her vegetarian lasagne again, I'm afraid, so practise your "it's delicious" face will you?'

'No worries, Dad,' grinned Toby.

'How's the maths? Done?'

'Not quite.'

'Toby . . . '

'It's no biggy, I'll finish it after I've gnawed through the raw aubergine.'

Michael smiled. His eyes swept the room.

'I thought the maths was easy.'

'It is.'

'So why's it taking so long?'

'Just got distracted. Cos it's so simple. Boring.'

'Alright. Make sure you don't leave it too late, you need your sleep. And—'

'Wash my hands before we eat. Yes, Dad.'

Michael nodded, fair enough, and left. Toby watched the door close, but he didn't move. His eyes were trained on the door handle which remained held down for a moment. After a long silence the handle was released and Michael's quiet steps retreated.

Toby relaxed. Then he pulled a drawer from his desk and turned it upside down. Underneath he'd made a little hiding place for the diary using tape and cardboard. He slipped the diary into his hidey-hole and put the drawer back in its place.

Then he hurried to his cupboard, and from the bottom of a bundle of clothes he pulled out a plastic bag with the logo 'Spy Trap' on it. Inside, brand-new, was a small box. The cover declared 'Spy Trap Microcam and DV recorder base'. Toby opened the box excitedly and took out a tiny camera, almost as small as a button. He carefully attached the fiddly thing to his belt. He then stepped back and examined himself in the full-length mirror on the door to see how it looked.

His finger shot imaginary bullets and he blew the nozzle clean. A miniature James Bond without the hair, the muscles, the looks, the weapons, the girl, the attitude or the licence to kill. Still, the hidden camera was a start.

A shout downstairs made him jump. Dinner! He hurriedly hid the box away again, then took another look at himself. He grinned, excited.

'Ready!'

Dinner at Toby's house was always a formal affair, repeated each night in order to 'maintain standards'. This was a phrase his mother, Laura, would use and Toby wasn't entirely sure what it meant. Laura was a straight-backed, greying lady who was prone to worrying. She insisted on a carefully prepared, home-made meal each evening, which always looked good but always tasted wholesomely disappointing. Toby glanced at his father as they politely chewed their way through her latest cooking experiment and pulled the right faces for Mum.

'And how about the history?' Laura asked, as she cut her food into smaller and smaller pieces.

'Yeah, good. Mr Philips was well pleased.'

'Not "well pleased". "Very pleased", or "really pleased"'.

'Pleased as Punch,' Michael interjected, and his parents shared a satisfied smile.

Toby sighed. 'Can't you just notice the bit about me doing really well?'

She placed her hand on his for a moment. 'Well done. I was going to bake a cake after dinner, but I'm running low on soft margarine. I was wondering if you'd mind, Toby, popping down to that shop on the corner.'

Toby gawped. He looked at Michael, who was also rather stunned. Their surprise meant they spoke at the same time.

'He's got maths to finish,' his father said sternly.

Toby said, 'What? On my own?'

Laura looked a little pleased by the fuss she'd made. 'Oh, it's only a few minutes down the road, five at most. I've been on my feet all day, I don't see why—'

'I'D LOVE TO!'

'Darling?' she said to Michael, and Toby turned eagerly to his father, his head bobbing up and down with excitement.

'Please, Dad, I won't do nothing, I'll—'

'Won't do anything, Toby, really.'

'I won't do anything, Dad. I'll finish the maths straight afterwards, it's dead easy, I've got about ten minutes left, honest. Honest. Honest.'

His dad stared hard at him, then glanced at his mum. Then he sagged. 'Alright. But you come straight back—'

'Yesssss!' Toby managed to resist punching the air, but only just. Laura stood up and reached for her handbag, pulled out her purse. 'You can get your father some extra-strong mints while you're down there.'

Toby jumped up from the table. 'You bet!'

'And wear your coat.'

'No problems.'

'And don't go wandering—'

'Mum!'

She waved him off and Toby rushed to the door, where his dad stopped him again.

'Oh, Toby. Take your mobile. Just in case.'

Toby nodded, stuffing the phone into the coat, hurrying to get out of the front door.

As soon as Toby took a step outside the house, he sniffed the cold, damp air deep into his lungs with relish. He marched down the suburban close and pulled his coat open as a tiny mark of defiance. His feet felt light – as though he could run forever. He spun around a lamp post and caught the attention of a woman walking her dog and waved at her before trotting on.

Further down the road, his mobile phone rang. It took him a moment to claw it out of the deep coat pocket. He checked the screen: UNKNOWN CALLER. Toby didn't usually get calls, so he answered the phone a little gingerly.

'Hello?'

He stopped. He didn't know the man at the other end, but he was happy to hear from him.

'Yes.'

A long pause, then he nodded again, answering the caller's question.

'Yes.'

And then Toby smiled. It was a different smile from the one before which was so carefree and childish. This smile felt more knowing, more relaxed, as though it came from the head, not the heart. He felt warm and calm and happy. He started to laugh and his pupils suddenly dilated – like a drop of black ink hitting still water. He threw his head back and his laugh turned into a wild scream.

And suddenly, Toby was awake. He was back in his bedroom, dressed in his pyjamas. It was morning. Standing at the end of the bed were his mum and dad. It took a moment for Toby to register that something was wrong, but then, when he sat up, he winced from the shooting pain that ran through his legs and right arm. Panic began to rise up within him.

'What . . . ? What did I . . . ?

His mother stifled a sob.

'Mum. I swear. I don't . . . what did I do?'

'We're going to be late for school,' his father said curtly. Toby could feel his anger bubbling within.

'But, what did—'

'We'll talk about it tonight.'

'But—'

'And you need to get dressed.'

'But I don't remember!' he shouted.

Laura looked down, hiding her face, and despite the confusion and the throbbing pain, Toby felt guilty. Michael didn't even look at him as he muttered, 'We'll talk about this after school. Your mother's made you porridge.'

Toby nodded okay and mumbled a faint sorry. Michael put an arm out, guiding Laura away. Toby lay there for a moment, trying to pull things together in his head. Suddenly he jumped from the bed and ran to the cupboard, pulling it open. Hidden beneath the clothes was the 'Spy Trap Microcam' recorder box – a little green light showing that it was still working. Toby opened it up, revealing a small screen. Eager, he pressed 'play' and, after a moment of fuzz, a picture emerged: Toby, staring at himself in the mirror, shooting imaginary bullets from his finger.

Toby let out a feathery breath of pleasure, then his fingers pressed 'fast forward' and he watched pictures of the camera heading downstairs, then sitting at the table where the picture became dark and obscure. More fast-forwarding, and suddenly he was moving towards the front door, grabbing a coat, heading through the door and out into the night . . .

Although it was dark, the camera picked out details with surprising clarity. Toby saw the street ahead and suddenly the camera whipped round in a disorientating circle as it recorded him spinning around the lamp post. Toby saw the woman with the dog smile at him. He smiled, just as he had the night before, excited.

The camera stopped moving. Standing still in the road. It just pointed forward, recording the empty street ahead. Toby waited. Any moment now . . . any moment . . .

But then the screen went blank. Toby stared at it, confused as it was replaced by grey fuzz again.

He pressed fast forward again. And while the digital counter showed him that the recording was progressing, the screen refused to reveal its secrets. On and on, the mist remained impenetrable, and eventually the recording ended with a tiny electronic beep.

Toby sat back, stunned. His legs were aching. He looked at his feet and saw that they were cut and sore – as though he'd been running barefoot across gravel. Or something. He examined them: the cuts were clean, washed, disinfected. His head fell and he had to wipe the swelling tears from his eyes.

There was a shout from downstairs. His father – a warning, they had to leave. Toby didn't reply. He just sat there, half-inside the open cupboard, too miserable to move. Finally he mustered the strength to place the box in its secret place, hidden amongst the clothes.

Then he stood and put on the school uniform that his mother had laid out for him at the foot of the bed.

The journey to school was quiet – too quiet for both of them – so Michael put on the radio. Toby sat silently, staring out of the car window, watching as grey buildings passed under grey skies. He looked down at his belt, where the tiny camera had once sat. It was, of course, gone.

His father tried to hum along to a pop tune. He didn't know the words or the tune, really, but Toby recognised the effort to lighten the mood.

'Dad?'

'Toby.'

'Where did you find me?'

His father drove on, stony-faced.

'Dad?'

'I don't know how you can bring it up.'

'But I didn't . . . '

Michael snapped off the radio. 'We were driving the streets all night, Toby. I was terrified we were going to get the call from the police saying you were hurt or you'd . . .' He stopped, and Toby realised how upset he was. 'Your mother never stopped crying.'

They drove on in silence. The red lights seemed interminably long.

'I guess it's because you're our only one, Toby. Your mum had so wanted a little brother or sister for you, but that wasn't to be. So we worry about you more. I know that can be a bit suffocating for you, but . . . I drove all night, Toby.'

Toby stared down at his lap. 'Sorry.'

His dad muttered something back under his breath, but Toby didn't catch it.

When he looked up again, they had arrived at school. A couple of stragglers were running in, trying to beat the bell.

'Just get into school. We love you.'

'Love you too, Dad.'

He got out stiffly, but didn't want to show it. He headed into school and turned at the gates. Michael was still parked there. Watching him. Toby waved, a little half-heartedly, then went inside. He wondered whether, if he turned and looked back outside again, the car would still be there, if his Dad was still waiting and watching. But then he saw some bigger boys coming towards him and he hobbled away to class, as quickly as his sore feet would allow.

THREE

Each time I see Jeff now, I feel jittery. I'm alright at home, but the way he laughs (his stupid bloody jokes) and the way he watches me only makes me more and more stressy. I thought this would all calm down but it hasn't. It's building inside me, I can't explain it right; it's like my body's really unhappy and my brain doesn't know why. At the end of every day, Jeff offers to drive me home, but I can't face him at the moment. I tell him I'm fine and say something about some job I want to tinker with. He's a bit unhappy about this, but eventually he lets me be and goes. I wander around the garage, restless and twitchy about things I just can't put my finger on. I feel worried, and not knowing why is just a bigger wind-up.

When I get home, it's quiet in the house. I go upstairs and find Carrie, Emma and Joe in our bed. She's reading a story for Emma, but Joe's crept into the bed even though he's too old for the book. They both listen with eager, earnest faces. Carrie looks up, smiles and carries on. I want to run over and hug them so tight. But I am still shaking inside. I listen to the story. The lines rhyme. It's witty, sweet, smart. Clear and easy.

I retreat to the boxroom. Turn on my computer. The machine powers up, but the screen is dead. I'm screaming inside as I bend down to check the plug, but it's in, on, so there's no obvious reason. I'll need my toolbox.

Carrie appears at the door. 'They want a cuddle before they go to sleep.'

All I can manage is a grunt. She comes into the room, puts an arm on my shoulder.

'What's wrong with the computer?' I say.

'No idea, I haven't had a moment free today. Joe managed to block the sink with . . .'

She keeps on talking, but I don't want to hear the details. Because they'll suck me away from where I am now. They'll make me feel safer and comfortable. I need the fix she offers, but I have to stay awake now.

And suddenly I feel I've been here a hundred times before. On the verge of opening my eyes and seeing it all, but deciding instead to turn my back, to slump down, to let it all slip blissfully away.

'The screen doesn't work, the computer's on but the bloody screen's buggered.'

She looks at me, confused. She was saying something and I've cut across her.

'Well, it has,' I mutter. 'You've not used it?'

'No. I said. What's with you?'

'I'll go see the kids.'

'No, hang on, you're all wound up. Did something happen at work? Was it that prick Jeff?'

It's nice that she doesn't like him either.

'I'm fine.'

'Balls.'

'Look, just ... it's nothing, I'm ... I had three pints at lunchtime, so maybe it's just the comedown, I don't know, it's nothing, honest.'

She studies me. Frowns, then nods. I push past her and go see the kids.

Joe tells me about a science experiment at school where the teacher made something go blue and Emma tells me that she needs another teddy, a brown dog, or the new one will get lonely cos none of the other toys like him. I play attentive dad. They seem happy enough.

Then I go back to my den.

I shut the door and stare at my desk. It's cluttered with junk. I see three envelopes with red bills in them. In the drawer are some old photos – me and Carrie before the kids. We're mugging it for the camera in a hammock.

I dig out more photos. Joe without his front teeth, Emma in the bath covered in chickenpox, all of us standing outside a collapsed tent in the rain. More photos, more memories. I stare at each one and I remember each moment. Then I stare at them all again.

Carrie comes back. She's in her baggy pyjamas and her hair's wet. I check my watch and realise that it's late and I've dropped photos all over the floor. I see her looking at me and realise I look like a mentalist.

'What's going on, Ben?'

I hear the stress in her voice. The anger seeps out of me like a long, slow breath.

'I don't know.'

She comes over to me, slips onto my lap, nuzzles her head in my neck. 'Do you ever get that thing,' I say, 'that thing in the morning when you wake up, you wake up and your mind's all blank? Like you're still in the other dream? I wake up sometimes and I'm lying there and I've no idea who you are or who I am, really. I lie there, and it's not scary, but I just feel as though I'm part of the other place, the dream. I lie there and slowly it comes back – you, me, the kids, work . . . it comes back, but it takes so long.'

'Everyone gets that.'

'Yeah, I know, you're right.'

She is right. But I'm not telling her the truth. Her hair is dripping cold water onto my shirt. I feel the trickle down my chest.

'Hun?' She looks at me with her beautiful big eyes.

'You're right. I just . . . I . . . sometimes even in the day I find it hard to see where the dream ends and where we start. Does that make any sense?'

'No.'

'No. Sorry.'

'Baby, you look so sad.'

She kisses me. I find myself wondering how many times we've kissed in our time together.

'Does this feel real?' she says. I see the smirk, the sexy smile.

'It might.'

Her hand reaches down between my legs.

'How about this?'

'Yes, I think I can be pretty sure that this is . . .'

We kiss again. And then the phone rings. It feels like an electric jolt through Carrie.

'Leave it,' I urge. I want to stay in this cocoon.

'No, no—'

'It'll be your mum. Whoever it is, let them wait.'

'No, get off, I must, I'll just—'

She's flustered, and all my worries flood back through me. It feels like she's fixing an expression for me.

'Get your clothes off, get under the covers,' she says with a wink. I sit back as she hurries down the stairs, hear her answer the phone. And I slip to the edge of the landing to listen.

'No . . . it's fine . . . I don't think we need to . . . no, nothing like that.'

A long silence as she listens to the person on the other end of the phone.

'We're okay. You don't need to . . . I'm on it . . . he's *fine*.'

The 'he' is me. And that's not her mother.

She hangs up, but doesn't move for a moment. I can see her, see her head sag. I can feel the burden. If I weren't so ripped up I'd want to share it with her. She's still holding the phone in her hand, caught in a terrible quandary that I don't understand.

I come down the stairs quietly, making sure she doesn't hear me.

'What's wrong?'

She jumps, turns, looks at me, confused.

'The call?' I say as casually as I can.

'Oh. Forget about it. Mum. Panicking about nothing. You know her, drama queen.'

She smiles. It's a natural, easy smile. And her confusion before seemed absolutely genuine. She grabs Joe's school bag off the floor and hangs it on the bottom of the banister.

'I thought you were gonna get naked,' she says, but the grin has gone now.

I go to the phone, pick it up, watching her the whole time. I dial last number recall. And her mother's number comes up. I was so sure I was about to catch her out, but, no, I'm wrong, totally wrong. I'm an arsehole. I see the look of disappointment on her face and then she turns her back on me, marches into the kitchen.

I follow her, saying nothing. She goes to the sink, dumps too much detergent into the bowl then starts bashing the saucepans clean.

'Carrie.'

No reply.

'I don't know why I did that. I'm sorry.'

She nods, but doesn't turn. Still, the plates crash a little more lightly in the bubbles.

'I think it's, maybe, it's cos I'm not sleeping properly. These dreams, Jesus.'

'You're booked in to see the doctor,' is her head-down reply.

'Yeah. Doctor McKay. Next week.'

A glass is placed on the rack. Her hand instinctively pulls hair behind her left ear. I don't know what to do. It's like that time we went to a nightclub and I got too drunk and made a fool of myself and she got so angry with me I thought she was going to mash me right there on the dance floor. But I have to know.

'He's just a GP, though.'

'You just said you only needed sleeping pills.'

'Yeah, but . . . what if . . . there's something more wrong with me?'

'More wrong? Like what?'

She turns and now I notice that her eyes are teary. I'm out of my depth.

'I don't know, that's what I'm saying. But my body's sore—'

'That's the rugby.'

'Yeah, sure, but there's that and my head's tired and I feel like shit.'

She sighs, the anger visibly fading with her.

'Go to bed, Ben.'

I stand there feeling big and useless.

'Were you talking about me. To your mum?'

Another sigh from her. 'No, I was talking about Dad. They're . . . she wants to leave him. And I just . . . she sees things, imagines things about him which are just not . . .'

And then she starts to cry. But I still don't go to her. I'm trapped in the doorway, trying to hold down papers in a gale. I imagine a fox, standing outside its lair, sniffing the breeze, its hairs on end, instinct telling it to run from a farmer's gun that it cannot see.

I find words from somewhere, not sure how. 'Why don't we go out tomorrow for a drink, and talk. Somewhere without the kids. Not anything big and boozy. Just, you know, if we tried to do it here then Emma would have nightmares or Joe would have a coughing fit or . . .'

'I'd like that.' She reaches for a drying cloth. 'Go to bed, hon.'

I nod, turn. Go upstairs. I slip into Joe's room. Crouch down and stroke his matted hair. He sleeps so deeply he doesn't stir. Sitting here in the dark, seeing the faint glow of the luminous stars that we stuck on the ceiling together, I wonder again what I have to worry about. A bad feeling. A glimpse of a face of a person I've never met.

I see the fox dead and decomposing. And the contents of my head feel wrong in my boy's room. So I clamber up and get out.

I head for the bedroom. But stop, distracted by the wonder wall. I see Carrie at her own graduation with the worst perm ever. There are her parents holding Emma up so she can see the penguins at the zoo. There's me and Joe pretending to be sumo wrestlers. There's . . .

Carrie appears at the top of the stairs.

'Bed.'

But I can't take my eyes off the photos. 'How come there are none of me up here?' I ask.

'Huh?' She comes up close to me again, an arm around my waist.

'Well, there's you when you were younger – there, about to do that bungee jump in New Zealand and there, there. And there are your folks, but . . . where are the ones of me? When I was younger.'

'I don't know. You tell me.'

'No, but—'

'You want to put some up, you dig them out.'

'But I don't know where they are.'

The hand around my waist is a tiny, tiny bit tighter.

'I don't know where . . . I, when I look back, when I try to think back about life before you, before the kids, I . . . I sort of remember stuff but I . . . it's so vague.'

'Same with everyone.'

'Really?'

'Yeah. Of course.'

'But I . . . no, cos I can tell you when I first joined the scouts, I can tell you what marks I got at school, but I can't *feel* any of it. I know it like I know dates in history, but I don't feel like I was there in any of them.'

It's so quiet.

'It's like ...' But I can't explain it. She waits. 'Do you remember how you felt when you were little?'

'A bit. Some things. You know, like trying on Mum's make-up when she was downstairs.'

'And what do you remember?'

'I ... the smell of the food she was cooking. Feeling excited. Feeling ... naughty.'

'Yeah. I don't ... I don't feel anything like that.'

'Maybe everyone's different. Maybe I'm the odd one.'

'Maybe.'

One of the photos shows Carrie at her hen night. She's surrounded by cackling, drunken gals, all in identical T-shirts, with devil's horns in their hair and an oiled-up stripper looking cocksure next to her. She's got a hand on his pumped chest. My stag do was a blur. But there's an obvious reason for that.

'Honey, you're worrying yourself for no reason. You need a good night's sleep. Come to bed. Come to bed, baby.'

I look down at my scratched hands. How can you think straight when you're this knackered?

Go to bed. Sleep with your wife. Be still. Choose the life you know.

I take Carrie's hand. Let her lead me there. Let her slip the clothes from my back. Let my hands take her.

We fuck. Slow, rhythmic, gentle, a little sad. I imagine us lost together in the jungle. Fucking in a bamboo forest. Green, hot, sweaty, silent.

She falls asleep with her arm across my chest. But I don't sleep. All I can think about now are my parents. I feel my mother's arm around my shoulders, smell her perfume. My father walks in from work and I run to him and he pulls me to him, laughing. I pull on his tie and he scolds me gently. This must be real.

Later, when it's safe, I'm drawn back to the wonder wall. I sit facing it, my back against the other wall. I look at every photo. I feel numb. Something inside of me is missing. Taken.

Breakfast is absolutely normal in every way. I look at everyone and it's almost like we're in an advert: 'the average family'. Carrie and I laugh and argue, then scold and chivvy the children to school. I head off to the garage with a smile and you'd never know that anything was wrong. Work at the garage is steady. I smile at Jeff and make the appropriate groans at his terrible puns. We get on with things and lose a few hours stuck under the bonnet of a choking engine.

I remember my father staring at the engine of our beaten-up Morris Minor, an oily rag in his hand, his head dripping with sweat. An ice cream van's bell rang out a familiar tune from a nearby street. He swore, angry, then saw me watching him and made me promise I wouldn't tell Mum. We fixed it together.

'Nothing more satisfying than fixing something with your own two hands, my boy.'

I must have taken it to heart.

Jeff revs the engine. It's sounding better.

'One more time,' I bark at him. He revs it again. I remember how different that old car sounded. Like a sewing machine. Tiny, simple engines for a smaller, simpler time.

'And again,' I call. Jeff revs the engine. We're nearly there.

Nearly there. I remember Dad saying exactly that as the car turned left and below we could suddenly see the sea and Mum squeezed my hand – the first time I ever saw the sea for real. I miss them. I miss them suddenly and terribly. I want to see them, want to connect with something that's mine.

'Again.'

I turn, even as he revs the engine and walk straight to my car. I don't even look back. As I get in, I can hear him calling to me, thinking I'm still stuck under the bonnet.

'Ben? Again? Again, mate? You happy? Oi! Ben!'

I rev my own engine hard. And I'm off.

It's a three-hour drive to the cemetery where my folks are buried, but I've got a full tank and the roads are empty. As I drive in, the sun breaks through the clouds and something superstitious in me tells me this is a good sign. It's been raining and everything is incredibly clear. I park the car. Outside the Chapel of Rest, a group of mourners wait to go in as another service finishes.

I slip into the graveyard itself, follow the path I know from old. My mum and dad died when I was eighteen, so I've been here many times. I look around: the old cherry tree is about to flower. Sparrows and blue tits bob around its branches. Suddenly it's warm with the sun out, so I pull off my jumper.

I stop at their graves. These seem remarkably well tended. And then I realise I've got the wrong ones. Someone else – Martin and Jemima King. Embarrassed, I turn, thinking I must be a row out or something. I move down, but stop. Turn back, try to get my bearings again. Stop.

I look at the cherry tree, the same tree I've looked at so many times before from this exact spot. It frames the chapel behind it. I am in the right place. But the names on the graves . . .

I walk away, walk around trying to work out where I've gone wrong. I do it ten times, at least. I know that the two graves in front of me should bear my parents' names. But they don't.

I feel sick and angry all at the same time. I look around, I'm choking on air, coughing. My knees wobble.

I start at one end of the graveyard and begin to check off each and every grave, slow and methodical. My mobile phone rings in my pocket but I don't even bother to check who's calling. I walk on, and with every name I don't recognise, anger continues to rise within me. Soon I'm boiling, volcanic.

I head for the Chapel of Rest, ready to take it out on someone. The man inside the room marked 'Staff Only' is pale and podgy, wearing the black suit and tie that the job requires. His hair's white, he could be sixty or something. He's got his head in paperwork, humming to himself, so I slam the door to get his attention. Before he speaks, I'm at him.

'You've got some explaining to do. Who the fuck gave you permission to dig up my parents' graves?'

The man is too astounded to speak.

'My parents, Jeremy and Patricia Jones. Buried here on March 16th, 1986. Out there. But I've just been out there and someone's . . . they're not there. So someone's gone and fucking moved them!'

The accusation seems to spring Podgy back to life.

'I don't think so, sir. No.'

'So, what's happened to them?'

'We would never, never move a grave, it's absolutely out of the question.'

'Did you dig them up?'

'NO! Absolutely not, we'd never, it's against the law, sir.'

'Those graves there, the two together – you can see them from here – those ones. They were my parents and now—'

'Those are, that's Mr and Mrs King. I know the family well. They were buried there over thirty years ago. Their daughters still visit regularly to change flowers and keep them tidy.'

Doubts again, doubts trickle around my head. They drip across my eyes like tar. Podgy can sense it, his confidence is growing.

'Sir, I've worked here for the best part of forty years. If I'd buried your parents then we would have met before and, well, I'm very sorry, sir, but I don't remember you.'

'No. I don't remember you either.'

I don't understand. I lean out a hand against a chair to hold me up.

'Maybe, sir, if you gave me your name, we could find . . . I'm sure there is an easy explanation. Has it been a while, perhaps, since you last visited? It's easy to become disoriented.'

He's right. And it has been too long. I try to remember the last time I came. Jesus, why won't my mind work better?

'Sir? If I could have your name? Did you say Jones?'

'Yes, sorry, it's, I'm – my parents were Jeremy and Patricia Jones. Jerry and Pat.'

He starts to type at his computer. Everything's on bloody computers.

'They died on March 12th, we had the funeral here on the 16th. 1986.'

More typing. He frowns.

'Right there. The cherry was in full bloom. Looked amazing. Everyone commented on it. Auntie Meg said it was a present from God, a sign.'

He looks up, shakes his head.

'And the vicar got the words muddled and we all giggled and ...'

'I can't find anyone who ... we've got plenty of Joneses, of course, but not those Christian names and not on any dates close to the ones you—'

He's embarrassed. It's clear he wants to help me. But I'm spinning now.

'Right there. It rained later and the blossom came down and we got soaked running to the car.'

'I'm sorry.'

'Stop it, stop messing with me. What have you done?' I take an angry step towards him. I feel the big man inside me, the one who challenged Jeff. 'Cos there's nothing wrong with my memory. It's you, this place. Check them again, check that bloody computer again.'

He starts to type. Both of us want the information to change and correct itself. Both of us know that it won't. And while he types, muttering apologies, I feel as though the sun has suddenly set, like something colossal is blacking out the sky.

Podgy looks unhappily at the screen.

'It's not my mind, it's not me that's fucked up,' I yell. 'I'm telling you. And Dad's old mate Ant gave me a fiver. Stuffed it in my jacket pocket and kissed me. See, it's not my brain, it's not me. Someone's been playing, someone's been screwing with your computer, with this place. I should make a complaint, you should, we should. I'm telling you, they should be there, just there, under that tree. THAT tree.'

I run out of words. He stares at me, too scared to speak. I realise that both my hands are clenched into fists.

'It's just . . . it's not me, my mind, that's not the problem.'

I look back outside at the grave. Standing there are two men. Big men. They wear sunglasses. One of them scans the grave-yard as though he's looking for someone. Both have short hair. And I find myself taking a step away from the window.

Podgy hasn't moved, his mouth's still open.

'Look, I . . . okay. Is there another way out?'

'I'm sorry?'

'I came in from that door. Is there a different way to get out?'

Something inside helps me out without anyone seeing. An instinct, or something taught and well-hidden, I don't know. Either way I slip over the metal fence, shielded by a tree, and if anyone's waiting for me at the gates they'll be disappointed.

Why would anyone be waiting for me?

There's nothing wrong with my mind. There's nothing wrong, nothing wrong.

I walk three miles then wait at a bus stop, leaving my car at the cemetery.

It's dark now. I sit in the shelter and try to work it all out. Buses come and go, their doors puff open and the driver waits, but I never look up. I don't want anyone to see my face.

Dark circles spiral beautiful, terrifying patterns in my mind, then crack and splinter. Roots wither and die. A beautiful sun rises behind my eyes then explodes, poisoning me with its deadly radiation.

I stare at my hands. I notice old scars beneath the fresh ones.

Another bus stops, its engine urging me to step on, but I can't move. A demon sits next to me, laughing, knowing everything.

The bus pulls away and it's dark again. Dark and quiet. Except for the laughter.

I don't know what time it is when I finally return home. The journey was slow and sore, but I barely noticed it. As I get to the door though, I realise that I'm soaked through. It doesn't matter, there is a red heat within me. I slip the key into the lock and hang my coat up as I have every day. It's quiet. The kids must have gone to bed long ago.

It's warm. Unopened junk mail lies by the door. The front mat is still dirty from the kids' muddy boots after our walk in the park.

Carrie appears from the kitchen. Her eyes are red. She stares at me – relieved and furious.

'You switched off your phone. No one knew where you were, the garage were very pissy about it until they realised how worried I was.'

'Sorry.'

'And?'

I don't reply.

'Ben!' her voice is higher and louder now. 'I've been worried sick. I had to get Carol to pick up the kids cos I was scared that if I left the house I'd miss ... the news ... that you'd ...'

She's nearly crying. But I won't move.

'I've been so worried.'

'I'm sorry.'

'If that's all I'm getting, we're going to have one big fucking fight because—'

'Please. Don't. Don't.' My hands. 'Do you love me?'

'Not when you behave like a complete prick—'

I find I'm screaming. 'Jesus Christ! I'm trying, I'm trying, I just need you to . . . do you love me?'

She looks at me, I see her expression change, and she rushes to me. Holds me.

'I like it, Carrie. How we are. Simple. All I have to do is worry about footie results and bills and how we can stop Emma sticking peas in her ears. I like it. And I love you.'

'I love you,' she says. Her face is so soft.

'But you've been lying to me,' I say, and she suddenly seems a little bit harder. 'I need you to be straight with me now.'

'I haven't been lying—'

'I need you to be straight with me.'

The reply is quiet. Not scared, but . . . I don't know. I love her too much to be able to read her.

'Okay.'

Okay. 'I went to Bolton today. And it wasn't like anything I remembered.'

She just shakes her head, doesn't understand.

'I feel like . . . half of my brain's been cut out or, I don't know, but I can't trust what's in here and that's really, really scary.' I pull away from her. Not cos I don't want to hug her tight, but the energy inside me is too raw. 'When was the last time we went to visit my parents' graves?'

'Honey, I think you shouldn't—'

'I want you to answer my questions.'

'Don't talk to me like that. I'm your wife. Stop it.'

A car drives past outside, the stereo's on full blast. It stops me for a second.

'I'm in trouble, Carrie.'

'So we'll see the doctor.'

'Who? Dr Mackay?'

'Why not?'

'You know, I've never met anyone else who goes to Doctor Mackay. They all go to the local surgery on Elm Street. Why is that? I mean, I've never seen anyone else in that waiting room. It always feels creepy, don't you think?'

'Let's just, let's just go in the morning, we'll worry about this tomorrow.'

'Don't we always say this? We'll fix it in the morning. We just fix everything by going to sleep.'

'I think you're suffering from some kind of depression or anxiety—'

'That's good.'

'—and I think you're starting to see things in a destructive way and I think you should maybe shut up before you do real damage here.'

'Seeing things in a destructive way? When did you eat the dictionary?'

'Alright. Imagining things.'

'Which things am I imagining, Carrie?'

Silence.

'Am I imagining the bit where I attack strangers in the night?'

'Yes! God! Of course you are.'

I stare at her. Flawless.

'No. I think I do.'

'Ben—'

'And I guess you think so too.' She's shaking slightly. 'I went there, to the cemetery and it was like I'd forgotten how to walk or, no I can't, that's not it but . . . I was so shocked because you trust what's in your head, right? I mean, we do things because of experience. Don't put your hand over the kettle's steam, cos you remember it'll hurt. I'm made up of everything I remember. But out there, nothing is . . . I don't know anything out there. So I come home. Cos this is the one place – the one place – where it should all make sense, but then I look at you and I know you're lying.'

'No.'

'You're lying. This is a lie. You are too. The kids, Jesus.

'Ben—'

'But I remember it all so clearly.' My voice is cracking, my chest is heaving, but I have to get this out. 'I remember holding Joe in my arms the minute after he was born. Remember the smell of the room. And I love him. I love my little boy to death, with all my heart. But he's not real. Is he? The dreams I have, they're not dreams, are they? They're real, they're the real things. But not Joe, not Emma. Not you.'

'Let's go see someone. Please. Anyone. You choose.' She reaches out a hand to me. But I don't take it and she starts to cry. 'Please, baby, please. Don't listen to yourself, you're just run down. We can fix you. Please, I just want the old Ben back again.'

She glances at the front door. It's a tiny glance, but it's a tell.

'Why did you . . . ?'

I go to the door, peer out of the spyhole. 'Are you expecting someone?'

She doesn't bother to deny it.

'Is someone coming? Carrie?' Her lip crumples. 'Carrie? Is this right? What's happening?'

I lunge for her. Angry. I grab her and pin her against the wall.

'What's happening to me?!'

She screams – but not to me. To the room, to the house. To others.

'Help me! He knows! He knows! Help me for God's sake!'

Her screams stun me and I let her go. She doesn't move, doesn't run. And when her eyes meet mine I see guilt and shame.

'Who were you talking to?' She doesn't reply. Another glance to the door. 'Carrie? What's about to happen? Hon?'

And then suddenly she pulls me to her, holds me tight, then whispers in my ear.

'Throw away your shoes, your clothes. Throw everything away. Never answer the phone. And run.'

I pull back, scared by the words, by the lips that speak them, so close to me. She looks at me fearfully. Her hands grab mine.

'I love you,' she whispers so quietly that I almost can't hear her.

A key turns in the lock and I turn, surprised. Suddenly three men charge into the room. They grab me before I can resist. I see a syringe. I try to avoid it but they are too fast, too strong.

Carrie screams. The syringe hits my arm hard. I feel its tiny sting and the darkness rises up and over. I try to call her name. Carrie.

Carrie.

Carrie . . .

FOUR

Each day, Michael would drop Toby off at the school gates, leaving him only a few minutes to make it into class on time. Today, however, a series of red lights had delayed them and Toby was late. As he hurried in, the corridors were quieter than usual. The bell had already rung and there were only a few stragglers left. He glanced in at other rooms as he passed, saw teachers arguing happily with pupils, heard a violin being played badly. He felt the sting of his socks as they rubbed against the cuts on his feet.

He pushed open the door into his classroom and kept his head down. Anna Price was standing at the blackboard. He glanced at her, muttered an apology and shuffled to his place. Anna watched him, pausing momentarily to express her displeasure but continuing so that the class couldn't make it an issue.

They were reading *Macbeth*. Toby found his book and sat quietly at the back of the class, turning pages when required. He looked up as Anna encouraged Raj and Paulette to read together in front of the class. Paulette was embarrassed, not wanting the public exposure, and as Anna tried to encourage them the whole thing quickly descended into chaos. Toby watched everyone laugh. He felt like he was seeing it from behind a cracked window. Anna finally got some control and Raj began to read in a quiet, slurred voice, massacring the old words as the class sniggered quietly and Anna watched with pursed lips and folded arms.

As Toby sat there, watching them, a memory jolted him. A sucker-punch to the head.

Thrashing about in dark water, freezing cold, unable to see, fighting to reach the surface.

The memory flashed and faded. But it left Toby short of breath. He looked around, jolted, but Paulette was still stumbling over the verse and the class was laughing at her.

Then another memory came crashing in.

Screaming under the water – the air from his lungs bubbling away from him. Screaming and screaming, but unable to pull himself up to the surface.

'Shit!' The word burst out of him involuntarily. It stopped the rest of the class dead and suddenly all eyes were on him. Someone started laughing. But Toby could still feel the burning in his lungs.

'Toby?' Anna came forward, surprised and annoyed by the outburst. Toby looked up. He could feel the horror of the memory tapping at the back of his neck.

'Nothing.'

'Excuse me?'

'Nothing, Miss.'

'Well, I'm sure it was something for you to interrupt the lesson like that.'

Toby just stared at his desk. He didn't normally get into trouble and he could tell that the class was thrilled to watch this. Much better than Shakespeare.

'Toby?'

'No thanks.'

'I insist.'

'Look, can we, can we just get on with the sodding play?'

A few gasps, then a lad called out, 'Hey, Toby's finally grown some balls!' and the class roared in approval.

'Right. That's enough!' Anna snapped. 'Toby Mayhew, detention after school. Raj and Paulette get on with it – and if I hear a word from anyone else then there will be big trouble. Do you all understand?'

The class murmured and grumbled, but no one really gave a shit. Paulette carried on reading, and soon everything was back to normal. Anna glanced at Toby, she caught his eye and her expression softened – what's happened? she asked silently. He looked down and didn't look back up for the rest of the lesson.

He continued to avoid her gaze during detention at the end of the day. Anna watched him from her desk, looking up between doses of a celebrity gossip magazine, but the boy remained sullen and withdrawn. Eventually, she'd had enough and got up, standing over Toby, waiting for him to give in and look up at her. But still he didn't move.

'So, what happened, Toby?'

He just shrugged.

'It's not like you.'

Again, nothing.

'I rang your father. He seemed, well, not that surprised.'

'Yeah, well . . .'

But he shut himself off before he could say any more. Anna leaned against the neighbouring desk and waited, exploiting the silence. Just as she thought she'd failed, Toby finally looked up at her.

'Is everything okay at home?' she asked, grabbing the moment.

'How do you mean?' He seemed genuinely confused by the question.

'Well, sometimes, when you're having trouble at school, it's actually because things aren't . . . going so well . . . at home . . .'

She raised her eyebrows to make her point, but Toby stared at her blankly.

'I saw you were limping, when you came into class.'

'It was my fault.' A pause and then he muttered, 'apparently.' It was said under his breath, but it was a shared whisper.

'What was?' Anna asked, leaning forward.

'Nothing.'

'But you don't think so?'

'Dunno.'

'If it wasn't your fault, then whose fault was it?'

He just shrugged, eyes down again. Anna's hands gripped the desk a little more tightly.

'If it wasn't your fault, Toby, then was it . . . your father's?'

Another shrug.

'Toby, is your father—?'

'I don't know!' he blurted out. It wasn't a shout and it wasn't aggressive. 'I don't know anything! It drives me mad, never being able to be sure about anything. I'm always told things and I believe it if they say it, but there's stuff in me as well, you know? Stuff that's not stupid, but I can't prove it. I mean, how do I get proof? All the things they say . . .'

And then the frustration ran out. A wound-down toy.

'Just drives me mad,' he repeated. He ran a hand through his short hair. It was the act of a much older boy. Anna stared at Toby and remembered the way Michael led him away from school. A hand on the back of his neck.

'Toby. If you're saying . . . what I think . . . then you need to talk to someone professional.'

'Done that. They just move me to another city, another school.'

'What?'

'I've been to four schools in five years. Didn't you check my report?'

'Well, no, I—'

'Never bothered.' It was said matter-of-factly, without accu-sation; an acceptance of the rules. 'No one checks. No one believes me.'

'I believe you.'

'No, you don't. Sorry, Miss, no offence, but . . .'

'I do.'

'You're nice, a bit concerned, just like the others, and I think you're a really good teacher too.'

'Thanks.'

'No worries. But you won't actually do anything.'

'Yes, I will.'

Something prickled within Anna. She had a thing for the underdog.

'What are you going to do?' Toby continued. 'Talk to the Head? Social services?'

From his mouth, the suggestions seemed specious.

'Well,' said Anna, bristling, 'what would you want me to do?'

Toby's sad eyes stared at her with doubt, but he was looking at her properly for the first time that either could remember. Maybe the first time since he walked into her class six months ago.

'Find me proof,' he said.

'Of what your father did to you?'

'Well, if it was him.'

'Okay . . .' she said warily, not sure where all this was leading. Toby seemed brighter-eyed all of a sudden and Anna was disquieted by this enthusiasm.

'You know how to get proof?' she asked.

'I guess. If you can take me there, so we can see it for real.'

'See what?'

'The place where it happened, of course!'

He stood up, overexcited, and Anna's stomach lurched.

Toby sat politely next to his teacher as her car squealed out of the gates. The further they got from the school the more he relaxed, and the quieter Anna became.

He pointed to the old railway bridge near the edge of town and Anna parked the car nearby as requested. He walked quickly along the narrow footpath that crossed the bridge next to the railway lines, his teacher following. The bridge was tatty, with crumbling paint and puddles in the corroding concrete potholes. He looked down at the river, twenty feet below. Its dark water swelled, choked with mud. The wind picked up and the dark clouds above threatened rain. He could feel the moisture in the air.

72

Toby stopped when he reached the middle of the bridge, looking around. Yes, he thought, this is the place. He closed his eyes.

And there he was. Stood in the exact same spot. Laughing as a train hurtled past behind him. The lights from the carriages illuminated him like a strobing disco.

'Toby,' Anna called, pulling him back.

'I've been here before.'

'But we're miles from your house.'

'Yeah.' He looked around him. The footpath was deserted. He closed his eyes again.

And he was laughing on the empty footpath too, but then he noticed a large camouflaged backpack that leant against the railings. And somehow he knew that it was for him. He peeked inside; it was filled to the top with rocks. He kicked off his shoes, peeled off his socks and then hoiked the heavy bag onto his shoulders. Then he tightened the straps around his arms.

Toby took a step towards the edge of bridge.

Although he was swaying under the weight of the backpack, he still was able to pull himself up and stand on the edge of the railings. He teetered slightly, staring up at the sky. It was a clear night. The stars were out.

'Toby. Come down, please,' the anxious teacher's voice broke through again. He opened his eyes and stared out at the dull water below. But he didn't step back down to safety.

He just laughed.

'Toby, please, it's not safe.'

No one saw him jump. No one heard the whoop of joy as he fell. No one was there to watch him sink. And sink. And sink. The rocks pulled him down. And as he sank, he continued to giggle.

Toby watched the water from the bridge. It offered up no clues.

Deeper and deeper. The light soon snuffed out.

Toby stared down and felt tears welling in his eyes. He felt hot, his breathing shallow.

Soon he needed air. He struggled to loosen the arm-straps. But they were too tight and the bag was too heavy. He hit the bottom hard. Glass and jagged rocks attacked his bare feet.

He blinked the tears away and was scared to close his eyes again. But he forced himself onwards. Downwards.

And then there was no air left. He writhed and struggled, finally getting one arm free from the anchoring backpack. But it was too late. He screamed, the bubbles rising and vanishing above him. He fought as the cold began to close him down, suffocating him with its cruel, clinical strength. The backpack finally fell from his trapped arm. Too late. As he pushed upwards, the cold and dark took him. His head spun, his lungs burned, and the darkness sucked him in.

'Toby. Please. Come down. You're scaring me.'

He was surprised to see Anna there. She seemed so out of place with the things in his head. But he liked her for that and she had a kindness about her that he felt he could trust.

'I get these nightmares,' he said. 'Well, I think they're nightmares, but sometimes they're so real, so real, I'm not sure. Sometimes I wake up and I still think I'm dreaming, like I can't even remember who I am. Mum says lots of people are the same. Is that right?'

'I don't know. Maybe . . .'

'Do you ever dream?'

'Of course.'

'Dream like it's so real that, you know, that it can't not be true. Do you ever?'

'Sometimes. Maybe.'

He nodded. She was not like him. Okay.

'I was here. I was down there and then . . .'

He took a step back to safety. Anna, clearly relieved, went to him.

'Miss, what's the longest you can stay underwater? If you held your breath and, you know . . . How long?'

'I'm not sure. A minute? Maybe two. Three?'

Toby considered this. Nothing made sense.

'Impossible. Dream. Must be.' He saw how concerned she was and it only made him feel worse. 'Sorry, Miss. I'm, we've wasted . . . sorry.' His head fell. She pulled him to her and he was grateful for the contact, muttering 'sorry' over and over.

'Can we go back to school, please, Miss? Don't want Dad to . . .'

He didn't need to finish the sentence. Anna led him back along the bridge. Toby walked stiffly, his injuries hurting more all of a sudden. As they walked, Anna stopped, seeing something glisten in a puddle, and she leaned down to pick it up. She peered at it.

'Well, look at that,' she said.

Toby's eyes widened. She was staring at his tiny camera, the one he'd attached to his belt the night before, holding it up to the light, staring at it unknowingly. 'I thought it was just a button.'

Toby's mouth twitched with surprise and excitement. He reached out and took the camera from her – she handed it over without question – and he stared at it in his open palm, cold and wet. She had found it and had not hidden it from him. This woman, who none of the other kids cared about or noticed, had uncovered the proof that he'd been searching for. He lunged at her, hugging her tight without explanation. And he didn't let go.

'Okay Toby. Toby, that's enough now.'

But he didn't move. He knew he'd have to tell her more soon enough and wondered what this might mean for her. But while he could, for that tiny fantastic moment, he would hold her and not let go.

The drive back to school was quiet. Anna glanced at Toby, waiting for him to tell her more, but he just stared out of the window, a dreamy smile on his face. Eventually, her curiosity and frustration won over.

'Toby. I don't understand. What happened back there?'

But he was just grinning to himself, whispering something over and over. She finally worked out that he was saying *I knew it, I knew it, I knew it.*

'Toby.'

He stopped, looked at her.

'Toby, you need to tell people about this. It'll carry on if you don't. We'll do it together.' The idea seemed to scare him. 'You trust me, don't you?'

'Yeah, yeah, of course. I mean, you found the camera and there's no way you'd have shown me it, if you weren't . . .'

'If I wasn't . . .?

He sighed. 'People don't believe me.'

'Well, we'll make them. We'll show them your scars.'

'Won't make no difference.'

'I'll make sure.'

'Yeah. But then something will happen and then they don't want to know.'

'That's what's happened before?'

'Yeah.'

'Well, this time it'll be different. I won't let you get hurt any more. I won't.'

'Thank you,' Toby said with a smile that blinked and died. 'But I don't think you get what this is.'

'I think I've got an idea.'

'No, this is just some kid and some cuts to you.'

'It's more than that, it's about you being safe about people not—'

'No, no, you don't get it at all.'

'So tell me.'

'I ... okay ... but you won't ...'

'*Toby.*'

'I bet you think—'

The blast of a police siren jolted them. The car was right there, close, like it had been stalking them for miles. It flashed its lights: pull up. Anna did so. But as she turned off the engine and turned to Toby she was surprised to see that he was white with fear.

'Toby? What's the matter?'

A gloved hand banged on the window by her face and they both jumped. The glove gestured for her to roll down the window and as she did so, a tall policeman in uniform leaned down, his face close to hers. He was gaunt, with greying cropped hair. His skin was newly shaven and his uniform perfectly clean and pressed. He looked at Anna then at Toby, with a slow stare like a scanner.

'Yes, officer?' Anna mustered.

'Toby Mayhew?' His voice was sharp, clipped.

Toby nodded.

'Get out of the car, son, I'm taking you home.'

'No, it's alright officer, I'm his teacher—'

The man's cold eyes shut her up. Then he looked back at Toby.

'Come on, lad, your mother's worried senseless.'

Anna tried again. 'But there's nothing to worry about—'

'Toby,' he snapped and the boy unbuttoned the seat belt and bolted from the car.

A second police car pulled up in front of Anna's, and Toby went to it. As it drove off, Anna saw that the policeman was still staring at her. But now his face betrayed a nasty leer.

'So,' he said.

'Look, officer—'

'You pick up a kid without his parents' permission—'

'I didn't "pick up a kid". I'm his teacher.'

'Take him for a nice drive, miles from home. I'm not sure that's allowed, is it?'

'This is crazy.'

'Get out of the car, Anna.'

A cold spike stabbed at her. How did he know her name?

'Where are we going?' she asked, not managing to hide her unease.

'You'll see.' He smiled. His teeth had a yellowish tint.

'No, thank you. I don't want to.'

He moved closer and she could smell the remnants of the morning's aftershave.

'Which station are you attached to?' she stammered.

'Get out of the car, Anna.'

'No.' She found some control in her voice. 'I want your name and police number. Please.'

'I'm sure you do.' He straightened, smirked. 'Take care, Anna.'

The policeman walked back to his car, got in and drove off. Anna watched the car turn at the end of the road and waited fearfully for it to return. She opened the glove compartment and reached for the packet of cigarettes that she'd resisted for so long, but then found she couldn't strike the match properly because her hands were shaking too much. Another nervy glance in the mirror, but the car was gone and not coming back.

She looked back at the seat where Toby had been sitting. The tiny button camera was all that remained. It was some sort of proof, but not understanding what it meant only worried her more. She felt as though a door had been opened somewhere. She could feel its chill wind and hear the distant cries, but she couldn't work out what they were saying. She didn't want to know. But the chill wouldn't go away. The door would not shut.

FIVE

They always tidy up after them. Always. Carrie remembered this as she came back down the stairs. The house was silent again. The van they'd bundled Ben into had arrived without a sound and was gone minutes later. It was her scream that had woken Emma, not their arrival nor the way they slipped him out into the dark. Tidy and polite. She couldn't imagine them screaming. But she had. And she knew that she'd be in trouble for it.

She knew she'd be in trouble, and it bothered her as she hurried up the stairs and soothed Emma back to sleep with kisses and lies. But when she came downstairs the house was still. The picture frames on the wall were restraightened, the rug on the floor was back in its place, the door shut and locked. Her heart could pound as hard as it liked, they had made everything normal again. She made herself a coffee just to give herself something to do. Someone would be over soon and she'd need to be sharp for them. Sure enough, she heard a key turn in the lock only ten minutes later and Diane slipped inside with a cheery smile and a stage whisper.

'Congratulations! You did it, you made it to the end!' She hugged Carrie tightly before hanging her coat on the back of the door and heading for the fridge to pour herself a juice. Carrie tried not to let this irritate her. They all had keys, and the way they behaved in the house made the message clear – this wasn't her home. The house was a shared space, owned by the Company for everyone's use. Carrie might spend more time here than the others, but she should never forget its true purpose. She'd been told often enough.

Diane wore a fitted skirt and white blouse which would look equally fine in the office or a wine bar. She perched herself on the edge of a battered armchair. She was a plain woman in her fifties with slightly wonky teeth. But she dressed well and had an expensive haircut. The combination could make you describe her as handsome.

'Bet you're relieved. How long? Six years?'

'Six in May.'

'Amazing. No one thought it would last so long. I heard Brian talking about it only a week ago. They normally blow up after a year, max. Angela had one recently who went totally bananas in the first week! The first bloody week!' Diane chortled and then glugged down the juice in one go.

Carrie shrugged. She felt exhausted all of a sudden but she'd never felt comfortable enough with Diane to crash out onto the sofa. It was the way Diane would run her eyes over you and the room with that calculating smile. She was always evaluating things, as if everything were an equation to be solved, a deal to be brokered.

'Don't be coy, darling. He only lasted so long because you were so brilliant. Watching the tapes, seeing the way you'd stop him worrying, the way you'd limit his thinking, it was stunning work. We'll be using a lot of it for training sessions. Transcripts and videos – it's a masterclass.' Diane smiled again, but her eyes were locked on the kids' cards which were stacked up on the window sill. World's Best Dad. Then her eyes returned to Carrie.

'Thank you,' Carrie replied warily.

Diane reached down to the smart leather bag she always had with her, and Carrie remembered their very first meeting. She was the initial point of contact all those years ago, after Carrie had answered the vaguely worded article in the local paper – something about smart, adventurous people with a purpose. She'd been impressed and intimidated by Diane way back then. Carrie had sat on her hands, trying to hide her chipped nails, feeling increasingly self-conscious about her short denim skirt which she'd tugged down as low as it would go over her bare legs. She'd listened with wide eyes at the way this cool, professional woman chatted to her as though they'd been mates for years. Back then, Carrie was a chancer, living off the dole and faking benefits, moving from man to man until they ran out of money or hit her, or both. She had eyed the classy, expensive jewellery on Diane's fingers and wrists, and felt a little giddy as this posh, educated woman held her eye and told her of her company's ambitions. For Carrie, it was an escape from a grubby life which only promised worse to come.

That first meeting in the cafe lasted about half an hour. Carrie had many more over the next few months and it only dawned on her later that Diane had left with plenty of details about Carrie without giving any back in return. After that there had been some odd events: a man who had been chasing her for money disappeared, and someone broke into her flat (spotted by the neighbours) but didn't steal a thing although she had two hundred pounds behind the boiler, which was where everyone hid their cash.

But Carrie hadn't given it much thought. Life back then was always chaotic and would shove shit at you whenever it fancied. Maybe that was why she was so impressed with Diane. She seemed untouchable. She read the posh newspapers and left generous tips without scraping around for money from back pockets. She would appear at odd moments, never ringing in advance, wanting to know more, congratulating Carrie for passing an unknown test or informing her that she was now on a shortlist; always tantalising. Diane was her new drug, and Carrie became more and more obsessed with saying the right thing, with being the right sort of person in order to please her and continue these meetings. She started to speak differently when she was around Diane. She lost the harsher tones of her accent and let her hair grow back to its natural colour. She would hold a wine glass the same way Diane did, at the stem rather than clutching it tight in case someone tried to steal it.

Eventually, Diane took her into the offices of the Company, sat her down at a long polished table, and told her that her life could change forever. The choice was hers. If she wanted to continue with the project, she would have to say goodbye to any family and friends and break all contact with her past life. ALL contact. Diane wanted her to realise how significant this was, but she was too excited at the idea of a new future to pay proper attention to Diane's concerns. Her parents were dead and she barely spoke to her estranged sister; her friends were just grifters and takers who she'd drink with one day and fight with the next. Leaving her shabby life behind would be no hardship at all. She signed every document without reading a word.

Now, as Carrie watched Diane reaching into her bag to retrieve more paperwork, she felt a stab of worry about what she had actually signed back then. She'd been dumb not to take them to a lawyer but, thinking back on it, she seemed to remember Diane hinting that this wasn't an option. She prided herself on her street sense and natural cunning – it had got her through the countless tests they'd put her through after all – so she'd signed away. But now she felt coldly exposed and didn't exactly know why. It made her feel stupid again, as though she were wearing that frayed denim skirt once more. Three months ago she'd thought she'd seen Leanne, an old mucker with whom she'd stolen and snorted. If it was Leanne, then time hadn't been kind. She walked with an unsteady, fragile step, like a beaten dog, and when she looked up at Carrie as they passed, her eyes had shown no flicker of recognition. But then Carrie would hardly recognise herself any more. Her performance was so complete she could hold Diane's eye without betraying a single true emotion.

Diane flicked through various documents. 'Okay, so . . . all this is just to tie things up now that the project's over,' she said. 'You know what they're like over at Head Office. Now, is it a C33 or a D12 you need?'

'It's definitely done, then?'

Diane looked up, a questioning smile on her face.

'Well, I wondered if he was, you know, fixable,' Carrie stammered. 'Maybe you could wipe his memory, start again.'

'Oh, no he's finished. Once they flip like that, there's no coming back. It's not fair on you, you're always going to be wondering if he'll go again. No, that one's run its course. It's company policy.'

Diane flicked through a document, muttered something, then chose a different one. She wandered over and laid it out on the kitchen table.

'Sign there. And then let's have a glass of wine.' She handed Carrie a pen. It felt heavy in her hand and she allowed it to roll in her palm for a moment before signing the paper. Diane whisked it away and returned it to her bag. 'Someone will be over later to do some drugs tests, you know the routine. Doesn't mean you can't have some wine, though. I'd have stopped off to get some champagne but they always want you there within fifteen minutes of an incident.' She snapped the bag shut. 'It's finally over! Can you believe it? Was it scary at the end? Must have been, what with the scream. That's not like you.' Diane glanced back as she walked towards the kitchen. 'Wine in the fridge?'

'Uh-huh.' Carrie looked around at the quiet house and wondered why she'd been so scared. Ben had been wild, for sure, but he was confused, not angry. Maybe it was knowing all the other stuff about him. She thought back to the first time she was shown photos of him. She had stared down at them on the office desk, trying to work out whether or not she found him attractive, while Diane described his character, his crimes and his cruelties. How different he'd been when he first opened his eyes and saw her. How bashful and charming, so shy and gentle.

Diane returned with the bottle and two glasses. She frowned at the label. 'Well, I guess something nicer would have been out of character, so congratulations on the authenticity. But now you're free, less of the supermarket own-brand, yes?'

Carrie didn't feel free. But she smiled anyway.

'You'll miss the kids,' Diane said, almost sing-song. Carrie nodded. The words kicked hard. She knew the day would come, or at least she knew that she'd been told it would. When she'd first been handed the children, she'd resented their arrival. Emma was only a few months old, Joe was two, and the whole thing seemed like overkill. But the project insisted on him being a family man, so she did as she was told.

'It'll be strange without them, that's for sure.' The words came from her mouth, but they didn't sound like her.

'We suggest you make it a quick clean break. Sometimes, when people know it's over they can get all gushy. That's frowned upon. And it's not fair on the little ones either.'

'What'll happen to them?'

'You know better than that,' Diane said. She poured the wine and when she looked up Carrie knew that she was expected to apologise.

'Sorry. Will they be gone tonight?'

'I imagine so. People will come.' Carrie took the glass she was offered as Diane raised hers for a toast. 'To you, Carrie. Exceptional.'

Carrie drank hard. As she lowered the glass, she saw that Diane was watching her.

'Why did you scream?'

Carrie almost gulped. There was bite in the question. 'Sorry?'

'You knew the drill. And if he was really scaring you, you just ask the three questions.'

'I screwed up. I said I was sorry. Did it disturb the neighbours?'

'Oh, you don't have to worry about them. Forget about it, I was just interested. It'll all go down in the case notes, so you can explain it then.'

'The neighbours didn't hear anything?'

'The neighbours are not a problem.'

There was something about the way she said this that bothered Carrie, but she didn't have time to dwell on it. Diane had other forms for her to sign, other questions and a list of tasks and chores for her to do over the next few days. The wine made her drowsy. She had no idea how late it was now.

'Go on, you go to bed,' Diane finally said. She put her hand on Carrie's cheek. 'Have a lie-in, enjoy having the house to yourself. Have a soak in the bath, chillax. See, I'm down with the lingo!' Diane rubbed her hand down Carrie's arm. 'We'll give you the mandatory time off – paid leave – and then we'll see whether or not you fancy a new case. Something a bit different but the same sort of work. I'm not going to ask you now if you feel up to it, I'm not a monster. But if you're worried about your future, then don't be. There's always a place for you with us. Always.'

Carrie wondered why the phrase scared her more than it excited her. After Diane left, she found herself humming the song 'Hotel California' even though she didn't know why. She went up to the half-empty bedroom and stared at Ben's discarded clothes by the door. She could hear Joe snoring down the hallway but she didn't dare go in to see him. She stood half in, half out

of the bedroom, trapped by Ben's crumpled jeans and the innocent growls of a boy she'd never see again. Her legs shook. Her
heart fluttered and tears pushed up into her eyes. She wiped
them away, shut the door, took three sleeping pills and climbed
into bed. She was asleep within seconds.

When she awoke, Emma was standing by the side of the
bed. It took her a minute to realise that this wasn't right.

'Mum. There's a woman downstairs.'

'What?'

'Dad's not here.'

'Hang on, Em. What's happening?'

'There's a woman, she's really grumpy. Says you have to come
down.'

Carrie's head was thick and heavy from too few hours sleep
and the pills. She dragged a dressing gown around her and
stumbled down the stairs. Diane was there, staring at Joe who
was munching on a big bowl of cereal. She was still dressed
in the same smart clothes, but her hair was down and she
couldn't hide the tiredness behind her eyes. Carrie looked at
her: what's going on? Diane glanced at Emma who stood on
the bottom step, watching Diane with a suspicion that was
beyond her years.

'Joe, honey, pour your sister some cereal, will you?'

Joe looked up, about to complain about this outrage, but he
clocked his mother's pale features and red eyes.

'Come on, Em, Mum got Golden Nuggets yesterday. See?' He
flashed the packet at Emma and she forgot about Diane in
seconds.

'He's a good boy, your son. Bursting with character,' Diane
said, loud enough for Joe to hear as she led Carrie up the stairs.

Neither spoke as they walked, but the phrase 'your son' made it clear enough to Carrie. Something was up. Diane shut the door behind her.

'Okay. We're going to keep this running for a few more days.'

'I'm sorry?'

'This house, the kids, you. It's still in play – and they'll be late for school.'

'Hang on, what's happened?'

'Nothing. They just want to wind this down more slowly. So we keep it all as it is until we're told otherwise.'

'Is Ben coming back?'

'No.'

Carrie waited for her to say more. Diane pulled a hair-band from her pocket and tied her hair back. In the daylight, Carrie noticed the lines and wrinkles on those elegant hands.

'Diane, if he's not coming back then . . . well, I don't understand.'

'Join the club, darling. When I know more, I'll let you know.'

'You'd only be back here if something had happened.'

'Oh, Lord, they're always changing their bloody minds, it does my head in to be honest. But a job's a job. Seriously, you need to get them to school.'

Carrie's mind was racing and the thought that clicked into focus jolted her.

'You said he's not coming back.'

'That's right.'

'What if he does?'

Diane looked down. It was the first time Carrie had seen a chink of weakness and it excited her. Diane adjusted the watch strap on her wrist.

'If he turns up, we'll take him away again. People are watching. You have nothing to fear. Alright? You're perfectly safe.'

'He got away,' Carrie said, realisation dawning.

'You don't need to be afraid, everything is in hand – except your kids, who should be in uniform by now. And the way Joe behaves, I imagine there'll be a milk lake on your carpet if you don't get down there and take them in hand.' Diane laughed and Carrie could feel how forced it was.

Ben was free. Diane didn't have all the answers. Anything was possible now.

Carrie's heart leapt inside her.

'How long?' she said.

'It'll be back in order in two days, max.'

'Okay. No problem.'

Carrie walked with Diane to the door then called out loudly as she closed it. 'Come on, rugrats, or we'll all be expelled!'

She found she was laughing. She felt stoned. Happiness and relief flooded her body.

Ben was free.

SIX

Toby didn't dare look up as the police car sped through the streets. The men in the front said nothing and the journey seemed to go on forever. Eventually the car slowed and he shot a glance out the window, recognising the neighbouring streets. Nearly home. Finally they parked outside his house and he saw the front door open and his mother hurry out. He didn't move; the fear of the journey had worn him out.

The cop in the passenger seat turned and looked at him hard.

'I used to run my parents ragged, kiddo. Then one day, me ma dropped down dead. Undiagnosed cancer, but I still blame myself for it. Even today. If I were you, I'd sort yourself out while you can. You follow?'

Toby nodded and pushed at the car door. His mother was there and she led him inside as his father talked to the cops. He caught a few words but little more. His mum's sweet perfume felt familiar and reassuring. He let her lead him up the stairs to his bedroom, and lay on the bed, quiet and embarrassed by her matronly concern. She left him with a gentle kiss on the forehead and he didn't move for a while. His mind drifted back to his teacher and the camera. It had all happened less than an hour before, but the memories seemed squashed now.

After a bit he got up and went to the window. The cops were just driving off and the road was quiet again. He spotted some neighbours who were looking out from their windows, but they soon gave up, bored. Everything was silent. But when Toby looked down, he saw his father standing by the front door. He didn't move, he just stood there, watching and listening to everything and nothing. He reminded Toby of one of those animals you see in a nature programme. Sniffing the wind, waiting for prey. Toby leaned back out of sight as his dad turned back and came inside. Toby heard the locks in the door snap shut, one after another.

He went through the motions during dinner. No one spoke much but he could feel his parents' eyes on him. Things like this had happened so many times before: embarrassing moments and wayward behaviour which could never be properly explained. His parents didn't speak, he believed, because they'd asked the same questions too many times before and he'd never been able to give them decent answers. He helped wash up, had a quiet bath and went to bed. His father popped his head around the door to check on him. Thinking he was asleep, he left him be and carried on with whatever grown-ups did late into the night.

Finally Toby pulled the sheets away and went to the wardrobe, opening the door where the full-length mirror hung on the inside. He stared at himself, wretched, and let his pyjamas fall to the carpet.

He looked at his battered body and ran a hand over the

embossed scar tissue along his stomach. Angry and upset, still no closer to the truth despite it all, he couldn't help the tears that rose up in him again. A naked child, helpless and hopeless.

He dressed himself again and got under the sheets, staring up at the ceiling. Slowly the exhaustion of the day won over. He didn't want to sleep, he wanted to find some sort of comfort from those heady moments on the bridge, but that all seemed so far away now. He had a memory, though it might be a dream, of a man calming him, offering him some sort of support. *Just close your eyes, kid, you'll be okay. Close your eyes, squeeze them shut and everything will be okay.*

Toby obeyed the voice of his memory. He felt the lightness in his head and body as it gave over to sleep, felt his mind relax and spin into kinder, safer worlds.

Anna was called to the headmaster's office as soon as she entered the school the next morning. A suspension was on the cards unless she could do a pretty amazing job with the parents. They were coming in, in half an hour.

Mr Benton, the headmaster, had a depressing, characterless office, rather like the man himself. Photos of his wife and children were the only personal details. Otherwise the room was just pine furniture and a tidy, organised desk. Benton was six foot three, naturally sombre, and was known as The Undertaker by the staff. Everything about him was grey.

'I don't quite know what you were thinking, Miss Price.'

'Anna.'

'I'm sorry?'

'Until today, you've always called me Anna. Why the formality?'

'Well, I imagine you know the reason for that.'

Anna had a flashback to her childhood: stamping her feet in front of her father who was dressed in a dinner jacket. He put on his raincoat, ignoring her sulk, then turned back and leaned down, tickling her under the chin. She refused to laugh.

'Have they said anything about me?'

'Only that they wanted to talk about this as a matter of urgency. I don't know if they'll want you to attend, but I think they should hear you out.'

It was the closest to solidarity she would get from him and she knew it. He pressed her again – a teacher taking a child out of the school without permission. In this day and age. How could he defend her? Anna bit her tongue.

'It was a serious error of judgement. You have to hold your hand up to that.'

Anna nodded and nodded as The Undertaker droned on. But her rage about Toby's abuse snarled and scratched within her. And when Mr and Mrs Mayhew were led into the office and The Undertaker grinned obsequiously at them, Anna wanted to scream at them all.

Instead, she stumbled through a muted apology. She knew she should have sounded more repentant, more genuine, but the anger wouldn't let her do any better.

Michael Mayhew was dressed in a suit and tie. His shoes were polished and buffed. He shifted unhappily in his chair.

'I allowed my concerns and my – er – my trust in your son to cloud my judgement,' she continued. 'In the clear light of day, I should never have—'

'Wrote this down, did you?' Mr Mayhew snapped at her. 'Feels nicely prepared.'

Anna was taken aback by the anger in the voice. She expected him to be defensive, at the very least.

'I don't want her teaching my boy. What did she want with him? You've done all the right checks on her, have you? If she's got form for this kind of thing, then you and this school are—'

'Mr Mayhew,' interrupted Mr Benton in his most reasonable voice, 'Miss Price is a valued member of my staff. She's explained her actions and apologised unreservedly for them. I think removing Toby from her class would only hurt his academic progress. As you know, he's already struggling with English and to put him in a higher stream would only—'

'Maybe he's struggling because she's not a decent teacher.'

'I don't believe that is the case.'

'If you want I can get a restraining order on her, but I don't imagine you'd like the publicity.'

'Mr Mayhew,' Benton pressed on, remarkably calmly, 'we're trying to resolve this in a fair and reasonable—'

'The way to resolve this is to keep that woman away from my son.'

Anna glanced at Mrs Mayhew. She was clearly embarrassed by her husband's behaviour, fiddling with something in her handbag.

The Undertaker took a sip of his coffee, his expression never deviating from its affected thoughtfulness.

'I don't wish to punish Miss Price for what I believe is a genuine error of judgement . . .'

'How many times are you going to use that phrase. Are we in court or something?'

'. . . but I also recognise that you are justifiably upset, Mr Mayhew.'

He could run the United Nations, Anna thought. Boutros Boutros Benton. She watched him sigh. Here it came.

'I'll move Toby into Miss Gilbert's English class. If he cannot keep up with the course work, then we should all meet again and reconsider the situation. In the meantime, Miss Price will make sure that she limits her contact with Toby wherever possible. Miss Price?'

All eyes were on her. She managed a nod.

'Good. Mr Mayhew, Mrs Mayhew, is this satisfactory?'

'Fine.' Toby's father stood, and his mother was there in his slipstream.

Anna stood too. She was flushed, and stared angrily at the floor to hide any more emotion from slipping out.

'Thank you for your understanding, Mr Mayhew,' said the headmaster, shaking both parents' hands. 'I'm glad you were able to help us sort this out.'

'Sure.'

There was an awkward pause as Anna realised that she too was expected to shake hands. She put her hand out, and her voice cracked as she spoke.

'Thank you.'

Michael smiled at her discomfort. He'd played his cards close to his chest until then, but now there was a nasty glint in his smile, betraying his previous anger as a performance. He held Anna's hand for a fraction longer than he needed to.

'Alright then,' he said with a voice that was suddenly generous and relaxed. He turned and walked his wife out of the room. Benton took another reasonable sip of his coffee and placed it back on the saucer. Anna walked away. The bell rang and pupils rushed around her. She wished one of them would jolt her so she could punish them, but even the kids wouldn't behave properly.

She walked along the corridor, wrapped in a storm. She entered the class and taught Year 9 with a bored coldness that the children noticed. It kept them quieter than usual, but their new-found attention didn't soothe her rage. She glared at Year 7 and taught them without care or attention. She didn't answer anyone's questions and she talked over confused but well-meaning pupils.

At break she hid from the staffroom and went, instead, to a narrow windy alley between two prefabricated buildings where she smoked her way through three cigarettes. Kath found her here and, apart from a raised eyebrow, said nothing for a while, smoking a cigarette herself. Crisp packets and cans littered the ground.

'He needed my help.'

'Says who? The kid? Sounds to me like he's got quite an imagination.'

Anna just smoked some more.

'Oh cheer up,' Kath said. 'You could have lost your job. Benton might be a prick but at least he stopped you getting into more trouble.'

'I guess.'

'You guess. Have you thought of how a newspaper would twist this? Secret trysts in the back of your car, parents weeping for the childhood snatched from their son, the crimson whore who's come to steal our children. You know what they do. The rules aren't just there to protect the kids, Anna, they're for us too.'

Still Anna didn't respond.

'Fine. Be like that. But it's done now. Move on. Leave the kid alone.'

'He's scared of them, Kath.'

'So go to the police.'

'I can't.'

'Why not? Anna?'

'I just . . . I don't know.'

'No, you don't. We're just teachers. Leave the rest for someone else, they can be the bloody hero. If The Undertaker says stay away from him, you do it.'

Anna recognised the sense in Kath's words, but she could not forget. Two pupils – a burly boy and a short-skirted girl – turned into the alley, holding hands, and were startled by the teachers' presence. They had guilt written all over their faces and they glared at Kath and Anna to make up for it.

'Don't look at me like that, Lucy Evans because I know exactly what you and Matt Long are up to,' barked Kath. 'Go on, piss off.'

The kids slouched off, grumbling kiddy swearwords.

'And use a condom, for crying out loud!'

The bell rang to signal the end of break time. Kath crushed her cigarette dead under her shoe.

'Lucky gits,' she said with a grin. Anna knew she'd said it to cheer her up, but she was still in her fug. 'Jesus, here I am, stuck behind the bike sheds with Anna Price. Where did it all go wrong?'

But Anna was too angry to enjoy the joke. She walked back to her class, settled behind her desk and glowered at Year 8 as they wandered cheerfully in. She snapped her way through the lessons for the rest of the day like this. When Toby's class entered, she wiped her sleeve across her mouth and tried to keep her eyes away from his empty desk. But the maelstrom raged within, unstoppable.

Toby sat in Miss Gilbert's class as she wrote up a series of quotations on the board.

'Today, we're going to discuss resonance within the text.'

Toby dutifully wrote the word down, then he felt a nudge from the boy sitting next to him. This was Jimmy Duthie – spiky hair, recurring acne, his tie always loose around his neck.

'Oi, Toby,' he whispered with a friendly, conspiratorial smile.

'Hi, Jimmy.'

'What are you doing here?'

'Oh. Nothing. You know.'

'Yeah, cos, we all thought you belonged with the mongs in Tiny Tits' class.'

Jimmy's eyes laughed at Toby.

'Don't talk about Miss Price like that,' Toby replied.

'Oh my God, are you banging her?'

Miss Gilbert glanced towards them, but she never bothered to get involved. She turned back to the blackboard and started to underline various phrases.

'Are you? Are you?'

Toby didn't reply, he just stared at the blackboard.

'Is she noisy? Does she like it—'

'No! Don't!' Toby's voice came out too high, embarrassing him.

'Don't!' mimicked Jimmy and one of his colleagues sniggered. 'No, she might be minging but she's not going to put out to you. So what's going on?'

Toby kept his eyes on the blackboard. Why wouldn't Miss Gilbert see this?

'Tell you what, why don't you explain it to me at break? Just you and me. How about that, eh?'

Don't look at him.

'Eh? Freak? Eh?'

Toby feigned a smile, as though something Miss Gilbert had said was suddenly interesting. But he could feel Jimmy's hateful stare.

Anna patrolled the playground during afternoon break. She watched the girls jabbering together and imagined hurtful gossip and bile. She saw violence as the boys jostled for the ball. Across the playground, Toby stood alone, waiting for whatever was coming next. They caught each other's eye and she offered him a forlorn smile. But then Mr Benton appeared and Toby turned away from her. Anna shouted something half-heartedly at a boy who wasn't doing anything wrong and he was suitably indignant. As he moaned at her, she saw Jimmy Duthie and two friends walking across the playground towards Toby. Their intentions were clear. Toby saw them coming and froze. Then he glanced at Anna who, in turn looked at Benton. He coolly, coldly, returned her gaze. Jimmy put a hand on Toby's shoulder, mock-friendly and the three boys led Toby away. Anna was rooted to the spot and a few seconds later, Toby and the boys were gone. Angry, she looked at Benton.

'Well, you can do something! Jesus!'

Mr Benton just walked away. Job done. Anna was furious. Her fingers dug into her palms as she tried to calm herself.

But as she stared at the space where Toby once stood, so miserable and vulnerable, she made a promise to herself.

Later, when Michael Mayhew walked through the gates, he found himself a spot a few yards ahead of the other parents. No one went to speak to him and his position was deliberately aloof. Anna watched all of this from the staffroom . She hurried down to him but found Toby ahead of her, walking towards his father, slower than the rest of the children. He was still limping, but now his nose was swollen and his hair was covered in some sort of gunk – it was purple, sticky. Toby walked straight past his father, ready for the car. Michael didn't seem bothered by Toby's appearance or any lack of 'hello'. He turned to follow him, but Anna stopped him.

'Mr Mayhew.'

He saw her and smiled, supercilious.

'Don't smile at me,' she hissed. 'I know you're hurting him.'

'No, you don't. You don't know anything.'

'Well, I'll make sure I do. I'm going to get you . . . you . . . you fuck.'

The word exploded from her lips. It shocked her. Michael stiffened, surprised.

'Well now,' he said, looking her up and down a little more closely.

'Whatever I said this morning, in front of the Head, forget it. I'm not stopping. I'm going to be everywhere he is. I'm going to find out exactly what you're doing to him and I'm going to let everyone know and I won't stop, I won't ever stop. Have you got that?'

Anger flashed across his face for a moment. But then he shook his head, mock-weary, and walked off. He unlocked the car with a click of the key and Toby bundled himself in. Anna followed, spoiling for a fight, but the driver's door slammed shut and the central locking snapped down. The car shot off and Toby glanced up too late to catch Anna's eye as the car drove away.

When Anna returned to her flat she dumped the bag of school books by the door, turned on the lights and poured herself a large glass of red wine from the carefully recorked bottle. She took three angry gulps, but it was too rich and she put it down, annoyed that she didn't have it within herself to be a big drinker. A nice tidy blouse and skirt, neat brown suede shoes, a dull mackintosh to cover it all up. She ruffled her hair and it fell back into its unexceptional place.

Anna's flat was small, acceptable, unfussy, in an unfashionable part of town. Partly this was down to her meagre teacher's salary, but her heart always sank slightly when she entered and she knew she could do better, somehow. Framed posters of old foreign films she'd never seen adorned the walls. In the hallway was the answerphone. It blinked with a message. She went over, pressed play, then wandered back to the kitchen to get her glass of wine. A man spoke after a moment's pause: throaty, sonorous, posh.

'Anna. It's the old man. I hope you're well, it's been . . . a while.'

She imagined her father sitting at the desk in his splendid study, toying with a paperweight or flicking through papers, wishing the call out of the way.

'I was wondering if you'd call me when you have a moment. There are things to discuss. Goodbye, love.'

A pause, a moment's hesitation, as though there was more he wished to say, and then the phone disconnected. Anna went to the answerphone and jammed her finger on the delete button. The call gave her the strength to down the glass and go for a refill.

In the kitchen she opened the fridge, took out some tupperware leftovers and placed them in the microwave. Irritated by the silence, she switched on the radio, but then switched it off again. She looked in at the dishes turning slowly and felt the tension of the day flowing back and forth across her, exhausting her. Then she headed back into the sitting room. She clicked on the TV, feeling the need to be doped tonight, and flicked through the channels, hoping she'd find something appropriate. In the kitchen, the microwave beeped. And as Anna turned to get her dinner, she noticed the television flicker for a moment. It was a fraction of a fraction of a second. But it stopped Anna dead.

The image on the screen was Anna. In the same clothes as she was wearing right then . . . holding the television's remote control . . .

She stared at the screen, her throat suddenly dry. She swallowed and looked again, but the picture was normal now. A reality show. A couple giggled nervously at the prospect of buying their first home. The presenter winked at the camera and Anna switched the TV off. There was her reflection in the blank screen – her clothes, holding the remote. Was this what she had seen?

Anna Price knew herself as a sensible, normal woman. Too normal for her own liking, and not prone to flights of fancy. But still she hurried from the room and returned with her small, orderly toolbox. She opened it, unplugged the TV, attached the right screwdriver piece for her needs, and then methodically began to unscrew the back of the set.

The phone rang again, but she ignored it and didn't listen out for the message. Soon she was pulling wires out of the back, knowing that she would never be able to reassemble them. Her delicate fingers removed the guts of the television, dumping electronic bits onto the carpet. She ran her hands over circuit boards and wires that made no sense to her until she reached a long black wire that had a small black box at one end ... and a tiny camera at the other, which was stuck to the inside of the television screen – pointing outwards. Anna held the camera up to the light, just to be sure. She fiddled with the black box, but it wouldn't open. She sat back amid the detritus of the dismantled TV, holding the camera in cautious fingers as though it were a baby crocodile. She put it to her lips, whispered quietly into it.

'What are you?'

And at that instant, the telephone rang again. Anna jumped. She looked at the thing in her hands and dropped it. Frightened of it. She went to the telephone – the answerphone was blinking again from the last message. She waited for it to pick up, but it didn't, it just kept ringing and ringing and ringing. Unable to bear it, she picked up, her voice breathy.

'Hello?'

No reply. Not even the sound of someone's breathing.

'Hello?' Still nothing. A fault on the line, maybe. 'Hello?' she said again, more confidence in her voice this time. 'Yeah, funny. Very funny.' Still nothing. She listened as carefully as she could, scrunching her eyes closed to help her. Silence. 'I'm not scared, okay?' she said into the receiver. She hung up. And immediately the phone rang again.

'I'M NOT SCARED OF YOU! DO YOU HEAR ME?' she shouted, and slammed the phone down again. And again it rang. Desperate, Anna ripped the phone line from the socket in the wall. Finally silence. Except for her panicked breathing.

And then, from her bag, she heard her mobile phone start up. Such a jolly ringtone. She stabbed it off. Turned off the phone. Put it in her handbag. Then pulled it out of the bag and ripped off the back, removed the battery and threw the pieces back down again.

Silence. It should have been reassuring. But the door was not locked, the curtains were not drawn . . .

Anna rushed to the door, pinned the scanty chain across it, locked it, then ran to the windows and pulled the curtains tight shut against . . . against what . . . ? She stopped and wheeled round and looked at all of the tiny nooks and crannies of her cramped flat. If there was a camera in the television, then there could be more. Anywhere. Eyes watching her right now.

'I'm going mad,' she said out loud to herself.

And then there was a knock on the door. A loud, sharp bang. Oh fuck.

She went to the door and peeked through the tiny spy-hole. But there was no one there.

Fucking fucking fucking . . .

She backed away from the door. But then something pushed her forward. She found her hands were undoing the locks, removing the safety chain. She watched her fingers reach for the latch and open the door.

Kath staggered into sight on teetering heels. She was holding a bottle of wine and had clearly had one already.

'WOO-HOO! Anna's hitting the town tonight! Anna's hitting the town tonight! Hang on: you're not going like that? Tell me you've got a sexy outfit ready and waiting. Tell me, tell me, tell me . . .'

Anna was so relieved that she threw her arms around her.

'Alright love, calm down. No need to get all lezzy on me. Jesus.'

Kath pushed her way inside and stopped when she saw the mess in the living room.

'What the fuck . . .?'

'Yeah, I – er – tried to fix it myself.'

'You big loon. And what's wrong with your phone? I kept ringing and it kept cutting out.'

Anna started giggling, unable to stop.

'Have you been on the sauce already?'

'Yes!' she laughed.

'Good girl! Tonight is going to be SO mental!'

SEVEN

Bloody hell, it's beautiful out here. From where I'm sitting, the land slips down and away and I can see for miles. There are ants by my feet, tugging away at leaves. I watch them for a bit, but then my eye's caught by the dew. It's sparkling on a spider's web. And the sky is a perfect blue, not a cloud anywhere. The cold is so bitter it makes me blink and I have to shove my hands into my pockets, but I'm not moving. Not yet. I watch the contours of the hills and the clean line of trees on the other side of the valley. Everything is so still, so perfect. Empty fields are divided by thickets and old stone walls. A big bird of prey weaves slow circles in the sky. And as I sit here, a deer – a young doe – clatters through the greenery and stops dead, suddenly aware of me. I don't move but its big, glassy brown eyes watch me nervously as it wonders whether to bolt. I see the tiny scars on its legs from barbed wire or thorny bushes and admire its fine brown coat. I smile at it, but the creature does not understand. It backs up slowly before turning and jumping easily through the thickets and away. I watch it bounce and bob through the trees and bushes and I find myself waving a traveller's goodbye.

I pull my hands out of my pockets and rub them together, blowing on them. Glancing down, I notice the blood. There's too much to wipe off casually and I'm cross with myself: It will be all over the inside of my pockets now. But then there's blood splashed across my thighs and ankles, so why should it matter? That's why the deer ran, of course. It saw what's behind me.

I'm sitting on the metal footplate at the back of a non-descript black van. It's new, clean on the outside. The interior has been modified; in the middle is the purpose-built stretcher and the restraints they used to hold me down. In a small suit-case are syringes and drugs. On the walls are various pieces of medical equipment – a defibrillator (that's what it says on the side), a heart monitor, an oxygen mask and tank. And the three men. They wear similar clothes – dark jeans and dull-coloured T-shirts – practical clothing for rough work. The first man lies on the floor of the van. It's hard to tell what he looks like cos he's face down in a pool of his own blood. The second is propped up against the side, his right arm hanging oddly (it's broken in two places), and if it weren't for that you might think he was dozing. The third man lies on the stretcher, his neck broken, his eyes open. The flies have found them already.

I stand and stretch. My body is a little sore from the fight but I feel good. I took them down in seconds. I think back to the moment, surprised by the instincts within me. I do not understand myself, do not know my own body. I put my hand on my arm. I don't lift weights but my biceps feel pumped. I run a finger over my knuckles and remember how they crunched into the second man's jaw, how easily I snapped the third man's neck. About three weeks ago we found a rabbit in the garden. A fox had been at it, but the poor thing was still alive, all wide eyes and fast little breaths. I didn't know what to do, had to use a spade, egged on by Carrie. But this morning I killed three men. My body has memories that it won't share with me. I get up and glance down at the steel ridges on the footplate, there to stop feet from slipping. When I look at the metal, I think of a serrated blade. I think of how I can twist it for best effect. And I worry that I think like this.

I have checked every detail of the van, but there is nothing here that can help me. The men have no ID and the phones they carry are new, pay-as-you-go, with no dialled numbers and no calls received. There is no paperwork, no map, no satnav to help me learn where they were heading. Even the medical equipment's serial numbers have been deleted. The thought, the care and efficiency behind it all scares me. It strikes me that the van will soon be missed. I bet they'll know where it stopped. Others will be coming for me.

I turn back to the beautiful view. My heart is thumping now, but I don't want to leave. I love the gentle curves of the earth, the way the crops sway, the grace of the bird that continues to cruise above me. I wonder where the deer has gone.

Time to move. I take clothes that are not too soiled and boots that fit me well enough, and my hands pull things towards me that will be useful.

Suddenly I'm rubbing my face hard with my hands; the weaker emotions have taken charge of me and I'm Ben again. Ben, the dad, the simple mechanic. I feel nauseous at the sight of all this blood and I don't know how I've managed to stay here so long. The noise of the flies is deafening. They'll be coming for me again. They're coming and I'm too weak and too scared to stop them.

I couldn't tell you the last time I went for a jog. I have a pair of dusty old trainers I put on when I need to do odd jobs around the house, but that's as active as I get. But I run and run at a steady, even pace and my body accepts it.

I stand under an old oak, invisible in the darkness, as my eyes clock the path forward – watching for obstacles, for lights, for any movement in the sky. Everything's still. I try to think back over the day that's passed, but I don't remember much. I was on some sort of autopilot, moving fast, following well-used footpaths to hide my trail, crossing streams without hardly getting wet. With my head down, I've become invisible to hikers, bikers, cars and busybodies.

Suddenly I'm starving hungry. I root through my things and find the few notes I was able to steal from the dead men. In the dark I begin to panic that there's blood on the money and that I'll be caught out when I try to spend it. I stare at the notes. Something moves near my feet and I nearly shout out with panic. I'm shivering. Even the tough old bastard inside me knows I need fuel and sleep.

Fuel first. I find a small town two miles further on. It's a dull place, its fine Tudor buildings now shops for the same old brands you see everywhere these days. It's quiet, except for a bunch of bored teenagers who perch on the edge of a bench playing with their mobile phones. I walk past them, pulling up the collar of my jacket as I get to the petrol station, the only place open at this time of night. There are no cars at the pumps and a bored Asian lad slouches at the counter, staring into space. I pluck up the courage to go in and grab the first bits of food I can see; a sandwich – I don't even bother to check what type – milk and crisps. But as I hurry to the counter, I suddenly become aware of all of the cameras. The lad scans my items without interest, but I'm desperate to get out of there. I feel the cameras staring down at me, watching, recording, making notes.

I get around the corner and cram the food into my mouth, gulping down a carton of milk too quickly so that I choke and spit some of it out and onto my clothes. I stand up and try to control my breathing. Everything is quiet. Of course it is. No one's noticed you. Tomorrow, they'll erase everything from the cameras and no one will ever know you were here. Calm down. Walk on.

I try to run but the food has swelled in my stomach and I start to cramp, so I'm forced into a bloated stagger towards the darker side streets off the high street where I can find some safety in the shadows. I stand still in the darkness as my body calms down, remembering what Carrie whispered into my ear. *Take off your shoes.*

The shoes were bugged? The shoes had some sort of tracing device in them? What did she mean?

Don't answer the phone.

The feel of her breath against my ear.

I find I'm nearly crying. *Take off your shoes.* I have, I now wear the second man's boots. But why should I think that these are any safer? I have this urge to rip off all my clothes.

I love you.

I'm so angry at everything that's happened, at the things

that have been done to me. I don't know where the rage comes from, but it swells up fast, so fast, from deep inside. I want to roar, to smash things, to take it out on something, someone, to tear things apart.

It is his bad luck that a man should step out of his house across the road at that moment and that he should be a similar shape and build to me.

As he lies on the ground, semi-conscious after my attack, he groans and snorts. The noises he makes are more animal than human. They're anger and fear, sucked in and out of his lungs. Maybe he'll die if I don't help him. I can't see any blood, but the noise is freaking me out. I pull the clothes from his body. He tries to struggle, but his eyes loll up into his head and he falls silent for a few merciful minutes. But then, as I tie the laces to his trainers he begins to snort again. His eyes are screwed shut but the noise is louder. Maybe, oh God, maybe my attack has left him brain-damaged. I stand over him and he must sense that I'm there – this dark monster – because he rolls away from me, into a ball, grunting and squealing. I make a decision and ring the doorbell to his house; hold it down long and hard for ten seconds. Wait. I hear movement in the house. I ring again – a few, short bursts – then turn and run. Maybe no one came. I don't know. I'm long gone, out of the town and smashing through the trees before any police search can be organised.

I don't see the branch which knocks me down, the sting and whip ripping into my cheek. I lie on the ground and something patters past, as scared of me as I am of it. My hand is wet and I don't know if I've landed in mud or shit or if this is my own blood.

The fucking noise that man made as he lay on the ground . . .

Get up.

It starts to rain. A brief shower and a sudden bluster of wind throws leaves and dust at me. I have grit in my eyes, but my hands are too dirty to touch them.

Get up. Don't stop.

I don't want to move. I just want to curl up and sleep, but I know that this is stupid. I look up: through a break in the trees I can see a brief glimmer of stars. Then the wind picks up, clouds zoom in again and another short burst of rain pelts against my face. I stand, but now I don't know which way I'm meant to be heading – or, rather, where I've come from. I turn in a slow circle, trying to find traces of the path I must have made to have got this far. My face is stinging. I think I've been cut quite badly cos it hurts so much. Another mark on my face to make me more noticeable and easier to find.

My trousers are wet and it's seeping through to my skin. Rain's settling in now. Fuck. Walk, you fool. Move. Make a decision.

Stiff, wet and cold, I find a road about an hour later. The rain won't stop and there are puddles everywhere.

I hear something coming behind me and lights flood the road. A truck. I keep my head down. It passes me and I glance up to see its brake lights. It's stopping. Shit. I have no option but to walk past it.

As I come to the window a voice shouts down to me.

'Fuck's sake, mate, you must be soaked through!' The man's voice is cheery, well-meaning. I look up to the driver's cabin and see a bearded face grinning down at me. 'Come on, hop in before you drown.' He laughs at his own joke, hilarious. He's wearing only a T-shirt – it's warm and dry in there. He could drive me miles away.

'Where are you heading?' I ask cautiously.

'What do you care? Have you seen the state of you?' Another laugh. There's something about his smile. Too many teeth. Why won't he tell me where he's going? 'Come on, pop on up.'

I hesitate. One hand has reached for the door handle, but my eyes are locked on his smile.

'Big truck for a small road like this.'

'Eh?'

'How come you're not on the motorway?'

'Cos my satnav's shit. You want a lift or not?'

I shake my head. Back away. 'Wrong direction, mate.'

'Well, let me drive you a bit, same way as you're walking. Save you from the elements, eh?'

Too friendly. Liar. Get away from him.

'I'm good, ta.'

I pull away and then run, can't help myself. I hear a shout from behind me, but I don't stop. I'm so wet now, the rain is in my eyes, all of my clothes are soaked. But I run and run – away from the road, back into the darkness.

I trudge and run for miles. I see an empty barn where I could rest till the morning, but decide it's too dangerous. The barn has been placed here by them. It's a trap. No, stop, think, you need to rest. But it might be a trap. It can't be. But it might. My fevered brain argues with itself, and I march on without direction.

I slip again and fall heavily on my shoulder, winded. Once again I think about Carrie and the kids. I see them at home:

hot chocolate in mugs, hot skin from their bath, waiting for me to come home. Wide, confused eyes. What am I doing?

I can't see because of the rain. My eyes sting and my head hangs low.

I love you.

Carrie. She beckons to me through the darkness. Get into the truck.

March, boy, march until you are ordered otherwise. Got it?

There is a wide, dark river ahead. It's hard to tell how fast the current is moving, but there's no obvious way across. I decide to swim, and start to take off the boots. Then stop. A moment's sanity tells me I'm being stupid. As I stand there, the moon breaks through the clouds like a helicopter's spotlight. I'm done for.

My knees give way and I slip to the ground. I'm overcome by exhaustion.

Don't sleep. Who said you could sleep?!

Carrie, my love, my beautiful love.

An animal shrieks in the darkness.

My head falls against the soft earth. It's like a pillow.

I hear the snort of the man I've hit.

The anger's there again and I pound my fists into the wet earth, over and over.

You bastards, you bastards.

My love.

The moon vanishes then suddenly it's back.

Let me sleep. Just ten minutes. Ten minutes and then I'll cross the river.

But they're coming.

Yellow eyes in the darkness.

My little boy. My darling daughter.

Just ten minutes.

I'll be strong in ten minutes.

My eyes flicker.

Just ten.

I wake up and I'm frozen stiff. I sit up, shaking, see my boots next to me and pull them on in a hurry. My head's just clearing from a dream. Something about a gun. It's the morning, I think. Well, it's light, anyhow. It's stopped raining, but it's a cold, dull day and my clothes are soaked through. I get up and look at the river in front of me. In the daylight it seems much less formidable. I'm cross with myself. My body's caked in mud, my clothes even more so. If I let myself go mad like that again, I'll end up killing myself.

And then I remember the man I attacked and I feel sick to my stomach with shame. I want to go back, I want to see if he's okay, I want to do something. But I don't know where I've come from, not really. And I'm too scared that if I did go back they'd be waiting for me. I put my head between my knees and squeeze my eyes shut. Where did it come from, that rage? It felt comfortable, a part of me, but now in the light I can't believe I'm capable of any of it. Yet there is a part of me that wants more. I make a quiet promise to myself that I will stop it and shut it down. I know, even now in the calm daylight, that this will be a hard promise to keep.

I stand up straight, roll my shoulders over. I put my hand into my back pocket and take out the few remaining soggy notes and count them. I can live for two days on this. Two days, and then what? Maybe I don't even have two days, maybe they're waiting, somewhere across the water. But then, if they knew where I was they'd have picked me up. I must have been asleep here for four or five hours, but no one has come. I am safe for now. I have time to stop, to think.

I look at the swirling river and follow a broken branch which spins slowly around as it's pulled along and away. I wonder about my dream and the gun. I know that I need to think about all my dreams now. There are answers there, buried in code.

The dark waters drift and drag, slip and slide. I watch the river with a strange admiration. There's such strength in the water. A slow, low-gear, bullish drive. I think about its long journey to the sea and decide that I'll do the same. I'll go and hide somewhere by the sea. I don't know why, but it seems as a good a plan as any, for a madman.

'Come on, have a tug, it's good for you. I promise,' teases Imogen as she passes the joint towards me. We share the back seats of a beaten-up car, along with bags and rubbish which cramp our foot space. I'm a guest, a hitchhiker who she and her mates picked up a couple of hours ago. And right now I'm Imogen's plaything. She's in her late teens (early twenties maybe) with long brown hair, and a pretty face made more attractive by her cheek and sparkle. Her bare feet are on my lap and she wears a tiny pair of tight, jean shorts and a skimpy T-shirt which reveals her small breasts and the pale, freckled skin on her arms and neck.

'Put him down, Imo,' says Fred from the front, who takes the joint from me with a grin and inhales hard. Fred's a thick-set man, twenty-something, with short hair and a square jaw. Apparently his real name's Alistair, but everyone calls him Fred

after the caveman cartoon. Next to him, driving, is Adrian –
same age, blond, quiet, wearing sunglasses. Imogen stares at
me with a crooked smile and tries to make me blush.

'You work out, Ben?'

'Jesus, Imogen,' groans Fred.

'I'm just being polite. We're giving him a lift, what do you
want me to do, ignore him?'

'Just don't fuck him on the back seat is all I'm asking.'

'Fuck you, potty mouth. Ben. Mister. You work out?'

'No.'

'So how come you've got biceps the size of my thighs?' She
runs a wide-eyed hand over her thighs, just so I'm sure to know
what she's talking about.

A growl from Fred up front and I realise (God, I'm dumb)
that he's in love with her.

'You got kids, Ben?' Fred asks, and I smile, relieved.

'Yes, two. Boy and a girl.'

They all nod politely. They've got no interest in this; grown-
ups, family vehicles, pot bellies, receding hairlines. They're too
cool for that shit. For the first time in an hour, Imogen glances
past me out of the window. We're on the motorway, travelling
fast. It's a sunny day and the fading autumn sun still has
enough heat to make the car stuffy. My shirt is sticking to the
back of the seat.

'You got any family, Imogen?' I ask and I see Fred smirk.

'Kid brother who's an idiot. And Mum.' She drops sunglasses
over her eyes.

'What about Brian?' taunts Fred, mock-innocent, and I realise
I've trodden in something.

'Shut the fuck up, Fred.'

We're quiet for a while. Fred passes the joint back to Imogen and her taking it seems to imply some sort of peace. She offers it to me again, but once again I decline. She shifts her position and I notice the small yin-yang tattoo on her ankle.

'Ben?' she says, playfully. (I decided to go with my own name. I thought of calling myself Angus or something, but then I thought that I'd only catch myself out.) 'How come you're hitchhiking?'

'Just mind your own business. Christ!' grunts Fred.

'No, come on dude, we're all like – hey, it's cool, having an old guy on board. But you're not exactly classic hitchhiker material, are ya?'

That's true enough. I think back to the hours before they saw me in that lay-by: changing into the new set of clothes I stole from the recycling bank, tying a bandage over the jagged cut on my thigh (thank you, barbed wire) and hoping the wound won't open up and draw attention. I have thought up a story – a family on holiday with in-laws, a broken car, a lost wallet. It feels suitably boring. But her naked feet on my crotch make me want to sound less like a loser.

'Oh, it's . . . stuff's happened, forget about it.'

She looks at me with intrigue and I regret my pride instantly.

'What stuff? Fred, look at him, he's gone all shifty. Hey! Are you . . . what are you? You're on the run, aren't you?'

'Yes. I'm armed and dangerous, Imogen. How did you guess?'

She looks disappointed. Maybe I am just a boring old forty-something-dull-guy after all. Fred lowers the window and out goes the burnt-out joint. He stretches, taking a slurp from a can, then glances at me, wondering if I'm worth any bother.

'Ben . . . come on . . .' she pines with a baby voice. 'Tell me something . . .'

Fred has given up and digs out a music magazine with earnest young men on its cover. The Next Big Thing, the cover declares in big red letters.

'Where's your wife? How come you're not travelling together? How come you can't afford a train, or a bus or a decent car?' She kicks the back of the driver's seat to make a point but Adrian drives on, oblivious. When we were introduced he shook my hand with his eyes on the road. 'Don't mind him,' Fred had said, 'he's a lawyer,' as if this explained everything.

I feel a poke in my ribs. Imogen's waiting for answers. Where's my wife? What a question. My face must have betrayed some emotion because the poke suddenly turns into a gentle hand on my arm.

'Just tell me to shut up, I won't mind,' she says, her eyes sad and empathetic. 'I talk too much.'

'No shit,' chimes in Fred.

'It's none of my business,' she says, cowed. Her hand rests on my arm. I can feel its heat. Her hair is frizzled and hangs loose around her shoulders and she smells of soap. Suddenly she bursts out laughing. It's self-conscious, embarrassed, but she doesn't remove her hand.

'Hey, remember Danny?' says Adrian, completely out of the blue. The name gets an instant reaction from the other two. A cry of excitement – Danny!

'He does, doesn't he?' says Fred and laughs. I'm confused.

'You remind them of a guy we met last year,' explains Imogen.

'He was cool, don't fret, man,' says Adrian. 'He was the dude who ran the local bar. Turned up in town first week of May, closed shop end of September. Made enough money to piss off to Thailand for the rest of the year. Man, he was wild.'

'Bloke never slept,' adds Fred. 'Fucking legend he was. Think he'll still be there?'

'Absolutely,' smiles Adrian.

Earlier, Imogen told me that they were heading down to Cornwall for a 'final fling' as she called it. An extended week-end. They'd called in sick from work and would drive back early on Monday morning.

'So what are you all going to do down there?' I ask.

'Do?' Adrian considers this. 'We're not going to do anything.'

Fred laughs at my baffled reaction.

'We'll surf, we'll smoke, drink . . . you know,' says Imogen, a little closer each time she speaks.

'It's the last weekend before everything closes down,' continues Adrian. 'The last bit of good stuff before winter.'

'Oh God, winter,' says Fred, and his shoulders hunch up.

Winter to them is work, I gather. The end of the party. But it's worse than that, it's like a forced hibernation, the way they talk about it.

'Work, eat, sleep, repeat till May.' It's like there is no life for them when they're not partying.

'But not this weekend. This weekend we're getting blasted. One final, fantastic fuck-off to the world!'

Imogen laughs. It sounds so shallow. But kind of brilliant too. And this is what they did all summer.

We pass a long line of trees and the dappled light strobes the car as we speed past. I can see them in a club, stoned, dancing to the rhythm of the sunlight. Imogen's hand still rests on my arm and I feel drowsy.

'Wanna come with us?' she whispers in my ear, and I smile through glazed eyes. What an offer – anonymous and carefree, sharing a sweaty bed with Imogen, burying my memories in her freckled skin. 'It's gonna be so out there.' I can feel the heat of her breath. I look at her, she's smiling, her eyes glittering with promise.

'You're teasing me,' I say. 'An old man, cramping your style.'

'Hey, you're thinking about it, though.'

I am. But . . . 'There are things I need to do.'

They're so bloody chilled, they'd drive this car off a cliff and they'd still be chatting about some rock band on the way down. They don't seem cool any more.

'Big plans, Ben?' scoffs Adrian.

And again the car is silent. I learn later that 'Brian' is Imogen's stepfather. The way she avoided the subject makes me think he's at best unwelcome in her life and at worst abusive. I understand her flirtation and the need to drive fast and far away. Adrian describes himself as a 'glorified photocopier' and it's weird how disconnected he seems from his work. They all do. All the things I thought were real and important just feel like dull tasks to them. I remember being excited and desperate to be cool, just like them. But I wanted adventures. I don't understand what they want.

Adrian moves into the slow lane; we're stopping at a service station ('piss stop!' he screamed gleefully) and I feel the tension creeping up in me again. Other people, strangers, maybe police. Maybe the men who are after me. He turns off the ignition and I'm trying to think of a reason why I'd stay in the car that wouldn't sound strange and suspicious.

'Coke and chocolate,' beams Imogen. 'You coming?'

I think I'll stand out if I hang out with them. A guy my age is much more anonymous on his own. 'I need a coffee,' I reply.

'Coffee? Jesus, that stuff's so bad for you. I'd do coke, whisky, smack even. But coffee, no way, José.'

She laughs, slipping her arm into Fred's as they skip off towards the shops. I hang back and follow a little more slowly. My eyes track everything around me: couples, commuters, businessmen, a group of lads on some kind of sports tour (football, I think). They all trudge around with the same bored expressions. Not sad, not hungry, just sort of empty. I'd never noticed this before. I guess I was always one of them. But now I've been shoved outside and I'm looking in and everyone else seems different. I know it's me, I'm the one who's changed, but it looks like everyone else.

I get inside and drop my head, grab a baseball cap from my back pocket and shove it on because there are cameras everywhere. Bloody everywhere. One behind in the coffee shop, one in the chemist's, one by the loos, one by every exit. Again, I never noticed this before. Why do they need so many? I don't understand. I see Imogen queuing for a magazine and there's a camera staring down at her and she doesn't give a shit. Okay, she's got nothing to hide, but still . . . she doesn't give a flying fuck about anything.

And then I notice the security guard watching me. I hold his eye for a moment too long and now he's interested in me. I turn and walk as slowly as I can to the loos, but when I get there I feel overloaded by fear and end up hiding in a cubicle. I'm sweating, imagining eyes watching me, seeing computers in cash machines which wait to track and expose me. I feel like I have a sign on me which says 'Other. Stranger. Danger.'

Like some sort of zoo animal. I try to control myself, shake my hands and take some deep breaths. Finally, I step out of the cubicle. No one's looking at me, of course they're not. No one looks at anyone in a public toilet. Get a grip.

The guard outside has gone, interested in someone else. All around me, people mill about doing their own, normal, average thing and I'm jealous of every one of them. I wander around the car park and find a small bank of grass on the far side. From here I can watch Adrian's car and make sure they leave without me. They're not right for me. Or I for them.

They wait for ages, bless 'em. They sit bored in the car park, then argue. After a while, Fred comes looking for me. When he's gone, I see Adrian and Imogen steal a furtive kiss. That Adrian will go far.

Fred finally returns and after some waving arms and pointing at watches, the three wearily head off. They look a bit glum. I wish them well.

I walk over to a second, bigger car park, clogged up with trucks. It doesn't take long for me to find a driver who agrees to take me further on my journey. We set off half an hour later and my mind soon drifts back to those three kids. I imagine their bovine summer, laughing crazily at jokes they won't remember.

I zig-zag my way towards the coast. I don't go anywhere in a straight line. But when I finally get there, and stand on the beach, I feel a thumping sense of disappointment. I had hoped for more from Stockton-on-Sea. Not glamour – I mean fair play, I chose this place because it was neither so small I'd be noticed, nor attractive enough to be touristy and expensive. But this place, with its shallow pebble beach and grubby fish and chip shop (which now only seems to sell kebabs) seems, well, knackered. There are a few drab houses that look out to sea. and further back, a sad high street with all the usual shop chains. There's litter trapped amongst the sharp pebbles, and the water is worryingly brown, with huge splatters of foam that make me think of detergent. There are no swimmers out there. The locals are clearly no fools.

Sitting down on a low wall that serves no real purpose, I look out at the fading sun. If you close your eyes and listen to the gentle rhythm of the waves, you could be anywhere. I wonder why this place got left behind. Maybe its time will come, but the floating beer can that's being knocked about on the pebbles makes me think otherwise.

I am wearing a slightly-too-trendy suede jacket that I stole the night before. It fits well, but I feel uncomfortable in it. Mutton and lamb and all that. I tap the stolen wallet in my pocket and feel a surge of guilt.

I'd watched him for over an hour as he chatted and boasted to his mates in a bar, having thrown his jacket so casually over a nearby chair. I waited and waited till they were drunk and inattentive, then grabbed the jacket as I passed without anyone noticing a thing. It didn't even feel risky. I feel as though I've done things like this before. It's that other part of me, the one that can run and fight. At least this time no one got hurt.

I feel lonely and tired. I stare out to sea and want to reach out and touch Carrie's hand, find her here – staring out at the sea herself, smiling that way she does. I try to remind myself of her lies, but it never works.

The next few hours I spend walking around the outside of hotels, but decide not to enter any of them. It's not that there are so many, it's that the five that I've found feel wrong. They have impressive views of the sea, and while their prices aren't huge, I fear that they're bustling with friendly, eager, intrusive staff who will ask me about my day, my business, the length of my stay. Maybe coming here was a mistake.

I stuff a kebab down my throat a bit too quickly and wander further back into the town, past the shops and the small car park. I notice a house on the end of the street with cracked render and flaking paintwork. A fading sign mentions Bed and Breakfast, but the lettering's almost invisible so I doubt if it still applies. I look at the house, at the grimy windows and the sad location. Stuck away, forgotten about. I suppose before the car park was built the house looked straight out onto the sea.

I ring the bell and am surprised that it works perfectly well. It's a while before the door is unlocked (three locks and chain) and an old man drags the door across the doormat.

'Yes?' His voice is forty cigarettes a day for forty years.

'I'm looking for a room,' I say, all friendly and polite. He looks at me with a wry smile.

'A room?'

'Are you not . . .? There was a sign . . .'

'The other places full, are they?'

'Er . . . Yes.'

This seems a satisfactory answer, I think, because he lets me in. I have a small bag with me (I'd guessed that someone at reception would ask about bags), but it has little to nothing in it. The old man doesn't seem interested and we trudge inside. There's a small booth near the front door which used to pass as reception, but it's clearly seen little use for years.

'Any idea how long you want to stay?' he says, as though the answer will be an irritation.

'Nope,' I reply with a smile. The gruffer he is, the better I feel. He doesn't seem bothered by my answer. Instead he fiddles with a small metal box, mounted on the wall, struggling with the small key until he flips it open. He reaches in and pulls out two keys. Two rooms. He looks at me, eyeing me up, deciding which room I deserve. Then he holds out one, and somehow I don't think I've done so well.

My fears are confirmed soon after. The room has a small window which looks out onto a brick wall. It smells musty and stale. Only one of the two standard lamps either side of the lumpy bed works. The old man looks around at the place. Nods. 'So?'

So? It's depressing. A dive. Carrie would have a fit.

'Okay.'

He nods. Good. He turns to walk out, then pauses, remembering his duties.

'Need anything?'

'No. Thank you.'

'Name?'

'Ben.'

'Surname?'

'I don't know your name.'

'Edward. You in trouble?'

I should say no. But I don't speak.

He frowns, his whole face crinkles. 'Hm.' He fiddles with his belt as he considers me. 'I quite like trouble. Police after you?'

'I don't know. I don't think so.'

'Who?'

'I don't know.'

'Is that going to be your answer to everything?'

I manage to smile before I reply 'I don't know.' Edward seems to like this. He looks at my small bag and nods.

'Breakfast's at . . . the morning.' He turns and walks away. As he reaches the door, a pipe starts to bang in the corner of the room. He swears something about plumbing and stalks off into the dark corridors.

I sit on the bed. The mattress creaks and sags so badly under my weight that I nearly slide onto the floor. I pull back the cover and find that there are no sheets.

I fold up my clothes as carefully as I can, then wrap myself up in the bed cover and prepare to sleep. I lie there and try to dispel all the usual thoughts that come chasing after me; Carrie, the kids, the sound of that man squealing outside his house in the dark.

But then a sound interrupts. The low bam-bam-bam of a stereo bass. Someone's having a party. I listen to it for a bit. And then it dawns on me that the music is coming from inside the house. I throw my clothes back on and slip along the musty passages, following the music. I stop outside a door: the music is blasting. Elvis Presley. I'm too nosy not to push the door open as quietly as I can.

The living room is large but empty. Once it must have been a smart room, filled with armchairs, sofas and coffee tables. You can easily picture a grandfather clock, thick rugs, an open window's curtains billowing gently from the sea breeze. But now the room is damp and stuffy. There are marks on the carpet and a brown stain running down one wall, the wall-paper rippled and scratched. All that remains is a boxy stereo on the floor. An old boxy stereo and an old man who is engaged in a very strange but energetic dance in the middle of the room. Edward shuffles and shakes, cackles and snorts as though he's dancing with an invisible partner. I stand watching him, but if he knows I'm there he pays me no attention. He dances with glinting eyes, a sweaty brow and a gleeful laugh. His fingers click, his hands wave in the air, his knees buckle and there's a drunken grin on his face. He's miles away. Maybe years away. Wherever it is, it sure seems fun.

'That's it, that's the way,' he grunts and laughs. He spins on his toes with a grace I hadn't believed possible. I slip away, slowly shutting the door. I don't want to interrupt his mad magic. I walk back to my bedroom and shut the door. Then I lock it. I collapse onto the rickety bed. He's crazy. I like that. Who'll come looking for me here? I'm tired, but I'm not scared, and that's a first. The music thumps on below as I let my eyes flicker shut.

EIGHT

Toby, quiet and sullen, sat next to his mother as she drove him to school, He stared out of the rain-smeared windows, avoiding her anxious glances. He'd become more and more introverted as the days had passed and the bullying had continued unchecked. He knew the boys would be waiting for him when he got there and he had no way of stopping them. He felt pathetic.

'I'm sorry it's so awful. I didn't like school much myself,' his mother said. He grunted back to her but nothing more. What else was there to say?

'But even so, Toby—'

'I know. You've told me. I know the rules.'

'They're for you, to protect you. We worry so much.'

'Sure.' He shifted in his seat, rubbed his nose, and they fell back into silence. He could see the school ahead and watched the other kids marching happily in while his mother fretted about where to park. Ahead was a spot and she lurched for it. After a couple of failed attempts she was finally able to turn the key and silence the engine.

'Look, darling. Your father is . . . your father. You know?'

He had an idea of what she was trying to say, but he didn't feel like indulging her. He was still thinking about the camera, about Miss Price and how she'd let him down. He was all alone.

'I'll talk to him,' she said. But still he wouldn't look at her. 'Oh, I hate this! It's just school, for goodness sake, you're a boy, you're meant to be happy!'

He glanced at her, not sure about this unusual outburst.

'That's it. You're not going in.'

What? This was not at all like his mum.

'Bugger the rules,' she said, stunning him even more with such a casual swear word. 'If you hate school, I hate it too. What do you say?'

'Er, okay.'

'You just want to be a normal boy, don't you?' Toby nodded, smiling – it was all he wanted.

'That's all I want too. And you never mean to hurt me, do you?'

'Never!'

Laura pulled him into an embrace. He felt overwhelmed.

'Why does it happen, Mum?'

'I think . . . I think maybe we spend too much time worrying about it. Right now you just need to stop worrying and worrying about us worrying and . . .' she gasped, threw her hands in the air.

Toby laughed, exhilarated.

'I know!' she grabbed his hands. 'Isn't tomorrow the school disco? Why don't we go into town and buy you an outfit? Something to make the girls swoon.'

Toby looked down, smiling, bashful.

'I don't know ...'

'Let them see how special you are. They just don't get you.'

Toby was warming to this.

'Well? Toby?'

'Okay.'

'Okay?'

'OKAY! Yes! Okay!'

Laura laughed. She turned the key in the ignition again and drove off, this time much faster. Toby stared back at his disappearing school, amazed.

Anna left school at the end of the day. She'd noted Toby's absence and had worried about it. So, instead of heading home she drove in the opposite direction. She parked her car in as visible a spot as she could find, worried about it for a while, then walked on. She could see her destination ahead – three ugly tower blocks which sat miserably in the centre of a run-down estate. Flimsy balconies were littered with junk, wheel-less bikes and broken machinery. Thin curtains fluttered through half-opened windows. The architecture was made up of cold, sharp lines. Litter was picked up by the wind and blown into waterless eddies. Graffiti on the walls was tired and old as though vandalism had turned its back on the area and looked for something more interesting. Anna eyed it all warily and walked on as quickly as she could.

Ahead of her was a bunch of teenage boys who were sitting on pushbikes, hoods up, looking bored. They were always here, so it felt. They watched her with cold eyes, like animals might do on the plains – discerning whether she was prey or predator. She ignored them and walked on, her shoes click-clacking on the concrete and echoing against the rough walls. She didn't understand the looks they gave her, couldn't read the emotions. She knew that drugs were for sale, but little more than this, and was glad to reach the stairwell. She glanced back and watched as one of the boys – they could be no more than fifteen, any of them – spat on the floor. He did it without thought or care and then dropped his chin onto the cold metal of his handlebars, settling in for more hours of waiting and watching. He seemed half asleep. Anna turned away and hurried inside.

In the lobby she stared warily at the battered elevator doors as she heard the shrieking lift slowly descending. The metal scraped and then stopped. She waited, but it seemed the lift had died somewhere above her, probably between floors. She decided to take the stairs.

Anna reached the top floor some time later. Her legs were hot and heavy from the climb but she didn't wait and rang the doorbell of a grimy flat, number 617. Paint was peeling from the front door and the numbers weren't evenly spaced. The bell gave off a buzz rather than a ring. It was eventually opened by Mary, an overweight woman with a face naturally set to 'scowl'. She was somewhere between late twenties and mid-forties. Her hair, that day, was blond.

'Hello, Mary,' said Anna. She didn't bother to offer a smile that wouldn't be returned.

'Oh bloody hell.' Mary walked back into her flat, Anna following her and shutting the door behind her. 'I don't know if he's in. Never bothers to tell me. If he is, tell him his Dad wants to kill him.'

'Will do,' Anna replied cheerfully and headed the other way to the last door along the short corridor. It was shut, but she

expected that. She knocked. No reply. Then something banged.
And then there was a shout. A young man's voice.

'WHAT?!'

Anna entered. Inside, standing nervously in front of a desk
with three computer screens on it (and a load of computer
gadgets that meant nothing to her, or to most people) was a
young man, nineteen years old. He was dressed trendily, his
hair was wild and his skin was that white, pale tone you get
when you've been inside for weeks at a time. His eyes were
always flicking about, his mouth twitched, his hands were
never still.

'Hello, Terry,' she said.

Recognising Anna, he smiled, relieved.

'Oh, hello. Sorry. It's just, when someone knocks, you know,
all polite and formal, I get bit nervy.' He paused, frowning.
'You look like shit, Miss.'

'Don't call me Miss. You know it winds me up.'

Terry grinned. 'So. Come in, sit down.'

The room was trashed. Empty pizza boxes and Chinese take-
away cartons littered the floor.

'I don't think I'll risk it. Haven't had my jabs.'

'Still got that teacher's sense of humour, I see.'

'Shut your face. How are you?'

'Yeah.'

'Still crashing stock markets?'

'Don't know what you're talking about.'

'I read in the paper that someone recently hacked into MI5.
Turned all their files into pictures of cartoon characters.'

'Really?'

'It's a waste of your talent. Like getting expelled from school just before your exams. Like not bothering to go to college when a certain teacher works her arse off to get you a place.'

'Yeah but it's a shit-load of fun. Seriously, you look awful. What's the matter?'

Anna didn't reply immediately. She looked around, but there really was nowhere to sit. She wasn't surprised. She'd visited Terry once every few months since he got himself thrown out of school and the room was always a tip. He'd become her 'cause', but she'd made little progress. He was clearly immune to her best intentions.

'There's a boy in my class,' she began.

'Found someone new to save? I thought I was your special project.'

'You were, but you've been deposed.'

'Wow, this one must be seriously tragic.'

Worry clouded her face again. 'This boy, I thought he was in trouble. I thought it was his dad, I thought it was all of that stuff, but now . . . now I don't know.'

She reached into her handbag and pulled out the camera that she had found in her flat. Despite the frayed wires it looked cool and sleek. She held it out and it hung between them like a dead mouse.

'What is this?' she asked. 'I found it inside my television set.'

Terry took the camera. He stared at it, ran his hand along its smooth edges, held it close to his eye. 'Inside?'

She nodded. 'It's nothing, right? It's normal.'

But Terry didn't reply; his focus was consumed by the camera.

'I don't know anything about how a TV works, about anything electrical, really. I'm sure that's meant to be there, yes? I just keep imagining things at the moment. A few days ago, everything was so straightforward. But now I'm scared. All the time. Please Terry. Tell me. Is that normal?'

Terry never took his eye off the camera, but his reply was the cancerous confirmation that Anna had feared.

'No. No, this ain't normal.'

'What is it?'

'It's cool. It was in your TV?'

'Yes.'

He went to his desk, pulled out a set of tiny, electrical screwdrivers. 'And you think this is cos of some school kid?'

'Yes.'

Terry tried to open the box, but failed. For some reason this seemed to please him hugely.

'You and a kid. Sticking it to The Man. Who'd have thought it? Well, Miss, for this, I'm gonna have to wash up a mug.'

Toby had convinced himself that his natty new shirt really would make a difference. He entered the gym with his hair flicked back and watched the girls dancing in the middle with their cool, bored expressions. At this, his confidence did waver slightly, but he wasn't going to fall at the first hurdle. There was a glitter ball and some silver streamers to hide the most obvious bits of school equipment, but the school disco was still a fairly bog-standard effort. What it lacked in presentation, it made up for in noise.

Toby bobbed over to a long table strewn with cans of coke and packets of crisps. He opened a can, took a big gulp and enjoyed a burp. Then he looked around. At the far end of the room, an older boy was pouring vodka into the punchbowl, unable to hide his excitement. Toby watched as the boy's buddy tasted the concoction and almost spat it out. They doubled over in hysterics. Toby looked away, worried they'd see him watching. Across the room he saw a couple snogging next to the fire exit. The other kids in his class were clustered together across the room, laughing and joking. Miles away.

He tugged at his shirt, suddenly uncomfortable. He looked down at the scuffs on his shoes and rubbed them on the back of his trousers. And as he did so, he remembered the time he entered the school before this one. He remembered how he looked at the indifferent, hostile faces of his new classmates and knew that it would all be just the same. His hand ran up and down his forearm, feeling the scars hidden beneath the shirt. He recalled the bullies at the school up in Newcastle who hung his clothes from the school windows. They had fluttered like flags against the bitter north-east wind while he, naked, shivered with cold and shame, unable to retrieve them without exposing himself to everyone. The teachers didn't bother to hide their smiles as they enjoyed the cruel japes at his expense. A new tune started playing and although Toby didn't know it, everyone else did. Suddenly they were all dancing while he clutched his warm can of coke, watching them.

He didn't last long. As the kids continued to throw shapes on the floor, Toby slipped out of the room. A cheer went up and for a moment he thought it might be about him. But it wasn't; a girl had accidentally spilled a drink down her top and the boys were leering. Of course. Nothing would ever be about him. He walked away, but stopped in the corridor. Outside, some kids were running around maniacally. They seemed crazed. He looked back at the disco, then at the quiet, cold corridors of the school. They had all been told that these were strictly off-limits tonight. He found a set of stairs, away from everything.

The door at the top wasn't locked, and Toby pushed through it. The night air greeted him; he liked the bite. The roof of the school building was made up of two tiled, pitched roofs with a central lead box-gutter between them. It was wide enough to walk along. Toby went to the edge of the roof and looked down. Below him he watched the banshee kids charging about, enjoying a rough game of British bulldogs. Further back, two boys lay on the grass, sharing a joint. One of them noticed him and nudged his friend.

Toby shuffled closer to the edge. He let the tips of his shoes peek over the drop.

Below, the two stoned kids stood up and started waving to him. Something about the wave wasn't encouraging. From where he stood, with the cool wind pushing and pulling at him, their arms were directing him down.

'I could jump. I could, you know,' he said, quietly. He looked down at the boys and saw them pointing at him, encouraging others to share their view. He saw kids pouring out of the building. They were shouting things at him, but the wind brushed the noise away.

'I might. I've done it before.' He stared down at them and strange, disconnected, jagged memories stirred up. A bridge, barbed wire, freezing water, hunting dogs that snapped at his feet as he ran. The images blurred as the cold wind blew around him. Below, a crowd had formed. They were waving at him and instinctively he raised his hand in response. Hello. The swirling breeze changed and suddenly he could hear their shouts.

'Jump! Jump! Jump! Jump!' Their faces came into focus. The waves and smiles were taunts and jibes. He could see that some of them were filming him on their mobile phones.

'If I did, what would you do then?'

'Jump! Jump! Jump! Jump!'

'I will. I can.' He edged further forward. The hysterical mob below cheered him on.

'And it won't hurt. Never does. Not until the morning.'

'Jump! Jump! Jump!'

'And then you'll see.' Toby breathed in the cold air. He closed his eyes for a moment, let his head fall back, wrapped up in delirium. His foot pushed towards the void.

But then the door behind crashed open and a gasping teacher – Mr Farlow – sprinted forward and grabbed Toby by the collar, yanking him backwards to safety. Toby crashed to the floor, jolted. He looked up, stunned to see this panicked teacher staring over him.

'Jesus, Toby. Are you crazy?'

Toby looked up at the strong, athletic man who towered over him, and he shrank under his gaze.

'I . . .' He couldn't manage any more. Instead he burst into tears. The teacher didn't say anything else, just stood over him. Toby assumed he was waiting for him to stop sobbing so he could bollock him some more. But he couldn't stop the tears.

Toby was still crying as he lay in his mother's arms, curled up on the sitting-room sofa. She held him tight to her and whispered soft things into his ears. He responded in turn, hugging her tight, squeezing his eyes shut against anything and everything. He heard his father enter, but he kept his eyes shut and Michael left soon after. He lay there, cuddled up against his mum for the rest of the evening. He'd let them down again. He'd probably have to change schools. Again. He tried to think of something positive. He was still trying when he fell asleep in her arms.

Terry had two sets of blinds on each window. That way, he explained to Anna, it was impossible for anyone to bug him using the windows' vibrations.

'Who would want to bug you?' said Anna, and his shrug reminded her of their days back at school when he was her brilliant, surly and near-unteachable pupil. She'd wanted to be the one to inspire him and put him on the right track. He'd responded by setting fire to a classroom. That should have been the end of it, except that once he'd gone he sent her an essay – three months overdue. The quality, the sheer insight and maturity of it, stunned her. It belied everything about him. And it showed that he cared. They'd become 'friends' though the word didn't suit their relationship. She would implore him to do more with his life and he would mock her sincerity. After their last visit she'd promised herself that she'd stop bothering with him. But then Toby appeared.

They'd been sitting in his stuffy room for hours, staring at a computer screen. He'd type things and say words that she didn't fully understand. She'd wait, hoping for an explanation, slowly getting bored and tired and irritable. On the plus side, Terry had shown Anna just what you could do with a computer, an internet connection and some know-how. He had always impressed her – his mind was a furnace – but Anna was surprised by his application, the calm methodical approach he showed. When she commented on it he sniffed and made some sarcastic comment about getting a good grade. But the truth was he had only ever been good at things which interested him. And everything that Anna showed him about Toby was fascinating.

Terry was obsessed by conspiracies. He would link anything he found on his screens to an anecdote about 9/11, about the Illuminati, the New World Order, about the way you could find Masonic symbols on the dollar bill and city-centre architecture. Everything, according to Terry, was about someone, somewhere up there who planned our demise and control with infinite detail. It had been a constant source of discourse between them.

'Yeah, well,' Terry would sneer, 'you're one of those drones who think that conspiracy theories are nerdy.'

'Well, come on—'

'See, they've got you programmed just as they want. Make it so anyone who questions the status quo is a wally. Genius, when you think about it.'

'Oh, I see. You're the great visionary, are you?'

Terry turned away from the computer and faced Anna directly. He cracked his knuckles and made a small sigh, as though he were dealing with a child.

'You're clever, right?'

'I like to think I'm doing okay.'

'You buy ready-meals, don't you?'

'What? Yes, I suppose so.'

'You don't think they're that good for you, though, do you?'

'Well, no.'

'But you buy them all the same. Why's that?'

Anna didn't have a reply handy and Terry kicked on.

'You watch TV most nights, soon as you get in probably. But there's nothing good on any more, is there?'

Anna didn't reply.

'Your life is flooded with American culture. Your interest in the news is half-hearted. You're more concerned with celebrities. Even if you think you're above gossip magazines, you'll find yourself checking out the front covers when you see them in the supermarket. You buy whatever is advertised or recommended by 'lists'. You vote for identikit middle-of-the-road governments, who all support business and corporate growth. You live in fear of your neighbours, of strangers, of young people, and you think you're always in imminent danger; the end of the world is creeping up on us through climate change or terrorist attack. And, most significantly, you do not believe that there is anything that you can do to stop this. Congratulations, Anna Price, your programming has been correctly installed.'

And with that, he turned back to the computer.

'What's that all supposed to mean?' she replied, irked by his confidence. 'How does me watching the telly prove that there's some evil Mr Big out there? It's silly.'

'You just don't want to admit that you might not be in control.'

'I know I'm not in control, I just don't believe anybody's that organised to have some master plan for world domination.'

'Alright, Miss.'

'Does he have a big white cat on his lap?'

'If you joke about it, then none of it could possibly be real. I'll say things that make sense; you take the piss.'

He said none of this with any acrimony and it made her feel a little childish. He typed on, and Anna was about to challenge him again when several files popped open on the screen. Anna and Terry leaned forward, their eyes scanning the information in front of them. These documents were school files and reports about Toby. They were quiet for a while as they read them.

'Well, there's nothing that odd,' said Terry. 'Four schools in five years, but that's because his dad's work has forced them to move.'

Anna shook her head. 'Toby said he got moved whenever he asked for help.'

'Well, there's no mention of anything like that in the reports. They don't mention anything bad at all. See? Hang on . . .'

A similar thought struck them both at the same time and instinctively they both looked more carefully at the words.

'This doesn't sound like the kid you described to me.'

'No. They make him sound normal and happy.'

Terry's fingers raced across the keyboard and more documents appeared.

'In each report, they all use the same language,' noted Anna.

'Yeah. Like they've all been written by the same person. It's also very neat.'

'What do you mean?'

'Well, normally, when I go after someone, like when I stuck all of that porn onto Mr Turnbull's computer—'

'THAT WAS YOU?!!'

Terry smiled, unabashed. 'Yeah, so when I was pulling all of his details off the web, it came in a jumble . . . bits here and there, discrepancies, errors, you know. But when you dig for stuff about Toby, you get it all neat and tidy. Like it's meant to be read.' He leaned in closer. 'I wonder how far back this goes.'

He started to type again, faster. But Anna pushed her chair away from the desk as though the information had a life of its own. She wondered if Terry's computer had its own camera which was also watching them. Terry dug deeper and asked questions that could not be answered. When she left his flat, late that night, Anna had caught his fever and she ran all the way to the car. She slept fitfully, her dreams tormented by faceless, laughing men with grips that couldn't be broken.

The next day, she drove to Toby's house and waited. She saw him come out with his mother and followed their car as they drove off. She parked discreetly in the supermarket car park and trailed mother and son as they wandered around the aisles. It wasn't long before Toby was tasked with finding a particular item and went off alone to find it. Anna followed him, looking back over her shoulder to be certain that his mother was far enough away before she grabbed her chance.

Toby was peering at a stack of cans, reading the labels when she came up next to him and said his name softly, urgently.

'Toby.'

'Oh, hello Miss.' He was clearly surprised by her presence. He glanced around him, a little nervous, then pulled a can of beans from the shelf. 'How are you?' he enquired with bewildering politeness.

'Me? I'm fine. Are you okay?'

'Yeah. Mum's making a big chilli con carne.' He held up the can.

'That's . . . nice.' He seemed so normal. She noticed that one of her shoelaces was undone, and her hand went to her hair to straighten it, to calm herself down.

'Do you need beans too?' he asked.

'No. I'm here to see you.'

'Mum says I shouldn't worry about all that other stuff so much. She thinks I make it worse that way.'

'Listen, before she sees me—'

'She said—'

'*Toby*. Just, just listen. Please. This is going to sound a bit odd. A lot odd. But, look, what's your earliest memory?'

'Huh?'

'I've been trying to find out about you, work out what's wrong. And everything about you, every fact I can find about you just stops before you're three. There's nothing I can find about you before you were three years old.'

'That's weird.'

'It is.' She looked nervously about her. 'I want you to think. Think back to when you were little. What's the earliest thing you can remember?'

'I dunno.'

'No. Think, Toby. It's important.'

'I dunno, I . . .' he blushed, self-conscious, like he was back in the classroom. Anna waited, her eyes glued to his mouth. She noticed a tiny scar that ran from his bottom lip to his chin. 'I mean, there's that teddy bear I guess, but, no, that's not right. Duh!'

'Tell me.'

'Well, there was this big guy and this teddy and he's holding it up above his head . . . but I've, like, I've never had a teddy.

A teddy, how weak is that?' He laughed and looked away, embarrassed. 'Anyhow, you don't really need me—'

But Anna had turned and slipped into the next aisle. She heard Toby's voice drift off as he realised she'd gone, then heard his mother's voice call out to him.

'Have you got them, love?'

The voice sounded maternal, kind and warm.

'You bet,' came his reply. Sometimes he sounded so much younger than his fifteen years, she thought. Like he'd been stopped from growing up. But then she thought about the way he would look at her and he felt a million years older.

'We'll need two tins,' his mother continued. She heard the cans drop into the metal trolley. They were walking away now. 'Tell you what, after we've got this into the car, why don't we stop off at that cafe – get a croissant and a hot chocolate? Doesn't that sound fun?'

Anna watched them pay for their items and load them into the car. Toby seemed so happy. Terry had made everything seem crazy and dangerous – a world of cameras and despotic control. She couldn't marry the image of this goofy kid with the paranoia he had fed her. But even after they had driven away and left her behind, even when she found herself flicking through a magazine near the check-out, still she found that her heart fluttered with fear of something unknown; something she was creeping towards without enough knowledge to do so safely.

NINE

'Don't moan about the heat, for fuck's sake. Moaning about the heat's like moaning about the food, you dickhead.'

We scrabble over the loose rocks and reach the top of the hill. It's so bright, the sky feels white, not blue. I'm dripping with sweat. I look down – everyone else is wearing boots, but I'm wearing sandals. My toes are cut to ribbons. The guy next to me is laughing. There are four of us, my good mates. One of them takes off his helmet and I wonder why I don't have one. Jacko pats me hard on the head and everyone laughs again.

Jesus, I don't have anything. I don't have water or food or proper boots or anything sensible, and it's only half nine and it's so fucking hot I'm going to die out here.

This is a dream. Come on. Wake up.

I do. I pull the sheets off and rush to the small dressing cabinet where an open diary waits for the latest entry. It's already half-full and each time the writing is scrawled, hasty, messed up by sleep. I write down as much as I can remember and then sit back. I stretch and yawn, then flick back through the diary. Jacko.

I find his name again in another dream. My scrawl describes him standing over me in a dark cave somewhere. In that dream I was a little scared of him. This morning I remember him as a mate. I flick through other pages – some bad drawings, lots of question marks and underlinings. It looks . . . insane. As I close it, there's a knock on the door.

It's Edward, still in his pyjamas, unshaven (a thin, patchy mass of white dander), with a tray of breakfast: two boiled eggs, some toast cut into triangles and two glasses of port. He grins.

'Morning, Ben. Sleep?'

'Yes, well, thank you.'

'I'm starving. Out the way, squire.'

He pushes past and dumps the tray on the desk while I move the diary to safety. He sits on the edge of the bed and tucks into his egg. This is the way each morning begins.

'Dreams?'

I nod. I've told him a little about my position and as a result he's become a confidant of sorts. I guess I couldn't hold it in any longer. Everything has been boiling away inside and he seemed as good a person as any. Better. He and I are loners and he's so bloody odd that no one would listen to a word he says. During my time here, we've had no visitors. The phone has never rung. I had to check it one day, assuming we must be disconnected, and was surprised to hear a dial tone.

Edward makes a routine trip to the supermarket where he buys discounted goods. He eats fruit that I would have chucked out weeks ago. His drinking is unpredictable. I once found him sleeping in the kitchen at five-thirty in the evening, a saucepan of baked beans charred on the stove. He's what posh people would call 'a character'.

'So. Go on, tell,' he barks, as he scoops up his egg and slurps the yolk down. I describe the dream and he laughs as he listens. 'You been abroad much?' he asks.

'Seems like it.'

'Mm,' he nods, taking a swig of his port. 'At least you weren't naked. Dreams like that, you always end up naked. Anxiety something, isn't it?' He finishes the port and reaches for the second glass. I smile – it's never for me, we both know I wouldn't drink at this hour, but he likes the delicacy of a big hit in two smaller glasses. 'Did I tell you the time when Martine ended up naked outside the house? Went to get the milk, trapped her towel in the door, it slammed shut and ripped right off her.' He starts to laugh, remembering it. I grin as his laugh gets louder and faster. He's always like this. 'And then, oh Jesus, apparently the door wouldn't open cos it had got wedged shut – was the wind or something, so she couldn't get herself decent and people were walking past with their eyes on stalks!' The laugh is a barking wheeze. He raises one hand to the sky, as though he can balance himself back into control. 'She had a fine body, my darling, before the years got to her . . . oh dear, I remember her telling me all about it over dinner that night and the kids were hooting and she went red just recounting it, my sweet little . . .'

The laugh is fading and his eyes are red. Every story ends like this. Sadder than its start. This is because he is talking about a family that has abandoned him. The laugh and the wheeze end and he finishes the port before sighing. He pats the sagging bed as though it were a faithful dog. I look down, a little embarrassed, still not sure how to deal with these moments. He'll talk about the family that left him so honestly and with so much self-hatred that I don't know what to say or where to put myself.

As far as I can work out – Ed's stories seem to contradict themselves at times so I have to pay attention – Ed was a happily married man: father of two and proud husband of Martine. But then he did something too shameful to speak of. Whatever it was (I think he must have got drunk and hit her, but maybe there was another woman), the family then upped sticks and left. And now he lives on his own, having sold everything but the house to keep afloat. The house itself is bare but for his family's rooms which are still tidy, awaiting their return, desperate for a sign that he has finally been forgiven. He writes to them once a week, posting the letters to the same address but never receiving a reply. I wonder if they live there any more.

I've started doing odd jobs for Edward around the house. I stopped paying hotel 'bills' – he stopped asking – and so try to make myself helpful to make up for it. I cook (occasionally and badly) and mend things which have worn themselves out. The wallpaper in his daughter's bedroom is today's task. I open a window before I start and pause to glance around the room. There is little personality here. No children's drawings on the wall or faded photographs. Just a girl's name (Tabitha) stencilled to the door (the letters have been touched up over the years), a bed, a pink beanbag and a desk with some old books lined neatly across it.

I reattach the wallpaper without too much difficulty. Smoothing it back with my hand, I find my mind pulling towards Emma. The desk we bought her came flat-packed in large cardboard boxes and took an afternoon of swearing to assemble. Tabitha's desk is older and far sturdier. I imagine Edward's little girl sitting here studiously finishing her homework. I remember Emma holding crayons like daggers, her tongue touching her top lip as she scratched formless shapes on scraps of paper. I wonder if she is still there.

Suddenly I find I'm about to cry. I miss my children. I miss my wife. I miss my old, dull, average life and I don't understand why I have suddenly been shunted into this weird, never-world. If I just went back, just said I'd gone on a bender, apologised, squeezed my eyes shut and went on as I was then I'd be able to rub my face in my little girl's neck. I'd be able to squeeze little Joe so tight he'd squeal with laughter. And Carrie would put her arms around me and hold me tight. If I went back.

I'm a crumpled mess when Edward walks in and finds me. He's carrying a small milk jug with fresh flowers in it – thin, delicate stems that have been snatched from the overgrown back garden. He places them on the desk and stands back to admire the effect. The pretty flowers are out of place, but he seems happy. His fingers twitch with pleasure.

'She won't see 'em, I bet, but you never know,' he grins. Of course she won't see them, they'll have wilted by the end of the day. I wonder how old she is now. Although Edward is cagey with the details, the family feel like they've been gone twenty years, at least. Does he not realise that his daughter will now be a woman? His little girl will never come running to the front door with a gummy grin and open arms. She'll stand by the car, a cold glare and a handbag full of recriminations.

'Yeah, you never know,' he says. 'You look like dog's mess. What's up, feller?'

He makes me laugh. I tell him I miss my kids and he puts an arm around me and nods, then pats my shoulder as he gets up to leave.

'I thought I'd do sausages tonight.'

'Nice.'

'You don't need any of those fiddly vegetables, do you?'

'They're for fancy dans, I thought.'

'Quite right. Get your vitamin C from the ketchup.'

'Dinner of champions,' I say, and as I say it someone starts banging hard at the back of my brain. Edward doesn't notice. He just waves a goodbye – a hand flung vaguely in my direction.

But I've just remembered something. Dinner of champions. The words come from cragged teeth, a northern brogue. A tall, muscled man standing on rough rocks in the blinding sun. Jacko. *'Dinner of champions, man,'* he spits out with a laugh as he gazes down at the barren wasteland below us. He wears a soldier's uniform. He is Sergeant James McFarlane. He is my colleague and friend. I am a soldier.

Before Edward leaves the room, I call out to him – a blurt of shock:

'I was in Iraq.'

He looks at me and sees my surprise. I notice his fingers start to twitch, like he's excited.

'Well, then.'

'I was a soldier. I remember . . . something.'

'A dream?'

'No. Real. I have a friend.'

A friend. Jacko.

Edward looks at me and frowns and walks away. I'm not

sure what his problem is, but I'm too wrapped up in this to worry. A hand has reached out to me from the darkness.

I walk to a bus stop at the far end of town rather than the one nearest the B&B. I wait half an hour then take a small, bumpy trip, away from the coast and inland, where I make two more changes. My map says I should be fifty miles from Edward's place now and I think that's safe enough. I stop in the nearest town and find an internet cafe. It's near the train station, on a run-down road with a youth hostel and an off-licence. I'm nervous of going in and find myself wandering around the town for ages before I'm ready.

A young man with an aggressive haircut and loads of piercings sits at a desk. He's reading a book. It's one of those big, thick classics by some dead writer that I don't know. I ask if I can use a computer and he's well polite in response; shows me a monitor, tells me the rate and that I should come back and pay when I'm finished. I sit down and am pleased that the guy can't see what I'm looking at. My hands pause over the computer. I glance back and catch the lad's eye before he slumps back into his novel.

I type the words into the computer, faltering. Sergeant James McFarlane. There are thousands of results and my initial excitement dies quickly – too many people with the same name. I limit the search to the UK, and after a couple of false starts I find him. His face pops up at me with a cheery grin that takes my breath away. It's him. Smiling at me. Jacko. Mate. Fuck!

I get the details in bits and bobs: his retirement from the army, his injuries and commendations. There's a photograph of him with two young children, in full dress. One of the kids bashfully holds up a medal. I never got to spend much time on the computer at home. Family life was always too distracting and I'm amazed by how much you can find with a few finger taps. I look at my friend and old memories bubble up. I suddenly remember sitting facing him in the back of an open truck, with other guys around. He's telling a story about sex with some tough nut's daughter – everyone's laughing, we're waiting to go. We're going to fight. He's telling the story so everyone can hear, but it's really just for me. We are best friends. He's joking that he's going to a combat zone because it's safer than facing this bird's dad. At least he can carry a gun out there . . .

I stare at the screen: Jacko smiles right back. I am giddy with the rush of old feelings. I have no real sense of the man, but I'm trembling at his grin and the faint memory of his matey laugh. I have to find him.

I find a website which tells me it can do what I want, but I need to pay. It's only five pounds, but I don't have a credit card. I go to the lad at the desk who laughs at me. You can get a free trial for a week. Apparently that's what everyone does. He shows me how to set up a free email address and then after a few clicks I'm in.

'Where have you been?' the lad asks. I think I get away with it by telling him I'm in my forties. But the question ruffles me. Where have I been?

The website does exactly what I ask and I get an address ridiculously quickly. I scribble it down on a piece of paper then delete all of the websites I've visited. I stand and go over to pay.

'Thirty quid, then,' he says, stretching.

'What?' I'm appalled. The price he'd quoted was five pounds per hour.

'Six hours. Thirty quid,' he says, as though I'm being difficult. I glance at my watch. Jesus Christ, he's right, it's late. I glance outside – it looks dark out there. I hand him the money without speaking and turn for the door, panicking. 'See you then,' he calls out sarcastically as I push through the door.

I've lost hours in that room and I don't understand it. Have I really been so wrapped up in that computer that I've not noticed the time passing? It doesn't seem possible. My neck is sore and I'm scared again. It's dark, it'll take me hours to get back to Edward's place on unfamiliar roads and I don't trust my mind. All I have is some cash – not enough cash – and an address for someone I may have once known but who may no longer live there. I thought I was over this, but now that the fear scrapes away at me I feel all of my old horrors all too well.

I duck into a back alley and hurry along, away from that place. I'm bursting with fear and need to get rid of it. I need to punch my way out of it. I want to mug someone. Jesus. I want to hit someone, steal something, hurt someone. Somehow that is going to make me feel better. I try to think about this rationally, but there's a woman on her own, right there, dropping her keys onto the pavement as she's about to enter her house. And I find myself walking towards her.

She turns to look at me as I get to her. She's pretty, a face that's open and trusting. The door is ajar and the house is dark inside. She's alone and if I do this now, no one will catch me. I feel like I've done this before. I look at her and I can see that she's scared.

'I'm sorry,' I stammer. I'm about to hit her. 'I'm sorry,' I say again. She's not moving, it's like she's waiting for me to do it, get it over with. The rage is still there, pumping inside me, urging me on. Her handbag will have money in it. There will be other stuff worth stealing in the house. She's well dressed. Easy meat. My ears are pounding, I feel saliva in my mouth, I can taste the urge to kick and punch and break.

I turn my back on her. I don't walk away, but I turn my back on her and I'm breathing fast. She hasn't moved. Get inside, please, get inside you silly cow.

'Are you okay?' she asks. Oh God.

I manage to nod. 'Yeah, fine, thank you. Sorry. You, er, I thought you were someone I knew.' I'm calming down. I'm not going to do it. I find myself walking away. I hear her door shut. Thank fuck.

I sit on a quiet bus and stare at my reflection in the dark glass. I'll be back at Edward's in an hour or so and am now miles from her. My face is blurred and distorted in the dirty glass. I stare at my wonky reflection, watch it smudge and smear as it stares back at me. It seems to be grinning. I lean in close, whispering to it: Who am I? Who am I? The answer seems to be coughed up from the depths of the engine and the tree branches that scrape the top of the bus, a slow repetitive rhythm that croaks out an answer.

Follow me and you'll see. Follow me. You'll see.

It's late and quiet as I walk through the back streets to Edward's house. You can hear the waves, but the air here is trapped between the buildings and everything smells foul, like it's all slowly rotting away with the salt and the damp. I'm calmer now, and although I stop regularly and check to see if anyone is following me (they're not), I do it as a precaution, not through fear. I'm a military man. I try to remind myself. Try to give myself the swagger of the squaddie but find I'm just walking like a man with constipation. I slip into the house. It's quiet. I was expecting Perry Como. I double-lock the doors behind me, untie my laces and lay my shoes by the door. Then I go looking for Edward.

He's asleep in the main room, a near-empty glass on the table by the armchair. I think of leaving him be, but I'm still too twitchy from today. So I sit down, more heavily than I need to in the seat opposite and he wakes immediately. His eyes are glazed and I see he's lost for a moment. Then his eyes focus on me and he smiles.

'So how was your sleuthing?'

'Interesting.'

He yawns, nods and stretches, reaches for his whisky glass. He looks at me – want one?

'Why not?' I nod back, and he goes to the shelf and pours two more meaty helpings.

'Are you holding back on me for dramatic effect?' he asks. 'Cos, really, you've not got much competition for an audience, sonny.'

'I think I know where he lives.'

'So he's real.'

'Yes.'

'Good. You'll visit him, things will fall into place. Maybe he'll put you up. Start of your new life.'

'You trying to get rid of me?'

'No, that was my attempt at petulance. It's as good as I can manage.' He passes me my drink and settles back in his seat.

'I was having a funny dream. Something about . . .' he tries to remember, his eyes narrowing, 'something about the kids and a swimming pool and . . .' he waves his hand the way he does – forget about it.

It's late, but he doesn't ask the time. He doesn't wear a watch. He'll wake when he wakes. He runs his finger around the glass, frowns.

'Something about Tabitha. She was little and grown up all at the same time.' He lets out a little sigh. 'Dreams. So your man.'

'Yeah. He's real. He's . . .' I dig out a piece of paper, hold it up. 'He lives here, or he did. Probably still does.'

'Soldier?'

'Yeah. We served together.'

'I like that word. You served, did you?'

'You did.'

'Didn't feel much like serving to me.'

'I can't remember how it felt. No, that's not true. I . . .' I falter because there's this big, imaginary glistening arm across my neck, pulling me backwards – strong, stinking of sweat. I look up at Edward, he's watching me carefully. 'I think I enjoyed it all a bit too much to call it service.'

'Damn right,' he smiles. 'Best bloody years of my life. Did I just say that? Jesus Christ, I'm a bloody cliché!' He coughs a rich laugh. 'But they were. Except when we were being shot at. Or mortared.' Another glug of booze. 'Remember hearing that Thomas had been born while I was hiding behind a burnt-out car in Ulster. I couldn't have been happier. We were running for our lives and laughing all the way.'

'When my children were born,' I say, 'I remember being in the delivery room with Carrie, pacing about, useless, too big, repeating everything the midwife said until Carrie had to scream at me to shut up.'

He laughs, but I'm quiet. The memory is too strong, too vital to be untrue. I want to get up and rush out of the door, go back to them all right this second.

'Maybe you're not a soldier after all.'

'Maybe I'm not.' My glass is refilled. The whisky swirls around the glass.

'What are you like with a gun?'

'Excuse me?'

'You heard.' He gulps his down, pours more in mine. He's watching me, chewing on a smile, a game up his sleeve.

'I've never touched a gun,' I say, but then there is, somewhere in my mind, a gun, a hand, my hand, my hand holding a handgun. Christ. 'I've . . . okay . . . I think I . . .'

I try to remember more, but the mist thickens again. It drives me mad.

'If you're a soldier, then you know your way around a gun.'

'I suppose so.'

'Shall we find out?' He pushes himself to his feet with a grunt and leaves the room. I don't move, I drink more, refill my own glass. It must be ninety degrees in here. I'm groggy from it all, from the day I've had. But then he's back, looming over me, waving an old-fashioned military pistol in the air.

'Bloody hell.'

'Clean as a whistle. I know how to look after a weapon, young man.'

'And I'm sure you know how to get a perfect crease in your trousers, but will you stop waving that bloody thing around, Jesus!'

He laughs, and his hands and fingers are twitching again the way they do when he's excited.

'Shoot something.'

'Excuse me?'

He waves the gun around and I'm wondering just how bloody drunk the old coot is. He points it at a porcelain vase on the mantelpiece with a faded pattern of blue and white flowers.

'Pow,' he whispers, one eye closed. For a second I thought he was going to shoot the thing then and there. But he just giggles.

'It's loaded?'

'Course it's bloody loaded.' And to prove it, he spins on his toes – with remarkable nimbleness – and shoots the bloody vase to pieces. The noise from the gun is unbelievable. I'm on my feet before I know what's happened, screaming. But Edward's just laughing. He looks at me, sees my disbelief, and doubles over with delight. 'Did you see that?' he cackles, 'Did you bloody well see that!?'

'Yeah, great, put it down, on the mantelpiece, there, that's it, put it down will you?'

He does a shoe-shuffle dance, the gun held high in the air.

'You'll bring the bloody police round.'

'No, no,' he scoffs, but he will bring the police if he carries on like this. And I can feel irritation and fear bubbling up inside me. That rage again.

'Edward. Stop this.' Please stop, mate, please.

'What? What's the matter with you? I thought you said you were a soldier,' he says, and walks over to fetch himself more whisky. He's a stubborn git. No wonder his family left him. The booze inside me thickens and burns.

'Edward. Put the gun down. I'm asking.'

'Oh, you're asking?'

'Yeah.'

And my tone finally gets through his thick skin. He stops. Looks at me. Sees the way I'm standing. And in that moment he's suddenly a frail old man again. He puts the gun down gently. Nods. There. See? I nod.

'Thank you.'

We stand apart. He waits for my signal to let him speak in his own home.

'Didn't recognise you for a bit then,' he says.

'No.'

'Didn't see it before, but you've got a bit more to you. Bit of a tough nut.'

'Yeah. Give it.'

He nods, grabs the weapon and shuffles quickly over to me. I could hold it by the nozzle and smash the butt against his chin. I could smash his jawbone, shatter it and leave him to die in this room right now. I take it from him and see him look at me with wary eyes. I take the gun and my hands dismantle and then reassemble the machine. I do it with hard, fast, effective movements. Old memories, hidden within my body. I should be excited or amazed, but this has happened too many times now. And I can feel my old self, too close to the surface, pushing up with closed fists, pushing and tearing his way out.

'You remember doing that before?' he asks. I don't reply. I try it again and I do it just the same. Well drilled. I look at him.

'You keep ammo in the house?'

He stammers a reply. 'Yes, yes. Upstairs.'

I point the gun past him – behind him, down the corridor. A blink, a shot and I smash the door handle at the far end. It's a good shot. Not amazing, not incredible, but better than any amateur would manage. Neither of us speaks. I can feel the heat fading. My head falls, I hand back the gun to him. He takes it and walks out. He comes back some time later. I assume he's hidden it.

'You scared me.'

'Sorry.'

'You ever been like that before, while you've been in here?'

'No. Not like that.'

'How about outside?'

I look up at him and he knows I am ashamed. He puts a tentative hand on my shoulder.

'Ben. I've done things that I, that are, you know. We all have.'

But I don't remember doing anything bad, not until I got away from that van. I rack my brains as I think back on my time with Carrie and the kids and I only remember good times. No affairs, no drunken fumbles, no fights, no theft, nothing to be ashamed of. I'd assumed this was normal, dull, a safe man's life. I'd imagined that all of this bad behaviour belonged to the newspapers and television, that it was another world's fiction. But I am the fairytale. And I am the lie.

Emma is climbing. Her face is a picture as she grunts and scrambles up the ropes to reach the top of the ladder. Go on girl. Eventually she gets there, to the top of the mast of a purpose-built kids' pirate ship in the middle of a children's adventure playground. She turns, thrilled with herself and calls down.

'Mummy! Mummy!'

Carrie's below, but she's distracted, trying to see where Joe has got to. He comes whizzing down a slide, trying to look cool. Calmer, she looks up at her daughter and waves, cheers.

'Look at you!' she calls back. But when she looks down I see how tired she is. She rubs her hand over her face. If you didn't know her you'd see a pretty, tidy woman in her forties enjoying a day out with her kids. But if you did, if you were her husband, you'd know that there's no energy in the way she trails after them. You'd know that smile because she used to give it to you when you came home late and she was tired and worried about something. You'd know – I know, that she's miserable.

Joe has made friends with two other kids in matching foot-ball kits – they're daring each other to go higher and faster. Carrie's glad that he's got people to keep him happy, but I want to warn him: they're older than he is and he'll hurt himself if he tries too hard to keep up.

But I can only watch. I'm hidden away, lying on my stomach about five hundred yards away, clutching a pair of high-powered binoculars. I'm spying on the people I love but don't trust.

Emma slips and hurts herself as she tries to climb down. She's got a leg stuck and she's crying and panicking, and Carrie, too big to climb up herself, has to get as close as she can and talk her down, soothe her, be her mum.

She needs her dad. But I'm lying in the dirt like a fucking thief. All I can do is stare as Emma finally makes it to the bottom and runs to her mum, who scoops her into her arms and covers her in kisses.

I let the binoculars fall and the lenses hit the dirt. I don't care, I can't look again. I thought coming here would give me some answers. I thought maybe I'd see Carrie with another man or with different kids or something. Something. No, I'm lying. I came here because I couldn't resist. It's torture, but I have to see them. I thought it would be wonderful, I've missed them so badly. But this isn't anything like that. It's not sad or melancholy or poignant or whatever the words are. It hurts. It cuts, it stings. I hate it.

My little girl. My proud boy. My beautiful love. I miss you all so much. And there you all are. Laughing, crying, kissing. There you are.

TEN

Anna knew that she was not allowed to ask when Toby would return to school. She knew she had to wait to be told and that the information was kept from her by Mr Benton as a punishment. Terry had stopped returning her calls, but he had a habit of vanishing when it suited him and she wasn't worried. She continued to teach by day and mark homework by night, ignoring the imprints that the broken television had left on her carpet. The fear had subsided for now.

One night, as she was writing an encouraging note in one of her pupil's books, she was startled by the doorbell. She didn't get many visitors, so she brushed imaginary crumbs from her skirt and went tentatively to the door. She peeked out through the spy-hole and recognised the ageing man who stared glumly at the corridor outside. Her heart sank.

'Dad . . . Hi.'

'Anna.' He smiled. His voice was rich and deep – tuned by long nights in oak-panelled rooms with cigars and brandy. Neither moved. 'Won't you invite me in?'

Anna looked at her father. He wore his age well, she thought. He was in his usual dark, well-tailored suit with the requisite

shirt and tie. His greying hair was cut just as she always remembered it. His shoes were recently polished. He made her feel
small. She gestured for him to enter without enthusiasm and
he followed her inside, shutting the door quietly behind him.
He removed his heavy coat, but then held it in his hands,
unsure where to place it. His eyes took in the small apartment
and Anna could see the disappointment in his expression. She
resented it and folded her arms, standing between him and
the sitting room, barring him entrance.

'You can hang it on the back of the door.' He hung his coat
on top of her mac because there was only one hook. She waited
for him to speak, to explain his visit. He never came, not any
more.

'I'd love a drink.'

'I don't have any whisky.'

'Wine, then.'

She shook her head.

'Water, if you can manage it.'

'I'll have to wash up a glass.'

'Doesn't sound like you. You're always so tidy.' Somehow
he'd managed to say 'tidy' as a barb and his face flickered with
annoyance. He pulled at his sleeves and Anna noticed the expensive cufflinks.

'Are you really going to make me stand here, by the door?'

'What do you want, Daddy?'

'Is it so odd that a father would want to see his daughter?'

'Here I am.'

'And you look lovely. Anna, please.'

She sighed. 'Come on, then. God.' She turned and walked
away from him. He followed her into the sitting room as she

went through into the kitchen and returned with a bottle of white wine and two glasses. She shook her head at him – don't say a word – and his small laugh in return broke the ice. He took the bottle from her and poured two big glasses.

'How's school?'

'Same as ever.'

He looked down at her marking, picked up an essay, but she pulled it off him.

'Don't.'

'Why not?'

'It's private.'

'It's homework.'

'They give it to me, not you.'

He looked away, gazed about the room. Anna saw him stare at the empty corner where the television had been.

'What happened?'

'What do you mean?'

'Your television.' They stared together at space.

'Oh. Nothing. Just, I – I don't need a telly. There's nothing on these days. Nothing any good.'

'Well, that's true.' He looked at her and she realised she was blushing.

'And it broke.' She drank the wine to stop herself from talking.

'Are televisions expensive?'

'You've got one. You've got a whole room set up.'

'Yes, I meant a normal one. Not as indulgent as mine.'

'You mean, can a teacher afford a TV?'

'That was the gist of it, yes.'

'Can my job, which you hate, allow me basic creature comforts?'

'I don't hate teaching,' he said. 'How can anyone hate teaching?'

'You think it's beneath me.'

'It is. You have a brain the size of a planet and you insist on throwing it away on charitable causes.'

'You think—'

'Can we not . . .? Can we not argue every time we see each other? We used to laugh all the time.'

Somewhere deep in her mind, hidden under many layers, Anna remembered herself curled up on his lap, laughing. They both drank again.

'Are you happy?' he asked.

'Yes.'

'You seem . . .' he trailed off, trying to find the right word. It came so much later that it almost felt detached from the previous sentence. 'Alone.'

'Well, I'm not.' She said it quietly, without defiance. And as she said it, she wondered if it were true. She wondered about Toby and Terry and that hateful policeman who had scared her so. She considered telling her father about these things, but when she looked into those well-informed, well-educated, well-heeled eyes, something inside her snapped shut. 'I am happy.'

'Good. It's all I want. You know they say a father is only as happy as his unhappiest child. So we're index-linked. That's meant to be a joke, but I don't really get it either.' His hands fiddled with the stem of the wine glass. 'I suppose it's a chemical thing, but I worry about you when I don't see you. I'm willing to accept that our relationship has changed, I can accept that. But I can't carry on with my stuffy life if you're . . . if there's anything that ... I ...' He put out a hand onto the table. 'You're my little girl.'

'I'm not little. Not any more.'

'No.' His hand stretched across the table and he ran a tentative finger over the back of her hand. Slowly, she pulled away from his reach. His hand remained on the table.

'I'll go.' He walked out stiffly, collecting his coat. She heard the front door click shut, then she put the kettle on and got back to her marking.

Each day that she parked her battered old car, she wondered if it would be the day that Toby returned. At first she considered the idea with butterflies in her stomach, but after a while she wondered about it idly; ready for him when he did come back, but less expectant. As she turned off the engine, she made a mental note to check on whether they were planning on moving him again. But by the time she was locking the doors, her mind had already slipped forward to how she could persuade Shontayne and Marika to read the balcony scene in *Romeo and Juliet* without causing a riot.

She nearly tripped over Paul Robertson, a spindly lad, who stood in front of her, eager for attention.

'Not now, Paul.'

'I got a message, Miss.'

'Take it to reception.'

'Can't. Terry said I have to say it to your face.'

'Who?'

'Terry. He said I was to say it when no one could hear. It's a bit weird too, like. But I've got to say it word for word or I don't get the money.'

'Alright, I'm listening.'

Paul frowned, concentrating hard. 'Okay, here goes. Dear Miss. Do not call me. I'll find you. Your boy is a fuck-load of trouble. Seriously. Seriously. Seriously. Seriously.' He smiled, embarrassed. 'He said I had to say "seriously" four times or you wouldn't get it. And sorry about the swearing, but he said that was important too.' He stuffed his hands in his pockets and waited.

'Am I supposed to give you some sort of message back?'

'Dunno. Don't think so.' He was bored already. 'See ya, Miss.' He wandered off. Anna watched him saunter down the corridor. He winked at a girl who shouted angrily at him in return. Anna felt sick.

The nausea faded over the day but rose again when she got home and opened one of her pupil's books for marking, only for a note to fall into her lap. On it was a postcode, a time (the middle of the night) and the letter T. All typed. She wanted to feel excited, as though she were on an adventure, but she just felt stressed. Stressed and deeply inadequate.

She left the flat later and went cautiously to her car, typed the postcode into the satnav, then drove for nearly an hour. She parked near a narrow footbridge which crossed a motorway. Trucks and cars roared past beneath. There were no street lamps. The bridge appeared deserted as she walked towards it and she assumed that Terry hadn't got there yet. But then a lorry growled beneath her and its headlamps picked the lad out, his hooded top pulled over his head at the far end of the bridge. He was just a shadow and once the truck passed, he was almost invisible again. Anna pulled her coat around her and went over to him.

'Agent T, I presume.' He didn't reply, so she felt compelled to talk. 'Licensed to drag me to the back of beyond.'

'Someone's trying to trace me,' Terry said sharply. 'I do some digging on your boy like you asked and now they're after me.'

'Who is?'

'Oddly, I'm not planning to get close enough to them to find out. If I wasn't so fucking clever I'd be somewhere between Guantanamo and Diego Garcia right now, and I don't look good in an orange jumpsuit, you know.'

'Oh come on!'

'No, shut up!' She was shocked by the outburst. 'They know we're meeting now. They'll have something in your satnav; they'll be watching. They might have something stitched into your clothes or in your shoes, but the cars, that noise is screwing that up. Now you're easy for them. They can have you whenever they want. But they're not having me.'

Anna couldn't help but smile. 'It's nerves,' she insisted.

'You need to take this a shit-load more seriously.'

'It's nerves! I'm not really smiling.'

'If you thought the same as me, then you wouldn't smile at all, however nervous you were. These people, they don't stop because you're a nice little teacher.'

Anna looked down and nodded. 'Go on.'

'Have you thought about why that boy is covered in scars? What they're doing to him?'

'You've found something, haven't you?'

'The little guy never beats the system, Anna. Never.'

'Terry—'

'If you stop now, let them know you're spooked and want to look the other way, then maybe they'll ignore you.'

'Terry.'

He paused, looked away from her, down at the cars which zoomed past below. It was a while before he spoke again.

'I'm going through it again like you asked, one last time and I find this article in the paper. Totally normal, and cos it's totally normal I'm about to skip over it, but there's one thing that stops me, that's odd – the photos are missing. Article's there, I found it on three different sites, but the photos have been removed each time. Why do that? Cos the photos are of a three-year-old boy. Called Toby.'

'You found him!'

'They think they can control the internet,' he said angrily. 'The fucking arrogance! They think they can control the greatest democratic creation in the last millennia, the fucking, fucking ... just shut us down ...' He reached into his bag. 'They think they can control us because we're lazy and stupid and we won't be bothered to do it in the old-fashioned way ...' He held up a collection of newspapers. Held them up like trophies. 'Well fuck 'em.' And now he allowed himself a smile. 'Read all about it.'

Toby listened as his mother lovingly explained the reasons she thought that it was time he went back to school. He'd been so happy at home, cocooned away from the bullies and care-less teachers, but the law was the law, she told him, and he could only hide away for so long.

'You'll fall too far behind if you miss any more and then we'll have to drop you down a year. And you'd hate that.'

He wasn't sure if he would. He hated school in whatever form it came, but he nodded anyway.

'It's not right, really, for me to be the only person you spend your time with. I'm not good at computer games and all those things that you like.' She took his hand. 'You need to live.'

He nodded, even though he wanted to argue that this wasn't what he wanted to do at all. 'Living' had, for as long as he remembered, been a complete fucking disaster. But he didn't want to let her down. She'd packed his things and he walked, head down, to the door where Michael was waiting for him. His father placed a hand gently on his son's shoulder.

'Come on, then.' The two adults stared at the boy. When he looked up, he seemed close to crying.

'It's only school, my love.' His mother pulled him tight to her. 'I'll be here at the end of the day. What would you like for dinner? You can choose. A favourite, anything you want. How about it?'

He smiled through the tears. 'Can I have steak?'

'Of course you can.'

'And chips?'

'A whole plateful!'

He grabbed his bags and took them to the back of the car. He dumped them into the boot, shutting the car door with a confident slam. His hands felt suddenly light without the heavy bags and he didn't know what to do with them. He noticed a scar that ran horizontally across his fingers. It looked like they'd been shut in a door, or attacked with a blade or . . . he couldn't remember. He looked up and saw his parents watching him.

'Pepper sauce on the steak?' called his mother.

'You bet!' He gave her two thumbs up and felt stupid and childish as he did so.

'Let's go then, beat the traffic,' said his dad, striding past him to the car. 'You can choose the music today.'

'Choose something really loud!' his mother called out, egging him on.

'Ready to feel your ears bleed, Dad?'

'Lord help me!'

Anna caught sight of Toby by pure chance. She was heading off to class because the bell was due to ring soon and only happened to glance out of the window to see him heading through the gates. Immediately she turned heel, grabbed a small folder from a locked drawer in the staffroom and went to find him.

He was skulking in the corridor, clearly waiting for the bell to ring before he entered his class. It was a classic sign of a child trying to avoid bullying. She went up to him and stood by his side as he peered nervously into the classroom.

'Toby.'

'Oh hi, Miss.'

'I didn't know you were back today.'

'No. Me neither.'

'Come with me.' She walked down the corridor, expecting him to follow, but Toby didn't move and she had to go back to him. 'Toby. Come on.' He hesitated, so she grabbed him by the wrist. 'Come on.'

She pushed open the door to a small, cramped music room. Music wasn't the school's strongest department and this solitary practice room was grubby and stuffy. She felt jittery as she closed door and turned to face the boy.

'Miss?'

'Sit down.' Toby did as he was told. Anna reached into her bag and pulled out a newspaper.

'Teddy bear,' was all she said. If he knew what she was alluding to, his face showed no sign of it. He just waited, politely, for her to continue. She flicked through the pages, found the one she wanted and placed it on the music stand so they could both see it. The big headline announced MIRACLE CHILD SURVIVES HORROR CRASH on faded, yellowing paper. Below it was a photograph of a car which had smashed into a tree: a mangle of crumpled metal. Two policemen stood by the car. One of them held a small boy in his arms. The boy, three years old, was laughing. Next to him, the other policeman held up a teddy bear – he held it aloft like a trophy and the little boy was staring up at the bear and laughing. His smiling features contrasted sharply with the bleakness of the accident. Although you couldn't see them, the photograph seemed to imply that there were people inside the destroyed vehicle. Dead people. Dead parents.

'See the small boy?' she asked. Toby nodded. His mouth was agape, his eyes locked onto the photograph. 'He's three. His parents were killed instantly in the crash, but he wasn't hurt.'

Anna took out another newspaper cutting. She passed it to Toby who took it and stared down at it.

'Here he is again. In hospital after getting the all-clear. Can you see that small scar by his right eye?'

Toby's hand instinctively went to his own eye. To his own identical scar. Anna knew she didn't need to say any more. She waited, resting against the battered piano. He looked up again at the newspaper article on the music stand, then at the paper in his hands. His head stayed down for a long time and just as she was about to speak, Anna saw a tear splash onto the paper.

'Can you remember what happened to you after that, Toby?'

He didn't reply.

'Toby?'

'I remember this.' He spoke with his head down, more to himself than to her. 'I'm sure ... I think ... the teddy was called Lolo.'

'Your real name is Toby Warner. Here.' She handed him a birth certificate. 'Those names there, those are your real parents.' He looked at the piece of paper, running his finger over its fine calligraphy. 'I'm sorry,' she said.

He looked up at her as if he hadn't noticed her for a while. 'This is just a piece of paper,' he said.

'I think it's the truth.'

'What were they like, Mr and Mrs Warner?'

'I don't know much. He was a plumber. She—'

'Did I go to their bed in the night when I was scared?'

Anna paused, took a breath. 'You had no other family beyond them. Their parents were dead and your father had an estranged brother who lived in Australia, who had never met you. It took the police a year to find him and tell him the news.'

'Did they read to me? Was she, Mrs Warner, did she rub my hair to help me sleep?'

'I think Michael and Laura—'

'Mum and Dad.'

Anna didn't know what to say. She knew the photos carried such a punch that the information was like a screaming siren. She knew that this poor boy needed and craved love. And why shouldn't he?

'I'm sorry. I just want to help. Stop you from being hurt. They're not your real parents, Toby.'

He handed the birth certificate back to her in silence, then with a sad smile he said, 'It's too weird, all this, isn't it? Which do you think is the weirdest? Is it that I'm a messed-up kid who keeps getting into trouble and drives his dad mad? A bit of an attention seeker. Or is that I'm . . . what? Snatched? That my mum isn't real, that she's hurting me? On purpose? She makes me spaghetti bolognese and apple crumble and then tortures me when I go to bed? Which sounds the craziest to you, Miss?'

'Toby—'

'No. No, I'm sorry, you're a nice lady, dead nice for a teacher, but Mum and Dad, they're . . . they're mine. Sorry. You've been really kind but this . . . Sorry. I'm sorry.'

And with that, he stumbled out of the room just as the bell rang. Anna came into the corridor as he disappeared into class. She heard a boy shout 'Fucking hell, it's back!' and a roar of laughter from within the class before the teacher inside cooled the hysterics. Soon the corridor was empty and her own class awaited. She sagged at the thought, then saw that Kath was watching her from the other side of the corridor.

'Kath. Hi.'

'Hey. What was that?'

'What?'

'You and that boy.'

'Oh. Me not following your advice again. Don't worry about it.'

'Right,' said Kath, frowning. When she spoke again, it was quieter. 'I do, though. You should be careful.'

'Yeah, well . . .' Anna crumpled the newspapers in her hands and started to walk towards her classroom. 'It doesn't matter anyway.'

'Why not?' her friend asked, walking with her.

'Whole thing's a waste of time.' Anna wondered how Toby could turn his back on her, on the truth as simply as that. She wanted to kick him. But something about his refusal was also a relief for her. This could all go away now.

Kath seemed pleased by this. Relieved, almost. Anna wondered why she should care, but then she saw two girls outside her class shouting and she forgot about her almost immediately.

Toby didn't even glance in Anna's direction as he walked out of the school gates at the end of the day. His father was waiting for him as he always did and greeted him warmly. They laughed together about nonsense during the drive home and his mother gave him a long, tight hug at the front door. He dismissed their concerns about the abuse he'd received that day as a trifle and chomped happily on the steak he'd been promised. That night, he lay in his bed with his hands behind his head, content. Ghosts laid to rest. He turned off the bedside light, closed his eyes and didn't move for ages, until a restless muscle made him twitch and his eyes flickered open.

He stared at the ceiling as the house got darker and quieter. He heard his father brushing his teeth, heard the loo flush. He listened to a murmured conversation about groceries from his parents' bedroom. And then the house hunkered down for the night. Outside, all was quiet.

Toby tried to hold his eyes shut. But a whisper fluttered, feather-like, across his thoughts. It twisted and turned. Toby Warner.

Eventually he could resist it no more. He pulled the covers off. Silently he tiptoed out of the bedroom. He paused on the landing, listening. He heard his father's heavy breathing and, emboldened, he slipped downstairs.

He walked into the dark kitchen, not sure what he was looking for. There was a big clock on the wall which ticked with an old-fashioned tock. Everything had been cleaned, tidied and put in its rightful place. He opened a drawer; it was full of familiar items – wooden spoons, a corkscrew, a ladle. He stared at them, then slid the drawer shut, enjoying the order, the silence, the reassurance of the clock's heartbeat.

In the living room, he sat on the carpet in the middle of the room. He collected the framed photographs of him and his parents that adorned every available surface and laid them out in a circle around him. One by one he inspected each photograph. He saw his grinning face between his parents on a beach in Cornwall, outside a museum in London, at the top of a fell in the Lake District. He stroked the frames, as though they were friends or pets.

His father's office was even tidier than the kitchen. A computer lay on a curved desk that they had bought in Ikea. Small piles of carefully organised paperwork sat in neat rectangles. All present and correct. Toby spun around in the office chair. There were graphs on the walls, a photograph of his parents on their wedding day, a paperweight and a stack of biros. Another photograph showed his dad on a fishing trip with some buddies that Toby didn't know. He held up a gigantic fish, laughing, exuberant. There was a joy and wildness in his features that Toby had never seen. Toby ran his hand along the bookshelf, but it was all work stuff which bored him. He slumped in front of the desk and pulled open the drawers which had nothing of interest inside. Except one. Which was locked. Toby glanced around, irritated. Then he remembered a set of keys his father always had attached to his belt.

The keys lay next to the telephone on his father's bedside table. The room was dark, with heavy curtains and a deep carpet that allowed Toby to slip into the room unnoticed. He watched his dad sleeping. It was something he'd never done before. His father's face was only inches from the keys on the bedside table and Toby felt a jolt of nerves. But he reached forward regardless and put his hand around them, clutching the keys tight to avoid any clinking. Carefully he raised his hand . . . and took five slow steps backwards and away to the relative safety of the landing.

Back in the study, he could feel his heart beating hard – he could actually see his T-shirt vibrate to the rhythm of his heartbeat. He looked at it for a while before sitting back in the chair, placing the key in the lock and turning it. He pulled the draw open and stared inside. Everything was neatly arranged. Some sterile cloths and wipes in one corner. Next to them were several small bottles. Toby pulled them out, one at a time, returning them to their exact original position. They had different contents. Some had pills, white and smooth. Others had liquids – pale yellow in some, colourless in others. They were labelled with names Toby didn't understand: 'Sinemet' and 'Amantidine'. It was hard to understand the chemical phrases, but the word 'anaesthetic' and 'disinfectant' stood out. He carefully opened a bottle and sniffed. The smell reminded him of his wounds in the morning. At the back of the drawer were several small, white, rectangular paper boxes.

Toby took one and opened it. From inside, a syringe slipped out onto his open hand. Each box contained ten syringes. The box he held was half empty.

Toby placed the box back in its place. He checked through everything inside once more and tried to imagine a reason for their existence. A locked drawer might just be to keep them safe, to prevent misuse. Maybe his father had a medical condition that he had hidden from Toby to spare his concerns. Maybe this was his medicine. He tried to think up favourable scenarios for each. But when he finally closed the drawer, locked it and returned the key to his father's bedside, he knew who the drugs were really for.

He stood on the landing at the top of the stairs. Below, by the locked front door, he noticed the alarm sensor fitted on the wall. Its red alarm blinked away, ever-ready. Until now, Toby had never paid it much attention. He'd imagined that, just like the many locks, it was there to keep the bad people out. But now he felt scared of it. He backed away, as though it could see him. Frightened and unsure what to do, he went back to his bedroom.

Inside, he stopped. He stared at the childish posters on his wall. He felt so much older than a boy who liked football and silly pop stars, but when he looked down at his pyjama bottoms and bare feet he felt small and feeble. He couldn't think of anything to do except get back into his bed. He pulled the covers up to his neck, then pulled his knees to his chest. He screwed his eyes shut and imagined that he had never opened that drawer. It was his mum and dad. Mum and Dad. They loved him. He saw it, he felt it every day. That must be the truth. He felt angry with his body as it spasmed and shuddered with emotion. He tried to imagine himself as a robot, with cool, ice-blue emotions, able to play the game, unable to be hurt. But the little boy in the bed couldn't stop the tears and the choked breathing. He pulled the sheets over his head and prayed for some peace in the darkness. In the morning, it would all be okay, he told himself. Dad would wake him up and Mum would cook him brekkie and it would all be normal and happy and fine and this would all, all go away.

He tried to imagine himself in the tent he was given for his eleventh birthday, the one his dad had helped him erect in the garden and in which he slept every night for a week. The wind and the rain couldn't drag him back into the house. He said he was going to be a cowboy. Under the covers, he tried to laugh, but the noise came out as a whimper. He knew that downstairs the red light continued to blink, never sleeping, malignant. It knew that he had been snooping and it would reveal his secrets in the morning. Things would not get better with the dawn. He knew that. He was only fifteen years old but the legion of scars across his body had taught him brutal lessons.

The window didn't open fully – there was a metal bar which meant it could only offer a narrow gap. But he didn't dare try to unlock the front door without waking his parents, so Toby forced himself through, scraping his head and his back with the effort. The tiles were cold and slippery and twice he thought that he would fall as he crawled across them. The drainpipe was plastic and couldn't possibly hold his weight. But he controlled his panicky breaths, gripped hard and slipped down with only minor scuffs and bruises. Even the clumsy fall at the end wasn't so bad.

He got up from the floor. There was no sound inside the house. Then he ran.

ELEVEN

A thick blanket of cloud moved in one night, unnoticed until the insipid morning that followed. There it stayed, shutting out the sun, and it wouldn't budge for weeks. Carrie gazed up at it from her bedroom window and thought of Ben. It had been weeks now since he'd gone, and while there had been plenty of visits, forms and questions still nothing was clear to her. A story was concocted – a sick relative to whom Ben had gone running – which she recited to her nodding children and half-interested friends. Ben would be back soon. When she asked Diane why she was claiming something which would soon be proved to be wrong, she was given short shrift. They were in a new stage of the operation. When asked what this meant, her question was answered with an evasion which irritated her. She couldn't work out the truth: was Ben out there or not? There was the chance, Diane admitted, that he might return, but the way she discussed it you felt it was all still part of the plan. Or maybe Carrie was reading too much into it all.

She slept fitfully. She would dream of Ben and wake with a jolt, the memory fresh on her tongue. The taste of his mouth against hers, the smell of his sweat, the rough feel of his big hands which would hold her tighter and tighter as the night wore on.

She had never been scared of him. The elegant old gentleman who'd told her about his past had described him as a thug, something dangerous. With her help, they would transform him; heal him. It would require deception and trickery, but this experiment was also an act of kindness – a rebirth. Carrie had tricked plenty of men before, that part wasn't hard, whether they'd been council officials, debt collectors, police or bailiffs. She guessed that was partly why they picked her.

When they first moved into the house the men had shown her where the cameras and voice recorders were. They'd explained how much medicine was needed to dope Ben if she was called on to do so, and where the drugs were hidden. Every movement was being monitored. She was in no danger. As a last resort, she could shout out and someone would be there within one minute. But this would rarely – if at all – be necessary. After all, Ben could always be controlled by asking the three questions.

The three questions, the man had explained, were part of Ben's hypnotherapy: three specifically worded questions, in the exact order, would return Ben to a place of peace and sanctuary. Such was the strength of these three questions that they could be asked by a stranger over the phone and the subject would immediately return to this calm, suggestible state. They'd done it in front of her and she'd watched, stunned, as Ben's pupils dilated, a childish grin formed on his face and he stood there, perfectly still, waiting to be led wherever was chosen for him. To do whatever was chosen for him. He was just a project. She would watch and record. He must love her and believe she loved him back, but she must be professional and feel nothing. She'd laughed at this. Men were easy meat to her. Ben would be no different.

But as she lay in bed, watching the slate-grey sky with no interest, she knew that her confidence in her own callousness was misplaced. He was too kind, too sweet, too loving, too gentle. He would pick her up and she would imagine herself as Fay Wray in the arms of King Kong. He would clown around with the kids, laughing, and roaring with mock-cartoonish anger, and she would find herself laughing with him. She would take his clothes off and pull him inside her and she would get lost in the moment. And she would see him hobbling and exhausted after he'd been taken away to do things that were never explained and she would dress his wounds and massage his tired muscles and she would forget that he was anything but her man. Her Ben.

Diane had spotted it first. Carrie had been reporting an event in the park which they hadn't been able to record properly – the recording devices in Ben's jacket had failed. (Issues like this weren't that unusual – there were plenty of sessions like this where Carrie's memory was pressed for every last detail.) Carrie had described how Ben had helped Joe down from a tree when he'd got stuck – his jumper having snagged on a loose branch. She laughed as she recalled the incident.

'You seem very animated today,' was Diane's smoothly barbed comment. Carrie stammered a reply and reported the other details as though they bored her. She carried on like this when she got home. Sure enough, Ben noticed the difference. At first he said nothing, but instead did all the washing up.

Carrie continued to push him away as he made her a cup of tea, cooked dinner, ran her a bath, all the time saying little but watching her, waiting for her to explain his sins. Eventually, she fed him a story about a girlfriend who'd pissed her off and had been on her mind. He was happy to buy the lie, happy to be welcomed back into her arms.

This was how it continued. Carrie would play the lover and mother a little too well, forgetting herself before pulling back. She would sleep happily in his arms, persuading herself that the closer she felt to him, the harder he would find it to spot her deceptions. She would reconcile the contradictory demands of her employers and her swelling emotions for Ben by telling herself that this total immersion into her case was a necessity for its success. She was helping Ben, she was helping the project. But when she reported back to Diane and pretended to be objective and uninterested, she became aware that she was telling more lies to her than to Ben. The realisation made her skin prickle.

But it was a half-hearted rebellion, at best. The Company approved of her loving behaviour, after all, and encouraged it. It didn't matter how tenderly she dressed his wounds, it didn't matter how sweetly she whispered lies in his ears. She was too scared to reveal the truth to him. But she desperately wanted, somehow, to let him know that her love was real. She wanted him to be able to feel, deep down, that her touch was hers, not theirs. But as long as they knew what she was doing, her rebellion was futile.

It came to a head one night. They'd been out for dinner (an approved, local restaurant) and would normally have headed home at that point, but had, by chance, run into parents from Joe's school and another bottle of wine had been opened, followed by spirits and, as chairs were pointedly put onto tables by the ever-less-smiley waiters, someone suggested going on to a club. It seemed ridiculous, at their age, on a school night. But the dad was very drunk, swearing loudly about 'raging against the dying of the light', and while Carrie had been sure to be the least responsive to the idea (in case they were listening), secretly she was thrilled.

They were nearly barred entry because of Ben's jeans, but it was a quiet night and so they were ushered in, promising the grumpy doorman that they'd be throwing money at the bar. Carrie followed them in, her heart pounding as they bounced down the sticky steps into the strobing, throbbing room. The mum turned to her and started laughing – shouting above the din – 'Now I remember why I don't come to these places any more!' Carrie laughed with her. But there was only one thought in her head: there would be no cameras in here. And no one could hear their words.

She drank the vodka and knocked back the tequila and danced and laughed just like everyone else did. She watched Ben as he and the dad argued about footballers, and then clung onto the mum and wailed with hysterics as the two men did their 'dad dance' in the middle of the floor to the bemusement of the cool youth around them.

Ben saw her laughing, caught her eye and grinned. She knew that everything he was doing was for her. He never even glanced at the young women in their breasty tops. He loved her with a totality that maybe was only possible because of the other senses and memories that had been taken from him. But it made his love no less powerful to her. As Carrie watched his terrible dancing, she suddenly felt like crying.

She ran to him on the dance floor and pulled him tight to her. He laughed, enjoying the embrace, turning it into a silly slow dance. But this wasn't enough for her. She needed him to feel more. She needed him to see her for real, for once.

She pulled him hard by his hair, yanking his face towards hers so that he was staring into her eyes. He winced with the pain.

'I love you, Ben.'

'Yeah, okay,' he laughed, trying to get her hands off his head.

'No, listen.' She pulled her mouth to his ear. She wanted to scratch his face, to make some sort of impression that could cut through all the lies, half-truths and performances. The music pounded all around them, securing them in a protective wrap. 'When it goes wrong, when stuff happens and you're not sure about me, will you remember this? Just remember this. Now. Will you?' Ben leaned in closer, scooping her up in his arms.

'Let's get that Ricky Martin song on and go *latino daddio!*'

He wasn't listening. She looked at him and wanted to scream. Immediately he clocked her mood and stopped dancing, staring at her stock-still in the middle of the dance floor as the music mphed and tsked.

'I love you, honey,' he said, his face cloudy with concern.

'That's not enough,' she replied and tears started to pour down her face.

'I can't hear you,' he shouted. 'What's happened? Baby?' He tried to grab hold of her and for a moment she wouldn't let him before a hopelessness swamped her and she crumpled into his embrace. 'What is it, honey? What did I do?'

Carrie held him tight. Then she whispered in his ear. 'I'm sorry. I love you. I'm so sorry.'

Ben had stared at her, baffled by the tears and the words. Then he grinned and started to dance again. 'You're off your face!' he laughed. She stared at his lumbering frame and felt sick. The music throbbed on as Ben and the Dad started doing the conga together, nearly starting a fight in the process. He looked like a happy, sedated panda, ignorant of his onlookers. He looked as though he didn't want to know. She wondered if he would cope if he ever did find out.

When they got home that night, Ben asked her if she felt better and tried to bring the matter up again. But here, under their gaze, with all ears listening, Carrie could no longer speak. That night they fucked hard and rough, as though somehow they were battling against the lies she fed. He fell asleep immediately afterwards, but she lay naked on top of the sheets feeling dirty and used.

The bed was now cold. Ben was gone and Diane was now her only companion. Carrie pulled a pretty cover over the sheets and tucked the corners in tight. Everything in the room was spotless. Diane ran her hand over the pristine bed cover and nodded her approval. Carrie knew she liked things tidy. She watched warily as Diane peered out of the window.

'Yes, I'm sorry it's dragged on. Fucking boring, really,' she drawled. Carrie folded her arms. Diane glanced at her, then continued to look out of the window. 'You know how Head Office can be. What can I say?'

'Can I speak to them?'

'I'm sorry?' She had Diane's attention now.

'I'd like to speak to someone. About Ben. About what's happened to him.'

'Well, I don't think that's going to help anyone.'

'I'd like to anyway.'

Diane frowned, then smiled, then frowned again. 'Why?'

'It might be useful.'

'For who?'

'Me. It might help me for the next case too.' She swallowed, worried that she was blushing. She could feel the heat in her ears. Diane gazed at her with that horrible stare that seemed to imply so many things without a single tell. Carrie remembered Ben at the end of the bed, struggling to pull his trousers on because of the pain in his back, and she felt emboldened. 'I think I've done enough for you to know more. I deserve it.'

Diane started drawing something on the window with her finger. A doodle of a sun. The silence was long.

'If I knew more then I'd be a help. I've been helpful so far, haven't I? It would be good, surely, if I had a better idea of how everything . . . clicked.'

Diane glanced up at her and she expected the stern warning look, but her expression was different and Carrie couldn't read it. She pressed on.

'There are things that don't make sense, things I've done and they worry me. There's so much I know about the project, but I know there's more too. After all I've done, I think I should be told what that is. After all I've done.'

Diane's finger paused on the glass and Carrie could see that the drawing was not actually a sun but an octopus with long, flowing tentacles. When Diane turned to Carrie she looked at her a little sadly.

'If you wish,' she said, 'I'll sort something out, send someone over.'

'I do. Thanks.'

But Diane shook her head, as if thanking her was the very last thing she should be doing.

'I don't think you'll see me again, then. You take care of yourself, Carrie.'

With that, Diane picked up her designer handbag and slipped out of the bedroom, closing the front door quietly behind her as she left. Carrie could feel the sweat under her armpits. Her pulse was racing. She was going to find out more. She was chasing after Ben and they were going to help her do it.

TWELVE

Everyone's always banging on about tighter laws and how impossible it is to get a fake ID, but all you need do is spend some time down at the arcade at the far side of town – and boy, is it a dive – and look for the shady guy in the thick coat who's always hanging around but never talking to anyone. Once you know him, he can get you just about anything, or so he says. He's got a leery way about him, always smirking and sniffing, and I'm not sure I want to find out what 'anything' actually means. Anyway, after I've given him the cash up front – which I wasn't happy about but what can you do? – we meet again ten days later. He hands over a fake ID and driving licence like it's the easiest thing in the world. Once I've got them, getting a credit card's a piece of piss. All this takes about three weeks. Once I've got these, I go to a small car hire company in the town about five miles from the hotel and choose something unremarkable. I'll only need it for a day, but sign for three, saying my own car is in the garage. They don't seem to care, which is just how I want it.

The drive from my shitty seaside town is surprisingly picturesque and easy. As I get closer, however, so the rolling hedgerows are replaced by wooden fences and dull lengths of grubby pavement. The houses cluster closer together. A pub, a garage, a row of tatty shops; another part of the country that no one really chooses to live in.

I stop and check the address against a map. Sergeant James MacFarlane lives, if he still does, two roads down. I drive around first and get to know the place. I look for speed cameras, for dead ends, for roundabouts and traffic lights. I keep driving back and forth until I worry I'll be noticed. I know the fastest way out now. Okay.

I wait until it starts to get dark, then I park one street down and walk the rest. I gaze into people's houses as I do so. The roads are identical – a square of semi-detached houses, some well-tended, some neglected. There are net curtains on the windows, but no one looks out. Televisions flicker inside.

And this is his street, just like the others. And here is his house. A small, tidy, semi-detached home with a varnished wooden gate which I hop over without any noise. I slip down the side entrance and am soon at the back of the house. Out of sight, I take a moment to check out the garden: lights from the back of the house show up the neatly mown lines on the tiny lawn; a small shed with a padlocked door; crazy paving swept clean. I could leap over the back fence and get away fast if I needed to, no problem. I move from the safety of the corner to the back window and glance in. An empty kitchen. A mug on the draining board, upside down. A trickle of water at its base. Someone's inside, or if not, they were only minutes before.

And then I see him walk into the kitchen and I nearly jump out of my skin, backing away, nearly tripping over myself as I try to get back into the darkness. But he doesn't look up and I'm able to stand there, only a few feet from him, watching him. And then, when he does raise his head, I realise that the light inside has turned the glass into a mirror – he's looking straight into my eyes, but all he's seeing is his own reflection.

Jacko. It really is you. But he seems so much older. His hair is thinner and he moves like a pensioner. He scratches his head then rubs his eyes and just, I don't know, sags. He stands in front of the sink, cleaning the same cup that he'd already cleaned before. I remember him always being tidy, a real stickler for it. I remember the way he'd position his polished boots at the end of the bed, the way he'd puff his pillow. I used to laugh at him for it. But this feels different. He looks crumpled. No – he looks shattered. Jacko, what the hell's happened to you?

He walks back out of sight and I stalk towards the back door. I check it – it's open. I enter and close the door behind me and stand dead still. No noise. I glance back behind me, check the windows of the houses that overlook this one, but there's no sign of anyone watching. I listen again. Nothing, then the faintest sound – a foot scraping on the floor, maybe. Then a choked cough. He's sitting in the next room. All I have to do is walk out and say, 'Hey, Jacko. Long time, buddy.' I've practised it enough bloody times. Fix the smile, say the words. Go on, do it.

Another cough. He's doing something, fiddling with something. I close my eyes for a second, try to picture his face as he used to be, just to give myself the confidence to walk in there. I see the guy standing on the bonnet of a military truck, shirtless, his muscles pumped, the eagle tattoo on his shoulder shining with sweat. Laughing.

I turn and walk into the living room. Jacko's sitting in an armchair facing a television which is switched off. He's holding a rifle. Its nozzle is in his mouth, his finger on the trigger. His eyes are red with tears. I stop and stare at him and my mouth flaps open but no words come out.

He sees me and his eyes widen for a second. Then he pulls his mouth away from the rifle's end and looks at me properly. But I notice that he leaves the gun pointed at his head.

'You choose your moments, don't you?' he says.

'Jacko,' I croak back.

'Where did you get to? We fucking buried you.'

'Really?'

'Yeah, really. You twat. You've been alive all this time and . . . What does it matter? Shit. If you want a cuppa you can make it yourself.'

'Put the gun down will you?'

'You gonna save me?'

'Not if you don't want me to.'

'It's hardly a cry for help. Not pills or shit, is it? Then again, I've been trying to do this for the last three days, so . . .' He lowers the gun. And then a craggy smile forms. 'You cheeky git. So you've been alive all this time. What happened?'

'I honestly don't know. Amnesia, I think.'

'Bullshit.'

'Mate, until recently I didn't even know I'd been in the army.'

'What did you think you'd done then? When you've got a bloody great army tattoo on your arm: 'No guts, no glory.'

I raise the T-shirt that covers my arm – there is no tattoo. His eyes widen.

'Come here, come over here.' He grabs my arm, stares close at it. Whistles. 'Wow. Must have cost a bit to get rid of that. Didn't know they could do that.'

'I had a tattoo?'

'Oh piss off. You'll be telling me next you don't remember Sarah.'

Sarah. Oh shit. Who the hell is Sarah? Jacko sees my confusion and bursts out laughing.

'Really? You monumental turd. She'd kill you all over again if she heard that. Well, she'd have to stand in line, what with you playing around with Jess and Pen at the same time. You were one sly old dog.'

Come on, brain. Remember. But there's nothing. Nothing. I sit down on the sofa opposite him and his hand grips the rifle a little harder.

'So what's this about?' I point to the rifle as casually as I can.

'Time. Catching up on me. Memories. You know.' And then he laughs. 'God, if you don't . . . Fuck me. I'll have what you're taking. I'd love to wipe the tat from my arm too, wipe it all away. Look at me.'

I do. He stares at me and I see his hard gaze become confused, then amused – he can tell I'm not the man from before. He shakes his head, amazed, leans back. A long silence. The only noise is his fingers tapping on the rifle.

'You a nice guy now then?'

'Apparently.'

'You remember what you were before?'

'Bits. They come and go. I dream a lot.'

'Dream?'

'Yeah.' And then I can wait no longer. 'Jacko. What's my name?'

He looks at me then laughs – a big, hearty laugh. 'Piss off.'

'I remember you. Bits of you. I remember some of my time in the army. Some of the things we did. What I was like. But I don't know my name.'

'What do you think it is?'

'Ben.'

Another laugh. 'Ben? Benjamin!'

'Please. Jacko.'

A pause. He looks at me, his smile fading.

'I'll tell you your name if you do something for me.'

I already know what he's about to say and he can tell because he leans towards me.

'You were my best mate. We stared into the devil's eyes together, you and me. Your dreams, they give you a clue to the sort of shit you've done?'

'Yes.' Yes, I know what that other part of me is. But I'm keeping the lid closed on that.

'Really? I doubt it. Cos your face, it's all gawping and sweet. That's not the Nudger I knew.'

'Nudger?'

'Want to know why we called you that?'

'Go on then.'

'Cos no one ever saw you coming. I wouldn't call it subtle, but you weren't the kind who'd chuck a guy off a cliff. No, you'd pally up to them, make them think they were going to be okay and then, then you'd just nudge them into oblivion. Like when we took down those towel heads on that sheep farm. You were one cruel bastard then, eh? Are. Still are, I bet.'

I don't remember any of this. But I believe every word.

'The guys were in awe of you. The way you could do those things and then sleep like a baby. Me too. Bet you never knew that.' And then he bursts out laughing, remembering my memory loss. He shouts it again in case I hadn't got it.

'Where's the booze?' I say, standing. I have to move.

He points towards the kitchen. 'Far left, top shelf,' he says. I get a bottle of cheap, garage-brand whisky and two glasses. I return and sit opposite him.

'Nudge. Mate. Best mate.'

'No.'

'Please. I've been sat here for days. My balls are dripping. I thought it'd be easy. It's only a trigger, it's only a tiny, little reflex action with my forefinger. Shot enough before, ain't I?'

'I don't remember.'

'Yeah, yeah.' He sighs. 'I was saying – I was in awe of you. Hid it from the boys cos I was meant to be top dog. I was the meanest bastard around, couldn't lose that crown. But keeping up with you came at a cost. Digger and the boys would piss themselves, but I'm too bloody soft.'

He runs his hand along the rifle. His eyes are fixed on mine.

'Nudger. Finish me off. You owe me.'

'For what? No, no, don't tell me. I don't want to know.'

He smiles. A little warmer, a little sadder.

'What's the last thing you remember about us?'

'Nothing. Not like that. Just some dreams. Just moments. You thought I was dead?'

'We were attacked – our convoy – about a mile outside Basra. Our truck took a direct hit. Ground to air missile, or, as they used them, ground to truck. I was thrown from the truck, Shakey lost his legs, the rest were brown bread. You were too, we thought.'

'How many died?'

'Five plus you.'

Five others. They're probably dead. But maybe one or two, maybe all of them, they could be out there too. Dads. Teachers. Doctors. I don't know. Forgotten shadows.

'You found the bodies.'

'Course. Six bodies, charred and all sorts of hell. Repatriated. Honours, funerals, the usual shit.'

'What's my real name?'

He smiles. Shakes his head. He has something to bargain with. He holds up the gun, go on, but I don't move.

'I'll ask you something. If you don't mind,' he says.

'Who's in a hurry?'

'Fair point. You, now, this new, improved super-you. You like it?'

'It has its problems.'

'Such as?'

'Men who want to kill me.'

'Oh. That's a pisser.'

'Yeah, it can really chaff.'

'Now that's Nudger!' he cries, excited. 'There, that was just like my old mate right there.' He smiles, points at me. 'Wotcher, Nudger.'

'Hello, Jacko.'

'Be a mate, blow my head off.'

'Who's Sarah?'

'I'll hold a pillow over my head, if you're worried about splash-back or noise and attention.'

'Jacko.'

'She's a girl. Your girl for a while. What's to say?'

'You know where she lives?'

'Alright, so here's the thing. Your life now seems a bit shitty, what with the men and the guns—'

'Jesus, Jacko, are you really going to spend your last few moments on earth bullshitting?'

'Why change the habit of a lifetime? Anyhow, this isn't bullshit. This is . . . fuck, this is almost profound!' He smiles, nods like he's a bloody guru all of a sudden.

'Go on then.'

'Right, so apart from the men and the guns, is your life really that bad?'

'That's like saying, apart from his curious relationship with women, wasn't Jack the Ripper really a top bloke?'

'Well, yeah, I'll give you that, but the point I'm trying to make – and you have to remember, Nudge, I always had a habit of coming to things in a roundabout way – the thing is, are you so sure you want to jump back into your old world? I'm only saying it because, well, if you look at me, who happens to be the only guy I think you know from the good old days – that's right, isn't it?'

'Yes.'

'Yeah. Right. So, you look at me and think "this fine upstanding ex-sergeant and servant of Her Majesty just happens to be suicidal". So maybe all's not entirely rosy in this garden. And maybe there are things from those glorious old adventures that might make you feel . . . not so rosy too.'

He has a point.

'What do you want to come back to all this for?'

'Who knows what we did, on duty?'

'No one knows what we did. Not our commanding officers, not even Scrappy.' He sees the confusion in my eyes. 'Jesus. Scrappy. David Doolly. Doolly Do. Scooby Do. Scrappy Do. Scrappy. Walked like he had a fucking melon between his legs. Wore his night-vision goggles in bed every night.' Still no reaction from me. 'Not a thing? You lucky sod.'

A pause. He stares at his rifle, while my mind whirrs with new information. He'll have a computer somewhere upstairs. He'll have address books. And he won't care if I take them.

'What was it like, when you woke up, when you first woke up? Where were you?'

How do you explain that there was no moment? No 'before'? My earliest memories involve me, four years old, watching our neighbours' cat cowering up on the kitchen units as our dog barks like bonkers below. And this memory joins perfectly with others, all leading naturally to the moment I met my wife. And onward. There is no army life at any point, no gap where men like Jacko should fit. My life was complete.

'I don't remember waking up.'

'You married?'

'What's my name?'

'What does it matter?'

'Don't be a tit.'

'Shoot me.'

'I'm sorry. I don't have it in me.'

'If you're chasing after yourself, the real you, you'll learn it again soon enough. You'll remember what we did and why I can't sleep. You'll start crying in the middle of the afternoon. You'll see faces of the women we ... we ... you'll be standing at the bus stop and some nice young lady with a pram will walk past and you'll start shaking.' His eyes are brimming with tears again. 'I deserve it, I don't think I shouldn't feel this, I'm trying to take my punishment but I've been like this for three years now. Three years and I can't ... it's too much. I deserve it and I'm so, so sorry but, but enough now.'

He reaches for the gun. I think seeing me has given him the strength – a reminder of what he needs to leave. And an audience. I jump forward and pull the gun away from him. And I do it easily. He has wasted away. I hold the gun and he falls to his knees.

'Please!'

'What's my name!?' I hold the gun above my head like a stick for a dog.

'Yeah, there you are again, Nudger.'

'My name! My fucking name!' He just grins. 'Why won't you tell me? What's in it for you ... not to tell me?'

Suddenly I imagine the men are at the door. That this has all been a ruse – a way of keeping me here. I turn the gun on him. He smiles. Grateful. No, there is no trick here.

'My name.'

'You know sometimes I thought I loved you so much I must be gay. I could sit in a car with you for hours and hours without either of us speaking. Just driving across that motherfucking desert. As long as I had you at my side I felt calm. Would've happily died with you next to me.'

'Jacko—'

'And I still do. Which is why I don't want to tell you your name.'

'Then you do it yourself.'

'Fine. Give me the rifle. You shouldn't want to know. You finally got out. Got a free pass. You want to run away from who you are as fast as you bloody well can.'

'Upstairs there will be photos, I bet. You and me. Maybe the regiment. It'll have my name.'

'Actually, you'll find a photo of us on the stairs, halfway up. You, me and the boys. It's got your name, your nice official name and rank. But it won't mean nothing.'

'It's who I am.'

'No. No, you silly arse, that's what I've been trying to tell you.'

I chuck the rifle across the room and go to the stairs. I hear him scrambling on the floor. Grabbing the gun. I walk up slowly. The stairs groan under my weight.

'If you see any of the boys and they hear how I went, well, tell them I was proud of them. Always proud of them. Just no longer proud of me.'

There's the photograph. Three short lines of strong men in green and khaki. Berets tilted. Smiles and thin eyes in bright sunshine. I step up so my eyes are even with the photo.

'You should be grateful!' the voice cries behind me.

There I am. One of the boys. Jacko next to me. A fixed grin. I count the names below to find my name, but a call below does the job for me—

'Staff Sergeant Lee Mackenzie! I love you! Remember that I told you to stop. Because you'll be doing this too, I bet, when you remember the rest.'

My tanned smile in the photograph gives nothing away.

The rifle does its job with a brutal, snapped retort. I hear him buckle and hit the floor, see a spray of blood hit the wall and ceiling. But I'm running upstairs to see what else I can find. I give myself five minutes before I must leave.

Lee Mackenzie is still grinning with his buddies as I slip back down four minutes later, my arms filled with papers and a lap-top computer. I stop, grab the photo too, then rush to the car. I am gone soon after. I hear no ambulance sirens or the glaring lights of a police car. James MacFarlane might well lie there for weeks before anyone finds him. I consider calling it in – a 999 call to stop him from rotting. But I'm worried that this will help them find me. They'll see the two glasses on the table, the missing papers, computer and photograph. And these will help them know what I plan to do next.

I'm sorry, my old friend. But we're all on our own now.

THIRTEEN

Diane was right. Carrie never heard from her again. She would still receive calls and visits – regular check-ups from various men and women who were always polite and formal – but she learned nothing more about Diane, about Ben, about anything. At least she still had the kids, but Ben's absence only made their time together feel hollow. Carrie behaved as she was meant to. She knew what was expected, but she hated waiting for news. The silence rippled around inside her.

Joe had just stabbed Emma in the hand with a protractor when the phone finally rang and a quiet, unprepossessing voice invited her to a meeting at the Company. Emma was screaming and shoving her hand in Carrie's face to examine 'the damage', while Joe himself was howling about something inexplicable. Carrie silenced them, took down the caller's details, hung up, then soothed her children's hysterics while a new excitement swelled inside her. She was in.

A week later, Carrie returned to the very room in the same offices where she had first been interviewed. She sat there with a glass of water and expected the elegant old man to come in and begin things again. But when the door opened, a younger man entered. Much younger, early twenties she guessed. He wore a simple dark-blue suit and white shirt without a tie. His hair was short and neat, in fact everything about him was tidy and earnest. He peered through the door at her.

'Carrie?'

She nodded and stood up.

'Hello, I'm David.' He walked over and gave her a formal handshake, not really meeting her eye. He carried two large files under one arm which he placed carefully on the table. 'I'm sorry about how long it's taken to get you in. Sit down, sit down, please.'

The room had a long central table, and David ushered her to one side then sat facing her on the other.

'So. What can I tell you? What do you want to know?'

She was thrown by the openness of the question. 'Er, well, anything. Everything.'

'Everything? God, I don't know if I'm qualified to go into all that!'

He seemed to think that this was rather funny. He had an uneasy laugh. It was as though the noise was somehow embarrassing and needed to be shut down as quickly as possible. He looked small in his suit, uncomfortable in his own skin. She watched his shoulders twitch and his hands move uneasily from knees to table to knees. She could tell that he dressed to make himself look important but he was really only an apprentice. Carrie tried to hide her irritation.

'Well, what can you tell me?'

'About what?'

'About the progress of the project, about where things are going. All the stuff they told me when I first signed up. I know it's part of an experiment, but there are things that don't add up, somehow. Like what Ben did at night, where he went. No one told me what happened then.'

'Right.' He frowned and stared at the table. Then he opened one of the files, looked at it for a second and shut it again. He looked up at her and scratched the back of his neck. 'Shall we start with Ben? Are you still interested in him at all?'

Interested? She nodded as casually as she could. 'Sure.'

'Well, he was hugely useful, a really ground-breaking case study. Changed the way we think about so much. There will be books about him one day, I bet.' A thought struck him and he hurriedly scrawled something inside one of the files. Carrie waited as patiently as she could. When he looked up at her, his face was blank.

'Oh,' he said, as though he'd completely forgotten she was there. 'Sorry, something popped into my head, wanted to get it down. Where were we? Ben. Yes. So, he was great and thank you from everyone here. I should have said that at the top. Sorry, I'm not so good with people.' He tapped his head as though this explained everything. 'Bit of a boffin, that's what everyone calls me. Anyway . . .'

He shoved one file to his right and opened the second.

'Well, now he's gone, we thought you might be interested in a new case. Same sort of work. You'd move in with the subject, they'd consider you their significant other, you'd record and observe, just as before. But obviously, no case is the same and I doubt very much that they'll last as long as that last one. First one's a pilot. Commercial jets, mainly long-haul. Second one would be more intense. A surgeon. He's suffering from exhaustion. What do you think?'

'They sound different.'

'Yes, they do. A bit posher, both of them, but that shouldn't be any trouble for you.'

'I meant, they're very different from Ben. They don't seem damaged like him. What's the point of them?'

He frowned as though he didn't understand.

'What's wrong with them?' she pressed. 'The point of the project was to help people, I thought. So how are we helping them?'

'Oh, right.' He looked a bit bored now. He flicked through the file without much enthusiasm. 'Here we go. The pilot's having nightmares about crashing the planes he flies. He thinks he really might do it, is struggling to tell whether he's awake or asleep sometimes. There's some interesting research we want to do here, about sleep therapy, about the way professionals cope under stress. And the other guy, he's got knife issues, it's all a bit bloody – but you'd be perfectly safe, really.' He snapped the file shut again.

'And I would just observe?'

'Sure.'

'And they would . . . what will happen to them?'

'Who knows? We never know at the start, do we?' He smiled as though that was that.

'Would they be taken away in the night as well?'

He didn't reply to this. He folded his hands on his lap, looked at her with a little more confidence than before.

'Maybe.'

Maybe he wasn't the boffin he was pretending to be.

'Can I ask you something else?' she asked.

'Please.'

'You said he was gone, Ben. What have you done with him?'

'Done? You make it sound like we've killed him,' he said with a laugh. Carrie forced a smile to join in.

'Would it matter, though?'

'I'm sorry?'

'If he was dead?' He still had his hands on his lap but Carrie felt that cool confidence in him again.

'I just found him interesting,' she lied. 'It would feel like a waste.'

No one said anything for a while. She noticed a harassed young woman hurry by the door, laden down by a stack of grey, cardboard files.

'You know the Sagrada Familia in Barcelona? The cathedral?' he asked suddenly.

'I've seen pictures.'

'It's a never-ending project. Men work on it knowing they will die before it's completed. That was the norm in medieval times, but to see it happening today, it's an incredible act of faith, don't you think?'

'I don't really follow.'

'We're a bit like that. Our work. Always watching, checking, monitoring.' He sounded excited as he continued. 'Billions of pounds, dollars, yen, euros. Everything analysed and considered. Tiny jigsaw pieces which will one day give us answers about the human mind. We'll all be dead too before the final answer comes, I'm sure. So – Ben, a waste? Hardly. He's just another step forward.'

'You're saying he's alive but in a different experiment?'

He leaned in. 'I'm saying that you are making a mistake if you think that we ever stop working, looking and watching. You have a mind too, Carrie.'

'My mind doesn't feel like it's going to teach anyone anything,' she said.

'Is that really what you think?' David's eyes were locked on her. He sat taller in his chair now. 'After all, you're so inquisitive.'

This didn't feel like a compliment.

'Do you want a coffee?' he asked, and she was thrown by this sudden change of direction. 'We've got one of those instant things where you can choose your type. They're actually quite decent.'

He sprang to his feet and marched over to the coffee machine.

'I'm fine with water, thank you.'

'Yes, you had three coffees before you came out, didn't you?'

They really were watching her. The machine dribbled a thin line of brown liquid into his cup. He stared at it, letting his last comment settle.

'Do you know what a panopticon prison is?' he asked.

She shook her head.

'The panopticon is a type of prison designed by an English philosopher called Jeremy Bentham, in, I think, 1780-something ... 1785. It's brilliantly simple, basically a circular building, but the point is it's designed so that the guards can see the prisoners at all times, but the prisoners can't see the guards. And when you're a prisoner in a panopticon prison and you're never sure if you're being watched or not, then your behaviour begins to alter – in case you are, you see? –

until you behave properly at all times. And yet there might be no guards at all. It's genius, isn't it?' He sipped his coffee. 'Yeah, really, surprisingly good.'

'Why are you telling me about this?'

He didn't reply for a moment. His expression was so cold. And then he was smiling again.

'How about a latte?'

She nodded, but only because she couldn't think of anything else to say. She wanted to run away from there. As the machine delivered its goods, he turned to her.

'You asked what we do, Carrie. We watch. That's the nature of our work. And it operates best when everyone is pushing in the same direction.'

'And Ben?' Her mouth was bone-dry, but his name forced itself onto her lips. 'Is he gone forever?'

'Why do you care?' He held the coffee cup, but he didn't bring it over to her. 'Carrie, the work you did was successful because you dealt with it in an objective manner. A scientific approach. You make it sound as though you felt . . .' He looked at her again, as though she were now more interesting but also more disappointing than before. 'Love?'

Carrie couldn't find the strength to deny it.

'God, once love gets into the mix, everything's fucked.' He spat out the last word. You didn't fall in love with the test, did you?'

'You've been watching me all this time. You know the answer to that.'

'Yes,' he said quietly. 'We do.'

He didn't move. Carrie felt naked under his gaze. This silly little man now terrified her. Then he snapped out of it and brought the coffee over. 'Honestly, if this was in one of those big mugs at Starbucks you'd have to pay three quid.'

She drank the coffee and joked about it tasting of piss and laughed at his mock-disappointment. But inside, her emotions spun and screeched. She had received his message clearly enough. She had been stupid to come here and wave her arms in front of them. They were watching her more closely now. She was part of the experiment. And there was no escape from its clutches.

When she returned home she didn't know whether it was safer to lock the door or not.

FOURTEEN

I leave the car in the town next to the B&B – I'll take the bus from here, over the hills, back to the B&B. Tomorrow I'll get the bus again and come back, pick up the car and move it once more, returning it in two days' time. If I return it early, then they might notice me.

It's nearly midnight now. I bought a small rucksack on the way with money I found at Jacko's and it's weighed down with the papers and files I took. The straps dig into my shoulders as I trudge along the dark streets. I can hear the sea and it is a familiar, reassuring sound now.

As I head towards the B&B I notice a light flicker inside a car. I stop and see two men sitting inside. One of them is using a lighter for his cigarette. In a second, it's extinguished. I watch the men as they sit there. I can't make them out in the darkness. They could just be waiting for a mate. Or they could be cops, interested in someone else entirely. Or they could be for me.

I turn and walk back, my head down, my hands stuffed deep into my coat pockets, hunched against the wall. If I do a big circle, come down through the back of the church, I can get back to the B&B without them seeing me. But if they're here, then they must know where I live. I stop. But if they know where I live, then why wait out here? But if . . . I go through a thousand possibilities in my head and get cross with myself. I get spooked too easily. I stop and take ten long slow breaths. In and out, in and out. Okay. Get back, be careful, move on tomorrow.

The diversion adds about twenty minutes to the walk, but it calms me down a little. I'm less manic as I slip over the church's low walls and head for the other side. It's dark here and the crosses and graves are a bit creepy. But then I bloody well slip over and everything falls out of the bag onto the mossy paving stones. If I was scared before, I'm bloody furious now and I'm scraping everything back into the bag as fast as I can, but the wind's pushing papers all over the place. I can't let any of it go. It might be the one sheet that tells me about Sarah or something else. And it might be the one piece of paper that tells them that I'm here. I scrabble about on the ground for ages. And then, when I think I've got them all, I sit there on my knees and shake my head. This is all so fucking ridiculous.

I'm about to stand up when I realise I've been looking at a grave without any interest, but the words on it have finally hit through. 'Martine Groves, faithful and loving wife, 1941–1989'. To the right and the left are smaller graves – Tabitha Groves and Thomas Groves – both dead on the same date. Both just children when it happened. Edward's family. Buried here.

They did not leave him. His family won't be coming back. They are dead and he's been lying to me.

I push the crushed papers firmly down into the bag and tighten the straps so they can't get out again. And then I look at the graves again, just to be sure. Why has he been lying to me? Why not tell me the truth? Why make up a story? Why did he let me in when he won't talk to anyone else?

I walk back, and I'm more scared and more angry with each step.

I enter the house and it's quiet, baking hot – Edward's gone mad with the heating again. There's something wrong with the thermostat, but he won't let anyone in to fix it. Doesn't trust workmen, he drunkenly told me, although he never explained why. He never explains anything properly. I drop the bag on the bed and pop open the top so the papers slide out again. I look at some of them but they're just bills, just details of a dead stranger's life. A link to my past, snapped out.

I walk through the empty B&B but it takes me a while before I find Edward. He's dozing in the kitchen, the obligatory bottle and glass of whisky in front of him. I pour myself a measure and stand over him. I'm topped up with nerves and aggression. He wakes and when he sees me, he stiffens.

'Hi,' I say.

He nods, trying to look calm, but his flicking tongue betrays his nerves. Is he nervous because of how I'm standing, how I can be, or because of something else, something that's about to happen?

'You found your man?'

'I did.'

'And you talked to him, did you?'

'Yeah.'

'You're awfully cagey.'

'He killed himself.'

He looks at me, cautious and quiet as he takes this in. 'Why did he do that?'

'I tried to talk him out of it.'

'I see. Poor fellow.'

'Yeah.' I find I'm pouring myself another drink, my glass already empty. 'Can we talk about something else?'

It's so quiet. No one ever rings, there's no post, no one visits. How can that be?

'So . . .' his fingers tap against his knees. 'What do you want to talk about?'

'What did you do today?'

'Me? Are you serious? Burnt some food, drank some booze. Are we really going to talk about me?'

'No one called?'

'No one calls.'

'No. Is the phone even connected?'

'Of course it's bloody connected.'

'So that your family can reach you, right?'

He doesn't reply, just swills the booze around his glass. Then he reaches over and pours more into mine. He's doping me.

'When did they last call, Edward?'

He's silent, then the voice that replies is quiet and tight. 'No one calls.'

How does a place like this exist? Ninety-degrees hot, every light on in the house, no calls, no neighbours, no letters, no cold calls. Nothing.

I watch him rubbing his thumb distractedly over his wrinkled, curled hands. I watch his eyes flick from me to the glass, then to his hands and then repeat the checklist over and over – me, booze, him. Until now I've always considered him a quirky eccentric. I felt guilty when I scared him before. But now my lungs are tight and his sweet old face betrays a wariness and cunning that I've never noticed before.

'How do you afford to live here?'

'You seem very interested in me tonight, Ben.'

'That's not my name.'

This shuts him up. He looks at me, his face creased with confusion.

'So . . . who are you then?'

'Yeah.'

'You said Ben isn't your name. You said it with some certainty. So . . . who are you?'

'I don't know.'

'You must do.'

'Why?'

'Why? Why? What happened today? Why are you being like this?'

I don't reply. The kitchen's so bloody hot. I can see growing sweat marks under the armpits of his dark shirt.

'If your name isn't Ben . . .' he says, pursuing my riddle with an uncomfortable smile.

'What do you think?'

'You want me to guess a name? Out of thin air?'

'Do I look like a Ben?'

'What does a Ben look like?'

I knock back the whisky. If tonight's going the way my twitching heart suspects, then I'm going to need a few glasses more.

'Well?' he says, almost pleading.

I just grunt back. Pour a glass for him.

'How come you never watch the TV?' I ask.

'I'm sorry?'

I just look hard at him. You heard.

'I don't like TV. It's all shit. Game shows and stupid presenters with flashy suits and big teeth. Not my thing.'

'But you don't listen to the radio either.'

'I don't understand, Ben—'

'I told you—'

'Whatever your bloody name is, listen son, I'm not scared of you. You sit there, you sit there all tough and hard, but I've done worse than you so cut out the attitude, you hear?'

I grin at the shaking finger he points at me. Good stuff, old timer.

'Edward. You don't get the paper, you don't listen to the radio, watch the TV . . .'

'Right.'

'You hardly go out.'

'I go out. I get food.'

'I've never seen you talk to anyone except me.'

'I don't like people.'

'Why not?'

'They let you down.'

'So you're a recluse. Is that it?'

'Yeah. So?'

'So why did you let me in?'

He pauses, a slight sag. 'I dunno. You seemed to need somewhere. You seemed a bit like me.'

We drink in silence for a few minutes.

'What's the date today?'

'I don't know, I don't care.'

'You must know!'

'Why?'

'What? The news, the day, the date, that's all useless to you, is it?'

'I've got no interest in the news, yes, that's right.'

'How do you pay your bills?'

'It's all set up. Direct debit thingies.'

'Sounds a bit hi-tech for you.'

'They did it years ago, when I was still ...' he falters. The lie's unravelling.

'And you've just shut yourself away.'

'I have.'

'Waiting for the day your family just roll back in.'

He can only manage a nod.

'How long since they left?'

'I don't want to talk about them.'

'I do.'

'Well, I don't. So fuck off.'

I lean in, the soldier's pushing up, *let me have a go*, he's calling, jeering. Edward doesn't shrink back. He just stares miserably at his glass, his hands finally still on his lap.

I push the chair away from me, hard enough for it to hit the floor. 'You are a liar, old man.'

Let them come. Let them fucking well come and try to get me. I'm ready for anyone now.

I storm past him, turning on the clapped-out old radio on the sideboard. It springs to life, playing a tune so modern it feels like it'll smash the china, but I'm not stopping in here.

I'm into the corridor, marching away as I hear his feeble cry, 'Ben, Ben, whatever your name is! What's going on?'

He'll be hurrying after me, I'm sure. I get to the lounge and click on the TV. It takes a moment, then the old machine wheezes into life, a dull picture slowly forming long after the sound has filled the room. But I'm not watching or listening, I'm off again.

There is a room, at the top of the house, locked by a key. I've stopped outside it a couple of times, but never bothered with it. I'd always assumed it was a store room and hadn't thought any more about it. But now – now I think they're there, behind this door.

The door gives way with three hard kicks, splintering and scuffing as the hinges collapse. I turn on the light using a switch so old I fear I'll electrocute myself in the process. The room is dusty and drab. There is no big secret in here. I look around, glancing back at the damage I've done to the door. The room has a drawn, moth-eaten curtain above a radiator that's screwed shut. It's much colder. No one has been up here for months, maybe years. An old rocking horse in a corner stares at the wall, dusty framed paintings are stacked up against each other, and cardboard boxes are piled one on top of another – the bottom ones have crumpled under the weight.

A little girl's pink wooden chair lies upside down on a small table splattered with dried, primary-coloured paint. I take it, place it on the floor and sink down onto it. I open a box; it's stuffed full of family photographs, old-fashioned paper folders with another unremarkable family's private moments inside. I glance in at Edward with the family, enjoying happy days, but soon drop the photos back into the box and fold the resisting lid down. I can hear the television blaring out somewhere below, hear Edward calling for me. I feel embarrassed. But why did he lie?

I reach for another box, open it – old clothes, children's outfits no longer needed. Everything neat and folded – by his wife, I feel. Put away for the grandchildren and then forgotten. I have a pang of sadness and Emma and Joe come dancing into my mind, dressed up for Halloween, over-excited, pushing and shoving over chocolates in an orange bucket. Carrie would carefully fold up their costumes in plastic and dream of dressing their children in the same outfits in years to come.

Edward finds me sitting in the light of the buzzing bulb, a tiny pink cardigan in my hands. He takes a second child's chair, bright green with smiley stickers all over it, and sits down near me, an arm's-length space between us. So he can duck my fists, I suppose. I look at him as he straightens the cuffs off his shirt.

'You saw the graves, didn't you?' he says.

'Why didn't you tell me the truth about them?'

He sighs. A twitch of his mouth, a nod. Then a shrug. 'I don't like the truth.' He says it so quietly I almost can't hear him.

'Say it again.'

'What does it matter? They're gone. Why does it matter if they're dead or they're just . . .' he falters again. His face creases, like he's about to sneeze. 'Who am I hurting?'

'Tell me. Just tell me what happened, I can't trust you otherwise, I can't . . . I have to know.'

His fingers make circles around the stickers on the chair. 'I'm ashamed.'

He looks at me for a response. He knows there's loads I'm ashamed of too, but I'm not giving him a thing. Not yet.

'Before they died, I was at my worst – drinking-wise. My wife would . . . she was very long-suffering.' He sighs and I can feel the history behind the words: shouting and screaming, broken belongings, locked doors. 'My kids too. They all loved me so much and never could understand why I'd keep on smashing things, pissing myself, all the stuff we drunks do all the time. They just wanted me to "get better". Like it wasn't my fault, like the drinking was a disease I couldn't control.' He shakes his head with disgust. 'Kids love their dad, don't they?'

Yes they do.

He's seen a painting, a little child's work, stuffed in the corner and he can't look away. I watch those red, crinkled old eyes as they study the picture then drop to the floor in shame.

'I was a cliché. I was meant to be running a business, but I was just drinking our profits and scaring the guests. But they didn't stop me. They would plead, sure, they would cry and hold my hand and nod and laugh when I promised them for the fortieth time that I really would change. But I only ever did that in the morning when I felt so shit I almost believed it myself.'

Again he pauses. There is no noise, only the faint, endless rhythm of the sea outside. 'Were you a nice dad?' he asks.

'I think so. Yes.'

'No sudden rages? No sudden bursts of violence?'

'That's . . . only come on recently. I think.'

'You think? Maybe you've just buried the bad bits away.'

'What happened?'

His eyes flick around the room. His knees are trembling.

'I don't want to be up here. I don't . . . I don't like it. Can we go downstairs?'

'No.'

He looks at me. He's so thin, so frail. His lips purse with anger.

'Christmas. I hate Christmas.' He pauses, his breathing a little faster. 'No, no, I'm not doing this here, I—'

He tries to stand, to barge his way out of the room, but I hold him down firm.

'Not in here, I'll tell you downstairs!'

But my grip on his arm forces him back onto the tiny chair. 'Go on.'

He sighs. He shakes his head, mutters something I don't catch.

'Go on, Edward. What are you trying to tell me?'

'I didn't push them away. That's what's so . . . I did every-thing a bastard could do to make his family loathe him but they never did. If I'd pushed them away then maybe . . .' again he trails off. But he knows he has to finish now, and the look he gives me as he continues to speak is laced with anger.

'We had a tradition that we'd do Christmas day here, just us and the guests and then we'd close down from the twenty-seventh to the thirtieth, opening again for a big New Year's bash. But those three days were ours. And we'd normally go down to Martine's mum. So we all get packed up to go. Well, they packed, and I slouched around the place sneaking drinks and being the thing I was. And when it came to it, I refused to go. Because I was at my worst, drinking-wise, see? I was as bad as I'll ever be and I knew her mum would go for me. And like a bloody child, I stamped my feet and refused to go. And when Martine took me aside and tried to reason with me, tried to point out the bloody obvious that these were the only days in the entire year when we could be a family without the hotel and guests and all of the other worries, I just poured half a bottle of gin down my throat right then and there, right in front of her, to make the point.

'So they left in the car together. And they waved as they went and I think I managed to raise an arm, or an eyebrow maybe, big effort on my part, then got back inside quick because the snow was coming down hard and there was no one to get in the way of me and my booze.' Another pause. 'And then I just drank and drank till I puked and shat myself. That's why I ran back inside so quick. To soil myself.'

I am no longer scared, no longer suspicious. I know this story has a terrible ending but I cannot tear myself away from it.

'I lay on the floor, staring up at the ceiling, I suppose, though I could have easily been slumped in a chair, I don't know. All those benders end up the same way. Chair, bed or floor. I just remember hearing the phone ring and not bothering to answer it. As pissed as I was, though, I knew it was the middle of the night. Those kinds of calls should have you running for the phone, all scared and shaky. But I just listened to it, like it was a tune or something. Eventually it stopped and I lay there some more. Lay there and mused about myself and how stupid other people were, and other drunk bollocks.'

'They found my wife about half a mile away from the phone box where she'd tried to ring me. She'd fallen, slipped on the snow, banged her head and not managed to get back up. They found my kids in the car, huddled together but frozen stiff. They'd got stuck in a snowdrift and the car had run out of petrol. I suppose Martine must have told the kids to wait there, told them she'd get help and would be back soon. And . . .'

He's crying now.

'They were dead, holding hands. Stiff little dead fingers intertwined. Oh God.'

His eyes are so red, so sore from this; his chest heaves with the difficulty of breathing with such an awful tale.

'And the car was . . .' He stops, sniffs, wipes his eyes and looks at me. There's an anger there; I've made him say these words out loud, brought it all back into the present. 'The car wasn't on the road to her mum's. It was heading back here. It seems that they'd decided to turn around and come get me. Decided that I was worth the detour, the extra four hours worth of journey. Cos I was their dad. You can imagine it, can't you? Martine saying come on, let's get him, eh? and them all cheering and laughing, thinking how shocked and pleased I'd be to see them. Not noticing that the route would use up all their fuel, that I wasn't even missing them, I was just lying there in my piss-stained trousers, not thinking of them for a second.

'Do you really not see why I lied? Can't you see why I pretend they're alive and try to make it be that they might actually come through that door one day? Is it really that hard to see why I want to imagine them laughing and hugging me, imagine them . . .'

His hands clench together. A prayer or a gigantic fist.

'If I drink enough, if I shut my eyes and pretend and pretend then I can almost feel them again, I can trick my brain, and for these tiny moments I'm happy again. I don't care what the truth is, Ben. I don't care what anyone says is real or isn't.

They're in here.' he taps his head to make the point. 'And in here they still love me.' He wipes his hand against his nose. 'You act like you're so different, the way you sit there. But you'd do the same. You're already hiding half the stuff you've done. Aren't you?'

I have no answer. My legs are tight and aching, cramped up on this tiny chair. A little girl once sat happily here and painted and laughed and I, because of my own insane paranoia, have forced a poor old man to relive his loss of her.

'You'd do the same as me, I know you would. I bet you'd do anything to forget all the stuff you've found out and go back to the way things were. Wouldn't you?'

Of course I would. I'd do anything. But the terrible genie won't fit back in the bottle. Suddenly I miss my own kids so much I find I'm crying as much as he is. I start to tell him my own story, and he nods and cries as he listens. We share our lonely tales and stories. About how fucked up we are, how badly we've screwed it all up, about what we've lost. We talk all night.

Outside, the sea licks and sighs, breaking rocks to pebbles, and pebbles to sand.

FIFTEEN

Edward stands at the front door, still in his pyjamas, pulling a cardigan around him to show his displeasure. I'm standing in the street, all my belongings in the small rucksack I bought the week before. I'm leaving, for good, and he's being very English about it.

'Not forgotten anything?'

I've been through all the files and papers I took from Jacko's house. Anything I didn't need, I've burnt. All I have now are a few sheets of paper and a spare set of clothes (thank you, Edward). They are my sole belongings in the world.

'If I have, you can have it.'

'What? Your dirty pants?'

'I'll see you around, Edward.'

'No you won't.'

'No. I won't. Take care.'

'Of who? Me?' he snorts with laughter.

'Can you just stop bloody talking and go back inside?'

'Listen, lad,' he says softly. I'd been hoping to avoid this moment. 'I'm not one for gushy moments . . .' he pauses, smiles and then shuts the door. And I burst out laughing. I nod, a silent thank-you, then turn and walk away from the old hotel. I should turn back and see if he's standing in bare feet, watching me, a cigarette drooping from his mouth, but my head is bursting with new-found memories.

I'd woken up after my fight with Edward with a sore back. Like I'd done ten rounds in the ring. Groggy and a bit embarrassed, I stuck to my room and worked my way through the papers. I didn't find much – mainly dull bills and debts which had got worse and worse over time. I checked out the phone numbers he rang, copying them onto a pay-as-you-go mobile. I got the phone with the cash I stole from a carelessly placed handbag. I'm sorry I took your stuff, young lady, but, well, there you go. Jacko made fewer and fewer calls over the last six months. It's weird how numbers can tell a story – the way he withdrew from the world and slowly turned inwards.

I pored over the old army photograph of myself and my colleagues for hours at a time. Some of the guys are still alive – so the internet tells me – but the ones I knew closely, the ones who could tell me more about myself than Jacko already did, well, they're all dead now. He was the last. I rang all the other numbers in his address book, but they were answered by voices that meant nothing to me and I would apologise hastily, hang up, and cross them off the list one by one, till there was nobody left. The whole task took me three days. There was no number for the Sarah girl that he mentioned, nor the other women. I don't know if I'd want to visit them anyway. I just want my wife and my kids.

Ever since I saw Jacko my mind's been on fire. I've been having new, vivid dreams that I remember well when I wake.

I see white walls, windows with shutters and row after row of beds with ties and restraints. And I remember doctors who would stare down at me, their faces half-covered by surgical masks. They would talk about me as I lay there, unable to move, too scared to struggle, powerless before the needle would drown it all to black.

One morning I woke with a start, a golden lion fresh in my mind. I rushed to the diary and wrote it down. A statue of a lion, on a plinth in a square. I'd seen this through the van's windscreen. I was meant to be asleep, but I saw it. And it was only a minute, maybe two from that place. The place with the doctors, the place with the endless corridors and the shutters that never let in the light.

That's where I'm going now: the square with the golden lion. I found a picture of it after a couple of searches on google. I'm calm as I sit at the back of the bus, my head down with a baseball cap on my head. There might be cameras and men waiting, but it's the only thing I have left. I'm going to meet my makers. I'm going to find answers. And I'm going to win back my girl.

It takes most of the day to get there. I travel away from the coast, pass by fields lined with long beech hedges, then join busier roads that lead to the city. Three changes later and I'm only half a mile away. My pulse is up and I stop in a DIY shop to buy two screwdrivers, slipping them into my sleeves, ready for I don't know what. Eventually I turn a corner and reach the square. I see the lion and it's just as I remember it. A memory, not a dream. They are near here. Somewhere. There is only one street, it runs down the south side of the square, allowing traffic. It's a one-way route which should make finding them easier. I just need to walk and walk until I find the back entrance: a basement garage with a steep sloped drive and black metal shutters that I spied before the van doors slammed shut on me. Black metal shutters in a side alley. That's all I have to find.

It's well-to-do around here. The cafes aren't the classic brands – they're bespoke eateries, all marble counter-tops with Italian names and labels. The people who walk past are mainly well-dressed – fine clothes and confident expressions. Their worlds are friendly, open places. I worry that I'm going to stand out too much so I keep walking, always looking. As I do so, I remember other people in the ward; their scared faces and that boy who cried out in the night. It seems incredible that these things could be going on around here when everything seems so posh and correct.

I walk and walk. I see side entrances and back alleys, but none are right. I stop and buy a sandwich and listen to an old man flirt with the girl behind the counter. It's funny and good-natured. I glance at a younger man, not so well dressed, who watches them the same way I do. I catch his eye and he looks away, then stalks off. I turn my attention back to the old geezer and his terrible chat-up lines. It's silly and harmless. It's so alien to me it sounds like another language entirely.

On I go, round in circles, trying to be methodical about this. I've got a map and I've worked out an area that should cover it. I get to an alley that looks promising, but there are no black shutters to be seen. And then I see that lad again, the one in the cafe. He's standing at the far end of the alley, his hands dug into a grey tracksuit top. He sees me and holds my gaze for a moment before turning and hurrying away.

Once is fine. Twice is worrying. I jog to the end of the alley, but he's gone.

It goes on like this for hours. I stop to fuel up with fizzy drinks and lots of bread – it's the cheapest way to keep going – then get moving again, walking around, checking the map, crossing it off, trying again. I can't be wrong. I just need to keep going, be patient. I pass laughing women with large shopping bags and smart long coats. I'm more and more depressed, miserable and tired, and their fine make-up and fancy ways feel like a kick in the shins. I walk back and forth, back and forth, but there's nothing. Maybe they're watching. Watching, and laughing at how pathetic I am. I didn't plan on storming the place or anything. Just finding it, just knowing where they were. Once I'd done that I was going to follow one of them, follow him home. And then I'd get to the truth. But here, aimless, clueless, running out of cash and dog-tired, I feel like there's some big fucking joke and it's all on me.

And then I see that lad again.

He's sitting with his back to the wall, just sitting there on the pavement. And he's watching me. His jeans are dirty, now I see him better, and his trainers are scuffed and old. He could be seventeen, he could be twenty-seven; his skin's pale and his eyes are red. And he's watching me. As I walk towards him he stands up and I find that I'm working out his weight, checking his hands and his shoulders to see how he'll throw a punch.

I go up close to him, but he says nothing. He glances either way down the road then meets my eye again. A nod.

'Looking for business?'

It takes me a moment to understand what he's talking about. He's offering sex.

'No. Wrong guy.' I turn and walk away, but feel his hand on my arm.

'You sure? You ran after me before.'

'I'm sure. Fuck off. Okay?'

But then I see another guy, like him scuffed and grimy, coming the other way. His eyes are on me, but he's walking at an angle, trying to hide his intentions.

I'm in a trap. I take a quick step away from the first one. I look to his hands. He'll have a syringe.

No, he doesn't. And neither does the second.

But I'm stuck in a back alley, with no one to see, and two guys who want something.

'Hey, don't be nervous,' the first one says. 'I'm sure we can do a deal.' His hand is back on my arm. I shrug him off. He looks around again, then whispers something. I don't hear what he says.

'What?'

The other one's still across the road. I don't get this. Then he says it again and I have to lean in. Suddenly he headbutts me and I see stars, then black. I hit the pavement hard. I feel his hands go to my jacket, trying to steal my wallet. He's shouting something, and then I feel the other one joining him, his hands rooting around my trouser pockets.

A leg kicks one of them hard – finding the knee, snapping it back so he howls in pain.

A hand strikes the other one in the throat and he's choking, his eyes bulging out, his hands clutching his neck to try to soften the pain.

And I'm back on my feet and I see how I could stamp there, kick there and there, how I could have them silent and bloody in seconds. I am Nudger, I am Lee Mackenzie. I want this.

The first one screams and it would be so easy to kick him hard in the face and shut him up. I'm not after his money, I doubt he's got any, I just want to punch things better. I've held back for so long, but now I can do it. Someone like him, a thief and a whore, is easy meat. I won't regret it. I won't let the nice Ben stop me this time. I'll have some, a little cosmic payback for all the shit that life's dealt me. A bit of justice. Come on, he's dirt. Come on, let's do it . . .

I stop running when my lungs give out and I have to lean against a wall to stop myself falling over. I didn't run from him, from sirens, or from men who might have seen me standing over him. I ran away before I started, before I hurt him properly. I ran to stop whatever it was inside me from taking over completely.

I lean against the wall and suck the air back into my lungs. I can feel the cruel man inside, Nudger, screaming in frustration. I stopped him. Just.

Oh God I'm going mad. I'm bi-polar or schizophrenic or something.

My heart's slowing now, the oxygen back in my system, my legs no longer shaking.

I was this close. It's like, ever since I left Carrie I'm losing a part of me. The Ben bit. And the old bit of me is rising back up. And I'm scared of this. If I stay away for too long, I wonder if I'll become him completely.

I'm not coping on my own. It keeps happening, this old temper, this cruel, spiteful bastard bit of me, and I'm scared one day it's going to take control. Like drugs or booze. I could have killed that guy. I felt it inside me.

I stalk the streets. I don't know what else to do. I'll never find them, not unless they want me to. I have nowhere to go. I'm scared and tired and hopeless. I stop in a busy street lined with shops. Everything's carrying on as normal. The sun shines, people gossip, music plays. As the anger fades, as everything carries on being so painfully normal, I end up standing dead still in the middle of it all. I am so lonely. I feel like a trapped animal that is too frightened to move, that allows its predator to feed off it without complaint. Shoppers mill past me. I'm stuck. Homeless and hopeless.

I watch an old couple make their own particular slow progress amongst the throng. He stands proudly next to her, a barrier from the kids on skateboards. She stops him to point out something in a shop window. I watch as they smile and joke about it. Instinctively, they reach out without looking and hold hands. Then they turn and shuffle on. I'm so jealous of them, I nearly cry again.

Several hours later I end up in an internet cafe. I sit at a computer but can't think of anything to type in. I have nothing left to search for.

'Those bastards.'

I turn to find out who's swearing and see two lads – kids really – with big headphones hanging loosely around their shoulders. They wear low-hanging shorts and T-shirts with strange logos – 'Give Peas a Chance' and 'Not Athletic'. They're hunched over a screen, excited about something. One's tall and very spotty, his greasy hair hanging down to his shoulders, the second is shorter and even thinner but with the same lanky hair. The tall one types something else, a pause and then they both gasp.

'No way, no way!' screams the tall one, spinning in a delighted circle as Thinner slams his fingers down on the keyboard so hard and fast I think he might break it.

'Try it.'

'I'm there, blud.'

'So do it already and cut out the fake gangster chat, you geek.'

'You're so two thousand. I'm street.'

'Sesame Street, sure.'

'Shut your fat mouth – oh!'

'Woah,' the other gasps in reverence.

'Here he is. How long till they find this one?'

'Let's time it – time it, bruv!'

I'm too intrigued not to wander over. The two guys are looking at a video clip of something on the screen. They see me and go quiet. I'm aware of how I look, but I try to be friendly.

'Hi guys. What are you looking at?'

'Who are you?'

'He's a spook,' says Tall to Thinner, fidgeting with the neck of his T-shirt.

'It's a free country, man, we can look at whatever we want.'

'Yeah, it's not fucking China, dude!'

I hear the words, but I don't understand a word they're saying.

'Yeah, so fuck off and send Kim Jung Un our best.'

'I just wanted to know . . . I'm sorry I bothered you.' I turn, scratching my head. I hear a shuffle of feet behind me. A whisper – *come on, look at him . . .*

'Hey, mister. You're not a spook?' calls out Tall.

'You mean a spy?'

'It could be a double-bluff,' says Thinner, wary.

'I guess I could be but . . . I don't know, I don't know how spooks work, but I don't think they hang out in places like this, do they? Are you boys a threat to national security then?'

A pause, then they both burst out laughing.

'He's alright.'

'For a spook.'

'So what if he is? We didn't post any of this. Look, come here, check this out. About a week ago, some kid nearly went and threw himself off a roof. Loads of guys caught it on their phones and posted it. So it's a big hit for a day, you know. We don't care, so what, right?'

'Right,' I say and I'm already a bit bored.

'Yeah, right, so what, exactly. But.'

'But—' jumps in Thinner excited, 'someone starts taking all the posts down. Gets them banned, removes them et cetera et cetera. Someone doesn't want us to see the kid.'

'His dad?'

'No, no way, not his dad. Cos his dad's just going to be some tragic bloke in his forties who thinks the net's about Amazon and porn. The people who are doing this – they're . . .' Thinner shrugs.

'Professionals,' says Tall.

'Not just professionals. They've got an agenda. It takes a lot of time and a lot of money to make someone disappear from the internet. You know?'

'So we're playing a game. Find the sites that still have the video and see how long before black ops take it down.'

'Black ops?' I ask.

'I don't know who they are, man, but you might as well call them black ops. They're like commandos. We found a site, I tell you, it was hard for us to find it and we're seriously good at this shit.'

'We're the best, bruv! This is what we do!'

'We find it and thirty seconds later, it's gone. I swear, if we weren't coded and encrypted, I'd swear they were tracing us. You feel me?'

'We found him again. Here, see? Watch it if you want, it's nothing special.'

Tall clicks the computer and a grainy, blurred video starts to play.

'Looks terrible, huh?'

It does. I watch the camera swing around – a load of drunk boys and girls, a grim building, a school, I suppose. They're all laughing, pointing upwards. The camera follows their gesticulations and it's dark, there's nothing for a moment, just a blur and then the camera zooms and focuses on a figure standing on the edge of the roof, staring down at us. You can hear the kids chanting – 'jump, jump, jump!' Little bastards, I think. And then the camera focuses on the boy on the roof . . .

It's the boy in my dreams. It's the boy in the bed, the bed next to mine.

He stares down at the camera, he's saying something, but the camera can't capture the words. He looks . . . happy.

It is the boy. I'm sure. It's the boy and they're trying to hide him.

'Shit quality, huh?' says Thinner.

'Did he jump?'

'Nah, some bloke stops him, you'll see.'

He's alive.

'That's the thing. It's not like it's against public decency or any of that legitimised censorship shit. There's an agenda here, dude.'

I look at the boy. He's staring down at me, through the camera. I want to wave.

And then suddenly the video freezes. A pause and then the image vanishes. Text appears in the box, replacing this image: *This video has been removed for breaching copyright terms.*

'BOOM!' screams Tall, and he and Thinner share a high-five.

'Two minutes? They're tracing us. They're like totally watching us, right now, man!'

They're giggling. Tall glances at me, sees my bemused gaze and laughs even more.

'You think that's the last one?' asks Thinner.

'Nah, but by the end of the day, they'll all be gone. Gotta hand it to them, they're ruthless!'

Another high-five. This is all a game to them.

'Who is he? The boy?' I ask.

'Who cares?'

'He's called Tony or Toby or something.'

'You don't know?' I try to hide the panic in my voice. They're so casual I could hit them.

'He's . . .' Tall taps at the keyboard. 'Here. Toby Mayhew. It's all down here.'

It is. On the screen are all the details of the boy I could ever need. His name, his parents, his school, his address. Thinner presses a button and the details print out in the corner. I try to be calm as I wander over and glance at the sheet. But the boys have forgotten me already.

'Come on, let's find him again!'

I take the sheet of paper and walk out of the cafe. The boys whoop and wail about some new discovery, but I don't need them now. I stop in the entrance, watching – always watching – then walk along the back streets, walking all night, not stopping. I've covered thirty miles by the morning.

I learn quickly enough that Toby is no longer at school. It's not hard to find out that his English teacher has also gone missing and the matter is a minor scandal. I see his parents looking worried. They pull all the right faces for an article in the local paper.

I stand in their garden in the dark, watching. They go through the motions, they look exhausted, I hear them argue and fight but the words are muffled. Maybe they are genuine. Maybe Carrie was genuine.

The teacher has a best friend called Kath. She likes vodka, single men and bars. She tells me she can't believe her friend would abduct a boy, but she's also not entirely surprised. The girl has secrets, she drawls, nudging her empty glass across the table at me. Some friend. We roll drunkenly out of the bar and she's put out when I don't invite her back to mine. She offers her place instead and leans in. I feel her bosom pressed against me, smell the booze on her breath. Maybe in another life I'd have been tempted. I let her think it's possible and we walk down the street together, hand in hand. I imagine the confusion then slow rage that must have filtered through her when she turned at the traffic lights and found that her new beau had vanished. Sorry, love, but I'm on a mission.

The teacher has a father, but she won't go to him. He's respectable, it says so on the web. No other family. She's almost invisible, but not quite. If a woman like her is going to run, then she'll run to someone; she'll have a plan. Not family, not friends, someone with no obvious links to her. Kath had blathered on about some kid she had befriended before and tried to help but he'd turned out bad. Two years before, she'd said.

I access the school's list, find the boys she taught two years ago. Find the boy who was expelled. Terry Miller. I have an address half an hour later. A flat high up in a shitty towerblock. I don't like it – there are no easy escapes from here. If this is another trap, I'm going to need weapons to get me out. I have checked out a couple of hunting stores, but the shotguns are far too well protected for me to risk a break-in. I buy a set of kitchen knives instead. I tie one to my thigh, strap two above my belt, out of sight but easily reached. Then I wait for nightfall.

There's CCTV on the ground floor. I watch the camera pan left to right, following a bunch of boys lounging on pushbikes with nothing to do. I slip past and jog up the stairs. I reach his floor and my lungs are pounding. I pause for a moment, get my strength back and then go to the door. I listen in, it's quiet. I break in with a credit card and a screwdriver, hardly making a sound. All these things I could do, they're coming back quicker and quicker.

Inside, a fat woman's watching TV, facing away from me in a room on my right. I see the plate of fag butts on the arm of the sofa and her yellow-stained, chubby fingers. She's no use.

I look left – there's a closed door, a light from under it. I go to the door, listen in. Voices. They're in there.

Stop. Think. If this is a trap, how do you get out?

I glance back at the woman – I can only see her fat ankles and slippered feet, but it doesn't look like she's moving any time soon.

I put my hand on the door, take a deep breath, then push it open and enter. Inside are three people. A lad who must be Terry Miller, dressed in the same sort of uniform as those kids in the internet cafe. His T-shirt reads 'I ♥ Slogans'. He sees me and jumps up, reaching for something in the drawer. I'm there in a second, pushing him to the floor, knocking the taser gun he has just grabbed away from him. I look up at the other two. A woman, bespectacled, scared – totally out of her depth. And the boy. The kid I've seen in my dreams. Here. Right here in the same room as me.

The lad beneath me is struggling, swearing and kicking. I pick him up in one easy motion and throw him onto the bed.

'HE'S GOING TO KILL US!' he screams.

But Toby doesn't move.

'No he's not,' he says, quietly. The teacher and the other lad look at him, amazed. He stares at me and then smiles. And I smile back.

'Hi,' I say.

SIXTEEN

Anna should have screamed when the heavy-set, wild-eyed man stormed into the room. He seemed to appear from nowhere, moving so fast, throwing Terry across the room. His clothes were dirty, his nose broken and his hands were tightly balled fists, scuffed and bloody. She should have screamed, but her mouth simply opened and closed, wordless, as the man turned towards her, took her in and then dismissed her. His gaze settled instead on Toby. She should have screamed or done something. But she just stood there, useless.

She'd been equally speechless when Toby had appeared at her door in the middle of the night. He was elated, overexcited; so thrilled to have run away that he had no inkling of the trouble he was causing. Anna had pulled him inside, packed a bag and driven straight to Terry's. She did it all in a daze, nearly crippled with fear, stunned that the boy had actually done exactly what she'd suggested to him. To her great relief, Terry took them both in without question. Toby was silenced with a store of pirated computer games and she was calmed by non-stop cups of tea. And there they stayed.

Stories appeared in the papers: lurid articles which painted her as a scarlet woman ('Sinful shame of school's sexy seductress!') and other cruel and hyperbolic character assassinations, but indignant as she was Anna knew that she could not answer back. There was no one left to trust. Not the police, not the press, not family or friends. Terry's conspiracy theories and paranoia didn't help, but there was no getting away from the fact that Anna was now the prime suspect in an abduction case and every hour, every day that they did nothing only further cemented her guilt.

At first, as they sat and wilted in Terry's bedroom, Anna began to worry that her actions had been hasty and ill-conceived. The phone didn't ring with voiceless messages, no men watched the flat from the streets below; in fact there was nothing out of the ordinary. And although Anna was still a good source of media gossip and innuendo, the papers were soon refocused on the affairs and fashions of actresses and other celebrities. But nothing could dampen the dread she felt when Terry got Toby talking about his dreams.

Toby had kept a diary, and he'd brought it with him. He showed it to them, turning the pages, explaining what each sketch and comment meant. They seemed like tales from a twisted adventure book or a comic strip. He would be chased by dogs, he would be caught in razor wire, he would hang from a building's edge. Toby would start each story with the same youthful exuberance he brought to everything, but the more he talked, the more he recollected the fear, the pain, the cuts and blows that he once thought were fantasies, the quieter he became. Anna would trace a scar across his leg and he'd tell her its source: a collision with a motorbike, a fall down a steep hillside covered in shale, a hand grasping a pipe that turned out to be burning hot. None of the adventures made sense. There seemed no obvious link or purpose. All they could be certain of was that one moment he would be living his normal life and the next he would wake with a start: sore, cut and bruised, having been dragged through something violent and nightmarish. Toby tried to brush the horrors away with glib jokes. It was a default trick to avoid the pain of his memories. And each time he did it, Anna became more determined to find the men who had done these things to him and make them pay for their crimes.

But this determination had collapsed when the man had burst into the room. And now he walked towards Toby.

'Hi,' grunted the monster.

'You're the man in my dreams,' Toby replied.

'Right back at you.'

'What the fuck?!' shouted Terry, clambering to his feet.

'Relax, alright?' the man responded.

Anna gripped a chair and sat down.

Terry was still hyper. 'Relax? Are you shitting me?!'

'It's alright,' said Toby. He went over to the man, up close. Anna watched them staring at each other, entranced by the other's existence.

'How the hell did you find us?' barked Terry, but neither Toby nor Ben seemed to hear him.

'Who are you?' Toby asked.

'Ben,' he replied. 'You're Toby.'

'Yeah. That's Terry and Anna.' But the man's eyes never left Toby. 'How did you get away?'

'Er, a bit of a kick and a shove.'

'Me too, sort of. Do you know what's going on?'

Ben let out a sigh, a little heavy. 'No.' Then looked over at Anna. 'I am sorry about the way I came in. I wasn't sure what I'd find, but I didn't mean to scare you.' His smile was surprisingly bashful. 'You're his teacher, right?'

She nodded, still sitting.

'I won't hurt you, I promise.' He looked at Terry. 'How did you get one of those?' he asked, gesturing to the taser gun which now lay on the floor.

'Internet,' said Terry, as though it was the most obvious thing in the world.

'How much of the other stuff do you remember?' blurted out Toby, his voice higher.

'Bits. I've started writing things down.'

'Me too!' Toby rushed off to the corner of the room where he pulled out his diary, bringing it back to Ben.

'Seriously, mate,' Terry interjected, 'how did you find us?'

Toby shoved the diary into Ben's hands and pointed at it, proud and eager. 'It was the only thing I took with me when I ran. Well, that, some cash and my ipod.' He flicked through the pages, pointing bits out to him. 'Look, that's where I got attacked by the guards in the forest. Did you fight them too?'

Anna saw Ben frown and scratch the back of his neck. She wondered what his dreams were like.

And then Terry's voice cut through. 'We need to get out of here. Right now.'

Everyone looked at him.

'What's happened?' Anna asked.

'How has he found us?' Terry pointed at Ben.

'He's alright,' said Toby again.

'I'm sure he's a tip-top geezer, but how come he's here? In my room?' He faced Ben. 'How did you know where we'd be?'

'Internet,' replied Ben with a smile and a shrug.

Anna stood up. The fear had hit her. 'You found us . . . just like that?'

'It wasn't easy,' Ben replied. 'A lot of digging, some guess-work, talked to some people but . . . yeah, just like that.' He faltered as he finished, seemingly aware now that there was something unhealthy about how easy it had been.

'He's led them here.'

'No, no!' Ben stammered. 'No, I've been careful. I've been running for months, I know what to look for . . .' Again he faltered. Anna could feel her heart pumping in her chest.

'Let's go then,' said Toby.

'Go where?' she asked.

'Who cares?' shouted Toby. 'If they're coming for us, then what are we doing waiting for them in here?'

'Alright, kid, shut up a second,' said Ben, and Toby did so, instantly obedient.

'Who says anyone's coming for us?' said Anna. 'And who's they, anyhow?'

No one had a reply to this and the room fell silent. Anna looked at Toby, but he was just staring at Ben.

'Let's do what he says,' said Toby.

Ben looked at Anna. 'Why did you come here?'

'Terry doesn't think like I do,' she replied. 'And I thought he'd also think differently to the people who would want to hurt Toby.'

Ben looked at her and nodded. She felt pleased by this small sign of approval. Then he turned to Terry.

'Do you know a place we can go where we won't be followed? No CCTV, out of the way, somewhere people ignore. Somewhere we can be for a while, not just a day or a week. A while.'

'Yeah. I know a place. Just . . . it's not exactly, er, comfortable.'

Everyone looked at Anna.

'Oh, thank you very much!' They all laughed nervously. Anna shook her head. 'After this place, I'm sure it will be paradise. And I'm not that much of a fuddy-duddy.'

'How much do you need to take with you?' Ben asked Terry.

'Two laptops, some cables and a toothbrush,' he replied, already grabbing at the things he needed.

'We've got our stuff there in that bag,' said Toby, pointing to a large holdall.

'What about your mum, Terry?' asked Anna.

'We're not taking her along, are we?' said Toby, and Anna glared at him to shut up. Terry finished packing the stuff on his desk. Maybe he hadn't heard her.

'Oh!' he said, and then smiled. 'I'll leave behind a little present for them.' He started to type fast at his keyboard. 'Just a little . . .' he typed some more, finishing with a flourish, '. . . booby-trap.'

'What? Like, they press a key and the whole room blows up?' asked Toby, sounding thrilled.

Terry gave him a withering glance. 'No, you tit, how am I gonna . . . ? I've set it up so anyone who comes in will automatically be recorded on the webcam. I'll pick up the link from the laptop – this way we'll get to see who these fuckers really are.'

'Come on, if we're going to go, let's do it,' said Ben.

Anna went over to Terry, a soft hand on his arm. 'Once we go, we're not coming back.'

'I know,' he said, his voice quieter now. 'Give me a minute, eh?'

He went to the door, and Anna watched him from there as he walked along the short passage to the lounge where the TV pumped out its cheery good wishes. She could see Mary, bovine, gazing at it through a thick haze of cigarette smoke. She didn't even acknowledge Terry's presence as he crouched down next to her. She just reached for another cigarette.

'Mum,' he said, quiet and soft, like a little boy. 'Mum,' he said again when she didn't reply.

'Yes, love?' was her groggy reply.

'I've got to go.'

'Right.'

'Out. For a bit. No, longer. A long time, maybe.'

Her eyes never left the flickering screen. 'Why's that then?'

'Got a bit of trouble coming, I think.'

A tut. She tapped the cigarette ash off, took a drag, breathed out and muttered something which might have been 'not again', but Anna couldn't hear her properly.

'I'm sorry,' he said. 'Will you be okay without me for a while?'

'Course,' she said, but her voice was distant, unconnected. 'I was alright before you came along, weren't I?'

'Sure. Sorry.' He stood. 'If anyone comes asking for me, Mum—'

'Yeah, yeah, I know the drill. Look, shut up will you? I'm missing the best bit.'

He did shut up, but he didn't move. He stared down at his mother, his head nodding slightly, his fingers twitching. Anna thought for a second that he was about to strike her, but instead he bent down and kissed her. Mary smiled, patting him gently on the cheek although she never lost sight of the television.

'You take care, my boy.'

'Will do, Mum.'

He walked back towards Anna, but he wouldn't meet her eye. He passed her, and went back into the bedroom. Toby was standing in front of Ben, mid-karate stance.

'Seriously. I was like, half-ninja, half-commando, half-batman!'

Ben had his arms folded, staring at the kid like he was a lunatic.

'Come on,' Terry said. 'Let's get out of this shithole.'

He grabbed his things and headed for the front door. There, he stopped and looked at them.

'And watch out for the cameras.'

Ben pulled his baseball cap down as he and Toby walked together along the street. They'd travelled away from the estate and towards the centre of the city. They'd avoided public transport and the busier streets where Terry would make covert gestures to the cameras that looked down from every vantage point.

The cameras. In Terry's company, they seemed to be everywhere. In shop windows, in doorways, on lamp posts and street signs. Ben glanced at the people they passed: shoppers, workers, mums with prams, men on phones, sly schoolboys truanting with cigarettes in their mouths. None of them seemed to notice or care about the cameras. He'd been like that.

They walked apart, trying to be forgettable. Sometimes Ben would walk with Anna. They spoke little. She seemed scared and fidgety, and he wondered why a woman so fragile would take such risks for a boy she barely knew. When he looked at her more closely he realised that she was actually very pretty. If she walked more confidently and wore more 'showy' clothes, then he thought she might be a real looker.

Each time they reached the end of a street, they'd regroup. Sometimes Ben would walk with Terry, who would mutter weird things about 'them' using 'speech recognition codes' and warn Ben not to say the same phrases more than once each day. Ben found him bizarre. On other occasions he walked with Toby and the boy stuck close to him, like a beaten dog next to its master. He'd noticed some of the lad's scars when they'd been in the flat, and from what Anna had whispered as they walked, it sounded as though he'd been in the wars. He understood the boy's need for protection. As big as he was, he yearned for it himself. Something familiar, something safe. Carrie's kisses, Emma's tight embrace. He was thinking about Joe and smiling sadly at the memory when Toby pulled at his sleeve.

'Can I ask you something?' Toby said.

Ben nodded, his eyes on the crowd.

'You know that place, the place where I saw you?'

'Yeah.'

'I keep seeing it, dreaming about it. All the time.'

Ben tried to hide the unease he felt. He looked around; no one was near them. Anna and Terry were on the other side of the street, a few yards ahead.

'Do you?' Toby asked. His hand still clutched at Ben's sleeve.

'Yeah, yeah I do.'

'And loads of other things are coming back too. The things I did, the things they made me do. Is that the same with you too?'

Ben nodded. He didn't want to talk about this. About knives and hammers. He shivered.

'It's sort of like,' the boy continued, 'sort of like now we're free from them, they can't keep it all stuffed away. It's all coming back up.'

Ben nodded again. He saw that Terry and Anna had stopped and were waiting for them at a street corner. Terry caught his eye and made a discreet gesture – we go that way next. Ben nodded to show he'd seen it, then felt another pull on his sleeve.

'If you don't want to talk about it, then I'm totally down with that.'

Toby hurried across the street on his own, leaving Ben behind as they'd agreed. He joined Anna and they walked on, a new couple. Ben walked alone for a while. Dark memories stirred within him. He tried to think about Carrie instead, to calm himself, but he couldn't picture her face. It was like she was falling away, as though she was just a dream too and he would soon lose her forever. No, he thought to himself. Never, never, never.

They reached the building a couple of hours later. Ben stared at it from the opposite side of the road – a grand, rather beautiful facade. From the outside, it looked deserted. Stained by soot, pollution and pigeon shit, its white front was now dirty grey. What would once have been a fine set of double doors was now a steel shutter, covered in graffiti. The windows were also boarded up, similarly tagged and paint-splattered. Cars roared past. Maybe a couple of hundred years ago this was a cobbled street with trams or carriages, or some such. Now the road was wide enough to suck through speeding trucks. Official notices were stuck to the building's door and to the lamp posts outside: a date for its destruction.

Terry grinned at Ben as dust and grit caught in his eye. 'Nice, eh?'

He led them around the block to the back of the building and pointed out a metal fence, which looked intact but had been cut at the sides so you could pull it up and slip underneath. The back was worse than the front – rubbish was strewn all over the place, asbestos had been dumped along with smashed glass and other detritus. Ben spotted a bloody syringe amongst the debris.

At the back of the building was a set of stairs, leading down to a basement. There was a sturdy padlocked chain holding the gate in place but Terry revealed that this was a facade – someone had sawn through the lock so that you could pull it open with ease. Once done, Terry carefully replaced the lock as he found it; to anyone not in the know, this place was a fortress.

At the bottom of the stairs he banged three times against the sheet metal. It seemed an age before someone called out from inside.

'What?'

'Daz, it's Terry. And some mates.'

No reply.

'Oh don't be a cock, open up!'

A pause, and then the noise of a drill or something, an

electrical whirring. Another pause and then the sheet metal was pushed open – a young man, thin with blond rasta dreadlocks, peered out. His nose, eyebrows and ears were pieced and his earlobes swelled with large African wooden discs. He wore beads around his neck, a brightly coloured mohair jumper and baggy green corduroy trousers. His toes peeked out beneath the trouser's turn-ups – bare feet. He stood half in, half out of the doorway, squeezed against the metal sheet.

'Hey, man,' he said warmly, then glanced at the others, offering a much cooler nod.

'We need a place to stay, Daz.'

'Yeah?'

'They're all good, I can vouch for them,' said Terry. 'They're in the shit, need a place to disappear for a bit.' He pointed to the sky, as though something up there was threatening them.

Daz frowned. 'They don't look the sort, Terry.'

'Do they ever, man? It came after them, you know how it is.'

'True words, my brother. True words.'

Anna glanced at Ben – what were they talking about? Ben shrugged back at her, equally lost.

'So come on, Daz, don't leave us hanging.' Terry's voice had changed slightly – from the scowling yoof to a more furry twang.

'How long do you need?'

'How long till we get world peace?'

'I hear you. Come on, brothers and sister.' Daz's teeth were crooked but his smile was warm and infectious. He pushed the metal sheet a bit further open and gestured for them to come inside. 'You don't want to be out there, it's well nasty, eh?'

'It's okay for us to come in?' said Anna.

'Of course. Anyone's welcome. Not like it's ours, is it?'

'All possession is theft, Miss,' said Terry with a wink. 'I'd have thought you'd have known that.'

Daz led them inside and the metal shutter slammed back hard behind them. He started to screw it back in place using a small electric drill – it was done in a matter of moments. Ben had expected dripping walls, crumbling concrete and rubbish on the floor – an extension of the debris from outside. He was surprised, therefore, to feel warmth, and see wall lights illuminating corridors which were carpeted and clean. It looked almost like an everyday, working office except for the posters, paintings and murals on the walls: a clenched silhouetted fist on a blood-red background, 'Love not H8', 'We Are Not The Enemy', 'I Didn't Vote', 'Who Would Jesus Hate?' – these and the word No! (with its obligatory exclamation mark) painted in every variety of shape and colour imaginable, lining every inch of every corridor. Daz led them deeper into the building, past various empty offices. Through the glass, Ben saw over-turned desks and scattered papers in some, while in others empty chairs were set in circles, as though ready for a meeting.

'What was this place?' he asked.

'Local council offices,' replied Daz with a yawn. 'Sorry, I'm not really a day person. So, um, the council owned it but wanted something more central, more swanky and corporate. Liggers. They moved out, we moved in.'

'We?' prodded Anna.

'Uh-huh,' said Daz. They had reached the centre of the

building. Stairs wide enough for three people to walk side by side led up and down, and there were also two lifts. Someone had written the word 'Heaven' next to the 'Up' button and 'Washington' next to the 'Down'. The lift pinged and the doors opened with a complaining screech.

'The lift's been a bit temperamental ever since Marco tried to get his piano in and bashed the doors. We had to drag the thing up the stairs, but you know what those Brazilians are like about their music.' He held the lift door open and gestured – after you. After a rather obvious hesitation, everyone got into the lift. A ping and a shudder, and the lift started to climb.

'So are there many people living here?' Anna asked.

'Hard to say,' Daz replied. 'Folks are coming and going all the time. I thought you guys would like Serita's rooms – she's gone off travelling and we're not expecting her back for six months.'

'Nice,' said Terry. 'Where's she gone? India, South America?'

'Sierra Leone,' said Daz with a slight glare. 'She's not a tourist, man.'

'Right,' Terry said, and everyone was quiet for a bit.

'How come you have power?' asked Toby.

Daz was pleased with the question. 'There's a guy called Alan, got an engineering degree from Oxford. He rewired the place, connected us to the grid. Every now and then some suit out there gets grumpy and tries to cut us off, but Alan always finds a way to get the power back. We had gas for a while, but that's gone now, the bastards. Still electric cookers do the biz and we've got wi-fi now.'

'Wicked,' smiled Terry.

'Yeah, it's secure, password-protected so you'll need—'

'Don't worry about that.'

'Oh yeah, you're one of those, aren't you?' said Daz.

'Daz doesn't like anything new,' Terry told them. 'He'd be hugging trees if he could.'

'No, no,' blushed Daz. 'I'm here, aren't I? I'm where I'm needed. Can't kick the system out in the forest, can I?'

Terry patted his heart with a clenched fist. 'Right on, brother.'

'Oh fuck off,' said Daz, but he was grinning. He smelled of stale incense.

He led them out of the lift into another corridor, this one daubed with huge red letters: 'No Logo!'

They walked on, passing more right-on quotes on the walls on both sides. Anna nudged Ben. 'Could this place be more of a bloody cliché?'

Daz must have heard her. 'What did you say?'

'Oh. Nothing, just how, it's really very kind of you . . . Darren,' says Anna. Daz looked at her, confused, then burst out laughing.

'No, no, it's not Darren, I'm Daz – you know, like the detergent – whiter than white. Name stuck cos I was always such a goody two-shoes.'

'Oh, I see,' said Anna. 'Does everyone have nicknames in here then?'

'This isn't a cult, honey. Whatever do you think we are?'

'I don't know. I've never seen anything like this.'

'You like it?'

'I . . . yes,' she said uncertainly.

'We're just a bunch of people who have found each other through the same ideology. We won't play the government's game. We don't do taxes, don't do ID cards, don't do plastic. We're a community of believers in a different way of living.

We're just a group who all looked at the way the world was and thought, we don't fit in. So we organise protests from here – try to stir up the students or the unions, you know. We're not running away, we're just . . . on pause while we work out a better way forward.'

'Cool,' said Toby.

'We march, we protest, it's like . . .' he tried to find the right words, his hand waving in the air, 'it's like that book, *War of the Worlds*. We've built our own little world in here, hiding from the invaders, waiting for our turn to reclaim the streets.'

Terry slipped between Ben and Anna as they followed. 'If there is hope, it lies with the proles,' he said with a smirk.

Daz didn't seem to hear this and walked on, finally stopping at a door which was painted red and green. Across it was daubed the words *don't trust anyone over 30*. Ben stared at it and then looked at Daz.

'Hey, don't get all steamed up, I didn't write it.' Daz pushed the door open and switched on a light to reveal a small, square room with a door leading off it. The windows were barricaded shut, so the only light came from the sterile strip lighting. The walls had all been painted in rich greens, gold and scarlet. Indian Gods had been drawn next to naked dancers who twirled and writhed around them. Ben nodded politely, but inside he was groaning. The carpet was faded and singed with small burns.

'Home sweet home,' announced Daz. 'You'll need some bedding, but it's dry. Don't try to open the window or take down the shutters. We don't want anyone knowing we're in here. There's another room through there and a communal shower down the corridor. Let us know when you're moving on. Good luck and may the force be with you.'

And with that, he was gone. Ben looked around.

'I'll get us some sleeping bags and a kettle,' he said. 'Some pillows and some basic foodstuffs.'

But Terry wasn't listening. He went to the other door, opened it and peered in. Ben saw another room, identical in shape and space but this time daubed in swirling purples and aquamarines.

'You stay in there, Miss, we'll share this other one,' Terry said.

'Thank you, but you've got to stop calling me Miss.'

'Yeah, yeah. So, shut the door, Toby.' Toby did so.

'Maybe I could get us a camp stove,' Ben continued. 'A can opener, some basic cutlery...' He stopped talking when he realised that everyone was staring at him.

'So, Ben,' said Terry, in a tone that wasn't entirely friendly. 'Fancy telling us everything about you?'

'Might take a while,' Ben replied.

Terry slipped down against a wall and folded his arms: I've got all the time in the world.

'Alright, sure. I'll tell you what I know.'

Ben leaned against the wall, stared at the grotty carpet and told them about his wife and children. He talked quietly about his dreams and his nightmares, about the aches and pains that would come and go. And, more falteringly, he told them how he became more confused and less trusting. He didn't tell them about the violence he'd meted out, but he hinted at a past that troubled him and actions which he did not wish to speak of. He told them about running, about the dead men in the van (although he alluded to a crash which had enabled his escape) and of his hunt for his true past. After a moment's hesitation, he told them that he was once a soldier, about the differences in his old life and the man he now believed himself to be.

Toby would occasionally interject with 'Me too!' or 'Yes, yes, just like that!' adding his own experiences, with Anna giving a calmer, clearer explanation of what they thought had happened to him. As Ben talked the mood became quieter, a little sombre. It was clear that, as much as they knew, they still knew nothing.

'And that's sort of it, I suppose,' said Ben, a little awkwardly. He looked at the others, unsure what more to say.

It was Terry who spoke first. 'You didn't say what your dreams were like.'

'Well they were . . . I don't know . . . just . . . dark, scary, me doing stuff that I wouldn't do, you know?'

'What stuff?'

'I don't remember any of it clearly enough.'

'Yeah you do,' Terry replied. Ben looked at him and saw the challenge in his eye.

'I'm not a threat to you.'

'Why are you saying that?' said Anna.

'You know what Toby dreamed of?' asked Terry. 'We do. Every bloody detail. They did terrible things to him, shitty, fucked-up things and he's told us all about it.' He spat out the last three words to make his point. 'Now what did they do to you?'

'It's okay, Ben,' said Anna. 'You can tell us.'

'I'm not making it up, I just can't, I don't . . . the details aren't . . .'

'Did they hurt you?' Anna asked.

'No, of course not,' said Terry. 'They didn't hurt him. He hurt them.'

Ben was silent, ashamed of the dirty secrets that were about to be exposed.

'You were a soldier, you said,' pressed Terry.

Ben nodded, staring at the cigarette burns in the swirly carpet, not wanting to catch Toby's eyes. He didn't care what Terry thought, or Anna so much, but he didn't want the boy to fear him or to hate him.

Terry got up, but kept his distance. 'Why do you think they'd take a bloke from the army? What do you think they'd make him do in his sleep? That he wouldn't do when he was awake?'

'I'm not like that,' was all that Ben could manage.

'Tell you what,' said Terry. 'How's about you have that room and us three will share in here?'

'He's not like that!' blurted out Toby.

'And how do you know that? In the – what is it, four hours? In the four hours that you've known him, what's he done to make you so sure?'

'Cos he helped me!'

'When?'

'In there!'

'Where?'

'In the place, the room, in that ... in that place ...' Toby stumbled into silence. 'In the lab,' said Ben, quietly.

Toby pulled his knees to his chest. 'We weren't going to talk about it,' he said.

Ben went over and sat down next to him. Toby eyed him like a child who's been tricked into a set of injections at the doctor's.

'What do you remember?' Ben asked gently.

'White walls,' Toby began reluctantly. 'Beds. Some nurses and doctors. Fancy machines. Windows with shutters.'

Ben nodded. 'Always closed.'

'Yeah. But you could hear cars outside sometimes, couldn't you?'

'That's right.'

Ben glanced at Anna and Terry who were silent. Anna nodded at him – keep going.

'I woke up once,' said Toby, 'cos of this loud car horn, right outside. Everyone woke up. And one man started shaking and ...' he squeezed his eyes shut, upset. 'He tried to get up, he was pulling at the straps and shouting and all the doctors were running to him. And then there was blood all over the ceiling.'

Ben put an arm around him, pulled him close and the boy nestled into him.

'Do you know where it is?'

'No. You never knew how you got there, you'd just wake up and you were there on a bed, tied down.'

'You don't remember going in or coming out?'

Toby shook his head.

'I think I do.'

'I remember going down in these big lifts. They had to be big cos they had to fit in a stretcher. And at the bottom there was ...' he paused, trying to remember.

'A van?'

'Yeah. Yeah, that's right, a van. I remember now. And they had to do that code. To open the doors.'

'The shutters.'

'A code. It was like a tune.' Toby hummed a five-tone melody. 'That was it.'

Those five notes ran clear in Ben's head like a long-forgotten nursery rhyme.

Terry stepped forward, pulling out his mobile phone. 'Sing it again,' he said.

Toby did so, and after a couple of failed attempts, Terry repeated the tune by pressing the right combination of numbers on his phone's keypad. He turned the screen to face Ben.

'Nine, nine, four, five, six. That's your entrance code.'

'And then the shutters would go up,' Ben said.

'What shutters?' asked Toby, confused. 'Oh. No, they changed those.'

Ben stared at him – what?

'Yeah, they had those old black shutters, but then they got changed. Don't you remember? They got that big metal door instead. Sank down into the floor. Wow, it's amazing how quickly it comes back. Must be because of you being here.'

Ben tried to remember a metal door. He could have been walking past it, several times, earlier. He could have been standing right outside without realising it.

'Do you remember him?' Toby asked, and his voice wavered, as though it were a question he'd nearly not dared ask.

Ben remembered a kindly old man's eyes that stared down at him. A wrinkled hand that would have nurses scurrying in different directions at the merest flick or gesture. He nodded and his grip around Toby tightened.

'He was quite kind to us, in a way, wasn't he?' asked Toby.

'Yes, he was.'

'You kept thinking he'd fall over, he was so old, but his eyes were always, like, twinkling sort of.'

'I remember that too.'

'And his hands, always moving.'

'Like he was conducting that classical music he always played.'

'Yeah!' said Toby. 'And his fingers would twitch along.' He was pleased with the shared memory. 'I sort of thought we were special to him.'

'I think we were.'

'Even though he told them to do those things to us.'

'He can't do them to you any more,' Ben said. 'He's gone. You're free.'

But Toby didn't seem reassured by this. He sat there, withdrawn, as though he didn't believe the nightmare really was over. And Ben felt the same unease and doubt. He sat quietly for a while before he spoke again.

'I think I know where it is.'

They all looked at him, amazed.

'And now we know the code to get in,' he added.

'You're saying that like it's good news,' Toby said. 'What the fuck do you want to go in there for?'

'To get answers.'

'You go in there and they'll catch you. Mash you up.'

'It's okay, Toby.'

'Are you on crack? You can't go back there.'

'I have to. Where else can we go? You want to live here for the rest of your life?'

'I don't mind. It's alright. Bound to be loads of hippy chicks in here and they'll be into free love and shit.'

Ben looked at Terry. 'We go by car first. Check it out. If I'm right, if it really is where I think it is, then we can have a think about how we get in.'

'And then what?' shouted Toby. 'Once you're in, then what'll you do?'

'I'll do to them what they've made me do to others.'

He felt absolutely calm as he spoke the words. There was silence in the room. He could tell they were scared of him. He'd talked about murder as though it were something casual, practical and easily done. Ben would never have talked like this, he thought. He found he was shivering again.

SEVENTEEN

There were three wards inside the lab. They took you up in a lift from the basement. Ben remembered a long corridor and that the wards led off it. There were other rooms and offices further along, but neither he nor Toby knew what they were for. Two of the wards, with white walls, hard-rubber floors and shuttered windows, could house ten or twelve beds. Doctors and nurses were always around checking on their patients, monitoring them, gauging their progress. It was normally quiet in there. The medical staff's footsteps were muffled by the floor and there was rarely much noise from outside. It was a place for recuperation, rehab and rest.

The third ward was different. It was smaller, and divided into three operating rooms. There were no windows here and the walls were lined with strangely shaped foam bricks that deadened all sound. And when you were brought in here, you'd be blindfolded and they'd put headphones on you. There were lots of machines in here; big, complicated beasts, covered in dials, switches and flashing lights. They made no noise. There was never any noise. When Ben and Toby spoke of this third ward they were noticeably quieter and more reticent. Whatever happened in there had scared them more than anything else had. In here was the man they spoke of; the old man who would control everything. This was his kingdom.

Sometimes things would go wrong in the third ward. Ben couldn't explain it properly, but he was sure that men and women had gone in there after they had become anxious or troublesome and they hadn't come back out.

Anna shuddered at the story, at all the tales that Ben and Toby had told that day as they steeled themselves to go back there: to see if Ben was right and the place really did exist as they said it did. She wanted him to be wrong. She was scared again, nauseous from it, and wanted all of this to be a stupid misunderstanding, a hilarious mix-up that could be happily explained away.

Ben had gone off alone later that night, returning with sleeping bags and other gear to make their stay more comfortable. And a car. Anna had expressed surprise that a rent-a-car company was open that late at night and had felt stupid when his wry stare revealed that he'd stolen it. She would have protested that she didn't do this sort of thing, but then again she'd stolen Toby.

The next day they ate cereal from cheap plastic bowls in silence, then prepared to go. Anna had delayed them by insisting on washing up. Even Terry had seemed nervous, moaning about computer access and wanting a couple more minutes before they headed off. Toby said nothing, pacing about the room, pale and fidgety. And Ben just stood by the door, lost in thoughts that Anna was happy for him to keep to himself.

They drove off once rush hour had passed. Ben and Toby sat in the front, Anna and Terry in the back. Terry had a laptop perched on his knees and he tapped away at it throughout the journey. Anna had no idea what he was up to, but she would have welcomed the chance for some distraction. Instead she stared out at the people, the shops, the cars and buses. Locked inside the car with this ragtag collection of strangers, she felt terribly alone.

They drove on, and after half an hour they stopped at a set of traffic lights. As they waited patiently for them to turn green, a police car drove up next to them and everyone stiffened.

'Just remain calm and look straight ahead,' said Ben, staring hard at the lights. Anna tried to do as he said, and no one spoke. The lights remained red. It seemed to go on forever.

'Oh come on . . .' gasped Toby.

Anna couldn't help but glance across to the police vehicle. The driver was a woman, a WPC, and she was talking to someone via the car radio. Anna watched her. Was she talking about them? Were they checking out the registration plate of the car? Why the hell were they driving around in a stolen car? And then the WPC turned and looked at Anna, looked her straight in the eye. It was as if she knew her. And Anna was about to shout out in panic, when the car jerked forward and took a right-hand turn, leaving the police car behind. It didn't follow. But still, Anna was shaken by that stare.

'See?' said Ben from the front. 'Just a cop car, driving around, not interested in us. We're fine.'

But she didn't feel fine. She felt that they were being played with.

Ben had explained to them how he'd worked out the rough location of 'the lab', as he'd started calling it, from a memory of a statue in a square. Soon they drove past this statue – a crouching lion, painted gold, on a tall marble plinth. It was just as he said. And although it meant nothing in itself, the mood in the car was buoyed enormously.

Toby had a map on his lap, but was rubbish at reading it and offered less-than-helpful directions. Terry, in frustration, used his computer to offer different instructions. The two boys would bicker and shout at each other as Ben would drive round and round, cursing when they hit a one-way system that slowed their progress even further.

But every now and then they'd reach a back alley, a quiet road that might be 'the one'. And then they'd all be silent as they drove along it and they'd all stare out, looking for those silver doors. At the end of the road, when nothing was found, Terry and Toby would resume their bickering. It was hard to tell if this was frustration or relief. As much as Toby said he wanted to know the truth, he had squirmed and argued hard against them trying to find it. It was just too dangerous.

Round and round they drove. Slowly Anna's fear faded, but it was replaced by car sickness. She began to believe that they'd never find these doors.

They found another quiet back street. Ben indicated right, took the turn and drove slowly along. Anna looked out at what must be the backs of office blocks or shops – the uglier, concealed back entrances which were hidden from public view. They passed a stack of large plastic bins and then the car stopped. Anna was confused for a moment, then she saw that Terry's face was turned away from her, pressed against the glass. She looked over his shoulder and saw a steep drive that dipped away from the street, leading down to a thick metal barrier, spotless and shiny. A metal door, close to the square with the lion statue, off a steep drive. Just as Ben had described it.

No one moved. The engine purred as they all stared at the metal door. Next to it was a small keypad on the wall. A digital keypad.

'Fucking hell,' whispered Terry. 'That's it, isn't it?'

No one else spoke.

Anna looked at Toby. She could see that he was shaking. She leaned forward and put her hands on his shoulder, but it had no effect.

'Let's go, just go,' Toby pleaded.

But Ben didn't move. His eyes were locked on the door.

'Come on, let's get out of here!' shouted Toby.

'They're in there,' said Ben. 'It's all in there.'

'Yeah, great, well done, cool. Now let's go!'

Toby was twisted and contorted in the chair, writhing with fear.

'Have you seen the keypad?' Ben said, turning to Anna. He seemed absolutely calm. She nodded. It was as close as she could get to speaking.

'Don't go down there!' Toby screamed.

'But it's the only way to find out the truth.'

'Fuck the truth!'

'Toby.' Ben put a hand on the boy's arm. 'We have to be sure. This could be the wrong place. Some rich guy's garage.'

'Or they could be there. Just waiting. You open the door and they'll get us.'

Ben seemed to have no answer to this. Anna watched him as he turned to stare back at the metal barrier. The silence was painful. The engine ran, idle. She looked back behind them, but there was no one there, no people, no police car. Terry started typing something new into his computer, but Anna just stared back at Ben, waiting for a decision.

'Come on,' he finally said, unbuckling his seat belt.

'No way,' Toby replied.

'Yes. Yes, come on. You have to do this.'

Anna could see tears forming in Toby's eyes.

'Why doesn't he just wait in the car with us?' she suggested. 'You know what the code is.'

'Toby,' Ben said, ignoring her.

'Come on, Ben, look at him,' she said. 'He's absolutely terrified.'

Ben glanced at her and then back at Toby. Then he nodded. 'You get in the driver's seat,' he said to her. 'If there's trouble, you drive. Just drive, okay?'

'Okay.'

She watched Ben get out of the car, rub his hands and roll the stiffness out his shoulders. Then he walked down the drive, towards the door and the keypad. Suddenly Toby bolted from the car and ran towards Ben. Anna wanted to shout after him, but she was scared of making too much noise. Instead she got out herself, closed the door he'd left open and got into the driver's side, pulling the door shut as quietly as she could. The seat was still warm from Ben sitting on it. Terry continued to type away in the back. She turned and watched as Toby caught up with Ben. Behind her, the typing stopped.

'You think this is it, Miss?'

'Don't call me Miss.'

'I do. I think this is the place. Fucking hell, I'm scared. I don't care who knows it.'

'We'll be fine,' she replied, a little too quietly.

Ben turned in surprise as Toby ran down the steep tarmac slope and stopped next to him in front of the big metal door.

'Better out here with you than in the car. She's a rubbish driver,' said Toby, pulling a face. Ben put a hand out and patted his arm gently. His nerves were shredded, but he didn't want the boy to see. He needed to be strong for both of them. He looked up at the building – the wall had a thick, even render, which had been painted white. High above were five sets of window shutters. Closed.

'You think this is it?' he said.

Toby nodded. The tears were in his eyes again.

Ben went over to the keypad. He was about to type in the code Toby had sung when the boy stopped him.

'Why do you think we've been dreaming about this place?'

Ben was confused. 'What?'

'Why do you think we both suddenly started dreaming the same sort of thing? Just like that. Now?'

Ben paused. He had no answer, he'd not considered the timing of the dreams important, only what he remembered from them.

'Do you think,' Toby continued, faltering, 'that like, maybe, they're still in our heads? Sort of, I don't know, sort of – they wanted us to remember this place?'

'Why?'

'So we'd come back here.'

Ben's hand instinctively jerked away from the keypad. He shoved it in his pocket to make the reaction seem less extreme. He looked at Toby, so fragile and so frightened in front of him. The boy would say anything to get away from here, he thought. But he couldn't deny the eerie logic.

'Sort of like we're programmed,' Toby said. 'Even when we're awake.'

The idea clawed away at Ben. But he shook his head.

'We've been here for five minutes. If they wanted us, they could easily have got us by now. Look at this street – only two ways out. We're sitting ducks.'

He looked around. The road was empty. He looked back at Anna and Terry who stared back at him from the relative safety of the car.

'No,' Ben said more confidently. 'If they knew we were here, they'd have got us by now.'

He turned back to the keypad.

'Why bother to get us if they know we'll just walk in anyway?' Toby asked, his voice tremulous.

'It's fine, it's probably not even the right place,' Ben replied. But it was. He knew it was.

He punched the five numbers into the keypad.

It made the exact tune that Toby had hummed.

But nothing happened.

Toby breathed out a shallow sigh of relief.

Ben tried again, adding an extra key – a green button – at the end.

Another pause. And then there was a tiny click, a slow groan and the door began to slide down into the floor. Slow and sleek, it sank away, revealing a dark room on the other side.

Toby nearly bolted, but Ben grabbed his arm. He was trans-fixed by the cool, slick motion of the door as it gradually disap-peared entirely into the ground. Then there was a small mechanical shudder and everything was silent again. Ben took one step closer and peered in. It looked like a large, empty garage. Parking bays were marked out by painted white lines on the floor. Big spaces. Big enough for vans. Nothing else, except a door at the far end and, next to it, the doors to a large lift.

He looked down at the sunken door and the cavernous opening. He took another step forward. There was something about the threshold, that sunken metal barrier that scared him. He imagined it springing back up once he'd crossed it, trapping him inside. But if he didn't step forward, he'd never know more.

Inside the car, Terry was muttering swearwords to himself, over and over. Anna's hands gripped the steering wheel, wanting to drive away, drive as fast as she could.

'He's not going in there, is he?' Terry asked, incredulous, as Ben took a tentative step forwards. 'We should get out of here, yeah? Now we know it's for real, we need to get the hell out of here. Yeah? Yeah? HELLO?'

Anna banged on the window, trying to catch their atten-tion. Come on, she thought, don't make me shout or sound the horn, just come back now, just come back. Toby looked up at her, his face pale. She gestured for him to come back to the car. He nodded, turned to Ben and said something. Ben replied, but neither moved.

'Why aren't they coming back?' she hissed.

'He's going in, isn't he? Oh fucking fuck.'

'It's okay, it's just, it's just . . .' but the words choked inside her.

Outside, Ben took another step forward. Terry coughed up a muffled squeal. She tried to find her most adult, practical voice to calm them both down.

'There's no sign,' she said.

'You what?'

'There's no sign to say who owns the building.'

'No shit. You think they're going to advertise themselves?'

'No, but maybe there's a sign on the other side, on the front of the building. We could find out who owns it that way.'

'I know who owns it, that's what I've been doing on my computer. It's a big holding company, the Rylance Group, but who gives a shit. Seriously, he can't go in there!'

He banged on the window himself, but neither Ben nor Toby seemed to notice.

The words hit Anna hard in the gut. She thought maybe she'd heard wrong.

'Who?'

'The Rylance Group. They're a big multinational, own all sorts, oil companies, airlines, computer companies, you name it. But they'll just be a front, I bet. Probably just renting out the space. Won't have a clue what it's really being used for.'

Toby had grabbed Ben's arm, trying to stop him from going forward. Anna watched them as she took in Terry's words. It felt like someone was sitting on her chest, crushing her lungs. She could barely breathe.

Her father worked for the Rylance Group.

Outside, Ben tried to pull away from Toby. But the boy held tight.

'Don't go in. You said we'd just check it out today. You said.'

'I know. But we're here now.'

'You promised!'

'Look, let's just go to the edge. Have a look. If it's at all odd, we won't go inside. I promise.'

Toby nodded reluctantly and Ben led him to the entrance. They stared in. The floor was clean, a little dusty, but well tended. Ben listened out, expecting the noise of charging feet coming to get them, but the room was eerily silent.

'Do you remember this?' Ben asked.

Toby shook his head. 'Not really. Just the other stuff. Upstairs.' He sniffed.

Ben pointed to the lift. 'They took us up in there.'

'Yeah.'

'We're not mad.'

'I already knew that.'

Ben was quiet for a moment. He wasn't mad. They had done things to him. And he really had done things to others. His wife had lied to him. His children were probably not his. All this wasn't just craziness in his mind. But the truth was worse.

And then he felt Toby's clutch on his arm tighten. He looked at him, followed his gaze and saw what he was staring at. A camera. A small camera attached to the wall, pointing right at them. Its red light blinked repeatedly: on, recording.

We see you. We are watching you.

Ben took a step back and they both turned tail and sprinted to the car.

Anna saw them coming and hit the accelerator as soon as they jumped inside.

'They saw us,' gasped Toby, who had thrown himself into the back seat. 'Oh shit, they've seen us.'

Ben had jumped in beside her but said nothing, panting slightly as she took a hard left turn and kept on driving fast. It was a while before he spoke.

'We need to dump the car. We're not safe until we do.'

She let him direct her to an industrial estate with long, empty roads, where they parked the car and walked away. It was a good twenty minutes to the nearest bus route, but the walk seemed to calm them down.

Except for Anna. She walked slightly behind the guys, trying to make sense of everything that had happened to her over the last few months. Her father worked for the Rylance Group. Soon after she'd got into trouble with Toby he'd turned up at her flat uninvited. Memories of her childhood flickered in her mind, but they didn't answer the questions that bit at her. Her father was a part of this. Which meant that she was too, in ways she hadn't realised.

Toby cheered up with each step they took away from the car. Ten minutes later, he was cock-a-hoop.

'We did it!' he cheered. 'And may I just say that you two were total pussies for hiding in the car!'

Terry thumped him and they started wrestling on the pavement, the relief pumping out of them.

Ben moved to pull them apart, clearly irritated by the spectacle, but Anna stopped him, her hand on his arm. He looked at her, surprised.

'I need your help,' she said to him quietly, so that the boys wouldn't hear. 'Let's get them back to the squat. And then I need you to take me somewhere.'

EIGHTEEN

Anna couldn't quite remember why she found it so hard to talk to her father. Their relationship had slowly deteriorated over time, starting when something had happened around the time she left university, and various rows and unintended slights had spiked their opportunities for a reunion. But they had been inseparable once.

She remembered happier days. She remembered playing on a beach when she was no more than ten or eleven, digging in the sand, laughing as the sea would sweep in and follow the trenches she'd dug for it. Henry sat in the shade, glancing up from a battered paperback, waving at her and worrying about suntan cream. When she stamped and pouted because his attentions were elsewhere, he'd laugh and crouch down next to her and together they'd build castles and cathedrals. She was never a princess, but always the master builder, an architect, and he was her trusty servant, berating their invisible workmen for their slovenly ways.

One time she looked up, having dug a hole so deep she was already down to her waist, to see her father had bought her a kite from one of the local stands. She was thrilled, and they flew it together all day. The kite was deep red with multi-coloured ribbons hanging down. Anna was so happy she slept with the kite on her pillow. But the next day, as Henry diligently smoothed the factor 40 cream onto her arms and legs, her hands became greasy and the kite slipped from her grasp. She wailed as the kite fluttered up and away, flying not out to sea but inland, above and over the steep cliffs that towered up behind the beach.

Henry listened to his daughter's pleas with a solemn face. He argued that the kite was most likely long gone, even if they did climb the steep, uneven path that zig-zagged up the rocky terrain. But little Anna was insistent and he relented. After packing up their belongings with a care that drove her to distraction, the two of them set off, holding hands, in search of the lost kite. Anna only had flimsy sandals on, and although she skipped along at first, soon her feet became sweaty with the heat and started to slip and slide. The rocks scraped and bruised her toes, but she tried not to show it. Henry walked ahead of her at an even, demanding pace, never slowing, only occasionally glancing back. By the time they'd reached the top of the cliffs, the sun was right above them and Anna was swaying in the heat, her hands and legs covered in the rocks' white chalky dust. Henry was waiting for her, having reached the top some time before. He gazed at her coolly and she tried to smile, knowing that this was all her idea. She could sense, despite her young age, that her father wanted her to grumble. This was a test. Ahead was a field, wire-fenced, covered with thistles and stinging nettles. Henry gathered Anna to him and lifted her up. For a moment she thought it was a cuddle of congratulation until her father pointed to a dash of colour, trapped amid the high grass at the far end. He'd lifted her up so she could see it. When he put her back down, Anna could only see the violent green of the nettles. And then her father took her hand with a firm grip that let her know she was going to come with him.

It took them twenty minutes to navigate through the field. Henry carefully lifted the kite out of the bushes, then held it up, inspecting it. The kite had no marks, no tears, nothing. He smiled at his daughter.

'See? It's perfect.'

Anna's legs were covered in pricks of blood, stung and scratched. She put her finger to a wound and tasted the blood. And then she looked up at her father, realising that he was watching her. He handed her the kite and she heard herself saying 'thank you'. She said it so politely, you would have thought they were strangers. Then she followed him back, the route made easier by the flattened path already travelled. When they reached the bottom, Henry washed her legs with seawater and although it stung, she didn't wince. And then he smoothed more sun cream onto her skin before returning to his novel.

Anna flew the kite for the rest of the afternoon. But she never touched it again after that day. And her father never asked her why.

She wondered why she remembered this moment above the others. Why didn't she focus on the time he bought champagne for everyone in a restaurant when he learned about her outstanding exam results? Or the long walks they'd taken together, arm in arm, them against the world? She shrugged the thoughts off and turned to look at Ben who was sitting next to her, driving the car he'd stolen only half an hour before. The car had been taken from a family home and he assured her that they wouldn't notice its disappearance until the morning. She'd told him little when he'd asked where they were going and why, and she was grateful to him for not pressing her further. He had his own secrets, she imagined.

They were close to her father's house now, entering one of the smartest parts of the city. The houses all shared the same white stucco frontage, protected by high gates and iron fences. Anna glanced at Ben as he drove. He wore a simple black T-shirt and jeans. She noticed his well-muscled arms, and despite the nerves and anxiety that meant she barely ate, she couldn't help but notice that he was handsome. Anna had never had much luck with men. A brief fling with Paul (Maths, married and coffee breath) last year was enough to have her retreating to her novels. And Ben, despite his kindness to Toby, was a strange, wild figure. They couldn't have been more different. Yet here they were together, alone in a car, unknown to the world.

Ben had explained what she should do if she were worried and where he would be waiting for her. He would flash the headlights when he saw her to let her know where he was.

'If you're unsure about anything, anything at all, then just run. Trust your fears and get the hell out of there.'

She glanced at his tough, scarred hands that gripped the steering wheel, then at her own pale hands. Blemish-free. When she looked up again, they were nearly there and the streets were wide and clean with old-fashioned street lamps and expensive cars parked in private drives.

Ben stopped the car where she told him. 'You want me to come with you?'

'No. Thank you. Why?'

'In case.'

'He's my Dad.'

'Right.'

Anna put her hand on his – I'll be fine. Then she got out of the car and Ben drove away. Suddenly she was all alone for the first time in ages. The quiet was delicious. She walked along the street and glanced up at the front door she knew so well. There was the spot where she had once sat, covering the stone steps in chalky flowers, suns and angels.

Lights were on inside the house. Although Anna had a door key, she did as Ben had instructed and walked along the spotless paving stones to the back of the house, passing the bins she had never had to take out, never even had to fill.

Past the bins was an imposing gate with wire above it. Anna, however, knew that you could jiggle it open if you did it the right way. She'd done so when she was a teenager, sneaking out to join Bella and Sophie when her father was away at a conference, taking a bottle of his Dalmore whisky to get the party started.

The garden was just the same as when she was a child. A long strip of lawn, a small pergola, a summer house at the end where she would play for hours. The kitchen had one solitary light on, but was empty. He'd be working in his study, just as he always had for as long as she could remember.

The fridge made a gentle hum, but otherwise there was no noise. The house had always been quiet – too quiet for some of her friends, who claimed it was weird to be this neat – but she had always liked it. She put her foot on the bottom stair, placed a hand on the banister, reassured by the slow tick of the grandfather clock. She climbed the stairs without a sound, just as she always used to. For a moment she saw herself as a little girl, ready to be admonished for interrupting her father's work, and she had to shake the thought away. She needed to be bigger and braver.

The door was open when she got to Henry's study. He used to close it, but now, alone, there was no need. He sat at his grand desk, glasses perched on his nose, a cup of coffee to his right and a glass of whisky to the left. Three expensive fountain pens sat on a silver tray in front of him. There were no photographs on the desk, just papers. The only concession to progress was a laptop computer, folded down and shut.

Anna stood in the doorway and watched her father sniff in irritation at something on the page before circling it with his pen. On the way here she had concocted a hundred questions for him: searing, penetrating accusations that would have his mouth flapping under the inquisition. But now, seeing him, they had slipped and spilled to somewhere unreachable.

He looked up and his eyes widened with surprise.

'Dad.'

'Anna, Jesus Christ.' He was on his feet, rushing around the desk to her, pulling her to him in an embrace. 'I've had the bloody police around here, you've been on the television, what the hell are you up to?'

She pushed herself away from him. She was meant to be the one asking questions.

'I'm fine.'

'No, you're bloody well not.' He rubbed her arms as the familiar awkwardness crept in between them. 'Come with me to the police. I'll get you the best lawyer, we'll sort it all out.'

'No.'

'Anna, this isn't a time for arguments, you're in a lot of trouble, child.'

'I know. But I'm not a child.'

He looked her up and down with the same old critical eyes.

'You look dreadful.'

'Thanks.'

'Well, you do. And you should. Where's the boy, this schoolboy? Did you really abduct him?'

'Of course not.'

'So he's not with you?'

'You know what, Daddy? I don't want you to ask me any more questions.'

He stood back, folded and unfolded his arms.

'Come on, then, what do you want?'

'Are you ...?' she stammered and was angry with herself for it. 'I'll have a drink, please.'

'Whisky and water?' She nodded and he poured from a crystal decanter. The drink was a welcome prop.

'Daddy. What do you know about all this?'

'No more than the papers said. The police were particularly bloody cagey.'

'Please. Don't lie to me. Not to me.'

He looked up at her sharply, but she couldn't tell if it was because she'd hit on something or because he was surprised by the accusation.

'What am I meant to know?'

'Don't make it a game, just be honest with me. I thought you were always honest with me. You could be cruel like that, but at least you were honest. Never hid anything from me. Not even Mum's death.'

She regretted this the moment she said it, and she saw his mouth tighten with hurt.

'I just tried to bring you up the best way I could. You were so clever, I thought you deserved it.'

'Yes, I'm sure, but look, I'm not hanging around here for long. We've agreed I'll only stay for five minutes.'

'Who's we?'

'Are you involved in all this?'

'All what?' His bewilderment seemed genuine enough to her. But that was not enough.

'Are you?'

'Hang on, are you saying you didn't run off with that kid? You think I've got him?'

'Daddy!' she screamed. 'You know what I'm saying. I'm your daughter and you know what I'm asking you. Tell me, please. Tell me what I should be scared of. Tell me how to hide. If you love me, help me. Tell me what you know.'

Suddenly he looked incredibly tired, incredibly sad. She'd never thought of him as old before, but now she saw the wrinkles and creases on his face. His eyes looked worn and weary. He stared down at his desk and she realised with shock that he was unable to meet her eye. When he did look up, he shook his head, an almost imperceptible movement. It was as though he was afraid to speak. Afraid to be heard. She looked at him and saw a man who was trapped in his own luxurious abode. As trapped and as helpless as she was. His eyes flicked across the room then back to her. But still he didn't say anything, his face lined with concern and doubt.

Neither spoke.

And then, as though he was aware of the silence lasting too long, he coughed loudly and stood a little taller, as though he was about to address an audience.

'Do you want money?'

She knew that this was all he could offer. Everything was incredibly clear. She could not trust him. She should not be here.

'I don't need money.' She turned away from him. 'Bye bye, Daddy.'

'No. Anna, darling, please.'

He chased after her as she walked calmly down the stairs and decided to walk straight out through the front door. Ben would be waiting at the end of the street. She'd be there in one minute. She put her hand to the latch and pulled the thick door open. She looked back and saw him watching her from the top of the stairs. She gave him a small wave goodbye. He seemed so small and frail.

She didn't bother to pull the door shut as she skipped down the steps, pulled open the iron gate and broke into a run. If her father called after her, she didn't hear him.

A car's headlights flashed nearby and Anna dashed to the passenger seat. Ben drove off immediately and soon they were miles away.

He didn't ask her a thing. She sat next to him with her head down, trying to think of something to say, but was overwhelmed by sadness. Her father had been her last connection to a happier, safer world. She was cut adrift now. Maybe she'd never been safe, not really, but she had loved the feeling, the lie. And that was gone now. She could never go back.

She started to cry as she stared down at her pale, manicured hands. They seemed so inadequate for the tasks ahead and she seemed so tiny next to the big man behind the wheel. She felt like a little girl in a woman's body.

Ben drove on in silence and neither spoke for the rest of the journey.

NINETEEN

Ben knew that he shouldn't go anywhere near Carrie. He knew that the men who took him before would be waiting for his return. And Carrie was a part of that. But as he drove Anna back from her father's, he found he was thinking about her again, remembering her sweet, shy shuffle, that infectious giggle, the way she'd bite her lip. He'd try to think of other things, but she would always find a way back in.

He dropped Anna off at the squat and told her that he'd have to dump the car far away so there was no possible link to them. She thought he was being careful, not realising that he was an addict, lying to her so he could get his next fix of Carrie. He told himself he would just drive past once, glance in, and then drive off. But, like an addict, he knew that he was lying to himself as well.

He parked in their road. Five doors down. He was being an idiot, he told himself. He was going to get himself caught. What made him do this? Was it some cruel programming they'd left ticking in his brain? He sat in the car, the engine off, the lights extinguished, trying to cool his head, work out what to do.

Get out and run away, his mind told him.

Start the engine, drive, drive and drive some more, his instincts screamed.

But Ben could not move.

And then he saw something, a slip of light, some movement at the door and there she was: Carrie, wrapped up in a coat, walking to the car. She glanced behind her and waved to a young girl – Keira, the babysitter – who waved back and shut the door. Ben was shocked by the sight of her; this young girl who had been an everyday part of his life but who he had completely forgotten until this moment.

What day was it? Tuesday. Book club. Ben watched as she went to the car, got in and started the engine. Inside, the kids would be bouncing around as Keira tried to settle them so she could get on with her studies. He tried to recall the course, but he had never paid her much attention. He had always found her presence awkward: a pretty, trendy girl with aspirations, and he a plodding mechanic. He'd make bad jokes and she'd smile politely and both would hope that Carrie would finish her make-up and get downstairs as soon as possible.

Ben's hand reached for the key in the ignition and he felt his salivary glands explode. He shoved the car forward, brain working hard to remember where she was going and how to get there before her. It would either be Heather or Sally. As her car indicated left he knew it must be Sally, and he made a hard three-point turn to go the other way. With effort and a little luck, he would make it.

If she was in on it, Ben told himself as he powered down the back streets, then she would be waiting for the moment when he appeared again. She'd be followed at all times, so all she would have to do would be to signal them, let them know when she saw him, and then they would take care of him once and for all. There would be no surprise for her. And he'd be able to spot it if she tried to fake the shock.

Ben remembered the surprise party he'd organised for Carrie, getting Sally to help him with friends and invitations. He'd dragged her unwillingly to a church hall, claiming his present was a set of ballroom dancing lessons ('honey, it's a lovely idea, really, you're sweet, but it's not quite what . . .'), and then he'd pulled open the doors and there they all were. He'd never forget her face that day.

He needed to see that expression. He'd know if she was lying. He'd told himself this over and over. Now he stood in the shadows, a few yards from Sally's gate, waiting for her to arrive. When she approached, he would step out, maybe even say hello, and he would see her face. And then he'd know for sure.

Ben shivered slightly as he waited. He glanced back at Sally's door and remembered the time he and Carrie had made their excuses early, gasping for each other, pulling clothes off frantically in the back of the car in this same street.

A car's lights swept into the road, turning slowly, the driver looking for a space. It was her. She locked the car, a bottle of wine tucked under her arm, and she walked quickly towards Sally's house.

As Carrie approached, checking the contents of her handbag as she walked, so Ben stepped out into the light of a streetlamp. He took his hands out of his pockets and although there were two knives hidden under layers, he was trying to make sure she saw him as he was, not a madman, not a fugitive. Her Ben. That's what she always used to call him. My Ben.

She looked up and when she saw him she faltered for a second. If you were watching from afar you might think she tripped on a paving stone. Then she walked on, straight towards him, their eyes locked. Ben felt tears welling up in his eyes. He was overwhelmed by this strange sense of weariness, exhaustion and absolute euphoria. If she held him now, he would curl up in her arms and sleep for a year.

Carrie walked on, the gap between them no more than ten metres now. Her face was blank and he was waiting for something – a slap, a scream of anguish; something. Her eyes stared at him but still she said nothing.

He was about to speak. Think of a line that doesn't sound too corny, you dope.

And then she broke the stare, turned and walked straight up the path to Sally's house where she rang the doorbell. Ben didn't move, confused. There was a weird silence before the door was pulled open and Sally's braying voice pulled her in.

The door shut with a heavy thump, leaving Ben still standing under the light.

Come on, then. Come and get me. Come on, you bastards. Here I am.

He stood there and didn't bother to move when a car drove past, but the driver was uninterested. He knew she must be making the call now that she was inside and safe. She hadn't spoken because she knew of the betrayal that was to come. He was a fool and he deserved what was coming.

But half an hour later, the road was still quiet and Ben was standing in the same spot, a suicidal sentry. Now different doubts drifted in on the breeze. Her refusal to speak . . . maybe it was to protect him? Maybe her actions were a carefully coded warning. A warning, and a sign that she did still love him and that he could trust her.

Inside the house Ben could hear women laughing.

Slowly, he walked away, casually running the stolen car keys along every car except for Carrie's. He eventually dropped them down a drain and walked on. It would take him hours to get back to the others, but he didn't care. He didn't care about anything at all.

TWENTY

Carrie stared out of the kitchen window, stirring a pot of bolognese sauce on the stove. She knew that no one could see her from here, but she still felt that she needed to maintain this performance. It was nearly time to pick up the kids from school and she'd need to look normal for the other parents. But now that she knew the cameras were trained on her, she found it harder and harder to maintain the artifice. A cold, shivery terror spread through her, and although days had passed since she had met David, the fear didn't diminish. On the contrary, it grew, burning with an icy fire that made her stare at strangers with mistrust. It turned her bedtime stories with Emma into a husky whisper and would push her into a curled-up ball in the far corner of the kitchen, hidden away, desperate for a moment that she could call her own. She felt she was falling apart.

Once a month, on a Tuesday, Carrie went to her book club. It had been set up by some studious mum with literary pretensions but had soon relaxed into a glass of wine, a bowl of pasta and a jolly good gossip. Carrie had fitted right in and the

Company had encouraged the night out – a small moment of release from her work as well as cementing her 'normal mum' facade.

Carrie had never read much as a child. She had scraped through school with no qualifications to speak of and so she found these evenings intoxicating. She listened to the five minutes each woman gave to the book (before the plight of finding a good cleaner took over) and found it easy to give her own version of what everyone else had already said. But after a while she realised she had her own opinions, and when she spoke the others listened and nodded. She really could be a middle-class mother and wife. She could be anything she wanted.

As she drove to Sally's house that night, she tried to remind herself that she was going to enjoy herself. She liked her friends, she was getting away from it all, just for an evening. But these thoughts couldn't cut through the cold fear. As she turned on the ignition, she thought about the cameras and mics that must be lurking, hidden in the car. She turned the radio up loud.

She reached Sally's house about fifteen minutes later and found a space at the far end of the road. She parked badly which annoyed her. She couldn't think straight and she kept losing things and forgetting others. She got out of the car and grabbed the obligatory bottle of wine. Sally's place was nicer than hers and no one crossed her threshold without wine or flowers. As she dropped her keys into her handbag, she wondered whether or not there was a bug right there inside it, something she carried around with her. It would be just like them, she thought. She peered into the bag, but couldn't see anything obvious. She resolved to check again tomorrow, no, she would buy a new bag and transfer only the bare essentials. But what did it matter? They knew where she was at all times and there was nothing she could do about it.

She pulled her coat closer to her, trying to gather her thoughts, fix a smile for Sally, perform as she was meant to. Then, as she worried about all of this, she looked up and saw Ben.

He was just standing there in the full beam of a street lamp. He looked terrible. He sported a beard, his hair was longer and he wore clothes she didn't recognise. But his face, his face smiled at her with an open longing that made her want to run to him. She stopped herself and the two opposing instincts made her foot slip for a second. She walked on towards him, not knowing what to do. She wanted to scream, but she was terrified of the noise. She wanted to laugh, she wanted to warn him, to push him away, to grab him and lock him to her. She wanted to take his hand and pull him along the street and run away with him. But the guards might be watching. The prison was working too well.

He smiled at her but didn't speak, his arms hung uselessly at his sides. He was free but he looked like he'd given up. But he was free! He was standing there and he was free.

Or he was a trap. A different part of the experiment. A new test for her. Maybe she was now the experiment.

His eyes were the same. Whatever had happened to him, his eyes, his beautiful soft eyes were exactly the same.

They were close now. She had to do something, say something that would make him realise that she loved him still. But then the fear reached up from inside and squeezed hard. Her heart roared, but she could not speak.

To her left was the gate and small front garden of Sally's house. Ahead of her was Ben. If she went to him now, they'd find them. If he really was free, then he needed to be far from her.

But it was him. And he stared at her and she at him. And she remembered the way he'd stare at her from the edge of the bathroom door as she bathed the kids. And she wanted to cry.

She turned left and their eyes finally unlocked. She hurried to the door, rang the bell and allowed Sally to ooh and ahh about something or other as she ushered her inside and took her coat. The door shut behind her and its heavy thump sealed the deal. No, she could turn back now, she could still run to him. But she let Sally lead her further inside and listened as the others chatted around her. A glass of wine was thrust into her hand. It was too late now.

She kept her back to the window so she could not be tempted to look outside. She sat politely on the edge of a sofa, shared with two other pretty mums, clutching her book and a glass of wine, trying to add enough witty comments so no one would notice just how terrible she felt. She'd seen him and now he was gone. He would think that she no longer loved him. He'd think that she'd abandoned him. Her legs were shaking so she played with the hem of her dress in an attempt to hide this. On the other side of the room, a plain woman called Ruth was moaning about a teacher. Something to do with her daughter, very talented, such a waste, seen the headmaster . . . The words drifted on and Carrie nodded with the appropriate expression. But all she wanted to do was scream. She'd failed.

The evening dragged itself out and she was able to get away relatively early without fuss or interrogation. She pulled on her coat and stepped outside, walking to the car, knowing that he wasn't there, but hoping, ever hoping, that he might have left a message, be hiding in the shadows, be about to tap her on the shoulder. But there was no sign of him. As she walked along, she could hear one of the women shouting angrily – someone had scratched her Volvo or something – but she didn't turn back. She just got inside and started to cry. Even as the tears poured down her face, she hoped that he might knock on the window and shock her out of her misery. But nothing happened beyond her loneliness and her shame.

She composed herself and headed home. As she did so, memories of her husband assaulted her. She remembered the way calls would come in the night, urging her to tell him this or that, and the way he would listen and nod as she fed him lies, trusting her because it never occurred to him not to. She remembered him sitting in the shitty office, worrying about bills that he never really had to pay, planning trips and holidays for the kids that would never happen now. She could imagine him sitting next to her, right there in the car, with his sweet, silly jokes.

Her thoughts were distracted by laughter outside the car; a happy gang of twenty-somethings lurched across the road in front of her at the traffic lights. She hunched down in the car, not wanting them to see her, but they were wrapped up in their own happy dramas.

She got home and dismissed Keira as quickly as she could. Normally they would have a chat before she headed off, but Carrie handed her the cash with few words and she was grateful to the girl for slipping away without any fuss. She checked on the kids, but couldn't stand the sight of her own empty bed, so headed back downstairs.

She was surprised to find David there. He was holding a bottle of beer from her fridge.

'You want one? Looks like you need one.'

She stared at him, confused. 'Hello?'

'I was worried about you. Well, they were worried about you. You were bawling away in the car so I got the call and came straight over. What's up?'

She hated him. However scared she was, she hated him more.

'I'm fine,' she said and walked to the kitchen to get her own beer.

'That's good,' he called after her and waited for her to re-appear. 'So what were all those tears about then?'

'The kids.'

'Understandable.'

'Still, they're not gone yet, are they?'

'Not yet,' he agreed. 'Then again, from what they're saying back in the office, I don't think it'll be long.'

'Why?'

'Why were you really crying, Carrie?'

'I told you.'

'Don't lie to me. Don't lie to us.'

He glugged some of the beer as though there were no threats in his words.

'I don't know what you want me to say.'

'You were fine when you left here, but apparently you were subdued and withdrawn at the book thing. So what happened?'

Someone at the book club was watching her. Reporting on her. Even there. 'Nothing happened. I'm . . . Jesus, fucking hell, David. I'm not a fucking robot. I do this work well and I find it hard sometimes. You all talk about it like it's a project, but, God, can't you see that it's not so simple?'

He watched her thoughtfully, then flopped down onto the sofa and patted the seat next to him.

'Excuse me?'

'Come and sit here with me.'

'Stop it. Stop being friendly! Stop screwing with me!'

'But I like you.'

'Fuck off!' And she threw the half-full bottle of beer at him. It missed but some liquid splashed across his chest and neck. He stood up, irritated.

'Carrie—'

'I don't care! I don't care what you think! What any of you think!' She screamed at the walls and the ceilings, to anyone listening. 'What did they do to him? You all talk like everything is straightforward and clean and professional, but you know it's not. You were meant to scare me last time, in the office, that's what you were really doing. That's what you all do. Whatever you say, what I've been doing has been . . . it's . . . there's something evil about it. Fucking horrible. Isn't there?'

Maybe men would burst in like before. She waited. Nothing.

'You'll wake the children, Carrie.' He went out to the kitchen, returning with a cloth to mop up the beer. 'It'll stink otherwise,' he said when he clocked her bemusement.

'What does it matter?'

He didn't reply, just diligently mopped up then went back to the kitchen and returned empty-handed, drying his hands on his trousers.

'You okay now?'

'No.'

'No. But you're calmer. Now: what made you cry?'

'I don't know. Really. Just being a part of that book group, everyone being so normal. I felt so alien to them.'

'But you've always been alien to them.'

'Yes. That's true.'

'You've never been a nice little mum. You know what you really are.'

'Yes.'

'So, what then?'

'I don't know. Am I not allowed to cry?'

'You were sobbing.'

Maybe they know, she thought. Maybe they put Ben there as a test. Maybe the more I deny seeing him, the worse it will be. Maybe Ben wasn't free. Maybe he was just like her. She considered this, then looked up at David and shrugged. She was like a naughty kid at school, busted and waiting for expulsion, too truculent to do anything more than shrug.

'We are all pawns, Carrie. We all feel like little cogs in someone else's wheel. You mustn't feel like you're alone. We are with you all the time.'

'Whether I want it or not.'

He acknowledged the comment with a tiny nod.

'I know you'll never tell me straight,' she said, 'but I have to ask. What has happened to Ben?'

He shook his head.

'Please. The reason I still have the kids is because he might come back. That's right, isn't it? He might come back and you don't know when.'

'We know everything.'

No, you don't, she thought. You didn't know that I saw him tonight. I'm certain.

David ran his hand over the empty beer bottle, as though he was considering a second. 'I keep thinking about the Second World War,' he said after a moment. 'You know those young men in the RAF who were sent out on bombing missions? Terrified on each mission – flying out in those flimsy planes, flying so low, dropping their load, rushing home, chalking off the missions, desperate for the war to end. They were scared witless, but they did it anyway, because it was their duty.' He shook his head, absorbed in his own story. 'What do you think it was like for the ones who flew over Dresden, slowly smashing that beautiful city to rubble? I don't see them laughing or cheering, somehow. I imagine their faces lit red by the flames, staring with those young, innocent eyes at the horror they'd unleashed, wondering how they'd do it again. And again. And again.'

He looked up at her, then checked his watch.

'I came because I was asked to. And I was glad to because I like you. But I did what I was asked. And I'll keep on doing it. Again. And Again. And you'll calm down. And you'll carry on. And you'll do what's asked of you. Again and again.' His voice softened. 'Carrie, it will never end. They're like the tide. I don't think what you do is evil. I think it's a stupid word, anyhow. And I don't think of myself as a bad person. I'm another cog, like you.'

He patted his pockets, checking he had everything. 'I hope I see you again. I don't know what the plan is. But if they say I can come back, I'll be glad.'

'But you'll do what they say.'

He nodded.

'That's me. That's you. That's everyone.'

TWENTY-ONE

Anna lay in her sleeping bag, thinking of her father, of his faltering gaze and the strange, awful silence that had engulfed and choked him. She had only ever thought of him as a man of utter confidence, until tonight. She tried to think back, remember other occasions when he had been cautious, unconfident, fearful even. But nothing came.

The night dragged past. She'd been surprised to find herself alone when she'd returned. She'd gone straight to her room and it was much later when she heard Toby and then Terry come back. There had been angry whispers which had then descended into giggles, but she couldn't hear what they were talking about. Finally, much later again, Ben returned. She only knew this because his presence silenced the boys. She heard a grunt and a sigh as he settled down on the floor, then nothing more.

She woke with a start to see light creeping in behind the metal shutters. When she went next door, the others were already up. Toby and Terry were crouched in a corner, watching Ben who was sat on his own, brooding.

'Morning,' she said quietly. The boys mumbled something back, but Ben didn't even acknowledge her presence. She went out to clean her teeth and have a pee, then returned to make herself some tea. The room was stuffy and smelly, and she had to fight the desire to hide away in her own quarters. She could feel the tension in the air. It was as if Ben were about to explode.

'Ben,' she said quietly.

If he heard her, he gave no sign of it. She'd made a decision in the night to tell him about her father, but his black mood made her uncertain. Her insides fluttered and when she put a hand on his shoulder he started in shock.

'What?' he barked. She took a step back from him.

'Alright, take a pill, mate,' said Terry from the other side of the room.

Ben glared at Terry for a moment before staring back down at the floor.

'What happened to you last night?' Anna asked.

'Nothing.' His clipped tone killed any response.

'Yeah, you were back well late,' said Toby. 'What's that about?'

'None of your business, kid,' Ben replied.

'You were back late too,' she said to Toby. He just stared down at the floor. Terry gave him a knowing nudge and the two boys started giggling. This seemed to wind Ben up even more.

'I'm going out,' he said, jumping to his feet.

'Where?' she asked.

'Anywhere, I don't know. Back to the lab, maybe.'

'What?' said Toby, scrambling up. 'Don't go there!'

'Well what else can we do?'

'But they'll get you!'

'So you stay here,' Ben replied. He was always more gentle with Toby, Anna noticed. He crossed his arms, then stuffed his hands in his pockets, uneasy as Toby pestered him.

'But I feel safer with you.'

'If you go out and they get you,' added Terry, 'then they'll know we're here.'

'You want to sit here for the next year?' Ben replied. 'What else have we got?'

We have my father, thought Anna. She was about to speak when Toby hit Ben hard in the arm.

'You selfish git!' he cried. Ben barely flinched. 'If you bugger off now, you won't come back, will you?'

'I will,' Ben replied, but Anna saw how he avoided the boy's eye.

'You've got it all sussed,' Toby continued, red-faced. 'You know what happened to you, sort of. I don't have that, I don't have anything. What are all these bloody scars about? How am I going to find that out without you?'

'I don't think chasing the past will help. From what I've found out, you're better off—'

'Don't give me advice when you're abandoning me.'

'I'm not your dad, kid!'

'Yeah, I got that. Thanks. But then you left your real kids, so what does it matter?'

Ben stiffened at this. 'Shut up. Yeah?'

'You think I'd want you to be my dad?'

'Okay, Toby,' said Anna, 'that's enough now.'

'I JUST WANT SOME FUCKING ANSWERS!' he shouted. 'I can't just bugger off like you. I'm too young, too . . . everything.

My dad wouldn't leave me. He was always there. Always. He was the best. And that doesn't make sense. Nothing, nothing makes ...' Toby stopped, upset. When he continued, he was quieter.

'Dad would always be testing me, always trying to make sure I was strong and independent and able to stand up for myself. He was watching out for me, see? Even when he was harsh and a bit cruel I knew he was just doing it to make me stronger. Like, one time, I was on a beach with him and I let my kite slip out of my hands. And it flew up, high up, away from the sea, landed on the top of the cliffs. And he—'

'Made you go get it with him,' said Ben.

'Yes,' said Toby, surprised by the interruption.

'And at the top, the field was covered in thistles and stinging nettles,' said Ben, 'but he made you walk through it anyway, even though you were in shorts and sandals.'

Anna felt the blood pounding in her head. She saw Toby stare in shock at Ben and noticed that Terry was also absorbed and confused by his story. She had to lean back against the wall for balance.

'I have the same memory,' said Ben to Toby, not noticing Anna. 'Me and my father. I let go of the kite because my hand was slippery from sunscreen.'

Anna felt the nausea rising inside her.

'I thought that one was real,' said Ben sadly.

Anna ran out of the room, pushing past them and staggering down the corridor. She was sick before she reached the end. Her stomach cramped and she doubled over, falling onto her knees. She didn't move until the final wave passed and she spat the last of it out onto the floor. She stood up, sucking in air, gazing down at the mess. What did it matter? She spat again for good measure.

When she returned to the room, they all stared at her, waiting for an explanation. She walked through to the other room and drank some water, swilling some around her mouth to clear away the taste. And then she went back and finished Ben and Toby's story for them. Their stunned expressions offered her no comfort.

'My father,' she explained, 'works for the company that owns the building we visited – the lab. I didn't know, I only found out yesterday. I think I'm the link between them and you. I think they've given you my memories.'

She shook slightly as she said the words. It was as though she was always out of breath.

Terry lit a cigarette. 'Why do you think they're your memories, Miss?' he asked.

'Because, well, it would make sense, that he took them from me. I'm the link to him and then he—'

'What if you're just like Ben and Toby?'

'But I don't have nightmares. Or any dreams or . . . anything like that.'

'Maybe the teacher bit is the dream. Maybe you were put there to meet Toby, to help him escape from his parents. Get him here.'

She looked at Toby and found he was watching her warily. They were suddenly isolated by suspicion.

'So what about Ben?' she argued. 'I didn't find him, did I?

'No, he just happened to spot Toby on the internet. Among a billion uploads, he just lucked out and saw him. Jesus, why didn't I see that before? No wonder he found us so easily. He was led all the way.'

'I don't understand what's going on,' Toby whimpered.

Anna turned to face Terry. 'What are you saying?'

'He's saying,' said Ben, taking Terry's cigarette off him and taking a deep drag, 'that we are doing just what they want. We always have. Awake or asleep.' He handed the cigarette back. 'You realise that means you're a part of their plans too.'

'Sod that,' Terry replied without much conviction.

'But why? What do they want?' she protested. 'It's like, we could run, we could go anywhere, but how would we know that we're still not just following orders?'

Ben just shrugged. It was as if he'd finally given up.

'We know what you were for, Ben,' said Terry. 'You killed people for them. I guess the point was, if you were ever caught, you'd look all confused and the papers would run a story about a nutter doing some random act of violence. God, I wonder how many of those were really true.'

'And me?' said Toby. 'I didn't hurt anyone. I just . . . got hurt.'

'Maybe you were in training, or something.' The words seemed stupid, but everything seemed stupid and everything seemed terrifying, and Anna had no idea how to tell the difference.

'What do we do?' she said. 'Do we stay here, do we run? What?'

'If they haven't got us, maybe they don't know where we are,' suggested Toby hopefully.

'Or they're waiting for the right time to use us.' Terry sucked on his cigarette, thinking. 'Maybe Toby's going to do some loony shoot-out at college or school.'

'No I won't.'

'Maybe you will. Maybe, Anna, maybe you'll . . .'

'Maybe I'll go mad and stab some of my pupils? It's ridiculous.

And it doesn't explain why we're here, all here together. And it doesn't explain why you're here too.'

'Why do all that stuff to me if I'm just going to end up dead anyhow?' Toby argued. 'This isn't right, we haven't got it right, there's something else, there has to be!'

'It's something to do with us being together,' said Ben. 'Us four. Why do they want us together?'

Anna looked at each of them in turn, noticing them doing the same, but they were banging against a locked door.

Finally Toby broke the silence. 'No one's making me do a thing.' He spat the words out.

'And how will you stop them?' said Terry.

'I'm free now.'

'Bullshit. None of us are free. No one.'

Anna imagined the kite slipping from her tiny hands and the way she lost sight of it in the glaring sun. She remembered turning to her father and the expression on his face as he dragged his eyes from his book to her tearful face. She tried to imagine Toby doing exactly the same thing, then Ben. She felt as though something had been stolen from her.

'Well, if they want to keep us together, then we should split up,' she said.

Ben nodded, pleased to hear this.

'But first, we're going to see my father.'

'Yeah, sweet,' sneered Terry. 'Gonna ask Daddy to make it all stop, are you?'

'In a manner of speaking,' Anna replied. Her voice was gruff.

'And what if he says no? I mean, he might be a big cheese, but I imagine that the company's plans might not include making U-turns because Daddy's girl says pretty please.'

Anna didn't bother to reply. She looked at Ben – are you ready?

'Seriously, Miss. What are you going to do when he blows smoke up your arse?'

'I'll kill him,' she replied. And right there, right then, she meant it. If he wasn't her father, if all her memories were false, then he was merely a stranger, a cruel torturer.

She buttoned up her coat and walked out. Her walk seemed more confident, as though she'd found an old part of herself from deep inside. Ben caught up with her and looked at her. She nodded at him, confident and purposeful. It was time for some answers.

TWENTY-TWO

The drive was understandably quiet. It had taken Ben ages to steal another car and Anna seemed far less confident when he finally picked her up. She fidgeted in the passenger seat, directing him towards her father's office. As they headed there, they worked out a plan. Henry Price was a man of habit and would leave the office for lunch at one o'clock. It was then that they would take him. Ben would knock him unconscious and they'd dump him in the boot before heading back to the squat. Once there, in one of the basement rooms, deep underground, isolated by thick concrete walls, they would finally get their answers. Ben didn't believe that Anna was actually capable of hurting her father. But he was. All she had to do was point him out.

The Rylance Group had several offices scattered across the globe. Henry worked in a smart but nondescript building in the centre of the city. They drove past it and Ben glanced through the glass frontage to see a bored security guard reading the paper at an otherwise unmanned desk. It looked just like any other office.

'He'll come out from the lift and stop to talk to that guy,' said Anna. 'He'll know his first name and all about his wife and family. He's like that.' It was sort of a boast and sort of an apology. Ben drove on and parked around the corner. He checked his watch and switched off the engine. They were early.

'I go up to him, stop him, and then you come from behind and you hit him,' said Anna.

'You said.'

'Yes, but I just . . . yes.'

She put her hands flat on her lap. And then her feet started tapping. 'Just don't hit him too hard, just enough to—'

'Anna, I know what to do.'

She drifted into silence for a while, then said, 'Should we be parked here this long? We might attract attention?'

He saw her feet go still for a moment then start to tap quietly again. He understood her nerves, he felt them himself. They were close to answers, to the truth. Finally. And he had no concerns about what might be needed to get it. A shiver slipped through him. Anna saw it.

'Are you scared too?' she asked.

'No,' he answered, but his voice was a little hoarse.

Ben stared ahead. They'd parked in a small side street between Henry's office and the small cafe that he liked to frequent. It was the obvious cut-through and he would come this way. Ben checked his watch. Half an hour to go, and then Anna would slip out of the car and confront her father as he turned into the street. And then he would get to work. He felt that shiver again and noticed that Anna was looking at him.

'I was thinking about my wife,' he said. 'I was thinking about the time we first met.'

It had been at a Christmas party; a work do at his boss's house which none of the guys from the garage had been keen on going to. But duty called and so they scrubbed up, put on their best clothes and made a deal to get out of there as soon as it didn't look too rude. Ben had always been awkward at those sort of things and soon found himself standing alone, clutching a warm glass of white wine, watching his workmates chat happily to strangers. Everyone else smiled and chatted as though it were the easiest thing in the world. He had tried to join in, but a faltering conversation with a smart woman who kept staring over his shoulder soon spluttered into silence and he was back on his own, in the corner, trying to edge his way out of everyone's eyeline but being pushed forward by an over-sized prickly plant in a huge terracotta pot. It was as though the plant were egging him on: go socialise, loser.

And then this pretty girl came over to him and started laughing. 'Who the hell keeps a bloody cactus in their living room?' she said. It was as though she could read his mind.

She chatted to him without the usual reserve or clever small-talk and he found that he was able to talk back. She told him her name was Carrie and that he was never, ever allowed to call her Caroline. She was there because her brother played football with the boss and she felt as out of place as he did. She had this funny way of touching her ear, as though she were adjusting an earring. It meant her shoulders would often hunch up, as if she were nervous, scared of something. It reminded Ben of a little mouse. Later, for many years, he used to call her Little M.

They stuck together for the rest of the night. She joked that they were the only sane ones – or the ultimate losers. And Ben thought she was lovely. She never turned away to check out other people and the conversation never felt forced or boring. They just clicked.

At the end of the evening, just as he was planning to give her his phone number, or maybe ask for hers (the whole thing was a little stressful), he was suddenly dragged into the middle of the room by his boss who was now hilariously drunk. He had his arm around Ben's neck, pulling other guys from the garage to him, telling them all how much he loved them, how much he owed them, and other drunken bollocks. One of the guys told him he'd like a pay rise, and for a moment it all looked as if it was going to get ugly, which made the whole thing even funnier. But then Ben looked around and realised that Carrie had gone. His boss still had a tight grip around his shoulder and would probably have fallen over if he'd tried to get away. Everyone was laughing and joking, but Ben was gutted.

When he finally pulled himself away, he knew it was much too late. He got out as quickly as he could, not bothering to put on his coat even though it was freezing outside. He stomped down the road, trying not to slip on the snow and ice, cursing to himself. But then he heard a shout. He turned and saw that it was Carrie. She came up to him with a face like thunder.

'You're a prick,' she said.

'Okay . . .'

'Do you get on with everyone, is that it? You find people easy to meet and forget?'

'No, no, not at all,' he stammered. 'It's the opposite.'

'So why did you just ignore me like that?'

Ben tried to explain himself, stammering and faltering as he did, waving his hands in the air. It was a pretty pathetic explanation and he knew then the words weren't doing what he wanted, which made him even more expressive and ridiculous. Eventually he gave up and let out a sad sigh.

'Cos, I'm a bit crap, I guess.'

Somehow, it seemed to do the trick. Carrie smiled. She looked so pretty there in the snow, shivering with the cold. She looked up at him, curious.

'Are you going to hurt me?'

'Never.'

'Promise.'

'I promise I'll never hurt you.'

And then she raised herself up on tiptoe and kissed him. A tiny, delicate kiss. Her lips were freezing and he realised she must have been waiting outside for him for ages. He pulled his coat over her and took her back to his cramped, dirty flat. She laughed at the socks on his radiator and pulled on his jeans which were so big on her that they came up to her chest. And she let him take them off and make love to her.

'And she never left,' he said to Anna, sadly.

He leaned back in his seat, looking down at the small gold band on his finger, twirling it with his thumb and forefinger.

'Do you think my story is real?' he said without looking at her. 'It feels real. It's not special or amazing in any way. So why shouldn't it be?'

Anna was quiet. Ben looked out of the window. The street was deserted. When Henry came, Ben doubted they'd have to worry about other people.

'How about the time when my son was born? Joe?' he asked. 'I was given three days off. We never left the house. Our little baby just lay on the bed between us and I don't think he cried once the whole time. We would play him our favourite songs, sing and dance for him. It was like we were wrapped up in this magic bubble and the rest of the world couldn't get in. And Carrie was so naughty. She'd be like "See, little Joe, this is what happens when I stroke your daddy's penis." And I'd be all blushing and embarrassed cos it seemed so wrong! And she'd laugh at me. Laugh and laugh. Jesus.'

He twisted the ring on his finger.

'You think that's from someone else?' he asked. 'You think some woman we've never met said that, did all that with some other stranger and now it's in my head?'

'I don't know,' was Anna's feeble reply. He nodded. How could she?

'And then there are the other things I remember. Ones I don't want to tell you about cos they're cruel and scary. The thing is, the longer I've been away from Carrie, the more I remember all that stuff. Like how I was before they got to me. How I got around, what I did.'

His face twisted with revulsion.

'It comes back stronger each day. And so it starts to feel more comfortable too. Like old clothes or something. I don't like what I was but ... shit.'

He scratched his head then clasped his hands together.

'The more I remember what I was like and the more I feel like that person, the more Carrie seems to drift away. I feel like I'm forgetting bits of her. Like there's only so much room in my head and as the old shit comes back so it's pushing out all of the bits about her. And my kids too. I was lying in bed this morning and I couldn't remember what colour eyes my little girl has.'

He felt so constricted in the car, he wanted to pound the steering wheel. He wanted to smash windows and hear things break.

'Blue,' he added. 'They're blue.' And suddenly Emma's giggle drifted through his head and he was smiling, quiet and calm again.

Anna gave him a tremulous smile, and he nodded, grateful for her companionship.

'Is she pretty?' she asked.

'She's my little girl. She's perfect. But one day I'm scared I'm going to wake up and she'll be gone. She'll have just gone from my mind. Carrie too, and Joe. And I'll never even know they ever existed. I'll just be him, the old me. I'll just be a thug and a drunk. Just wake up one morning and it will all be gone.'

He looked down at the gold ring next to his bruised, scarred knuckles.

'I don't know how to stop it. I've started writing it down, everything I can remember. But I feel like I'm sliding down this sandbank. And it doesn't matter how hard I try to claw my way back up, at the end, she'll go. I'll wake up and she'll be gone. It's like she's dying in front of me, bit by bit, wasting away.'

Tears welled up in his eyes. He wiped them away and then checked his watch again.

'Come on, it's nearly time.'

He knew that Anna was still watching him and he felt her hand go to his and give it a delicate squeeze. And he knew also that this was all she could offer. So he cleared his throat and muttered something about checking the side mirrors. He couldn't think about any of that now.

About ten minutes later, Henry Price turned the corner and walked into the side street, bang on time. Ben nudged Anna and she stepped out of the car, just as he reached them.

'Daddy,' she said, as Ben slipped out, unseen, and approached Henry from behind him. He saw Henry smile at his daughter, delighted to see her, before he hit him hard on the back of the head. He crumpled with little more than a grunt and Ben grabbed him before he hit the ground. Then he pulled him up into his arms and looked up at Anna to see that she was frozen in shock.

'Anna, the boot!'

His words galvanised her. She ran to the back of the car, opened the boot, and Ben heaved Henry's body into it, dumping it inside as delicately as he could.

Moments later they were driving off. Ben waited to hear sirens, glanced around for cars that would suddenly intercept them, and checked his mirrors for the quiet vehicles that might follow from a suitable distance. But there were no interruptions to their journey. And there was no noise from the boot.

Later they stopped in a lay-by. No one could see the car here and Ben opened the boot. He stripped a still-unconscious Henry of everything, throwing all of his belongings onto the roadside before they drove off again.

They then made a long, meandering circle back towards the squat to flush out any followers. Neither spoke. Ben's eyes scanned the road and junctions ahead while nagging thoughts pushed and prodded at him.

'I thought I was going to recognise him,' he said.

'I'm sorry?'

He heard surprise in her voice and turned to her. She was holding a knife in her hands, the one he'd put in the glove compartment. For emergencies. She was white as a sheet. She looked at him, then the knife, and then shoved it away again. She's having second thoughts, he guessed.

'Your father,' he said, trying to distract her. 'I thought he was going to be someone I'd met.'

'But he wasn't.'

He shook his head. 'I thought it would make sense, when I saw him.' His fingers tapped on the wheel.

'What are you thinking?' she asked.

'It's been too easy.'

'Yes,' she nodded, fiddling with her fingers.

'If they're watching us, why let us get away? I don't get it.' He looked around, but the road was now completely clear. The calm silence seemed all the more sinister for it.

'He'll tell us,' Anna said. 'You'll get him to, I know you will.'

But Ben wasn't so sure. He frowned, trying to see a pattern, some design in all of this. The car passed a big advertisement hoarding that promised bargains and happiness.

'You're one, I'm one,' Ben said. 'Toby's one, Terry could be one, who knows? Is everyone—' He stopped himself, unconvinced by his train of thought, then started again. 'They must have put us together for a reason. We're doing something, or we're in place to do something . . .' He let out a stressed sigh, cursing quietly at so many dead-ends.

'You found us because they led you to Toby on the internet, is that right?' Anna asked, and Ben nodded. 'And what before that? If they led you there, they must have led you to whatever happened before.'

'No, no, before I was just running. I was holed up with this strange old guy and . . .'

Ben fell silent. He drove on, almost on autopilot, as his mind raced back to the B&B and the sound of lapping waves. The roads were busier now as they got closer to the squat, and the car slowed in the traffic. Ben glanced left and right. There was nothing particularly untoward. Two young men were pushing each other, swearing and scuffling over the contents of a plastic bag, but Ben wasn't interested. His mind was busy with its own battles.

'Anna. Describe the scientist to me. The one who led the experiments.'

'I've never met him.'

'I mean, from the way I've talked about him. And Toby. Tell me what we've said.'

'Well, you said he was old. And kind. Or kindly. He had perfect manners, you both said. Something about classical music, and the nurses being intimidated by him. What else . . . Oh, he cared for you, and . . . I don't know . . . What is it?'

'Please. What else?'

'I don't know. Really. That's all you said. Oh, Toby said he always fidgeted. No, not fidget, but he said he was always doing stuff with his fingers. And his hands.'

Ahead was a bus stop. Ben's hands felt light and shaky on the wheel and he had to stop the car and think. He pulled in and parked, then put his head in his hands, closing his eyes and picturing the musty old B&B where an old man, his only true friend in the world, would laugh and joke about the good old days, his fingers twitching excitedly in the air. Ben pictured his face: sweet, old doddery Edward. And as he did so, he remembered a different man with the exact same face staring down at him in a white coat, his hands waving in the air to the music, asking polite questions before indicating that it was time for his sedation.

He knew that Anna would be staring at him, desperate to know what was going on, but he kept his eyes clenched shut, trying to pull answers from the darkness.

'They needed me to be the muscle,' he said, his nose squashed against the wheel. 'They needed Terry to help you, give you the clues and make you believe that you were doing it for real. They needed Toby to make you care enough to do it. And they needed you, Anna, to kill your own father.'

He opened his eyes and saw that her mouth twitched with a smile that died as the words hit her.

'How can you be sure?'

'I can't. I don't know anything except that all I've done, everything, has been planned by them. So, if we're planning on hurting or even killing your dad, then that's planned by them too.'

'So is there nothing we can do?'

He was silent at this.

'Ben. If we're already doing what they want ... then what do we do?'

Ben looked down at his battered fists. They seemed to be the only things he had left. He pushed against the car door and stumbled out, not bothering to shut it as he walked away. He heard Anna calling after him but he ignored her cries. If they wanted Lee back, then they were going to get him in spades.

Inside the car, Anna called after Ben, watching him break into a run then disappear into the crowd. She sat limply in the passenger seat, alone and bewildered. She didn't know what to do. If every movement, any action, was predetermined by others, then what could she possibly do that wouldn't simply be following their wishes?

A few minutes later, a car pulled in behind her. Three suited men strolled towards her with an easy purpose about them. The first was a good-looking man in his twenties. He opened the door as though he were a valet at an expensive hotel.

'Miss Price? Are you alright?'

She nodded, feeling stupid. She glanced behind her and saw the other two men were opening the boot of the car. She wondered how they had a key to do so.

'Don't worry, Miss Price. Would you like to come with me?'

She got out because she didn't know what else to do.

'Is my father okay?' she asked, rather pathetically. It struck her that she wasn't scared. They'd caught her, finally, but she felt nothing. Numb.

'Yes, Ma'am, everything is fine.'

TWENTY-THREE

Toby began to fidget roughly one minute after Anna and Ben had marched out of the room and left him and Terry behind in the squat. He sat down on the floor, got up, rolled up his sleeping bag, puffed up his pillow and then, fresh out of ideas, sat down again. Terry was hunched over his computer, obsessing about some new mind-altering chemical that 'they' were putting into children's cereal, and didn't want to be disturbed. Toby muttered to himself, '*I'm nobody's puppet, I'm nobody's puppet.*' He muttered it over and over as he wandered along the corridors, looking for something to do or someone to talk to.

He stared at the slogans on the walls.

Our Principles Are Not Negotiable!

Amandla!

One Nation Under CCTV.

The words seemed empty and smug. All these stupid words and catchphrases were just a substitute for action. Stupid, idiotic, clichéd hippies, he thought, just wasting their time in here with their clever, empty phrases. Too clever to do anything.

He thought about his parents, and he imagined them laughing about him. Why didn't we go for them? he wondered. They knew more than they said, he was sure of that. Why didn't Ben and Anna listen to him? Why go without him?

Toby created furious arguments and answers which defied logic, his anger focused on two people, fired by Anna's words: 'I'll kill him.' Her words pushed him along the corridors to the exit. He unscrewed the metal door to the outside, unseen by anyone.

Standing in front of the squat, a little dazed, a little scared at how he'd be able to travel alone, Toby nearly turned back. But then he felt the cash in his pocket and remembered the night before. Stung by shame and anger, he marched ahead.

The night before had started badly and then got worse. After Anna and Ben had dropped them off, Terry had bumped into Daz who had invited them to a 'session at his pad'. At first they were both excited, imagining naked chicks handing out spliffs and free love. And while their hopes were raised when Daz opened the door and they spied two women kissing behind him, they soon found themselves being berated by bearded men with pseudo-intellectual diarrhoea. Everyone seemed angry, no one seemed to like anyone else, and even the massive black dude who was smoking something fruity refused to share his junk with them, calling them 'liggers'.

It wasn't long before Terry and Toby were standing alone, alienated, by the door, ignored by everyone. They did try to join in, but what they thought was a harmless conversation would suddenly split into raised voices. Phrases like, *Could you be any more bourgeois?* or *You just can't free yourself from your colonial instincts, can you, General?* spilled out of any and every conversation. And when they tried to talk to the lesbians again, they were sent packing at the line, 'Every man's a potential rapist, accept it and stop apologising.'

Soon, he and Terry slipped out and returned to their room, where they sat on their sleeping bags without much to say.

'So much for the revolution,' said Toby. Terry smiled, powering up his computer. Toby went over. 'Got any games?' he asked, crouching down next to him, but Terry pushed him away. His screen fizzed with data that Toby couldn't understand.

He lay back on the floor. Someone had painted various constellations against a dark-blue wash. It was a paltry substitute for the real thing. He sat up again and threw an empty can at Terry. It missed but Terry glanced up at him.

'What?'

'Let's do something.'

'Go hang out with the dykes if you're bored.'

'I dare you to go down there and call them that to their faces.'

'No chance. They'd wear my nuts round their neck as a bloody trophy.'

'Terry, this is shit. I'm so bored.'

Terry shut the laptop. 'So what do you want to do?'

'Go out.'

'No way.'

'What, we're just going to sit in this shit-house for the rest of our lives?'

'Last time we went out, you pooped in your pants.'

'I didn't, and screw you very much, but that was different.'

They were grinning now. 'Come on, mate. Let's go out, sink a few. Be normal. No one's going to find us.'

Toby jumped up and rushed over to Ben's bed, pulling out a roll of notes from the bottom of his sleeping bag.

'You know that guy kills people with his bare hands?'

'Come on ... please ...'

Terry eyed the money in his hands. Toby winked at him.

'You know you want to.'

'Okay,' said Terry, 'one pint. But if you ever tell Ben or Anna then I'll cut your throat while you're sleeping.'

Tiffany's was half dead when they trotted up to the door, and Toby could tell that the bouncer was giving serious consideration to barring them. But then he sighed and ushered them in, muttering something about Toby's age. Once inside, they ordered the strongest lager available and sat excitedly at a table. It was the beginning of a great adventure. They were onto their third pretty soon, and if they had ever planned on leaving early those thoughts were long gone. Toby was so happy to be there, he even let Terry loose with his latest conspiracy theory about the way Hollywood deliberately posted 9/11 images into their movies, although it wasn't exactly clear why.

Toby was about to question him about this when Terry stiffened.

'Bloody hell, matey. Bird o'clock.'

Toby followed his gaze and saw two girls, late teens, who were watching them. As he caught the eye of one of them, she looked away but then glanced back at him a moment later. To Toby's horror, Terry gave them a big grin and a wink.

'That's it, screw the New World Order, we're in,' he said. 'Come on.'

He got up and headed over towards them and Toby had no choice but to follow. The girls introduced themselves as Bea and Lara. Toby sat awkwardly at the table, but slowly relaxed when they laughed at his jokes and when he realised they weren't nearly as old as they first appeared. When they went off together to the loo, Terry patted him warmly on the shoulder.

'You're in, nice one. I'll have Lara, you can have the other one.'

The other one. Bea. Straight dark hair, a small run of spots on her jaw line and breasts pushed forward by a low-cut top.

'Terry, I'm not really that, um, you know ... experienced, when it comes to birds.'

Terry knocked down his beer. 'Mate, relax, you're the shy type, some girls dig that. Stop worrying. We'll just get them a bit more oiled and then see where it takes us.'

Toby did what he was told. He glanced nervously at Bea every now and then, especially when Terry suddenly leaned over the table and kissed Lara hard on the mouth and she responded enthusiastically.

'For fuck's sake,' screamed Bea. 'Get a room!'

'That's the plan!' leered Terry, and all four of them laughed, Toby a little less enthusiastically than the others.

More drink. Toby's head started to spin as Lara told them all about her favourite characters in some American reality show and who was dating who (which Terry seemed to find fascinating). He didn't understand a word of it. He looked around; everywhere people chatted and laughed animatedly. So this is what it's like, he thought. And then he felt a hand on his leg, under the table. It was Bea. She looked at him with a smile so shy he almost didn't recognise her. So he smiled back, squeezed her hand, and then suddenly she was laughing, pulling her hand away so she could wave her hands around, emphasising just how incredible some film was.

Later, he went for a pee, and when he returned only Bea was at the table.

'They left,' she said with a coy smile, taking another sip from her glass, and Toby realised he was meant to take the lead here. His heart hit his boots. Clueless.

'You, er, you want to go too?'

'You got a place?'

'Yeah but no.'

'That's just what your mate said.'

'Right.'

'So what are we going to do?'

Oh Christ, oh no, here comes the laughter, he thought, here comes the sickening moment. At least Terry's not here to witness it. Just grab your coat and run.

'If we go back to mine,' Bea said, 'you can't speak. Mum's home, but she's always on the diazepam and if we're quiet she'll never know.'

'Cool.'

'You have to swear though.'

'I swear. I swear!'

'And you can't stay the night.'

'Er, alright.'

If this was a trap, Toby's drunken mind thought, then it was the sweetest and cruellest trap ever. She stood and put on her coat, pulling her hair free. When they got outside she nestled into him and pushed her lips to his, her tongue snaking into his mouth. It was his first kiss.

Bea didn't hold his hand as they took the bus back to her

home. She chatted about school and how annoying her teachers were. He murmured the appropriate comments, but all he could think about was what she would look like naked and how her breasts would feel in his hands.

Bea lived in a house not much different from his last one. They crept up the stairs and slipped into her bedroom. And as Bea slipped off her top and turned her back to him as she unclasped her bra, so his eyes were dragged away to the little-girl posters and the teddy bears on the bed. And then she was naked and to him she looked like a model in a magazine. His legs were shaking and he was praying the jeans were hiding this. Her hands went to his belt and undid it but then she turned and rushed across the bed to a drawer where she pulled out a condom.

Toby could feel how hard his heart was pounding in his chest.

'You're beautiful,' he said. She put a finger to her lips, irritated, and he gestured a 'sorry' back at her.

'So ... ?' she mouthed, and then whispered loud enough for him to hear, 'Get your kit off.'

But he couldn't. There was a scar on his arm that was suddenly burning and he didn't want to ruin this moment, didn't want to see the disgust on her face when she saw what was underneath his clothes. But here was a naked bloody girl on the bed, holding a condom and wanting him to screw her brains out. He wanted to touch her so badly, wanted to kiss her again, put his tongue in her mouth, taste her. But still he didn't move. He knew that this was as close as he'd ever get to being normal.

Bea looked at him warily and pulled the sheets over her body.

'What are you doing?' she whispered harshly at him.

Toby didn't say anything for a while. He just stood there and began to cry. It was too late now to do anything else. Eventually he looked up and saw her staring at him with worried, hostile eyes. Yes, he thought, that's more like it.

'Normal service is resumed,' he said. She didn't understand and just glared at him, like the kids all did at school. He noticed his belt and flies were undone and wearily reorganised himself, then he turned and left, walking down the stairs and out into the darkness. As he went, he thought he heard her laugh.

When he got back to the squat that night, he was all alone. Anna might have been next door but he didn't want to disturb her and he was happier to be alone anyhow. Terry returned about an hour later and although Toby let him pretend that everything had been brilliant, inside he seethed.

Marching away from the squat the next day, he heard Bea's laugh in his head. He saw the sneer on her face, the way she'd pulled the sheets over her to protect her from him. He was so angry and ashamed that he took two buses in the wrong direction before he realised his mistake. Eventually, however, Toby reached his parents' house. It was getting dark and they hadn't yet drawn the curtains. He could see his mother inside, folding one of his dad's shirts. He watched her for a moment before going to the front door and ringing the bell. It struck him that most kids his age had their own key and he wondered why he didn't, but then the door opened and his mother was there. She gasped, her hand fluttering to her mouth before grabbing him and holding him tight to her.

'I've been so worried,' she said. 'Oh my love, oh my darling boy. Michael! Toby's home! He's home!'

Michael came running through and Toby couldn't help but grin at their warmth. He needed it. But as his father embraced him, he remembered the way his hand would rest on the back of his neck, guiding him this way and that. Controlling him. And he heard Bea's cruel laugh again.

'Where have you been?' Laura said, shutting the front door behind him and ushering him inside. 'Oh, you're freezing!'

He let his mother fuss over him, pulling off his wet clothes before running a bath for him. It was as though nothing had happened. But this time, he wasn't waking with a start, with no inkling of what he'd been through. He had entered the house with eyes wide open. He stood in his old bedroom and looked around at a place that should have felt so familiar but which now felt fake, like a wobbly film set that he could push to the ground. He sat at his desk and pulled out a drawer, turning it over to see where he used to hide his diary. He wondered why he'd allowed himself to be conned for so long. Because he was young. Because he was little and gullible and stupid. Because they'd trapped him and hidden him from real life. The anger snapped on again and he left his room to find them.

Michael was on the phone when Toby came down the stairs, but he hastily hung up. Laura appeared from the kitchen.

'Are you hungry? You must be starving. What can I make you?'

'Don't you want to know where I've been?' he asked.

'I assumed you'd tell us when you thought the time was right,' his mother replied. Her face clouded with that hurt, anxious look she always had. But Toby's emotions would not be calmed so easily.

'I'm not all beaten up, like I usually am,' he said. 'Am I?'

'Well, that's something, yes,' she replied.

He was studying their faces, waiting for the performance to end. But they just stared silently back at him.

'I keep remembering things,' he said, his voice a little jittery with emotion. 'Loads of stuff, all coming back to me. Like this one time, I remember climbing this building – so high, Jesus! – and then climbing along this rail and hanging there, just hanging there for ages, until I fell. Why did you make me do that?'

'We didn't make you do anything, darling,' Laura said.

'Yes, you did. I know you did.'

His father put a hand on her elbow. 'It's time we stopped this.'

'No, we're fine,' she said. Her voice had an edge to it now though.

'I know who my parents really are,' said Toby. He felt like crying. Like screaming.

'Is that what you think?' his father replied.

'Yeah. Yeah, I do. So who the fuck are you?'

'Okay. Enough,' his father said. 'Your name is Toby?'

'Yes,' he replied, confused by the question. But something stirred in him when he heard it.

'Toby Mayhew?'

He felt calmer all of a sudden, but then his mother's voice cut through. 'Oh for God's sake, we don't need any of that.'

The anxieties lurched back into his stomach. His dad stared angrily at his mum.

'What?' she snapped. 'What's he going to do? You think we can't handle him without having to resort to that?'

'What are you talking about?' Toby asked, but they ignored him.

'I'm doing what they said we should,' his father replied with a shrug of his shoulders.

'Oh, yes, you're always good at kissing arse,' she replied. She sounded so different now, Toby thought. She looked at him and her gaze was cold and impatient.

'Go to bed, will you?'

'No,' he said. 'No, I want you to tell me the truth. For once, tell me the truth.'

'Laura . . .' His father raised an eyebrow. But she waved an angry hand at him.

'So he finds out, so I tell him some things. And . . . ? Who cares. They take him away, wipe his mind clean, and then he's back to us with the same old, same old. Don't you get fed up pretending? Making up stupid meetings and bogus reports for that non-existent bloody job?'

Toby couldn't believe what he was hearing.

'At least you came back, I suppose,' his mother continued. 'Makes some things easier; less questions, less paperwork.'

'Mum . . .'

'What? What do you want?'

This wasn't how it was meant to be. They were meant to be ashamed, he was the one who should be confident and angry.

'I met another one, like me,' he said, trying to will some control into his voice. 'And he'd been in the army and they made him do things to people. And we're going to stop you people.'

She didn't even bother to reply.

'But what I don't get is why. All those things I did . . .' He pulled at his shirt, exposing the scars that littered his frame. 'What were they for? What was I made for?'

'What makes you think you were made for anything?' she replied.

'Oh, Jesus,' said Michael. 'I'm going to have to call in about this.'

But he didn't move. Toby had always thought of him as being in charge, but now he twisted his fingers unhappily, waiting to be told what to do.

'I must have been doing all those things for something,' Toby said. 'There must have been a plan, right?'

'Listen to him,' she scoffed.

'No, no, come on. What were you going to make me do?'

She shrugged.

'What?' he cried.

'As far as I know, there were no plans.'

The words made no sense.

'His face!' She laughed cruelly. 'Little boy, you were just a test.'

'Laura, shut up,' his dad hissed.

'He thinks he's special,' she jeered. 'Listen, love, you know those models they have in cars, the ones where they drive into walls and then inspect the damage? That's you. That's all you are.'

Toby was silent, his mind spinning and empty. A crash test dummy. He felt sick.

'They just . . . a test?'

'A lab rat,' she said, and it felt like she took pleasure in the words. 'As you are, you're a puny specimen. But then they play with your mind and you seem to be able to do so much more. So they wind you up and see how far you go.'

Toby saw himself jumping gleefully from that bridge.

'They tried it on the military, this sort of thing – adrenalin patches and so on. But the public are rather attached to their good old boys.'

He imagined himself diving off that bridge again and again until finally his body snapped and could no longer be sewn back together.

'For God's sake,' his father snapped. 'You can't talk to him like this.'

'A rat?' Toby spluttered; but his mother had turned away from him.

'So he hears the truth for once. So what? I'm so fed up with pretending all the bloody time. Go on, make your call, you pathetic little man.'

Toby's head was spinning. This couldn't be right. There had to be something, a point to his life. Some bigger reason that would explain everything. But his mother's cruel taunts had exposed a horrifying alternative. No point, no story, no end, no answers.

He pictured Bea, scowling at him from the bed. He thought of Ben and the way he and Anna had abandoned him. He thought of all the schools he'd attended and the same cold callousness that had greeted him at every one of them. This was his life. He could run, bolt for the door, but wherever he was, the truth was the same.

His parents continued to argue while he stared at his feet. He heard his father shout something about 'protocol', but he didn't care any more. He went back up the stairs. There was a bath waiting for him. He sat on the edge, his finger trailing in the water. Below he heard more shouting.

Is this it? Is this the rest of my life? He tried to picture different endings, different versions where he was heroic or victorious or simply significant somehow. His finger drew an invisible circle in the water and his mind was blank, empty, useless.

Just a test.

He went back out and stood at the top of the stairs. He saw his mother stride past without bothering to look up at him. He was home after escaping and they had no interest in him at all.

Soon he would be taken back to the lab.

He pictured waking up the next morning, sore and confused. He thought about returning to school where Jimmy Duthie and his pals would be waiting to bash him up again. He shuddered as he imagined the next tests that might be planned for him.

No happy endings.

He found what he wanted in the bathroom cabinet. He closed the door on the bathroom and realised for the first time that there was no lock on the door. Still it didn't stop him.

He pulled the razor blade across his wrists. It was tougher to do than he expected and he had to cut harder and deeper before the blood really began to pour. He did the same to his legs, just above the ankle. The blade stung like hell, but he didn't cry.

His head began to get woozy and his feet slipped slightly on the wet floor. He put his hand out and banged the door. From below he heard his mother call out his name. He heard the exasperation in her tone and was pleased.

Feet clumped up the stairs without hurry. But this could not be undone, not now.

His eyesight was fading. He sat on the edge of the bath, only just able to maintain his balance. Things drifted into black and white.

Toby smiled as his mother pushed open the door and stepped in, only to slip and fall. He looked down at the floor. It was everywhere. He had no idea there would be so much. It was a delightful surprise.

His mother started screaming as Toby's eyes fluttered closed and he fell back into the bath. He could feel her clawing at his body, trying to pull it out of the water. But she was too late, he could feel it. He smiled, delirious.

He was telling his own stories now.

TWENTY-FOUR

Anna sat in the empty boardroom of the Rylance Group's central office. It was high up, with tall windows which offered spectacular views of the city below. The room was silent but for a steady low hum from the air-conditioning system. The long, polished table could seat at least twenty and she cut a small, fragile figure as she waited. Her hands were not tied and no one guarded the door. Since the young man had helped her into the car, everyone had been polite and respectful. A jug of coffee and a small pot of hot milk had been put in front of her and eventually she helped herself.

Her father came in. He was dressed in his suit again, with a swelling bruise under his jaw. He sat next to her and gazed at her with such affection that she wondered whether she had imagined her murderous plot.

'I was going to kill you,' she said. Her words sounded ridiculous to her now.

'Yes.'

'So, why are you smiling?'

'It was planned this way.'

'For me to kill you?'

'For you to try. When you had reached the point where you intended to kill me, then the experiment was over. It was a finishing line, if that makes sense.'

'No. It doesn't make any sense at all.'

'No, it won't. I'm sorry. But you've proved today that you were right. I was against it, I was so anxious, but you were always bolder than me.'

He poured himself a coffee.

'Who am I?'

He looked at her. 'You're Anna Price. My daughter. But it's a good question.'

'You know about my memories, don't you?'

He nodded.

'You know that I remember the same things as the others?'

'Yes.'

'So, what does that mean? Does that mean they're mine? Are they real memories or are they stolen from someone else?'

'What do you think?'

'Are you going to answer every question with another question?'

He placed the cup down on the saucer. 'I'm sorry. Ask away.'

'That time on the beach when I was a little girl, was it me?' she asked. 'Or was it someone else? We came up with a phrase for it in the squat, for Ben and Toby. We called them "sleep-walkers". It seemed a nice way to describe something so dreadful. Am I one of them? Or is it me on the beach?'

Henry didn't reply for a moment. He stared out at the city and she wondered if the delay was theatrical.

'The memory you refer to belongs to a man in his forties called Steven Dawson.'

Anna's mind reeled. The light was too bright, there was no air in the room.

'Who?'

'He's no one important. The memory you have of a pet rabbit, the one where you leave the latch unlocked and in the morning—'

'In the morning it had been savaged by a fox.'

'Yes. That came from a woman called Karen Dixon. They are just average people who do not even know why we have borrowed and copied their remembrances. We have thousands of these, all from different people.'

'So I'm not your daughter.'

'Of course you're my daughter. I love you. And this, this phrase of yours, sleepwalking, it demeans you. You don't understand how special you are.'

'Oh, I'm a special sleepwalker, am I?'

'No. Yes . . . God, you're not a sleepwalker, it's everyone else, down there, them, they're . . .' He sighed, frustrated. 'Look. The programme is not what you think. You imagine all sorts of things, like a child imagines monsters under the bed. But the programme is entirely, absolutely for the greater good.'

'I don't believe you.'

'It is designed to help certain individuals who have suffered extreme trauma. It's an ongoing project, intended to move beyond the old-fashioned limits of therapy and psychoanalysis. We're removing the trauma from a patient's mind, giving him or her a chance to live free of the memories and experiences that have scarred them.'

'What?'

'It is a project in development which intends to control a damaged mind. To remove what is malign and hurtful and replace it with positive, empowering emotions. Your friend Ben was badly injured when fighting in Iraq. His friends died slowly and painfully in front of him and he has been unable to overcome the experience. We have been trying to help him. Toby too. After the death of his parents in a road accident, he has struggled to cope with the trauma and has moved from foster home to foster home.'

'And me? What was my trauma?'

'You have no trauma, Anna.'

'I don't understand.'

'The head of this project, the pioneer. It's you.'

Anna stared at him, dumb with shock.

'It was in this very boardroom that you explained the project, explained its goals and ambitions to a collection of sponsors in the hope of raising funds for further research. To prove the validity of the project, you proposed to have the work done on yourself. You would have your memories removed and we would watch as an unlikely English teacher inevitably plotted the murder of her own father. Your experiences would be recorded and documented. A camera was placed inside your television set as a means to this end.'

The coffee tasted too bitter. 'Is there any water?' Henry pressed a button on the phone and after a few moments the door opened and a young man entered with a jug and glasses. Behind him, Anna saw a figure walk past the doorway and pause for a moment. It was Kath. But she was dressed differently – smarter and with her hair straightened. She saw Anna and nodded, a little bashful, almost apologetic. And then, in a second, she was gone.

Henry poured her a glass of water and she drank thirstily.

'The programme,' he continued, 'meant that you would live as a completely different person, someone with a different character, different friends, employment, accommodation. A life that had no recall of any past experiences beyond your relationship with me. I wouldn't let you cut all our ties, I couldn't bear it. You chose an English teacher. We were all surprised.'

'Why?'

'Because, you were, you are, very different.'

'What am I like?'

'You run the research and development department of a multinational corporation, specialising in neurology. You run a team of thirty of the brightest minds in the country. You have a beautiful flat in the smartest part of town. You're driven and tough and ambitious. And you don't suffer fools.'

'I don't think I sound very nice.'

'You're not nice. Nice is . . .' he sighed. 'You are brilliant.' He reached for her hands and she was too confused to stop him. 'I love you. You are my girl. We've only had each other since your mother died and these last couple of years have been terrible. Looking at this nervy stranger in those terrible clothes.'

Anna stared down at her clothes. She'd always thought she'd dressed rather well.

'Now it's over, you can come back. The real you. You can come back and show what an incredible success your work is.'

'It's all about trauma victims?' she could hear the incredulity in her voice.

'Yes.'

'I'm not sure I believe you.'

'Come back to me, Anna. Let me find you again and you'll see everything clearly.'

She sipped on the water. 'What if you're lying?'

'Anna—'

'What if I am the person you say. This big cheese. But what if I'm not into therapy? What if I'm into brainwashing, for different purposes ...'

'You've been listening to your friend Terry too much. This is a major, major scientific breakthrough, and until we get you back it's never going to be finished. People need you.'

Anna thought about this for a while before speaking. She stood and went to the window. You could see all the way across the city from here. Below her, cars were stuck in traffic. Commuters were buffeted by the wind.

'Ben said that he did terrible things.'

'No.'

'And Toby. He's covered in scars.'

'From all the stupid escapades he got himself into. He was a wild boy.'

She turned away from the glass. 'You talk about it all like it's good, like it's fireworks when maybe it's gunpowder.'

He didn't respond to this, just shook his head as though her arguments and protests were childish. Were all her nerves just because of who she was? Because of the person inside that she was denying?

'You could just make me revert to the person I was. So why don't you?'

'Because you're my daughter.'

'If you did, would I remember everything that has happened?'

'Yes, of course.'

'So I'll remember how I felt? How scared I've been?'

'It's all recorded, Anna. It's valuable data.'

It was starting to rain outside – water spat against the thick glass without a sound. Everything seemed so small from up here. People looked like ants. She shook her head, still unconvinced.

'I'm not sure.'

'Christ,' he sighed. 'Don't you want to find out the truth? You want to stay on the outside? Really?'

Outside, far below, there seemed to be a world teeming with people who had no interest in 'the truth'. Anna thought of her bovine pupils, of Terry's mother.

Henry put out a hand to her, palm up. It was like a key. Anna wondered what would happen if she took it. She wondered if she'd laugh at the kind, sensitive girl she believed she was. She wondered if, even now, she had any choice in any event that had ever taken place.

'I want to go home,' she said.

'Which one?'

'The one I know.'

Anna slept badly in her old flat, waking often, jolted by innocent noises from the street. The next day, her father arrived to pick her up and led her to the foyer of an expensive block of flats where the doorman gave her a familiar, respectful nod when he saw her.

'Miss Price, it's a pleasure to see you again.'

She noticed his eyes flicker across her clothes with a moment's surprise but her father led her to the lift before he, or she, could make anything more of it. They rose in silence. When they stepped out, Henry handed her a set of keys and gestured to a door. Polished oak flooring beckoned her in and the place smelled . . . wealthy. She glanced at Henry who was smiling at her.

'Welcome home, darling.'

She entered tentatively. It looked like something from a magazine – designed to seem effortlessly cool and sophisticated. She ran her hand over a sculpture; an antique wooden head with opal eyes.

'You picked that up in Bali. You've got a thing about travelling,' he said as he sank into a sofa, picking up a small remote control. When he clicked it, a section of the glass wall automatically retreated, revealing a small terrace. Anna stepped out and leant against the railing and stared down at the river and the city below.

'I can afford this?'

He shrugged. 'I helped set you up a little, I admit. But you've earned it. Believe me. People are very happy with you.'

People.

She turned back and wandered through a smart dining room into a smaller study. Its shelves were lined with books – some were reference books with academic titles, others biographies of the rich and famous. None were the English novels and plays that she had taught her pupils. She sat down at the desk. The chair was at just the right height. She didn't touch the computer in front of her, but flicked through the papers and notebooks, opening one and recognising the handwriting as her own. But the words were unfamiliar and made little sense to her.

Her gaze fell upon a series of photographs in silver frames. One was of her and Henry: he in a dinner jacket, she with her hair up, wearing a designer ball gown and diamond jewellery. She stared at herself, saw the laughter on her lips and wondered if she'd ever laughed like that in her present incarnation. Anna pushed the frame away and chose another, showing her alone, high on a mountain top. In another she stood in a bikini with three laughing men, dripping with water, turquoise seas behind them. She remembered none of them. As far as she could recall, the most exotic place she'd been to was Spain, where she'd suffered food poisoning and had spent most of the trip in a darkened hotel room.

Henry appeared in the doorway.

'Go away, please,' she said. He nodded and left. She listened to his hard leather shoes on the wooden floor and wondered what the people below would think. And then she considered that flats like this were probably designed so that you never had to worry about such things. She leaned back in the chair; it was incredibly comfortable. She let herself swing around like she might have done as a schoolgirl, probably the brightest student in her year. What must that feel like?

She rifled through the drawers, finding bank statements which shocked her (in a good way) and letters from strange men – some pleading and lovelorn, others confident and flirtatious. There was a vanity about everything here which Anna disliked – the photos in the flat were always of her – and she wondered if this was simply narcissism, or maybe a facade for a deeper loneliness. If it was this, the money would certainly help to alleviate it.

She left the study and passed through the elegant kitchen, its cool marble worktops completely bare except for a fashionably retro coffee machine. She walked on, eventually finding her bedroom. There were two others for guests, although she couldn't imagine this woman tolerating other people's company for long. The longer she stayed in the flat, the more irritating she found it. It was smug and unreal. But she felt less uncomfortable in her bedroom. For a start, there were none of the posed photographs that she'd found elsewhere. There were only two: one of her father at Buckingham Palace, proudly holding up a medal to the camera, and the other, a faded snapshot of a woman in her thirties turning and laughing, surprised by the snapper. The photograph was crumpled at the edges as though it had been handled a great deal before being framed. It had faded to pale pinks and blues. One day the image would fade from sight entirely. Anna studied the laughing woman. It was her mother. She knew it instinctively. She sat down on the bed and ran her finger over the picture.

Later, she opened what she thought was a bathroom door but was instead the entrance to a walk-in wardrobe. She rummaged through the clothes, stopping only when she found the dress that she recognised from the photograph in the living room. She put it on and tied her hair back. Then she hunted for the diamond necklace and earrings. She finally found them in a large, leather jewellery box, put them on, and examined herself in the mirror before heading out to find her father.

He was standing on the terrace, looking down at the river below. When he turned and saw her, he was visibly shaken.

'It's you,' he said after a moment. He took a step towards her, as though he wanted to take her hand, but then she shook her head and he stopped, unsure, not wanting to upset or annoy her.

'We used to be inseparable,' he said. 'Your boyfriends found it unsettling. One of them called it creepy. Stupid bastard. You were only eight when your mother died. She was so beautiful, your mother, she would light up a room. I don't care if it's a cliché because that's what she did. She'd be there and everything was brighter and better.'

Anna remembered the photograph.

'I didn't think I'd ever get over it,' he continued. 'She died so suddenly. It was just meant to be a routine operation. I still don't know what went wrong exactly. All I could think about was you; how you'd cope, how I was going to tell you. On the way home I worked out some words for you and I sat outside the house for an hour preparing, trying to compose myself so you'd know that even if your mother was gone, you didn't need to be scared because you still had me. But when I saw you, I started to cry. I sobbed in front of you, but you didn't. You took my hand and stroked it with your little hands. 'There, there,' you said. Those were your exact words. 'There, there, Daddy. We'll be okay. Don't cry, Daddy, we'll be okay.'

He then told Anna how she had grown up with this same fierce determination; refusing to let events affect them. He wondered if her special desire to succeed in the sciences was somehow related to her mother – a fairy-tale desire, perhaps, to bring her back from the grave. He told her she had listened to him read her Mary Shelley's *Frankenstein* with wide eyes, and from then on he'd pushed her away from such fantasies – fantasies that hinted at the impossible. Instead, he'd paid for sports courses and chemistry sets. She was a classic only child – driven by her parent's intense desire for excellence – but one who had her own burning needs that pushed her far beyond her peers. It made her a loner, he said.

'A loner, or lonely?' Anna asked.

'I fear the latter. I was always there, of course, but I don't think a father should ever be a girl's sole company.'

Anna imagined herself in this enormous flat, devouring books and journals late into the night, not allowing herself television or any frivolous luxuries, always reaching for impossible standards. She thought of the photo of her on top of the mountain and knew that the smile was forced – that the peak had felt like no victory, that there would always be higher mountains to climb. She almost felt sorry for herself.

'I think your loneliness was what made you so brilliant,' her father said. 'I think it's why your don at Oxford, Sir Edward Clitheroe, noticed you and insisted you join us. The protégé of a genius, I couldn't be prouder. Together you have already pushed back the boundaries of what we considered possible. Mapping the human mind, uncovering its secrets. I'm just a manager, it's way over my head.'

Anna caught sight of her reflection in a gilt-framed mirror and saw a stranger who stared warily back at her, despite all her finery.

'Don't you want to come back?' he asked.

She gazed at herself and imagined her other self: brilliant, sadder, no longer fearful and confused, but driven by a pure sense of purpose. Breaking barriers. If she remained who she was, she would forever be running.

'If I go back, will I be able to help Toby? And Ben and Terry?'

'Yes, of course. You worked with them before and you'd continue to do so.'

'I treated them well?'

'You were magnificent.'

'There is a lab, then?'

'I'm sorry?'

'They talked about a lab where they'd be taken at night. Where we'd hurt them.'

'Hurt them? Hardly.'

She remembered her own fear, alone in her humdrum flat. She could feel her old self urging her to shed this skin. She was embarrassed at how much she had coveted the clothes and scents that were already hers. She remembered the fading photograph in the bedroom, her bedroom, and wondered if she could trust this as a sign that she was a kind person, deep-down. If she went back, maybe she would laugh with her father at how she was right now. Perhaps she would become cruel. Ben and Toby might become mere numbers on a file that needed to be dealt with. Maybe the project was a front for something darker and crueller. She didn't trust her father's claims that their memories were falsely imagined and she worried that this was not the only lie he'd told her. She believed Ben and Toby when they said they had been taken in the night. She believed everything they'd told her. But how could anyone willingly choose to remain ignorant? She had no choice, she told herself as her hand slipped to the expensive jewels around her neck.

'So,' her father said, interrupting her thoughts. 'Will you let us make you better?'

She paused, then nodded.

'Ask me,' he said.

'I'm sorry?'

'Just ask me and then I'll make it all happen.'

She paused for a moment, confused by his words. But then she shrugged and said, 'Whatever. Please make me like I was. Happy now?'

TWENTY-FIVE

Ben reached the B&B in the dead of night. He knew the town well and felt an odd sense of homecoming amidst the tatty facades and dank, foetid smells of the back alleys. This time, however, he walked without fear. After all, he was already inside the cage. Knowing this made his anger burn. He'd been scared of such feelings before, but tonight he was happy to let rip.

There were lights on inside. As he rang the bell and banged on the door, he could hear faint music from somewhere inside the house. But it wasn't the old rock and roll of before, it was something classical now – sweeping strings and clashing cymbals. Eventually the door was pulled open. Edward stood there with a welcoming smile on his face. But he was different somehow. It took Ben a moment to work it out and this slight disorientation stopped him from hitting the old man right there on the doorstep. Edward was wearing a tie. No, a suit and tie. A perfectly fitting dark suit with a cream shirt and blue silk tie that matched his eyes. He had shaved. He seemed taller. He looked at Ben with that same twinkling grin, but it was clear that he was stone-cold sober.

'Lee,' he said, and his voice was posher now. 'I knew you'd come back. I even dressed up for the occasion.'

'You're laughing at me. I wouldn't do that.'

'No, no, not at all. This is a very big moment for me. We can finally be honest with each other. Please, come in.'

Ben stepped over the threshold and Edward locked the door behind them. Ben's hands curled up into tight fists but when the old man turned back to him, he showed no signs of fear.

'I'm going to kill you,' Ben said. 'You do realise that, don't you?'

'Well, you're certainly going to try,' Edward replied. His voice was definitely posher.

'Got back-up? I seem to be able to take most men down.'

'Yes, you're very handy. And no, there's no one else here.'

'Aren't you scared? I know who you are, old man. I know what you did to me. And tonight, I'm going to stop it all.'

'Why would killing me stop it all?'

Ben was thrown by the question, unnerved by how calm and collected Edward was.

'I want you to tell me things,' Ben said. 'Before I do it.'

'Okay.'

'Not here. Let's go into the sitting room.' Ben produced a roll of rope from behind his back.

'You've planned ahead.'

'Don't mock me.'

'I'm not mocking. This is all being recorded, by the way. You wouldn't expect otherwise, would you?'

Of course. Cameras were everywhere. There was nowhere in the world where one could hide out of sight any more.

Something tightened in Ben's throat. Edward suddenly didn't seem so vulnerable.

'Are they watching now? Are they coming for me?' Ben asked quietly.

'No one's watching right now and no one's coming. I told you. It's just you and me.'

Edward's fingers twitched lightly by his sides.

'I remember you,' Ben said, his voice clearer as he spoke. 'You're the one who stole me. It's you that destroyed my life. I see your face staring down at me. You. You are the thing in the night. I've been so scared of you for so long. But not any more.'

Edward merely nodded.

'Now we're going to go into the other room and you're going to answer my questions. Every single fucking one.'

'I will,' Edward calmly replied. 'But first. Your name is Ben?'

'Yes.' As he heard his name, the tension seemed to ease from inside him. It was as though a cushion had been gently wrapped around the back of his neck.

'Ben Jones, is this you?'

'Yes,' he replied, and found that he was starting to smile. He wasn't sure why, but he suddenly felt happy. Anxieties drifted off and away from him. He began to wonder what he was doing here. He knew, somehow, that a third question was coming.

'Ben Jones, are you ready for us now?'

'Yes.'

And suddenly nothing mattered at all. He felt so happy and calm. His fists uncurled. He tried to remember why he'd come here, but his head was in such a delightful fug that such thoughts just weren't worth the effort. He stood there, a stoned grin on his face, swaying slightly. He waited to be told what to do. Whatever it was, he'd do it.

Edward put a hand on his arm and led him away from the door, into the other room. Inside, Ben saw that the few remaining pieces of furniture had all been removed and had been replaced by a small leather armchair and a high, long table, the sort used for massages, perhaps. But a masseur doesn't use restraints.

Ben gazed at the table with heavy eyelids. Edward gestured for him to lie down. And he did so. And as Edward slowly and carefully used each restraint to tie down his arms and legs, so Ben started to hum an old-fashioned nursery rhyme. And then, happy, doped and utterly mellow, he closed his eyes and went to sleep.

Ben woke with a start. He pulled up sharply, but was held tight by the restraints on the table. It took him a moment to work out where he was. He'd come in, he'd threatened the old man, he was going to hurt him and then . . .

He couldn't remember any more. He looked down and saw that his legs and arms were bound tightly by thick leather ties. He pulled against them, but there was no give. And then he noticed Edward sitting in a leather chair nearby, still dressed in his suit and tie. It was dark outside. Ben guessed that, at most, a few hours had passed. He looked at him, then down at the restraints again.

'You might try to hurt me otherwise,' Edward explained.

'I'd kill you, yes.'

'Well, you might try.'

'What was all that about? The old drunk routine?'

'Was I any good? I'm not a big drinker and it was starting to take its toll.'

'My question.'

'It was so I could spend time with you. See you close up, first-hand. I've watched you for years, but it's always been through a lens or a recording.'

'You've been playing with me.'

'My work has no time for games.'

He held Ben's stare, sitting straight-backed in the chair. He was not the same man at all.

'Who are you?'

'My name is Edward Clitheroe. The other Edward, Edward Groves, whose family are buried in the graveyard, he left here about four months before you turned up. His loss, his story is true, even if it isn't mine. But I'm a bit of a magpie when it comes to stories. Like those other gravestones – the ones you thought were your parents' until you visited the place for real.'

'So where are my real parents?'

'Dead. A cremation in Southend-on-Sea.'

Ben tried to remember this. Nothing came, but somehow it felt true.

'How did you know I would come here?' he asked.

'It was planned. We control you.'

'If you control me, how come you have to tie me down? Let me up and let's see how much control you've got.'

'You shouldn't be so angry. I saved you, Lee.'

'That's not me.'

'Why not? Because Lee was a thug? Because he drank, screwed around, stole from his friends?'

'I'm nothing like that.'

'No, but you're starting to feel more like it each day. Isn't that right?'

Again, Ben was silenced. The old man knew too much about him. Everything about this conversation was one-sided.

'Who am I, really?' Ben asked. 'Tell me. Tell me what you've done to me.'

Edward leaned back in the chair. His eyes were incredibly blue. His face seemed so alive, buzzing with thoughts and ideas.

'You were a soldier, serving in Iraq, but you already know that. We had tabs on a number of men like you. Men who had no family, who had a penchant for violence. When your unit was attacked, you were badly injured and taken to a military hospital. We had contacts there and your records were changed. Dead on arrival. You were then transported to a private hospital and patched up. And then, when you were well enough, you were brought to me.'

He stood and came closer.

'My speciality is the mind.'

'You're the one who put all those dreams in my head.'

'Which ones?'

'The ones where I . . . did stuff.'

'I think you know that those aren't dreams.'

Ben was out of breath. He'd just remembered a woman in a hotel room, falling backwards from the door as he attacked her with a small hammer. He shuddered at its intensity.

'What have you just seen?' Edward asked, peering down at him.

But Ben didn't answer. He didn't want to acknowledge that other part of himself that seemed to be swelling inside him, spreading like a cancer.

'They upset you. I'm sorry. I could get rid of them, if you'd like.'

'You talk like you're God.'

Edward ignored the jibe. 'At least I gave you Carrie and the kids.'

'Fuck you.'

'But you were happy.'

Ben suddenly remembered Emma, six months before, dancing to some pop group's song. She danced so seriously that he and Carrie were left weeping with laughter.

'I'm just an experiment, aren't I?'

'Everything is an experiment. We test, we learn, we improve. I'm just one of many.'

'And there are more like me.'

'Hundreds.'

The number shocked Ben. Edward turned and walked to the window, opening it slightly, then digging into his pocket and pulling out a cigarette which he lit. He blew the smoke out of the small opening.

'Control of the damaged mind,' the old man said. 'Removing the more dangerous elements and relieving it of unnecessary thoughts.'

He blew a thin line of smoke through the window.

'You made me kill people,' Ben said. 'Didn't you?'

Edward shrugged. 'Sure.'

'Sure? Fuck! How does that help my mind?'

'It's not just your mind. It's everyone's.'

He gazed out of the window. Ben could hear the sea behind him.

'Imagine, Ben, that you wanted to arm the police. The public, right now, would say no. They say this because they are sentimental about the good old British bobby. But you know that criminals are importing weapons into the country at a terrifying rate and that they regard our police service with increasing ridicule. You know that the police need to be armed. Fact. So you create an event, a shock, which helps change the public's thinking.'

He exhaled again, a low slow breath of absolute calm and confidence.

'It could be a massacre at a school, perhaps. Or the shooting of three unarmed police women in the middle of a park. A shock. Turning public opinion.'

'And I would do this?'

'One of you.'

'It's disgusting.'

'It's extreme, that's all. Look at climate change. No one will agree to anything. The planet will boil and die unless we do something. Wouldn't a small shock be worth saving the planet?'

'There was a woman, in a hotel ...'

'Yes. She was having an affair with one of our patrons. And she was about to print some material that was damaging to the cause.'

'That's not saving the world.'

'Did you care? No, you were happy with your son.'

Ben imagined lying in bed with Joe, his son's head nestled on his shoulder as he listened to a story being read to him.

'But I hurt her, I ...'

Another memory flickered into focus. A man, his age, jogging along the towpath of a canal. The low winter sun lit his breath as he ran. Ben followed until he was sure that no one was following. And then he pulled a knife from his jacket and stabbed him. He left the man staring up at the perfect sky, trying to speak: stunned, scared, slowing fading. Another memory clattered into this one, a newspaper front page. The same man on the cover. Ben felt sick as he realised what he had done.

Edward looked down at him as though he could read his mind.

'A man, a politician.'

'Yes. The housing minister. He was very unpopular before he died. But after that, people were clamouring to uphold his memory. A law was passed as a result, protecting working-class families in council homes. His death has benefited hundreds of thousands.'

'How many have you made me kill?' Ben gasped.

'None that you can blame yourself for. You simply answered a phone call. Like all the others. One call, three questions and then whatever we asked. In the morning, you remembered nothing except the new memories we'd supplied: rugby games or drinks with friends.'

Ben squeezed his eyes shut, scared that more memories, more grotesque violence would seep in. He felt a hand on his shoulder. Edward gazed calmly down at him.

'I can make it go away. I can give you back Carrie.'

The punch of her name nearly winded him.

'If you want her, that is.' Edward's eyes gauged and scrutinised. Ben felt that there was nothing he could hide from him.

'She misses you. So do the children.'

'Don't.'

'Is she fading yet? It should start about now. We got rid of the clutter in your mind so you could be Ben. But the longer the gap between treatments, the more your old self and your old memories rise to the surface. There are two opposing personalities within you. We gave you Ben. Without us, Lee will take over.'

'No. I'm Ben.'

'Lee would spit on Ben if he passed him on the street.'

'Lee's dead.'

'No, Lee is very much on the way back. You may have resisted it for now, but the feelings will overwhelm you. Unless you let me help.'

He leaned forward, his fingers twitching again.

'Carrie wouldn't touch Lee with a bargepole,' he added. 'Without me, you've lost her forever.'

'You've got me strapped down, just do it if you want to.'

'No. You must ask.'

'What?'

Edward's hands were suddenly still. He stood up and moved with a speed that belied his age. He untied one of Ben's arms and then the other. Ben sat up, undoing the restraints on his feet. He swung his legs over the table and now the two men faced each other. One lunge and Ben would have the man in his grip.

'I want you to ask.' Edward said. 'Ask and I'll wash it all away. You'll wake with a start and there will be Carrie. And everything will be as it was.'

'And the other bit?'

'You'll still do that. From time to time, when we require.'

'I can't.'

'I thought you loved her.'

Ben was silent. He was unbound, but scared to move.

'Without us, she'll fade away. You'll remember her vaguely, but you won't be interested in her. You'll chase other women.'

'I love her.'

'I made you love her. Do you get that? I put love into your damaged mind. Without me, you are just another selfish, stupid man.'

Ben's eyes were red and he bit his lip to control his pain. 'She's my girl.'

'No, she's mine. You're mine.'

'Carrie!' Ben screamed. Rage burst out of him and he overturned the table, sending it crashing to the floor. 'Carrie!' He screamed her name over and over as though he could summon her there and then, as though her name proved that his love was real and permanent.

Edward was unmoved. 'Ask me.'

'I'll run away.'

'You'll forget her.'

'No. Never.'

'How did it feel when you attacked those men?'

'They attacked me.'

'Was it exciting? Did it bring it all back?'

'I'll stop you.'

Edward's contempt was all too visible.

'I will!'

'What are you going to do? Go to the police? Join a student march? A riot?'

'I'll hurt you. I'll fucking torture you till you give her to me.'

Edward's eyes narrowed, but there was still no fear.

'Is that you, Lee? Are you back already?'

Ben shrank from him. He really could feel those old cruel emotions. He could taste it in his mouth. And he hated it. The old man watched him with his relentless gaze. Ben couldn't move. He couldn't fight him. He couldn't outwit him. He had nothing.

'Just close your eyes and nod if that makes it easier. Think about your wife, Ben.'

Ben closed his eyes. He could see Carrie smiling, waiting. All he had to do was nod.

'Ask me.'

If he refused, he would lose her forever.

'You'll be so much happier.'

Little Emma would grow into a fine young lady. And he'd never see it.

Joe, his best boy, needed his dad.

'Come on now. Nod your head.'

That was all he had to do. That tiny gesture. Just be ignorant. Close the door again, ignore what he'd seen and heard. Just do what everyone else did.

'You have been scared of us for so long. But there is no need. We are not interested in forcing people to do our will. We've learned this over time. We control their damaged minds and help them see things as we do. So they want it. The whole world, Ben. Just like you. Asking us to control them. Asking not to think, not to question. Now. Ask me.'

Maybe it was the blatant arrogance or the slip of cruelty in his words, but it forced Ben's eyes open.

Edward barely had time to react as Ben charged past him and threw himself at the patio doors on the far side of the room. The glass shattered as he barged against the wooden frame, breaking the doors open. He smashed his way out and ran. He heard a call from behind, but he was too far away too quickly. He felt stinging pain on his face and hands, but he didn't stop running.

He didn't know where he was heading. He didn't know if they were following him.

Carrie's voice whispered in his ear.

Run.

His legs burned and his lungs begged for oxygen, but on he charged into the darkness.

He finally stopped at the peak of a long hill and he turned and looked down. He could see the lights of the town far below and the moonlight which glistened on the sea's swelling waves.

He was all alone. The cage was broken. He stared out and wondered where he could go next. He waited for images of Carrie and his children to come back and haunt him. He expected to hear her whisper on the night's cold breeze, a taunt at his stupidity for running away from her arms.

I love you.

But nothing came.

The night seemed so much colder in the silence.

TWENTY-SIX

Terry never saw any of them again. He waited at the squat all day, then began wandering the halls, pestering Daz and the other militants, but no one knew anything. He stayed for another night and then, spooked, moved to a room on the other side of the building, in case they'd been rumbled. After a week he gave up and returned home. As he turned the key, he wondered if there might be someone waiting for him but the flat was just the same. His mother sat watching the TV, muttering about unpaid bills, and his room was untouched. He checked his computer, but there were no images of intruders on the secret camera that he'd set up. He felt oddly disappointed.

Each day he wondered if Anna would appear. Or maybe it would be Toby, panicked and wide-eyed, banging on the door, begging for his help. He posted his experiences on various blogs and conspiracy websites, but even there no one seemed to take him seriously. He wandered the streets again, trying to find the lab. He couldn't remember the exact street, however, and although he was sure he'd found the right place, there was a different set of metal shutters at the back, so he wasn't entirely certain. He stood outside and waved his arms, swore, even threw stones at the windows. But he got no reaction. Everything, it seemed, had been turned off.

He got a job in computer programming, something to pass the time and pay the bills. In the evenings he'd go to the pub where he'd argue angrily about mind control and the faceless men that watched and controlled our lives. But people rarely argued back. They just turned away and talked about something else until the landlord finally gave him a hard tap on the shoulder and showed him the door.

Every day he read the papers, circling stories that might prove his theories right. A shooting here, a bomb there. Wide-eyed suspects who claimed their innocence; a haunted stare for the camera. Every night he returned home a little drunk and swore at the news on the television. His mother would groan and put the kettle on.

Sometimes he woke in the night with a start. The room was empty and there was no noise. But still, the lights against the window and shadows under the door made him wonder. Were they still watching? Deep down, he knew that their punishment for helping Toby, Ben and Anna was that he would never know. And even if he did discover the truth one day, no one would ever believe him.

TWENTY-SEVEN

Carrie's friends might have been awkward when it came to mentioning Ben's disappearance, but she was sure that as long as the Company let her keep Emma and Joe, there was hope. So she did what she was told, waited and focused on the children.

She and Emma became zealous bakers. They started with biscuits, but were soon making elaborate cakes which Emma would deliver to school with a proud grin. So popular were the cakes that soon Emma was bringing friends home and the house would be transformed into some sort of créche-cum-bakery, where mothers would pick up their daughters with more than a little envy, taking home the goodies and wondering why Carrie hadn't become fat and spotty.

Joe was a harder nut to crack. He missed his father and would sulk and smash monsters to bits on his computer. So Carrie joined him, buying a massive television so they could play together once Emma had gone to bed. It was their time alone and each cherished it as much as the other. Joe started smiling again, even began talking at breakfast. Comments from school percolated back that an improvement was noticed and Carrie began to feel that she was putting her family back together.

All that was missing was Ben, and during those long, cold nights when she couldn't sleep, Carrie would feel the emptiness of the double bed and angrily tell herself that he would never come back. As she lay there, she remembered the click of the door when they brought him back, unconscious. She'd help them settle him in the bed, then follow one of them downstairs to go through a checklist of expected injuries, strains and pains that he'd suffer. Once they were gone, she'd go to the secret stash of medicines in her hidden draw and then tend his wounds, listening to his quiet, gentle breathing while she ran her finger over his newly acquired scars and bruises. My poor brown bear, she would whisper. Poor, poor brown bear. And then finally, in the morning, he would open his eyes and see her. And he would always smile.

David would come to the house and check on this and that while awkwardly attempting small-talk. But his visits became less regular and, while she never believed that they weren't always watching her, Carrie began to think that they were becoming less interested. And she wasn't sure why.

She continued to be the obedient, compliant employee that they desired. But when she was outside of the house and she felt safer, she would tell the children stories about Ben. She'd remind them about the time he carried both of them on his shoulders across a muddy lake, nearly making it to the end before slipping and all three of them fell into the slime. The children screamed with laughter as Carrie described Ben pulling himself to his feet, covered in green gunk from head to toe, laughing at his own ridiculousness. She told them about the time they went camping in Cornwall and Ben tried to put up the tent in the middle of the night, making such a hash of it that they all had to sleep in the car. Joe called him a 'dufus' when he heard this, but Carrie reprimanded him.

'Your father's an amazing man. Most men can only be strong or soft. Your dad could be both. He's my champion. And you must be my champion until he returns.'

Joe grew three inches that day.

At night, alone, she'd remember his laugh and his touch. She'd roll onto his side of the bed and pull the odourless sheets close to her, trying to imagine him there next to her, gazing at her. She might lie here alone forever. It seemed a just punishment for her infidelities. And not knowing, never being sure beyond the faint hope that the children provided, was cruel yet utterly deserved.

'I love you, my darling,' she'd think, but never dare whisper out loud. 'I love you and I'm waiting for you.'

And then one day she received a call from a woman whose voice she didn't recognise, telling her that the case was closed. She would pop over later to get Carrie to sign the necessary forms.

Closed.

Carrie hung up and felt the tears spring to her eyes. They were coming to take the children away. They would move her on to another case, another man. And Ben must be dead. She sat at the table, utterly desolate, hope extinguished.

The woman turned up an hour later. She let herself in with her own key, as they all did. Carrie was still sitting at the table and gave her a cursory nod but no more. The woman walked over and stared at her. Carrie looked up.

'Hi, Carrie,' she said. 'I'm glad to meet you finally.'

'Sure,' she grunted back. The woman took off her coat and laid it on one of the chairs. She was pretty, Carrie noted, and she liked her clothes. But it was her stare and the way she held herself that made Carrie wary. She seemed important.

'Do you want a cup of something? Before we begin?'

'I'll do it,' Carrie said, getting up and heading to the kitchen.

'Tea, please. White,' came the call, but the woman didn't follow her in. Snooping around, Carrie thought, irritated. Fuck it, what did it matter anyway? She brought back the teas a few minutes later to find the woman cradling a framed photograph. She looked at Carrie and smiled, a little embarrassed.

'Sorry.' She put it back down. Carrie saw that it was a photo of her and Ben.

'I'm Anna, by the way,' the woman said.

'Right.'

They sat facing each other at the kitchen table. Carrie didn't say anything. She saw no point in being friendly.

'So,' Anna said. 'Well done and thank you. This particular experiment is now complete. It has been extremely revealing.'

Carrie stared down at her mug. She could feel the tears rising but she didn't want the woman to see it.

'The only questions now are what we do with the house, the children and you.'

'Yes.'

'But our interest in this case is closed.'

Carrie nodded, waiting for the appropriate paperwork to be shoved in front of her nose.

'The cameras have been turned off,' Anna said, more softly. Her hand reached out and touched Carrie's. Carrie looked up, surprised. Anna nodded, her expression surprisingly gentle. 'Every one.'

Carrie said nothing, not trusting her. Anna took a sip of her tea. Her eyes ran across the room before they returned to Carrie. Like Diane did, but somehow more natural. Carrie wondered if Diane had been trying to copy her. This woman felt much more original.

'What happened to him?' Carrie finally asked, not managing much more than a whisper.

'We don't know,' Anna replied. 'Not for sure.'

'So why have you stopped?'

'He's been away from us so long that the memories we placed in his head will be gone. He won't be chasing after us and we're happy to let him run wild. He's no use any more.'

'He's free?' Carrie shifted in her seat, trying to remain calm.

'In a way.'

Neither spoke for a moment.

'I met him, you know,' Anna said. 'Spent a bit of time with him. I liked him.'

'Ben was the best.'

'Yes. Ben.'

'Are you going to take the children away?'

'Why? Do you want to keep them?'

Carrie watched Anna from across the table and realised that she couldn't read her at all. At times she looked kind and gentle, but then her eyes also seemed wiser, more worn somehow. She decided it was best not to answer the question.

'He loved you,' Anna said.

Carrie was jolted by the comment, it seemed to come out of nowhere.

'I know,' she replied, a little upset, a little angry.

'We created a wonderful little family here,' Anna said.

'No. I did. Ben and I did.'

'Alright. But either way, it's gone now. I'm sorry about that.'

'You're sorry? Are you in charge then? Did you do all those things to him?'

'I'm in charge of some of it. It's taken me a while to realise that I'm really just another drone. But I'm sorry anyway.'

Carrie watched as Anna reached into her elegant leather bag and took out some papers. She slid the papers across the desk.

Carrie feigned a shrug of indifference and signed where little yellow stickers indicated she should.

She dropped the pen onto the document and shoved it back at Anna, who flicked through the papers to make sure that it was all done properly. 'It's funny because I received an uncon- firmed report that he'd been seen in Cornwall, hanging about near a campsite. I dismissed it. Destroyed the report, actually.'

A campsite in Cornwall. Carrie just shrugged as though this meant nothing to her. Anna was watching her more closely now though.

'The man will now call himself Lee. He'll spend his life in bars, do some menial work on building sites, cash in hand. We give him three years, max, before he gets himself killed in a fight. It's inevitable.'

She checked through the paperwork and nodded.

'Good, all done.' She sat back and drank some more of her tea. 'Yes, that report was ridiculous. Like the idea someone had that he might still be watching your children.'

Carrie wanted to grab her. She leaned forward, her hands

on the table, inches from Anna's. Anna held her intense gaze.

'We made him love you, Carrie. We control him. God, we control everything. He cannot love without us. If he did ...' her voice trailed off, 'then my bosses wouldn't control everything after all.'

A flicker of a smile crossed her lips for a moment.

'If someone else had seen that report, they might have wondered why a man who could not remember you, let alone love you, would show up at that particular campsite. They could, if they'd been more thorough, have checked other places that you and your children had visited. And had someone done this, they might well have found evidence that suggested that he had visited these locations too. Almost as though he was trying to hold onto the memories that they offered. But since I'm the only one who saw the report and I've destroyed it, I think we can discount this theory.'

The small smile faded and was replaced by a sadder look.

'There was this boy,' Anna said. 'He was so full of life, one of those funny kids who everyone laughs at but sort of loves as well, always grinning, always the fool. You know?'

Carrie nodded, not sure where this was going.

'You get so caught up in your work sometimes, you're always chasing the future. You get so excited by what you could do. Everyone's reaching for the sky, trying to outdo each other, to be the best, so you don't notice ... the cost ... sometimes. Good intentions, the road to hell, you know.'

She picked up her mug then put it back down, realising it was empty. She seemed very different now, Carrie thought. But then Anna straightened and the softness fell off her.

'It's strange work we do. Sometimes you feel like you're a

pioneer. Other times, it feels harder to justify. I get the feeling you've had enough.'

'You too,' said Carrie.

'I've made my bed,' was all Anna said. She pulled at the sleeve of her top, pensive for only a moment. 'But you should move on. Maybe enjoy some travel.'

Carrie pulled a face. Travel?

'Go back to the places you used to visit, maybe. Take the kids.' Her eyes bored into Carrie's. 'It would be a lot less messy if they stayed with you. The Company would be very grateful.'

Run.

'I can finesse the other bits. Privilege of my position.'

Keep the kids.

'I'll give you a couple of days. Then the house will go on the market. You don't need to contact me with your decision.'

She stood, put on her coat and strode to the front door. Carrie followed her and suddenly they were very close together as she put her hand on the latch.

'Carrie,' she said, her voice low, 'he might not remember you. He's probably behaving exactly as we predict. We don't get much wrong.'

She took a breath to continue, but then said nothing. Outside a car was waiting for her, the driver standing by the door with his hands behind his back. Anna's mobile phone started to ring. She looked at the screen, then at Carrie. Before she answered it, she leaned in a little closer and her whisper was almost drowned out by the ringtone.

'Good luck.'

Then she turned, talking fast into the phone, barely acknowledging the driver as she slid into the back of the car and continued her conversation.

A few moments later, she was gone. Carrie turned back inside. It was then that she noticed the envelope on the table. A thick, A4 envelope, bursting with papers. At first she thought that Anna had forgotten the forms, but then she realised that this was a different envelope altogether. She tipped it upside down so the papers fell out onto the table.

Out they spilled. Hundreds of pages. Thousands of stories. Carefully recorded memories.

Memories from all walks of life.

Collected, refined and injected into one man's mind.

TWENTY-EIGHT

'It's too hot, I'm dying!' Joe cried as they scrambled up the rocky slope. Carrie, a few yards ahead, stopped and turned. Her son was glaring at her, arms folded, while Emma had sat down on the ground, on strike.

'I'm thirsty!' she mewled. Carrie made her way back to them and crouched next to her daughter. The sun beat down on them and she adjusted Emma's sun hat to protect her, then handed her the bottle of water. It was already half-empty and Emma guzzled greedily.

'It's just over the hill,' she said. 'Come on, guys, we'll hold hands, go up together.'

They were in Greece and had been for three days now. Before that they'd travelled to France and to Spain. They'd trawled beaches in Cornwall and seaside towns, trooped around cities and hung around tourist traps. They followed the clues that Anna had left behind on the kitchen table, checking off each memory, one by one. At first the kids had been excited about their adventures. But now, not knowing why they were away from home for so long, they just wanted food they recognised, television in English and their own beds. But Carrie was un-deterred. She grabbed their hands, cajoling them on. Her weary children got back to their feet and staggered up the uneven road. There were olive groves on either side; ancient trees with bent trunks. Somewhere nearby Carrie could hear the tinkle of goats' bells.

'It's just at the top, I promise,' she said. In truth she wasn't sure. The file had described a holiday on a Greek island. A tiny villa with views onto a harbour. Sunburn and sex. She was on the right island, but there were so many villas.

Working her way through the file had been like reading a secret diary. She knew many of the details already – the Company had needed her to understand him as completely as possible. But still, she felt a strange longing as she worked her way through them, finding herself in events she didn't know about, chasing after Ben. It felt intimate and voyeuristic. And it made her miss him even more.

They'd left the car half a mile down the track after the bumpy road had become impassable for vehicles. On the other side of the hill should be the small, white-walled villa and the view of the sea. She should be excited, but after all the disappointments she was more wary this time. No, not wary – she was dreading it. Dreading reaching the top and finding no one there again. They were running out of dreams to chase.

The sky was perfectly blue and the sun glared down. The back of her T-shirt was caked in sweat. The breeze had disap-peared and the slope seemed impossibly steep, but somehow they clambered their way to the top, and there was the villa. Behind it the land dropped sharply away and the sea shimmered in the harbour below. You could see a collection of small white fishing boats. She smiled at how beautiful it was.

'Mum! Emma's finished all the water!' Joe grumbled.

'We'll get some in there,' she said, pointing to the villa.

'But that's someone's house.'

'Yes, but it's a holiday home. I'm sure it'll be fine.'

'What? We've got to beg for water from strangers? That's embarrassing!'

'Oh shush and come on.'

All the shutters were closed, but that didn't mean that no one was inside. He could still be there, she thought, and now her heart was racing. There should be a patio around the other side where she was meant to have sat wrapped in his arms, staring out at the wonderful view. She walked slightly ahead, her nerves jangling.

'There's no one there,' whined Emma.

She turned the corner and saw the stone patio. Empty.

'I'm so going to die and it's all your fault!'

Then suddenly there he was, walking out from the villa, gazing out at the sea, oblivious to her and the kids. He'd shaved his head and lost weight. In his hand was a bottle of beer. He clutched it tight, then drank it all in one heavy glug. His eyes were narrow, his mouth twisted slightly, as though about to shout something. He looked rougher, harder. A dangerous stranger. His bare feet shuffled against the stone floor and he sniffed nervously.

He looked so different that Carrie stopped dead in her tracks. She tried to remember how he used to be, the way he'd laugh and let his head fall back. Kinder, softer gestures. The man on the patio muttered something under his breath and stalked back into the villa.

Carrie didn't move. Her children caught up with her and stopped.

'Oh, that's great, that is,' Joe griped. 'I knew there'd be no one here.'

Carrie reached out, wanting to take Joe's hand, but then the man came back outside, disturbed by their appearance. His head snapped around to face them. His movements were sharp, driven by fear. He put a hand to his eyes to shield them from the sun.

Joe saw him. His mouth fell open and then he charged away from her. She heard him scream 'DADDY!' with such excitement that she could hardly bear to look.

Joe ran at the man. He charged onto the patio, about to hurl himself into his arms.

She closed her eyes and waited for the scream.

'Mum! Mummy!' Joe shrieked.

Still, she didn't dare look.

'Carrie!'

Her name. His voice.

Open your eyes, she thought. Blink away the tears. Open your eyes, and run to him.

Carrie looked up. Ben stared back at her.

And they ran.

ACKNOWLEDGEMENTS

Thank you to George Faber and Charlie Pattinson at Company Pictures for getting this started and to Patrick Spence for his help in its previous incarnation. Thanks to Anna Wilson for being its first reader and encouraging me to take it 'out there'. Thank you to David Nicholls for opening the door and to Jonny Geller and all at Curtis Brown who were there to greet me on the other side. Thanks to Jane Wood and all at Quercus for making it real. And a lot better. And lastly, thank you to my parents for pushing that first pencil into my grubby hands.